NOT
ALL
SECRETS
STAY
BURIED

TIME of DEATH

CARRIE ▾ MERRILL

PARANORMAL THRILLER

Time of Death, *Not All Secrets Stay Buried*
by Carrie Merrill

Copyright © 2020 by Carrie Merrill
All rights reserved.
First Edition © 2020

Published by
Christopher Matthews Publishing
Gleneden Beach, Oregon 97388

ISBN-13:
978-1-944072-41-4 (hbk)
978-1-944072-39-1 (pbk)
978-1-944072-40-7 (epub)

The events, peoples and incidents in this story are the sole product of the author's imagination. The story is fictitious, and any resemblance to individuals, living or dead, is purely coincidental. Historical, geographic, and political issues are based on fact; the stories of the children of Central America are based on truth, however, the names have been changed to protect the innocent.

Every effort has been made to be accurate. The author assumes no responsibility or liability for errors made in this book.

Cover / book layout & design by Suzanne Parrott
Ghost woman with dead tree in background, ©Joe Prachatree / Shutterstock.com
Dry tree isolated on white background, © saengla / Shutterstock.com

Library of Congress Control Number: 2020916473
paranormal thriller / medical suspense / ghost / horror / murder mystery

Printed and bound
in the United States of America.

For the nurses, staff, residents and attendings
at St. Francis Hospital:
You helped me survive residency,
even if I came out of it with some grim tales.

Books by Carrie Merrill

— Angel Blade Series —

Angel Blade

Daemon

Archangel

Harbingers

*

The Key, the Outlaw and the Treasure

Time of Death

* * *

Follow Carrie Merrill at
CarrieMerrill.com

By the pricking of my thumbs,
Something wicked this way comes.

"MACBETH" 4.1.45-6, William Shakespeare

Chapter 1

"I need the retractor," Evan said, her bloody, gloved hand reaching to the scrub tech, who slapped the silver instrument into her open palm. She didn't look up to say thank you. Never take your eyes off the operating field, especially with a clamp holding a bleeding vessel. Every resident learns that in their first day of a general surgery rotation. She placed the retractor into the patient's abdomen and the medical student at her side grasped the handle, just as he had been trained to do.

The operating room lights cast harsh halos down to the table, broken only by the overhead lighting that filled the cold space. Those same lights shone bright inside the open abdomen of the man that lay under the sterile blue surgical drapes. Her gloved fingers tied a suture around the vessel, pushed the knot down the length of the thread, and moved on, retracting aside a jumble of pink intestines. It was a surprise that there hadn't been more damage so far. But there was still a problem in this mess somewhere because a pool of bright red blood welled over her fingers again.

"Damn it," she muttered, half to herself, behind her mask. "There's another bleeder in here." She opened her hand out to the nurse again. "Sponge."

She felt the firm placement of the white gauzy towel against her palm and pressed it into her operating field. Blood stained it as soon as she plunged her fingers into the pool.

Nobody said much, not tonight. Usually the room was a background milieu of chatter and the clang of equipment around the operating table. An anxious quiet had descended over the room now, one that held no peace or solace. Evan understood it, and appreciated it. She needed to concentrate and the constant noise would only be a distraction.

The wad of small intestines spilled across her hand and then she saw it. A rend in the once-pink wall of the bowel. The opening was jagged and the organ had nearly been severed save for the thin strip of tissue that tethered the two ends. It never took long to find the damage, even though there were several feet of intestines to examine. That one small injury would eventually make itself known. From the moment she made the first skin incision until now, she didn't doubt that the bullet had done something in here. Forget trying to retrieve it, though. The CAT scan showed that it had lodged in one of the vertebral bodies in the patient's lumbar spine. Fishing that out would be up to the bone and nerve guys. The orthopedic and neuro jocks.

No bullets coming out tonight. She had been called to do a much more important job: retrace the path of the bullet and stop the hemorrhaging before this guy died. Anything else could always be fixed later when he was more stable.

"I need suction," she said, and the medical student to her left responded by placing the suction tip into the red flow of blood that gushed up from below the bowel. His hand trembled and the edge of the suction device quivered in the pool of blood.

Her fingers slipped over his and grasped the device. "It's okay," she said to him. "I've got it." It was the student's first night of call on his surgery rotation. He may not have ever seen this much blood before, and there was no need in having him pass out on his first surgical case. As a resident in her fourth year of training, Evan had seen enough med students drop to the floor shortly after the shakes started, and now wasn't the time to see another one do it.

"Can you see the source?" the older doctor across the bed spoke, his voice calm and smooth. Dr. James White, her supervisor – her attending. Thank heavens he was on call with her tonight.

The even-cadence of his voice eased the little quiver she had in her gut. It always did, and she respected him for that. He never lost his cool during emergencies, which helped when she was a new resident. It made times like this easier to handle. And now, four years into this program, few emergencies rattled her anymore. No more shakes. No more sweating under the surgical mask. Just here to do the job. Fix the problem at hand.

"This looks like it," she said. Her blue eyes gazed down through her clear protective goggles. "Hemo-clip."

The nurse pressed the instrument into her open hand. With a slow and steady breath in, she drew the clamp down to the pumping vessel. *Calm fingers. Easy peasy.* The clip slipped around the vessel and tightened. The flow instantly ceased with the closure of the artery, and she released the breath that she had held for the last few seconds.

Dr. White leaned further into the surgical field and gazed down at the shrinking pool of blood as it was sucked away into tubing, thanks to the medical student who handled the suction with ease now. "I think you solved the biggest problem."

His matter-of-fact tone made her smile. *As simple as finding a leak in a hose*, as he would often say.

"Very good, Dr. Jensen," Dr. White spoke. "Now let's see what we can do for the small bowel. How are we doing up there, Dr. Patel?"

The anesthesiologist stood, his face visible over the edge of the blue drape that shielded his station, the small space where he monitored the patient's vital signs. He glanced over the monitor, its lights steady and calm. "We're doing well. The patient is stable, but I'm going to infuse four units of blood as soon as it gets up here, if that's okay with you."

"Excellent," Dr. White spoke and turned again to Evan, watching her as she examined the damaged sections of small intestine. "What would you like to use to repair that?"

"I think we can patch this with an endo-GIA," she spoke, and Dr. White nodded.

"Sounds good to me. Proceed."

The surgical nurse handed the tool to her and she began the task of excising the damaged portions of the small intestines. As she worked, Dr. White discussed the impact of the gunshot wounds and trauma with the medical student. This turned into background noise to Evan, as the attending-student mini-lectures often did. She had heard them so many times, the same lectures every six weeks with a new batch of students each time. One more year, and she wouldn't have to hear them anymore. Then she would be out of the General Surgery residency and into the Trauma Fellowship, and get to hear a whole new set of mini-lectures in the background.

After removing the more damaged sections of the small intestine, she slipped the instrument around the organ and ran the clips through it. It sealed the intestine shut. No more bleeding. No more green bile oozing from the ends of the bowel. No other injuries in the rest of the intestine. She handed the tool back to the nurse and started the routine task of sewing every layer of the guy's abdomen back together. Doing this enough had left the muscle memory in her hands, and she didn't have to really think about it anymore.

A ripple of thunder shuddered against the outer walls of the operating room. The circulating nurse glanced up from her paperwork as the sound rumbled along the walls. The darkness beyond the frosted windows lit up with flashes of lightning. Dr. White glanced behind him to the windows as another growl of thunder vibrated against the glass.

"That's quite a storm moving in," he spoke.

Evan continued the suturing. Sure, she had noticed the thunder, but at this time of year these storms moved through almost every day. The only time she paid attention was if a Code Black came blaring through the overhead PA system. Tornado warning. Then it would be time to take action. Until then, another day, another storm in downtown Chicago.

The permeating sound of a beeper erupted through the silence of the room. Evan's ears had long since trained to the sound and she glanced back to the shelf where the black pager rested. The circulating nurse stood from her place and grasped the pager, silencing the persistent sound. For a moment she gazed to the display of numbers and then picked up the phone. Evan continued to work under the hot lights and heard the nurse's voice over the hum of the ventilator.

"Dr. Jensen, it's the ICU," the nurse said. "They said it's about Mr. Ceglinski. His blood pressure has dropped very low."

Evan's stomach turned into knots for the first time since stepping foot into the operating room tonight. *It's time. The old man will die despite everything I've tried.*

"Go ahead, Evan," Dr. White said. She glanced up to him. "Young Student Doctor Marks here can help me finish closing up." He ticked his head to the medical student at her side. The student's eyes widened and the shakes started in his hands again.

She nodded and stepped away from the patient, although the thought of not finishing made her cringe inside. The suture job on the outside of the body was the only thing the patient saw, and if it didn't look good, then the rest of what happened inside wouldn't matter. But someone else needed her more right now.

Her gloved fingers pulled the blue surgical gown from her body. She scooped up the beeper once again and stepped from the operating room. The smells of the corridor changed, leaving behind the sharpness of alcohol-based scrub solution and blood for the sterile scent of hand-sanitizer. The cool air hit her face as soon as she ripped the mask from her around her neck. With the latest trauma patient in Dr. White's skilled hands, she now had to worry about the other three patient's she had scattered throughout the hospital. Mr. Ceglinski had been the sickest, however. She wasn't surprised that the ICU called now. The biggest surprise was that he had lasted as long as he did.

As soon as she walked out of the surgical unit, she pulled the blue cap from her head. Long strands of blonde hair had come loose from the tie that bound her hair in a messy wad at the back of her head. *Just don't look in a mirror.* With the static that pulled her hair all over the place and the dark circles she most likely had under her eyes, she must have looked like a zombie. Because that's how residency training always looked. Work all day and on-call all night. Good luck getting to sleep when you weren't working, now that her circadian rhythm was all out of sorts. No wonder the higher-ups had made restrictions on resident hours, not that it did much good.

She found her long white coat on the hooks outside the operating room doors and pulled it on over the periwinkle blue scrubs with *St. John's Hospital* printed all over them. Like she would ever forget where she worked.

The beeper sounded again and she cringed at the relentless noise. She continued down the empty corridor and silenced the beeper at her hip as she slipped into the stairwell. Another floor down and she entered into the critical care and cardiac units, where the sickest patients in the entire hospital were kept. Harsh fluorescent lights glared down upon the dark blue carpets. The hall seemed endless as she moved past the quiet entry desk that usually bustled with activity during the daytime hours. But at eleven o'clock at night it stood quiet and isolated. She rounded the desk and entered the long corridor that led to the intensive care unit.

Her pace quickened. If that beeper went off again before she got there, her head might just split open. After all, she could only go so fast. It's not like there was anything she could do when she eventually arrived.

The hall extended down the length of the south wing to the ICU. Here the fluorescent lights had been dimmed to half-light, an energy-conserving approach in the middle of the night, but it left everything in darker shade of its natural color. Windows along the hallway allowed the brilliant flashes of lightning into the hall as she moved. Rain spattered against the glass in torrents and shimmered with the lights of the city outside St. John's Hospital. What would normally be an impressive view of the Chicago skyline was now a smeared mess of liquid light in the rain that cascaded down the glass. She stepped through the dim shafts of fluorescent light toward the double door that barred the entrance into the ICU.

A faint shuffle sounded behind her and she stopped. Evan glanced back to see who had entered the hall, but the corridor remained empty with the lights flickering overhead. The effect was so subtle that she probably wouldn't have noticed it unless she had stopped. But now the flicker turned into an uneven strobe. When she had walked past the desk, she was sure that nobody else had entered the unit with her. Living in this city for four years had taught her that much. Always be aware of your surroundings. Even in a hospital. And just as she had suspected, she was still alone in the hallway.

Rain pounded against the glass with relentless fervor and she glanced outside. Perhaps it was the sound of the storm that had caught her attention the first time and made her stop. Like seeing faces in a cloud. Hearing voices in the thunder. Lightning flashed again and a rumble shuddered against the hospital's foundation. The lights flickered and faded for a moment as if straining to hold on to the last bit of energy that supplied them. The lights then blinked out, leaving the corridor in darkness with the exception of the glow from the city and the electric storm outside the windows.

Evan held her breath. Her pulsed pounded like a jackhammer in her ears and she froze. The hospital had lost power only one other time since she had started here and that was only for a few seconds in a storm very similar to this one. At that time, the generators had kicked in fast.

But now the dark held, and she counted the time with every beat of her heart. Her eyes must have grown huge. It was a silly thing, but she was alone … in the dark … in the hospital … in the middle of the night.

Five seconds. Ten. Fifteen. Was this going to last forever?

The emergency lights at both ends of the hall sprang to life in a sudden and loud click that made her jump where she stood. Thank hell nobody was around to see that. The floodlights cast harsh, narrow circles at the base of the doors, but left very little light for the center of the hall where she stood.

You're okay. The small reassurance was a habit she had formed growing up in the isolated farm house in Colorado, the basement had always been a dark and closed-in space, but that was where her dad had kept the canned food. A once-a-week trek into the basement had been enough to stir up that little voice to talk her through it. *You're alright. It's only dark, that's all. The power will come back in no time.*

Evan turned away from the windows and headed once again for the doors beyond the spotlight. Lightning flashed, illuminating the dark corridor. A growl of thunder. She approached the spotlight and her black clog stepped into the circle of light.

"*Evan*," a whisper spoke behind her, low but definite.

The breath caught in her throat and she spun around on her heel to gaze back down the corridor. Someone had to be behind her. Maybe one of her fellow residents, taking advantage of the power outage and playing a joke. But the hall still remained as empty as it was before, the silence only broken by the rain and thunder. In that instant, the fluorescent lights flickered back on with a hum. Evan reflexively swallowed. Her throat had gone dry as soon as the power had cut out, leaving her without a drop of saliva to use her voice.

With the bright overhead lights now on, her eyes scanned the windows and down the length of the corridor. No shadows. No places to hide or sneak away. Just a hallway connected between two doors. The heaters along the base of the walls hissed and clicked as they came alive with warm air, a sound that would have scared the life out of her when she was ten. They sputtered for a few seconds and then quieted with a steady flow of heat.

Not a single person stood in that hallway with her. Nothing else could have made the voice that had whispered.

The beeper rang out once again and she jumped, startled at the instant sound. Her trembling fingers turned off the sound and she laughed at herself once again. The damn beeper, a hold back from medical training twenty or thirty years ago. Now only residents and drug dealers carried them, and the drug dealers might have upgraded by now. And tonight, it served to scare the life out of her while standing in a dark hallway. She clipped the beeper back onto the waist band of her scrubs and took in a slow breath in hopes of steadying her nerves.

You're just tired. Working eighty hours a week could do that.

She glanced back down the corridor one last time. This storm was bound to pass sometime. Growing up in the Rocky Mountains, the storms would roll across the valley and be gone within a few minutes. But Chicago was another story entirely. Here, a thunderstorm could hang around for an hour or more and dump inches of rain by the end of it. Hopefully it would be gone by the time she was off call in the morning. Until then, the beeper was bound to go off again unless she showed up in the ICU soon. She turned away from the empty corridor behind her and pushed through the double doors of the intensive care unit.

The doors opened into an expansive twenty-room unit reserved for post-surgical patients, as opposed to the medical ICU that stood one floor above them. Electronic beeps and the hum of ventilators filled every square foot of the sterile white environment. A single strip of flowered wallpaper along the walls attempted to break the white monotony and provide a warmth that this place otherwise lacked. Bright light overhead lit a path around a curved nurse's station that arced around the wide expanse of rooms, like a central hub in a wheel. The alcohol scent of waterless hand gel perfumed the unit but could not mask that underlying odor of the dying.

Evan stepped through the doors and a nurse glanced up from her work. She stood and rushed to meet her. Her dark purple scrubs and colorful scrub jacket were a stark contrast to the white room.

"I'm sorry I paged you again, Dr. Jensen," she spoke in a hushed voice. "But he's going downhill fast."

The nurse led her to room nine at the far east end of the unit. Despite the illuminated department, this individual room remained dim except for the occasional bursts of lightning through the window. The glass wall and door that bordered this room from the brightly lit corridor had been covered with the privacy curtain, most likely the doing of the nurse.

Evan stopped at the door and her eyes fell upon the man she had pitied all week. Peter Ceglinski was an unfortunate soul, a Polish immigrant, who at the age of eighty-three continued to work as a cab driver. A week ago, his route on Chicago's north side brought fate to his small car when someone attacked and robbed him. Then, the same fate brought him to Evan on that terrible night. He lay in the emergency room, half-delirious and his abdomen swelling with internal bleeding. Upon operating, she had found his bowel hemorrhaging and necrotic, all complicated by his use of heparin to thin his blood, a typical treatment for a man who once had a blood clot that had traveled to his lung. Now, despite Evan's best effort, Mr. Ceglinski lay dying in the ICU, the remaining bowel in his abdomen slowly losing its blood supply and his belly distending once again. Perhaps another surgery could have helped, but his weakened heart would probably not tolerate this. Then, three days ago, his grandson and only living relative arrived, requesting that his grandfather should be allowed to die in peace: *do not resuscitate, DNR.* His signature had made it official, and he was probably right to do so. Evan was not so sure that Mr. Ceglinski would survive another surgery.

The man lay motionless upon the bed, an oxygen mask hissing at his mouth and nose. His gaunt frame appeared even thinner than before. Multiple intravenous lines pumped saline to help maintain his blood pressure but it seemed futile now. Evan's eyes fell upon the blood pressure reading as it monitored continuously through an arterial catheter: 61/32, and this was dropping. Soon the plummet in blood pressure would affect his heart.

She stepped to the bedside and her fingers found the pulse at his wrist. It was weak and thready at best. The arterial catheter reading was real. She swallowed and felt her dry mouth against her tongue. This was the worst part. Nothing in medical school or college prepared you for moments like this: when a person lay before you and his life slips away, and there is little you can do about it. There was always something cosmic about it, beyond the science and the textbooks. This was real; this was death. Some of her colleagues watched this moment as a collection of numbers and ratios that changed continuously until the moment that they reached zero. But she refused to see it that way. She never wanted to see only a number and forget that it was once a man, a man with a family, a job, a life. At moments like this, the air thickened and became difficult to breathe in and out, as if something greater and unseen filled the room. She couldn't hear his raspy breath any longer and the blood pressure continued to drop: 40/25, 38/22. The electrocardiogram registered heartbeats that now grew further apart.

"Do you want me to do anything?" the nurse whispered, her tone giving a hint of respect for the same sensations that Evan always felt around the dying.

Evan shook her head. "Just let him go."

The nurse nodded and stepped from the room. Evan slipped her fingers from the pulse at his wrist to his cold hand. Like a cool, wax figure, his hand was stiff and lifeless but she held onto him. Perhaps it would be the only comfort she could provide to him in his last minutes.

His hand suddenly clasped about hers in a crushing grip. She gasped and almost cried out at the vice that latched onto her wrist. Then his eyes flashed open, two pale orbs surrounding ghostly blue, senile eyes. Pinpoint pupils turned toward her and his face grimaced in agony. His free hand fumbled to pull the oxygen mask from his face. Halting gasps escaped his throat beyond his yellowed teeth. He looked to her in desperation and his mouth moved, eager to speak. Lightning erupted through the window, illuminating his fearful eyes that stared at her with desperation. Evan leaned closer to him, her hand gripped tightly in his.

"It—" he muttered and fought to speak. "It . . . comes . . . soon." A rasping, rattling breath filled his lungs and his eyes widened in horror. "Go" he hissed. "Get out now." A pained gurgle welled from his throat and he grew limp, his hand falling to the bed.

Evan slipped her throbbing wrist from his grasp and stepped back. The alarms of the heart monitor rang out and displayed the twisted, erratic pattern of ventricular fibrillation: the writhing, non-functional pumping of a dying heart. Then she gazed down upon him but he remained still, the breath in his lungs now gone. The nurse appeared at her side at the sound of the monitor alarms.

"There it is," she muttered. "Fibrillation."

Evan rubbed the pain from her fingers and watched him as though he would awaken again. "Did he say anything to you today?"

The nurse furrowed her brow. "No. Actually he has been non-responsive since his grandson was here three days ago."

Evan said nothing. Perhaps Mr. Ceglinski had a quick blood re-perfusion of his brain, drawing him to confused consciousness for a brief moment. It wouldn't happen again, though. The monitor turned from the twisted writhe of ventricular fibrillation to a dampened flat line.

Evan sighed and glanced up to the room clock above the bed. "Time of death: 23:47."

Chapter 2

Water swirled and bubbled beyond her ears with each stroke of her arms, but with the soft earplugs, it only sounded like a dull roar. It dampened the rest of the noise in the aquatic center. Kids screaming in the shallow pool. Moms yelling at them to stop running. Normally, all that sound wouldn't be there. But Evan had a harder time than usual getting out of bed and a swim was the only thing that helped with the post-call headache. The same one she got when she drank too much caffeine during a shift just to pull through another surgery after midnight.

The water always helped. It flowed down the length of her back and rushed with each kick. The red line along the bottom of the pool came to a stop just before she turned her head to the right and took in a quick breath. Her fingers reached ahead of her with one last, long stroke. And there it was. The concrete wall touched her hand with the exhale. Her body glided to a stop and she lifted her head.

With her ribs still moving in a quick rhythm to catch her breath, she pulled her wrist from the water and clicked the stop on her watch. 4:48:26. Slower than usual for the 400-meter, especially the freestyle, the same stroke that got her a full-ride through college. But that wasn't unusual after being on call and every joint in her back ached.

She pulled the blue rubber swim cap from her head with the polarized goggles and rested along the edge of the pool. It didn't matter what her time was, as long as she made it into the water today. It was getting harder every day to get a swim into her day the further she got through residency. Getting up at four in the morning on most days to get to the hospital by five and then home by seven or eight at night, and that was when she wasn't on call. That was just to get the work done.

But the water helped to get rid of all those worries from the day.

Evan closed her eyes and wiped the moisture from her forehead. Swimming laps and then finishing with the usual 400-meter freestyle had loosened her joints and cleared her brain. She pulled herself out of the water and paced back to the locker room.

The rest of the day stayed quiet. Thankfully. She just wanted time alone before she had to return to the hospital in the morning.

With the fatigue setting in her muscles from the swim, she stretched out on the small sofa in the front room of her apartment and let the television run in the background. It didn't really matter what was on. Scrolling through social media on her phone proved to be the most entertainment for the night. What was everyone else doing on a Wednesday night? Because there was no way she was going to go out once she had settled on the couch. Almost everyone else she knew worked at the hospital as well, and pretty much was either working tonight or doing the same thing she had planned. Absolutely nothing, and that was the best part.

Just scrolling through her feed on the phone. This is what Julie had for dinner. This is the workout John did this morning. Here are some cute cat pictures. Brainless entertainment, and nothing that she had to think about too hard. A funny meme now and then made her laugh.

Her finger stopped and hovered above the screen when she saw the picture. *Here's a memory from seven years ago, hope you enjoy it.*

The colors of it ran into a blur with the tears that welled in her eyes. She remembered that photo. She took it during the summer just before she graduated from college. The day had been hot, but the river was nice and cool. Their drift boat sat anchored along the shore line with the line of mountains in the background. A perfect stop for lunch, some fishing, and a memorable photo.

Dad had leaned in close, the bristles of his white beard tickling her cheek. She had cringed at just the moment her finger hit the button on her phone, taking the picture of her face contorted into a grimace. He had insisted that she keep it and they laughed about it for days. Just her and him, like always.

It had always been the two of them since her mother had left when she was four years old. An only child, and apparently too much to handle from a woman that wanted a life in southern California to become an actress or something. She had never seen her in a single film or television show, and if she had, she would have turned the damn thing off. Dad had been the one that raised her, and that couldn't have been easy. A single machinist and a teenage girl whose moods changed constantly.

He had always made time for her, though. Just like that day on the river.

And then she had had to make time for him when the doctor gave him the diagnosis of mesothelioma. A lung cancer, probably acquired from years on the job and exposure to all the chemical and structural hazards that came with it. He had made it to her college graduation. He made it long enough to know that she had gotten accepted into medical school.

He didn't make it long enough to see her start her first day as a medical student. And just like that, she was on her own. Just her and the money that she had inherited from his accounts and his pension. The only time she had seen any other relatives was on the day of the funeral. Some aunt of her father's had approached her, a woman with a pinched mouth and too much rose-scented perfume. There was no way she would ever remember the woman's name after that day, and it didn't matter because she had never heard from her again.

And her mother hadn't even come. Maybe she had never heard about it, and Evan had no way of letting her know.

So, she sat on the chair at the funeral home with people she didn't know giving her hugs and condolences and potato salads until she was sick of them. The only other person she knew in that room lay as still as wax in a coffin only feet in front of her.

A small measure of relief came the day she got the letter from her dad's former lawyer. It had been a cold and miserably rainy day and she had just gone through a series of med school exams when it arrived. But it made her smile as she read it. A class-action lawsuit brought about by families and victims of mesothelioma had resulted in a powerful win. Her dad would get some justice for what had happened to him, and as his only heir, she received a payout that had helped keep her head above the cost of medical school and now residency.

And here was his picture, seven years later. *Hope you enjoy it.*

That smile of his, lips always together. He had hated his coffee-stained teeth and refused to get them whitened. His smile had beamed anyway because he reflected it in his eyes.

No more scrolling. That was enough memories for tonight. Any more and she might not sleep. She rolled to her side but kept the screen awake with the photo on it. The picture turned as she tilted the phone to its side and propped it against a book on the coffee table. Her dad's smiling eyes stared at her, and she ignored the grimaced look she had on her face seven years ago.

Love you, daddy. Miss you so much.

Especially now that the glittering silver and crystalline trinket sparkled next to her phone. Damn. She had forgotten that it was there, still strung through a silver chain, and nestled among a mess of books, bills and other junk mail on top of the coffee table.

The engagement ring. She still hadn't put it back on since she first got it last weekend. What would her dad think of her now, too scared to put on a stupid ring and too scared to admit that she wasn't ready for any of this.

And it was going to stay there for now. No sense in worrying about it tonight. She reached to the table and shuffled the papers on top of it until she couldn't see it anymore.

With the remote in reach on the table, she punched up the volume on the TV until the program was loud enough to drown out her thoughts.

The chill of the auditorium left goose bumps on her arms. Evan hugged the lapels of the long white coat around her torso and squinted into the room where the lights had been dimmed. The projector screen in the front of the auditorium glowed a harsh white, awaiting the education conference that was about to begin. Every Tuesday morning. A necessary evil of residency, even if the caffeine hadn't kicked in yet.

Four rows from the front and in the center of the small auditorium, the seven guys that comprised the rest of her residency group sat and talked among themselves. Other residents sat scattered in their own groups throughout the auditorium, but the surgery residents talked the loudest with little care of anyone else in the room.

"Hey," an elbow jabbed into her ribs.

Evan turned to see the woman who stood behind her with two cardboard cups of steaming coffee in her hands.

"I got you one," the woman said, her brown eyes a little too bright this early in the morning. Brandy held out one of the cups to Evan.

"You're a lifesaver." Warmth pulsed into her fingertips with the cup nestled in her hand. The instant bitter taste perked up her brain.

"How was call the other night?"

Evan sipped at the coffee, bitter and strong. "Busy. Had a gunshot wound come in, totally shredded the guy's bowel."

"Gross," As a Family Practice resident, Brandy didn't spend much time in the operating room, and that's how she liked it. Not everyone was made for surgery. The long hours. The guts and the smell. Her nose scrunched up and Evan recognized the familiar aversion.

"You wanna sit with us this morning?" Brandy said and ticked her head toward the small group of residents sitting in the front of the auditorium. "Or is it back with the Jock Squad today?"

Evan glanced once again to the group of her fellow surgery residents. Not that she minded hanging out with them, but she just wasn't sure she wanted to deal with the obnoxious jokes and *bro-talk* today.

"Or let's just sit in the back," Brandy said with a smile. "Maybe Dr. Sorenson won't call on us if we're in the dark."

"That man has x-ray vision. He could see us through the walls if we were standing outside," Evan said and followed her to the back row.

They settled into their seats and Evan took another sip of the coffee. It hit her stomach with warmth and the magic of caffeine welled into her brain.

"So," Brandy spoke, low enough so that nobody else could hear them. "I need to see it. Why aren't you wearing it?"

A twinge of fluttering started in her chest. This had to come up eventually. It was definitely something she didn't want to talk about just before grand rounds, but Brandy's arched eyebrow implied that she wasn't going to let it go. The news must have spread through the residency ranks already, despite her best effort to keep it under wraps for now.

Evan curled her finger around the chain along her neck and the ring drew from under her scrub top. Brandy grasped it between her fingers and held it into the dim light.

"It's gorgeous," she said, the diamond winking at her. "But seriously, why is it not on your finger?"

"I don't want to lose it," Evan said. "You know how it is when you constantly have to take it off to do surgery. These things get lost all the time, always removing them and putting them on the scrub sinks or in your scrub pocket. I don't want it to be another casualty."

"Details. How did he propose?" Brandy asked.

Evan sipped at the coffee again. It was still too hot, but anything to give her a few seconds to push down the quivers that turned her stomach into knots. "We just went out to dinner and he asked."

"Come on. I said details."

"That's it," Evan said with a smile. "Not much to tell."

"Well, you don't seem that excited."

"No, I am. Just kinda wasn't expecting it."

"You do love him, don't you?"

The jolt of it shuddered into Evan's chest. "Of course I do. We've been together since med school. It's the next logical step."

"This isn't about logic, sweetie."

Evan took the ring and slipped it onto her finger with the chain still dangling from the edge. "I know. I just never thought of myself as a wife." Was that it? Being someone's wife, just like her mother had once been her father's wife. Yeah. She turned into a real piece of work.

"You can do it."

"Alright," a man's voice came over the speaker system. "Let's get started."

They both glanced up to the podium, where Dr. Sorenson stood and worked at the computer before him, bringing up the presentation on the projector screen. He stood tall above the podium, a button-down shirt and a blue tie below his long white coat. His pepper gray hair was neatly styled and his face cleanly shaven. He still looked just like the huge picture hung in the main lobby of the hospital, along the wall of hospital administrators and financial contributors. The overlords of St. John's Medical Center. As the Chief Medical Officer of the hospital, he had power over everyone in this room, and the silence that commenced as soon as he took the podium reflected that dominance.

Evan followed his gaze that floated among the young heads watching him from the auditorium, but they never seemed to drift toward the back. Maybe Brandy was right: he wouldn't notice them back there. The white screen behind him lit up and flashed to the initial slide of his presentation and his voice carried into the room. Respiratory illnesses, also known as *the topic of the day*. Dr. Sorenson had worked at St. John's for over thirty years and had chaired the OB/GYN department for most of that time, yet he seemed to know everything about all medicine. Not just the female stuff. Evan guessed that was why he was the chief medical officer. He was just too smart just to keep in a private clinic.

The initial slides clicked through and she barely noticed them. Lung infections had their treatments. Something she had studied a dozen times since med school. With the caffeine buzzing in her veins, she glanced down to the ring on her finger. The diamond glinted back at her, but the hollow pit formed in her stomach again.

The scene from the restaurant played over in her mind, just like it had all weekend. Paul smiled at her from across the table, the candlelight glinting in his dark brown eyes. He said something that she couldn't remember now. And then he reached into his pocket. She knew what was happening before he pulled out the small velvet box. That's when the panic first set in. It had jumbled up her thoughts and her mouth had gone dry. He said the words, and even now she didn't recall hearing them. She just knew that they had been released like a flock of birds.

And then she let go of her own flock of birds before killing them. She said yes before she realized she had done it, and the memory of that moment still squeezed at her insides.

What's wrong with me? Paul is the best. Stop this.

"Dr. Jensen?" Sorenson's voice boomed through the speakers. Her heart dropped in her chest and she glanced up to him. The heads of the other residents turned back to her.

"Well," he said. "Do you know the answer?"

Damn. She hadn't even heard the question.

"I'm sorry—" she stammered.

"What is the primary treatment for *Pneumococcal* pneumonia?"

This was so easy, but the answer escaped her. All she could think of was Paul down on his knee with a sparkling ring in a box, and everyone in the restaurant gasping and murmuring with joy at the scene. This ring had made her stupid. She was sure of it.

Chapter 3

The late October fog rolled in across Lake Michigan, moving like a thick cotton blanket under the mass of storm clouds that hung at bay over the sparkling skyscrapers. The humidity was heavy with the charge of electricity that had previously lit up the evening sky. But the city didn't notice. Headlights raced by in an endless line down Lake Shore Drive, flickering beyond the guardrails and glistening on the still waters of the Chicago River. Rain had washed down the smog, leaving that familiar tart odor against the cement. Despite the recent storm and ever-approaching bank of fog, the city moved and throbbed, and its heart beat at the center of Navy Pier. The lights of the Ferris wheel were now softened halos in the encroaching mists.

Evan relaxed back against the hard metal of the folding chair and perched her feet on the cement ridge. The parking garage still remained a resident's favorite haven: eight stories high, outside the hospital but still a part of it, quiet and with a great view over the Chicago skyline even at one o'clock in the morning. She brought the bottle of water to her lips and sipped as if were just something to occupy her time.

The water that slid down her throat had warmed significantly since she had purchased it from the vending machine hours earlier, when she thought she would have had time to drink it but the beeper went off again. That ghoulish little device forever strapped to her hip. It summoned her to yet another trauma and another gunshot wound. She sipped again and for the first time felt the ache in her shoulders, that same ache that always came this time of night, at every single call she worked. But resting was not an option; it never was. Another trauma was inevitable. Somebody in the hospital would always need the general surgery resident on call for the night. She only hoped, as she did at every call, that it would change when she graduated from residency.

But everything always seemed to hinge on the future. It had ever since high school. *When I finally get into Princeton, then it will all be great. When I finally get into medical school, then it will all be great. When I finally get into residency, everything will be better. When I finally become an attending physician . . .* but what then? Residency was like purgatory, as she thought of it. A waiting game, making it through each day, through the experiences the attendings said would "make you a better doctor, a stronger doctor." So why did it feel like ridicule and humiliation so often? But in some way, perhaps in a twisted sado-masochistic way, they were correct. She had come so far since internship and she *was* a better doctor.

Just as she thought, the beep was inevitable. It came without warning and burrowed into her head like a jackhammer: that repetitive buzzing sound that hummed from the beeper. The little demon strapped to the waist of her scrub pants. Evan pushed back that cringe long enough to glance down to the electronic display of the device. The all-too-familiar number glowed back at her — the emergency room. Her nighttime skyline and water break was done and it was time to continue working.

She swallowed the rest of the water in two big gulps and gazed at the twinkling lights of the Hancock building and then to the flashing antennae of Willis Tower. The humid air drifted across her face with the smell of car exhaust and a haze of the Chicago river, but then came the pungent memory of the ICU the other night and the cold hand of a man at his last breath. What had he said before he slipped away? *It comes soon.* He must have sensed his last few seconds.

With one final glance out to the city and the few cars that sped down the streets, she took in a slow breath. *I saw a man die last night. How many of you can say that?*

She turned to the elevators and began her descent to the emergency room.

Evan opened the door to the back entrance of the emergency room and the flood of lights, noise, and the smell of exhaust that exuded through the ambulance bay filled her nose. She stepped down the long corridor lined with small rooms occupied with the urgently ill. Children, men, women, the old, the young, the drunk. All the variety of humankind converged in the ER in their most unpleasantness. Eyes watched her as she stepped past their rooms, eyes that wondered if she was there to see them, to help them in some way. Evan averted her glance as she moved to the main station. Nobody wanted to be stared at in their suffering. She just needed to get in, do her job, and get back out before they called again.

She rounded the corner and the corridor opened into a bustling station of nurses, technicians, and physicians. The wide, curving charting desk arced around the front of the emergency room and faced the four main trauma rooms, which appeared surprisingly empty tonight. The ambulance bay doors opened and two paramedics rolled their gurney into the brightly lit emergency room. Evan stepped aside and allowed them to pass as she spied the elderly, demented man on the cart. The smell of old urine wafted as they passed by and the man mumbled unintelligibly.

Evan held her breath until they passed by her and then she stepped up to the ER census computer. Names listed next to a room number followed by the patient's symptoms. She scanned the collection of complaints to see if any of them possibly required the consultation of general surgery: anything to not speak to the ER secretary, who was usually cranky and overworked.

Hands grasped her waist from behind and lifted her off her feet.

The force of the arms around her pushed the air from her lungs and her fingers grasped to the muscled cords that held her. She turned back to face the man's familiar brown eyes. A breath of relief escaped her lips despite her rapid heart rate and trembling hands. But those eyes shined as he smiled: perfect teeth to a perfect smile. His dark hair a warm sable with the fluorescent lights behind him, hair cut short and his jaw angled in such a way that he reminded her of the gorgeous elves in Lord of the Rings. And when he smiled, those dimples appeared in his cheeks.

"My precious. I've lured you here," he said with his best Golem voice. "All part of my master plan," he smiled and eased up next to her, a chart in his hand.

This was always a part of his usual routine. Doctor Paul Williams. Third-year ER resident from Austin, Texas. His time spent away from home had dampened his accent but, although subtle, it was still there.

And he was the cause of her anxiety all weekend. But looking at him now, it was no wonder she couldn't think or speak right around him. Those nervous flutters turned into something else that held her attention to him, like she never wanted to turn away.

"I had to page you," he admitted and held out a clipboard chart to her.

"I'm sure you volunteered," she smiled and accepted the chart.

He laughed and that boyish grin showed up again. "Actually, I did."

Evan glanced across the chart: a 15-year-old girl with stomach pains and nausea. Her mother brought her in when the girl woke up in pain. Negative pregnancy test. Temperature in the ER was 102 degrees.

"CAT scan shows probable appendicitis," he spoke. "We gave her some antibiotics and a little morphine. All ready for surgery." He leaned in closer. "What are you doing this weekend?"

Evan smiled and lifted her eyes. There was that magic grin of his again. "What room is she in?"

"Four," he spoke and rose with her as she hooked the chart into her elbow. "I can get us reservations at *Tru* this weekend."

Her eyes narrow. "No you can't. And we couldn't afford it even if you did."

"Yes I can," he said and lowered his voice while he still smiled. "I've got connections."

"I'm sure you do." Just as she tried to turn, his fingers reached to the chain at her neck that plunged below the edge of her scrub top. The ring dangled at the end and the diamond sparkled in the harsh fluorescent lights.

"And you can finally wear this on your finger instead of on a chain," he said.

"You know I don't want to lose it when I'm operating." She grasped the chain and tucked it under her top.

Evan stepped away from the desk but Paul moved around the end to stop her before she went back down the hall. "Maybe we can talk about finally setting a date."

The flutter settled into her gut again. Does that have to be done so soon? All the saliva dried in her mouth but she still smiled. She grasped the lapel of his white coat and pulled him close as she lifted onto her toes, planting a quick kiss on his lips. "Sure. Now, I have to get to work."

The last tingle from the kiss still lingered on her lips when she turned away from him. Just leave them wanting more, she thought and smiled as she felt his eyes still on her.

"I'll be waiting right here when you're done," he called after her.

Evan flashed him a smile as a middle-aged nurse stepped around him and shoved another chart into his chest.

"I wish you would hop like that when I walk into the room," she spoke with a grin and eyed him.

"Margaret, I always do." Paul pointed at her and then glanced back to Evan before she plunged into room four.

Chapter 4

Matt hated hospitals, especially when they put him in the Crisis Room.

Too many voices. Too many people. But here he lay, in this damned emergency room, handcuffed to the gurney just like one of those psychopathic sickos you see on television. The same two uniformed police officers that brought him here now stood just outside his room chatting about inane garbage that would never matter.

Matthew Logan Pearce (that's what the mug shot would inevitably say), with a gash in his hand and one above his left eye. They would never understand why. Not that nurse at the desk, not that brown-eyed, pretty-boy, jock doctor that seemed to have Matt's chart now and occasionally glanced into the Crisis Room with apprehension. That's what they called this place, the room in the furthest corner of the ER but not so far that you couldn't keep an eye on it from the front station. The crisis room: the place to put people who have a "crisis". But, his situation now couldn't be called anything less than a crisis.

"Hey, Margaret," he heard the jock-doctor calling out at the front desk.

The nurse turned to him and the doctor ticked his head toward Matt's room. "What's the deal with this guy?"

She moved closer to him and turned her back to the room. "Police brought him from the north side. They said they were

called to a disturbance and found him in a restaurant screaming and tossing dishes. He tried to escape by throwing himself
through the front window. He has lacerations on his left hand
and on his face that need stitching before he goes to jail."

"Do we have toxicology on him yet?"

"Not yet. Enjoy, Paul," she spoke as she walked away with
an evil smile.

The jock doctor, with his cheek dimples and narrow jaw
and perfect brown hair, looked far too young to be working here,
and he had the same look that they all had. Nervous. The bob of
his Adam's apple when he swallowed as he looked over the chart.
Anxious, despite the two officers that stood outside his room.
The doctor approached the gurney and pulled up a metal stool,
the legs screeching against the linoleum. The faint scent of alcohol hand gel and men's body wash followed the young doctor.
The harsh overhead lights blinked on and Matt squinted, but this
just opened the blood-caked laceration above his eye once again.

"I'm Dr. Williams. Alright, let's have a look at you Mr.
Pearce," the doctor spoke as he set aside the chart.

Matt rolled to his back, feeling every ache that now lingered
in his muscles. The handcuff clinked about the side-rail as he
turned to face the doctor. Fresh blood trickled down his temple.
The cut must have opened up again with this much oozing down
the side of his face.

The doctor pulled his latex gloves on as he glanced over
him. Matt's black hair hung over his eyes, hair that needed cutting almost a month ago. His brown eyes looked at the doctor
and couldn't help but think at how opposite the two of them
were. Had the doctor even noticed that Matt wore a suit and tie?
Or did he just assume he was some lunatic pulled off the street?

Gloved hands touched the laceration above his eye. He

dabbed a gauze pad around the wound that sent painful shocks through his head.

"So," Dr. Williams said, "do you want to tell me how this happened?"

Matt winced as the swab touched the wound, but the doctor continued to clean. "Just a misunderstanding."

These people would never know, or comprehend, the things that happened tonight, or any night in the past three years for that matter. But after what happened at that restaurant — why he had gone there in the first place — it would be hard to predict any longer. He had suspected this, though. Things had become worse over the last several months and it was becoming too difficult to disguise. This doctor would never understand, and just like everyone else, would probably think he was insane. So, he just had to lie.

And it all came back to why he hated hospitals; this was like the county fair for *them*. This kind of place was a beacon, like one of those bug-zappers to a moth. Horrible things happen here every day, and that tended to leave its thumbprint, its greasy, bloody thumbprint on everything it touched. It hung back in the corners, in the shadows, even under the brightest light. Parents often tell their children that a light will chase away the biggest monsters, but not here. That doesn't seem to work in a place like this. Those things hide in the brightest of daylight; only normal people cannot see them—or they don't want to be seen. Even now, despite the humidity and oppressive warmth of the emergency room, Matt sensed the chill that coalesced in the recesses of that Crisis Room.

The young doctor finished his work on the facial lacerations and turned his attention to Matt's hand, but the bracelet of the handcuff obstructed the laceration.

"Excuse me, officers," Dr. Williams spoke as both men turned. "I can't repair this with the handcuffs in the way."

The older, grayer officer entered the room and drew the keys from his belt. "Are you gonna behave, Pearce?"

Matt nodded and felt the instant relief of the handcuff clasp releasing. The doctor worked at the wound and the officer returned to his post, continuing the inane conversation with his partner about going to Wisconsin last summer. Just moronic gibberish that eventually drew the attention of a fair young nurse who joined in on the conversation. Everyone oblivious. Everyone distracted by the mundane. Nobody can hear or see. *But I can.*

Despite the bright lights shining through dull light panels, the room narrowed and darkened when the chill descended. Matt sensed it in his bones like an oppressive fog that rolled across a deserted shore. A crushing, choking fog. The core of his body trembled with the cold and fear that pulled at his insides. Small beads of perspiration formed across his brow and below the gauze dressing taped above his eye. If only the doctor would work faster before he could no longer hide his distress. But it continued to approach like an unwanted guest. Closer. Colder.

"Alright, Mr. Pearce. You're done," the doctor spoke and finished taping the last dressing over the wound. "We just need to wait for the results on your blood work and you'll be on your way." He stood and collected the suture items. "Just try to keep them clean and the sutures will be taken out in about five days." The jock-doctor absently nodded and slipped out of the room.

Just as he had departed, Matt almost wished he had stayed. Then maybe the thing would leave him alone. The lights overhead flickered; one could have missed it if not paying attention. The chill intensified and the heavy air pressed down on his chest. He curled to his side, his eyes searching frantically through the door for anybody who could feel it too. He trembled in the chill of the room, his heart pounding in his ears. In short, quick bursts, his breath moved past his lips and now condensed into wisps of fog.

It was near now, and far worse than the one at the restaurant. This one wanted to be heard, and damn was it big.

Matt pinched his eyes closed and muttered his memorized whispers under his cold breath: poems, song lyrics. Anything to drive it away. Prayers didn't usually work, only quick distractions helped a little. *Jack and Jill went up the hill, to fetch a pail of water. . . .*

That was when the whispers came. More like screaming in a voice that couldn't muster the energy to be heard any louder.

He cringed and whispered between clenched teeth. *Jack fell down and broke his crown . . . .*

It raged with such torment and violence that it shook his frame and drowned out the sound of the nursery rhyme. His eyes flew open and sought for any hope, any solace out in the light. But there it was, watching him, waiting for something in all its fury and hideousness.

Paul approached the staff desk, just as Evan emerged from room four, chart in hand. Again, those brown eyes beamed at her as she placed the chart on the counter and proceeded to fill in the surgical note. She purposefully ignored his smile, this time. No more distractions tonight.

"So?" he asked.

"I agree with you," she said. "It's appendicitis. The operating room will be ready in thirty minutes."

"I also scored two tickets to the Cubs game this Friday," he said and leaned over the desk.

Evan finished signing the last of the surgical consent forms. "Is that before or after we set our wedding date?"

"I'll let you decide."

Margaret cleared her throat loud enough to interrupt their conversation. "Your test results, Romeo."

He accepted the paperwork she shoved at him as she huffed away to another patient.

"What the hell," he muttered, his brow furrowed and his eyes squinting down to the results. "I was sure this guy was high on something."

"Another crisis patient?" she said and tucked her chart into the rack behind the desk.

"Yeah," Paul said. "Don't really know what his deal is though. Apparently it's not meth or cocaine."

A shiver ran up her spine, an unexpected sensation that drew her attention away from him and left his words as hollow echoes. The hair on her neck prickled. The pen in her hand slipped to the floor at that moment. The noise of the ER dulled into a hollow sound. A faint puff cloud of white breath slipped from her lips in the chill that had closed around her.

Something watched from behind her; she was sure of it. She turned and gazed back to see only the busy traffic back and forth along the main corridor. Nurses. Radiology technicians. Laboratory staff. All the usual cast of a night in the emergency room. Another pair of paramedics wheeled their hapless patient through the ambulance bay. A nurse walked a patient through the main doors and to the triage room, stepping past a pair of police officers chatting with another nurse.

And then she saw it. Those eyes, scared and searching from under flickering lights in the crisis room. The man lay curled against the bed rail with absolute terror in his eyes, but his steady gaze on her never wavered. The shivers came again and she turned away.

"Is that him?" she whispered to Paul.

"Yeah," he said and glanced over her shoulder to the room. "Guy went crazy in a restaurant. I had to sew him up before he goes with the cops. But I thought he was high on something. Maybe he *is* just crazy."

Evan knew those eyes still burrowed on her. *Right. Maybe just crazy.*

Matt gasped when the woman arrived at the desk. The screaming suddenly stopped, leaving only a dread silence and chill. But it still waited out there, this gruesome, sad, angry thing. Waiting. Watching. Twitching with fury. To his surprise, it turned and faced the woman doctor, focusing all its energy upon her, and he knew that this woman couldn't hear it, just like everyone else. Matt could, though, and its anger intensified, dropping the temperature of the room again.

Never before had he witnessed this. What did this thing intend to do? It gathered its energy, but for what purpose, and who was this woman that it should care? The one thing he could be confident of was that this entity grew more frustrated and something bad was going to happen when it finally snapped. He saw things clearer than ever before. Enough is enough. The restaurant was one thing, but this was completely different. He had to do something.

The woman, her golden hair falling down over collar of her white lab coat (he could only assume she was a doctor too), whispered to the jock doctor, was it Dr. Williams? Clearly, he was enamored of her, and why wouldn't he be? She was beautiful. Young. Athletic. He would not leave her side, though. How could Matt speak to her, warn her? Who was he kidding? There was no way she would ever believe him.

The angry thing watched and neared her with calculated motion. There wouldn't be much time left, whatever its intentions. Matt clenched his cold fingers into a fist and then pushed himself upright upon the gurney while a plan formed in his brain. *Only one chance. You've got one chance, Pearce.* As he held his breath, he slipped from the edge of the bed, his eyes focused on the guards. The officers continued their conversation with the pretty nurse. But beyond them, the angry thing remained.

Yes, one chance. Point of no return. His cold fingers clasped together to buoy his courage. A quiet step forward in silence and the thing still knew nothing about his intentions. The cop shifted his legs and the pistol in his holster seemed to grin at him. Then the lady doctor moved from the desk and approached the rack of printed forms directly across from his door. Now or never.

Matt lunged through the door, grabbing the gun as he raced beyond the two cops. The officer flinched in surprise but couldn't react fast enough to stop him as he leapt across the corridor. The next few seconds seemed an eternity as Matt grasped the woman doctor's coat and pulled her against him. Screams of horror erupted from the nurse at the door as the other cop reached for his gun. With the pistol held firm in his hand, he heaved it up to the blonde doctor's head, pressing it against her temple more powerfully than he had planned.

The doctor felt small in his grasp, her shoulders trembling against him. Her feet stumbled as he pulled her back.

The other cop upholstered his gun.

"Stop! Put it down!" he shouted at the cop and pushed the gun against her head much harder. She winced as her neck craned against its force. The cop halted but kept the pistol in hand. "Throw it over here or I'll kill her!"

The officer hesitated and Matt could see his desire to shoot his suspect and be the hero. But the cop waited and then tossed the gun toward the ambulance door.

"Everyone to the ground, now!"

His voice carried sharply across the room and many flinched, their eyes fixated on the gun in his hand. Several of the staff dropped to the floor in a trembling mass. Most went down, except for that doctor, that jock. He stood, his arms held out before him.

"Just let her go, Mr. Pearce," Paul spoke, the shaking evident in his voice. "You don't want to do this."

"Shut up! You know nothing about me!" Matt pointed the gun in his direction. "Get down now!"

Dr. Williams wanted to diffuse the situation. Matt understood that, but he couldn't afford to let the woman go. She was in far more danger that any of them knew. He had to stop the thing that stalked her, the thing that now slithered into the shadows of the crisis room.

The jock doctor eased himself to the ground but kept his gaze on the lady doctor in his grasp.

Matt kept the gun pointed out to the crowd and then glanced to the ambulance bay door behind him. There in the parking lot was what he had hoped for. He trained the gun down to the first cop that lay splayed on the floor.

"Give me your keys," he demanded.

The officer fumbled at his belt and finally unclipped the key ring. With a shaking hand he reached the ring out to him. Matt released his grip on Evan and leaned into her ear.

"Get them from him."

The woman froze until he nudged her toward the cop. She cautiously took one step forward and stooped, his hand clutching the back of her coat. Her fingers grasped the metal key ring when the overhead PA system came to life with a woman's voice.

"Code Silver. Emergency Room. Code Silver. Emergency Room."

He pulled her back and she crashed against him. "What does that mean?" he spoke.

"Code Silver," she stammered, "it means there's a safety alert. Security is on their way."

He had run out of time. He wrapped a strong arm about her shoulders and placed the gun at her temple again. Matt pulled her back with each step he took toward the doors and her feet stumbled to keep up with him. They neared the ambulance bay and the automatic doors slid open. He pulled her along, the gun hard against her skull.

"If anybody follows us I'll kill her!" he shouted and pulled her through the door, which slid closed as they entered the humid nighttime air.

Chapter 5

Evan didn't notice the usual smell of exhaust fumes in the ambulance bay. Only harsh lights cast down from the upper floors of the hospital contrasted by the dark of the Chicago night. The pounding heartbeat in her ears and the scream that stuck in her throat couldn't pull the fear of the moment from her chest. With the barrel-end of the gun pressed against her head, the guy wrapped a rigid arm around her and moved into the dark of the parking lot. Each second that ticked by drew her further away from the hospital, the repetitive peal of the floor alarms growing more distant. Her feet stumbled beneath her but it didn't matter: he pulled her to the first row of cars and raised the key fob in his hand. On first glance, she had mistaken him for a lanky, thin, drugged out weak man, but he was a lot stronger than she had suspected.

A flash of headlights and a resounding electronic beep startled her. Everything that she had seen on those TV programs about self-defense shouted in her brain. *Don't let him take you away. Whatever you do, don't get in the car.*

Scratch him. Bite him. Whatever it takes.

His grip had wrapped around her torso and pinned her arms. No scratching. The race of thoughts whipped through her mind. She raised her knee and pounded her heel back against his shin. The guy stopped for only a second, pulled her off her feet and moved faster toward the car. She no longer had any leverage left. And they were right beside the car, a dark blue sedan with a police light bar on the roof.

The movement sickened her. The rear passenger door opened and the blur of light left her dizzy. She fell against a cold vinyl surface and the slam of the door sent rigid chills down her legs. Her spine froze and she stayed pressed against the seat. The driver door opened and slammed shut, and then the engine roared to life. Tires pealed across the pavement, leaving the smell of burned rubber to waft into the cab of the police car.

The car jolted and she could only imagine that he had driven over a curb or something. It almost made her scream but she pressed her palm against her mouth. Any sound could enrage him or draw more attention to her presence in the back seat. The street lights zoomed by, each one faster than the last, and they cast a gridded shadow from the iron cage that separated the driver from the back seat. The place where the prisoners are locked in place. No handles. Shatterproof glass. Everything to keep her confined.

Why couldn't she hear anyone coming after them? No sirens. Nothing.

Evan lost count of the times the car turned and then jolted forward again, but the street lamps dwindled in numbers, leaving longer stretches of roadway in darkness. Her assailant said nothing in the minutes that felt like hours. Only the sound of tires humming against the pavement.

Then the roar of the engine faded to a steady thrum. The urgency of motion flowed into a slower cadence only broken by seams in the road that drummed when the tires rolled over them. The violence of a speeding car had rattled her nerves and seized at her chest, but the slowing of their progress was more sinister.

He didn't have the need to race away from anyone or anything. This meant that nobody else knew she was here with him right now. The cops didn't follow them. She was alone with only the man behind the wheel.

The car slowed and turned into a bank of shadows. Evan's fingers gripped the strap of a seat belt with the centrifugal force exerted on the turn and then the final ease of the brakes. They had stopped and the engine shut down. She held her breath and gripped tighter to the seat belt. If he was going to pull her from the back seat, she was ready to make it as difficult as possible. Her gaze flashed to the door at her feet. Maybe she could get a good kick into his groin if he grabbed at her. But what if he came from the other door? She shifted her glance to the window and realized her significant vulnerability at that moment. If he came from this way, she had no leverage. He would find her pressed onto her stomach against the seat, her only defense was a weakened grasp onto a flimsy seat belt. But her fingers squeezed hard against that strap. It was all she had.

"Are you okay?" his voice came from the front seat. The sound startled her and she glanced up to the grid of bars that separated them.

This wasn't the angry voice of the man that had put a gun to her head in the emergency room. His voice trembled, the rage absent.

"Hey, I said are you okay?" he spoke again and the car rocked as he turned back toward her. The top of his head shone as a silhouette in the dark against the bars.

Her throat had tightened but she forced her vocal cords to move. "I don't know."

A sigh whispered from his lips and he pressed his head against the grid. "I'm sorry about this. I really am. I don't want you to be afraid."

The white of her knuckles faded as her grip loosened on the seat belt but her heart still pounded in her chest.

"I'm not gonna hurt you," he said, his voice so small now.

The lump that had formed in her throat threatened to choke her. She swallowed and lifted her head from the seat, just enough to see the faint light reflected in his eyes.

"I didn't plan to do this tonight," he said and met her gaze. "It just happened. I didn't know what else to do."

She licked her dry lips. "What are you going to do to me?" There was no point in trying to stop the shaking in her voice.

A sad smile appeared on his thin lips. "I swear I'm not going to hurt you."

"Then why am I here?"

"It was the only thing I could think of. I needed to save you."

Her fingers slipped from the seat belt and she glanced away from him. He must be psychotic, delusions of paranoia. Unpredictable and terrified. The worst kind of person to be alone with right now.

"What do you mean?" she said and placed her hands on the seat under her. The tremble in her breathing quickened.

"There's something wrong with that place."

"The hospital?" Her breath collided against the vinyl and brushed warm against her cheek.

He nodded. "Yes. I had to get you out of there."

The delusion was strong. It must have gripped him from the moment he stepped into that hospital. He seemed protective, but that could snap at any moment if he ever felt threatened by her as well.

She had to see his face. Otherwise, his unpredictability could take her off guard. Her hands pushed against the seat and she pulled herself up to look at him. He lifted his head away from the grid but still watched her.

"What would have happened if I stayed there?" she said, trying to keep her voice steady.

A frustrated laugh escaped his throat and his forehead creased. Evan pressed back against the seat, the furthest spot away from him.

"You think I'm crazy," he said. "Just like everyone else."

The hollow of her stomach squeezed. "No, I don't."

"Yes, you do. I can tell by the way you're looking at me."

"I don't think you're crazy. I'm just scared, okay." Keep him talking. *If he likes you, he might be less apt to hurt you.*

He shook his head and the smile faded. "People like you always think I'm crazy, but you're wrong about me. Everyone is wrong. You don't know me. You just don't understand."

She forced her spine to move and she shifted closer to the grid. "Then tell me something. Anything. Tell me your name."

He stilled for a moment and looked at her. Although shadows cast over his features, she knew he studied her. His head tilted to the left.

"Matthew, but everyone calls me Matt." He glanced down.

Finally getting somewhere. "Evan." Her trembling fingers touched the grid. "So tell me, Matt. Why am I in danger?"

His eyes shot up to her and the breath hitched in his throat. Creases formed beside his eyes and he grimaced. Whatever it was, he fought to keep it secret but there was no way it could stay hidden.

"There are things in there that . . . that are not good."

Maybe it was his anxiety flowing through the bars and infecting her, but a shiver moved down her back. "What things? I need to know."

He shook his head and pressed his forehead against the grid again. "You know, I used to be a normal person. Lived my life like everyone else. Worked. Played. Ate. Slept. My life was boring. Things were just fine, and then this happened."

"What happened, Matt?"

"I went to the Bahamas on vacation, my usual trip in the winter. Or whenever I wanted. Hell, I had the money. And the law firm provided the jet."

This slap of reality hit her and she sat up straighter. "Wait, you're a lawyer?"

He glanced up to her and smiled. "No. An accountant for a law firm. Like I said: boring and happy." His eyes drifted beyond her and into the dark outside the car. "It was January 7th three years ago. Geez, feels like it was just last week." A weak laugh broke through his tight throat. "Scuba diving like I always did when I went there. The waters were choppy that day. I surfaced and a boat came out of nowhere, struck me in the head. I didn't see them, they didn't see me. I don't remember much after that until I woke up in the hospital." His voice faltered for a moment. "They said I had died for two minutes in the ambulance."

The silence between them chilled and Evan swallowed.

"But they brought me back and I was in the hospital for another month after that. Cracked skull. Blood on my brain. Lucky to be alive, they said." A pitiful huff escaped his lips.

Of course, a head injury. That would explain the delusions, the paranoia. He had a head injury three years ago and now he still suffered.

"But I seemed to get better. I was able to return to Chicago, go back to work. The headaches were the only down side. Otherwise, I was feeling pretty good. And then things changed."

He had gone silent again, but she had to keep him talking. Keep him engaged. "What happened?"

"It first started as cold spots, funny odors, things like that," he said and glanced out the passenger window. She followed his gaze to the bridge overhead that obstructed the city lights and left the car in shadows. The dark water of the Chicago River flowed under the pier, barely lilting the few boats docked there. Quiet and isolated between the warehouses. A perfect place for her murder.

"I didn't pay much attention to it at first," he continued and this drew her attention back to him. "I mean, hell, I just survived a near-death experience. My skull had been cracked. I just chalked it up to being side-effects of the whole thing. And then it started interacting with me."

Evan's fingers curled against the grid. "Interacting? How do mean?"

"Whispers at first. It was only at home and I couldn't make out what they were saying. But then it got louder.

Paranoia. Just as she had suspected.

"I tried to read as much as I could. Psychiatry books called it delusions, and I really thought I was going crazy. But the voices started telling me things about themselves: names, where they lived, sometimes how they died."

"Did they tell you anything else?"

"Like what?"

She feigned a shrug. "I don't know, maybe they wanted you to hurt someone . . . ."

His brow wrinkled and he shot her a glance. "No. Like I said, I'm not crazy, okay. They said things that I could verify. If someone told me his name was John Smith and he was murdered in the alley behind Coleman's Shopping Plaza, I could find it somewhere in the news. And then I started seeing them."

Matt shifted to fully face her, his eyes wide now. "I read something where spiritualists called it channeling. Where people had a near-death experience and when they came back they were different."

"What do you mean different?"

"Something about the brain changes after it has *crossed over*, so to speak. I don't know, maybe it leaves a door open to the other side or something. It's different for everybody, though. But that door allows us to step into the realm between us and that other place. And that's where they live."

The sounds of the pier vanished with his words and his determined stare. "What do you mean *they*?" she asked.

He only stared at her, his eyes widened and his gaze shifted around them, looking for anyone else who might be listening. But it was only the two of them, hidden in the car among the shadows of the bridge.

"Matt," she said and brought his attention back to her. "Who are they?"

His voice faltered and dropped to a whisper. "The dead."

The delusion he had developed reached so far into his psyche. The hallucinations had formulated into a reality for him that ingrained itself into his life. She had seen this happen to so many people she had taken care of during her time spent in the psychiatry ward as a medical student. The disease disrupted so many lives and debilitated those affected by it. He just needed help before something bad happened.

"Do you see them now?" she asked, her voice low to match his.

"Not yet," he said. "They're not around all the time. Only when they want attention, but they're getting more aggressive.

That's why I got arrested tonight and ended up in your ER."

"You saw them tonight?"

He shook his head. "One of them told me to go to that restaurant, didn't know why but that's how it usually happens. So I just showed up to find a super powerful one there. I'd never seen it happen before, but it could actually pick things up and throw them around. Like a poltergeist I guess. But the moment I walked in there it grew so much stronger. It just started throwing silverware and dishes and tables, and then it threw me right out the window. And then everybody thought I had caused it; they called the cops and so here we are."

Her throat went dry again. "Right, so why am I here?"

"You can't go back there, to that hospital." His voice trembled. "I saw something there, something I've never seen before. Whatever it is, it's pissed. I heard it, well sort of. It just mumbled and screeched. It lives in that hospital and by the way it reacted, it's been trying to get your attention." He sighed. "Have you heard or seen anything weird lately?"

She glanced away from his concerned stare. The way he talked about his delusions made her skin crawl. A small niggle of concern wormed its way into her thoughts. The single moment in the hospital corridor outside the ICU. She had thought it was just her nerves and she had been so tired, but she could have sworn that she heard a voice that night. No, she couldn't let him get into her head like this. Everyone has had that moment before, a single instance when they felt someone watching or heard things in the wind. Matrixing. That's what it's called. When your brain tries to make sense of the stimuli and turns it into something more familiar. That's all it was. The brain playing tricks.

Matt's gaze fixed on her with those pleading eyes. "You know when they're near because they drain the energy from everything around them. I think maybe that's how they can be seen or heard. I don't know. The electricity coming from lights, the static in the TV or radio, even the heat in the air. Everything gets cold. Lights flicker. That's how you know they're coming."

She couldn't look at him, not with the flash of doubt that welled in her chest. Yes, she had seen things like that. But everyone has experienced that at one time or another.

He pressed closer to the grid, his gaze boring into her soul. "You have, haven't you? You've sensed something wasn't right."

"No." She set her jaw and pushed back against the seat.

"It's okay," he said. "I know how it feels. It doesn't matter if you believe in them or not, if you see them or not. They're still there and they see you. There's something terribly wrong in that hospital. Whatever she is, she wants something from you."

Evan tilted her head and watched him. "Wait a minute. She?"

"Yeah, I think so," he muttered and pinched his eyes closed. Wrinkles formed over his nose and around his eyes. "She's young, maybe in her late teens, early twenties. Long dark brown hair, wearing a hospital gown. But something's wrong with her. There's blood all over her, covering her from head to toe and flows down her legs like she's still bleeding. I'm not sure what any of it means."

She let out a steady breath and leaned forward again. "Matt, I want to help you, okay."

His head fell and rested against the grid, his gaze turned down and he breathed steady, saying nothing. Evan waited for him to move, to speak, anything. But there was only silence. Then he shifted around and stared out the windshield.

A click sounded and the driver door opened. Matt slid from the seat and a flash of metal glinted in his hand. The gun, shining in the faint light. Evan froze, her fingers once again finding the seatbelt strap. He stepped to the back door and it opened with a squeak of the hinges. The breath stopped short in her chest. Only the shadow of him stood there and she could see him just from the chest down, with the gun pointed down to the ground at his hip.

Chapter 6

This is it. This is the end.

Even in the middle of summer, the air around her chilled and sent goosebumps over her arms.

He stood there, silent and unmoving. The faint lap of the water at the pier echoed under the bridge. This dark and lonely place, with only the sound of the black water. This was where she was going to die.

He stooped down and gazed at her. "Get out."

There wasn't anywhere to run that he couldn't catch her if she ran. Especially with the gun in his hand.

"Get out of the car now."

The gun waved in the air, urging her to exit the vehicle. The humidity of the night air drifted heavy into the car like a fog. Her heart pounded against her ribs but her eyes couldn't waver from the tip of the gun. He would only wait so long for her and there wasn't much time left. She released her white-knuckle grip on the seatbelt and willed her limbs to move. Every inch closer to him made her joints stiffen. He stepped back just as she placed one leg and then the other onto the hard dirt. She forced her knees to hold her up and she stood to face him.

He didn't back away from her and the space between them threatened to suffocate her. Matt looked down to the ground, the gun still held against his thigh.

Although the dark still shrouded him, the move of his hand startled her. Her hands clenched into fists, ready to protect herself at any moment. He stepped back and the metal of the gun glimmered as it skimmed through the air and landed in the weeds far from the car. Gone into the dark abyss and thrown away by the man who had kidnapped her.

"I told you I wasn't going to hurt you." He forced his stare at her again. "Now get in the front seat."

She froze, her hands still clenched against her torso.

"Please?" he said and tilted his head.

"Why?"

He let out a quick and breathy laugh. "I could leave you here, but that would be wrong. It's not a safe place. Just . . . let me take you home or something. Anywhere but here or the hospital."

For the first time tonight, this was the only thing she believed about him. He was not a murderer – mentally ill, maybe – but not a murderer. Just go with it; play the part he has created in his delusion.

She loosened her fists and nodded her head. "Okay."

He stepped aside and allowed her to move around the front of the car. She slid into the front passenger seat as he eased behind the wheel again. The engine roared with a turn of the key and rolled back out into the night, slow and steady without the fervor of the high-speed getaway that he had driven before coming to the pier.

"So, where do you want me to take you?" he said. The car veered onto the main street leading away from the warehouse district.

"Um – head north – Evanston."

She stared forward, the glare of the street lamps passing by one at a time. Some of it was familiar, but definitely not anywhere that she would just jump out of the car and run. These dark alleys were no safer than in the car with Matt. A green and white sign floated in the headlights, indicating the coming on-ramp to the interstate. He didn't say anything, and Evan could see the white-knuckle grip he had on the steering wheel from the corner of her eye as he drove.

The silence thickened between them and Evan steadied her breathing. "After you take me home, where will you go?"

He shook his head. "Not sure. I've never done anything like this before, trust me."

"But you're afraid, aren't you?"

He shot her a sideways glance. "I am, but not of prison. There are far worse things out there, but I promise I won't bother you again after this."

She hoped that was true. As long as she got out of this alive and never saw him again, she didn't care what happened after that. *God, help me get out of this.*

Her lips parted, the next words ready to fall, and that's when the red and blue flash behind them lit up the entire street. Another car approached them from a side street, lights blinding and sirens wailing. The lump stuck in her throat and she glanced in the side mirror. More police cars joined them, at least half a dozen now. It only took a second, but she knew what her kidnapper would do next.

She turned toward him. "Matt, don't . . ."

It was too late. His foot slammed down on the gas pedal and the car shot forward. The massive engine on the other side of the dashboard roared and they sped at tremendous speed, leaving the army of cars behind them, but not for long. His eyes darted up to the rear-view mirror, the flashing lights reflecting against his face. She had seen that look before: terrified, confused and desperate.

"Please, stop the car," she said, her ribs seizing and her fingers clutching the side door handle. "You can't outrun them."

"They're driving the same thing I am," he said and the car surged faster. It veered with a quick lurch to the left and rolled onto the on-ramp at the last second. The car raced onto the open freeway. Thankfully, the lanes were mostly open with little traffic. Matt steered the car beyond the few vehicles that occupied the road, but the flashing lights still approached from behind them.

Evan pressed back into the seat and glanced to the glowing lights of the speedometer: 127 miles per hour and climbing. Her throat had gone dry. She pried her fingers free of the door handle and clutched the seat belt. With shaking hands, she pulled it and slipped it around her to the clip. Metal clanked against metal. Why wouldn't it connect? Street lights raced by them, and she only saw the seat belt clip in brief flashes. One more burst of light and she found the clip. Snap. The belt connected and she turned back to the side mirror.

Red and blue lights closed in behind them.

"Matt," she called out to him. Maybe he would listen to her if she forced him to. "They'll stop us somehow and when they do they'll kill you."

He just stared forward with an occasional glance into the rear-view mirror. The engine roar blared in Evan's ears and the road vibrated under her, rattling her spine.

Please God, get me out of this.

A bright flare of white light descended on the car from the sky and followed them down the freeway. Evan pressed against the side window and followed the light to a helicopter moving with them from above. That had to be a news helicopter, or maybe something from the Chicago PD. Either way, everyone would be watching this whole thing unfold. In the chaos of the moment, with hands clutched to the seat belt, she pulled away from the window. A tug at her neck caught her attention. She released her shaking fingers from the belt to pull the chain that dangled below her scrub top. The engagement ring, glinting with the flashes of blue and red behind them. No matter what happened now, she couldn't lose it. She pulled it free and slipped it on the fourth finger of her left hand.

Evan clutched the seat belt again. "Please stop the car," she shouted above the sound of the engine.

"I have to get you home," he said through clenched teeth, both hands on the wheel now.

This was getting out of control and far too dangerous. She placed a trembling hand on his shoulder. "I don't want you to die."

For only a moment, he glanced at her, his eyes glassy and pupils wide. The engine's roar calmed and the car's momentum slowed. The speedometer needle drifted backward: 115 . . . . 100 . . . . 95 . . . .

Flashing lights loomed closer behind them. Matt turned his gaze back to the road, but it was too late. His headlights caught the reflections of two police cars on both side of the road, their lights off and waiting like predators for something big to happen. Matt gripped the wheel and locked his elbows. A glint of metal stretched across the freeway before them. Evan held her breath and pressed back against the seat. And everything went silent for an eternal second.

First came the double thud before the tires exploded over the tire spikes. The wheel rims caught the pavement and the car jerked to the side with violent force. She clenched her jaw at the same moment Matt reached an arm out to protect her from crashing into the dashboard. The forces changed and her fingers clutched the seatbelt.

So much noise, metal tearing against metal. The car flipped into a roll, over and over. Evan squeezed her eyes shut. Glass shattered around them and then a ripping pain tore into her skull.

Everything fell into dark silence.

Chapter 7

Paul couldn't have done anything else.

When Pearce grabbed Evan, Paul tried to stop him but everything had happened so fast. And now only the fluorescent lights burned into his retinas and his ears rang. It was so loud he couldn't hear the cop speaking although he was only a foot away from him.

She was out there with a mad man and there was nothing he could do about it.

"Doctor Williams," the cop said and this time he heard it, which was a little hard to miss with the cop snapping his fingers next to Paul's ear. "You okay, doc?"

"No, I'm not okay," he said, his arms still folded over his chest.

"We're working on it," the cop said and placed a meaty hand on Paul's shoulder.

Working on it. That meant they still had no idea where she was or if she was still alive.

"Hey, doc," Margaret called out from the nurse's desk. Paul turned from the cop. "Get over here now. It's all over the news."

He turned away from the cop, not even an *excuse me* because he just didn't have the energy to say it. This was now all over the TV. Something was happening out there and he was stuck in the ER. His insides quivered and threatened to explode, but he clenched his jaw and marched forward to the station where everyone gazed up to the TV mounted from the ceiling.

The ER fell silent, even the cops milling around and the crime scene photographers with the clicking cameras all stopped.

"Turn it up," someone demanded from the edge of the crowd. Margaret said nothing and just raised the remote control until the sound from the speaker bled into the station.

Dramatic music with drums blared with the flash of "Breaking News" across the screen, and then a live shot from right outside the front entrance of the hospital. A young reporter, a woman in her twenties, stood there with her microphone in hand and began speaking as soon as the news anchors tagged her.

"Thank you," she started. "I'm at St. John's hospital where an armed assailant reportedly attacked a police officer and then proceeded to abduct someone from the emergency room. He then managed to escape in a stolen car with the hostage. We still have no word yet on the identities of either the assailant or his hostage. What we do know is that the man had been arrested earlier in the evening and brought to St. John's Hospital emergency room for medical care before being taken to jail. We are learning that . . . ."

The news anchor from the main station interrupted and the camera view returned to the brightly lit desk. "Sorry for cutting the feed, but we are now receiving word that there is a high-speed pursuit. We will turn to the footage, live with Steve who is now on Chopper 5 and assessing the situation."

The screen darkened except for the shimmers of red and blue lights down on the Interstate. The camera shook a little but kept trained on another police car ahead of the others, its lights out and speeding down the road. The helicopter followed it with a halo from the spotlight.

The dizzying spectacle of the camera work made Paul nauseated. He clenched his arms tighter around his chest even though Margaret pressed beside him for reassurance.

"Yes, we are following above the scene of the chase now, proceeding northwest on the Kennedy Expressway. By the looks of it, the car has been going well over a hundred miles per hour and there are police cars in pursuit. We believe this to be the suspect that had fled St. John's emergency room less than an hour ago."

The police scanner on the back desk screeched with garbled speech, but Paul clearly heard, *we are in pursuit.*

The voice of the main anchor broke into the conversation. "Do you see anybody in the car with him? Is the hostage still with him, Steve?"

Static crackled before the man in the helicopter spoke. "It's unclear at this time. With the car's speed and the lighting along the road, it's hard to tell if anyone else is in the car."

This is 827, in pursuit. Suspect accelerating. I believe I see a passenger in the car with him, over . . .

Paul turned away from the television and to the little black scanner as though it could show him something the screen refused to.

Be advised, 827, there is a blockade about three miles ahead. Tire spikes have been deployed, over . . .

They were going to stop the car. In mere seconds, this would end. Paul glanced back to the screen where the helicopter's spotlight still followed the speeding car.

Chopper Steve spoke again over the sound of the helicopter. "It appears that the driver may be slowing down."

Then officer 827 responded. *10-4, tire spikes deployed. Over.*

But the car was slowing down. They didn't need the spikes. He had seen the results of such counter measures when these people came into the ER. Their cars didn't turn out so well and sometimes, neither did the drivers.

Paul's heart hammered in his chest and he held his breath. The spikes were right ahead of the car. They only had seconds left, and now he was sure the Evan was still in that car.

He held his breath and then it happened.

The camera in the helicopter didn't capture the sound of the tearing metal when the car struck the spikes. Smoke from burning rubber billowed under the wheels that still whirred despite the rupture of all four tires. The car had to still be going over 90, and when the driver lost control of the wheel, it flipped. Over and over, toward the grassy median. Sparks showered around it as it collided against the pavement, metal shrapnel spearing outward with each roll until the car landed in a smoking mess upside down against the posts of a billboard.

Several gasps around the emergency room whispered out to him, but Paul still held his breath. Smoke ballooned in thick black clouds from the car's undercarriage.

The camera in the helicopter focused, now keeping a steady eye on the still car. The police squad that had chased it now surrounded the vehicle, small figures clad in black creeping toward the overturned car, only visible in the flashes of blue and red light until they entered the harsh white spotlight of the helicopter. It didn't take a genius to know they had guns drawn, every single one of them. Guns aimed at a wreck where Evan lay, alive or dead.

Paul drew his fingers together and rested his forehead against them, allowing a small and careful breath out. But his eyes never left the TV screen. Margaret placed her hand softly on his shoulder, muttering under her breath, "oh Lord."

Chapter 8

The acrid smoke burned into Matt's nose and his eyes flashed open. Drops of blood trickled into his eyes and his nose throbbed. Blurred light stabbed into his eyes with every blink. So much noise and smoke, and his head pounded. He swallowed and blinked again, and then he understood why everything looked so odd. Matt glanced to his window and found the world had turned upside down. Wet grass and mud slaked against the shattered driver's-side window, but only at the top of it where it met the roof. A billowed white sack lay limp in front of the steering wheel: a burst air-bag.

The last few minutes still hung in a fog within his brain. The last thing he remembered was that he had let his foot off the gas pedal. The cops were behind him, and she had her hand on his shoulder.

She. Evan. Oh no.

He called her name but only a croak sounded in his throat. Despite the sharp pain in his neck, he turned his head to the right and squinted through the smoke. There she was, hanging from her seatbelt, arms limp and dangling over her head. Her locks of blonde hair hung and almost touched the roof, trailing threads of blood until it pooled below her body. Macabre red splatters decorated the deflated airbag that draped from the passenger side dash board. Oh, god. There was so much blood. And she wasn't moving. Was she even breathing?

Matt reached his right arm toward her but it just didn't move right. The terrible sharp pains that rose into his shoulder made him cry out. The abnormal angle of his forearm explained everything about that pain and he gritted his teeth against the muscle spasm down his arm.

"Evan," he whispered her name, afraid of what she wouldn't say. He pushed himself away from the driver's side door and inched closer to her. His gaze moved along the dashboard above him and to her legs. The car had crumpled inward and her legs disappeared in a mangled mess below her knees. Hot tears streamed down his face and dragged blood into his eyes. He called her name again, but she didn't move. Silent, in her beauty and gore. A torn paper doll.

"I'm so sorry," he cried. He had promised he wouldn't hurt her, but he had lied.

"Pearce," a shout bellowed beyond the smoke and broken glass. "Out of the car, now!"

He could never forgive himself. In his fear and desperation, he had killed this poor woman. And she had every right to come back for him with her vengeance. The others were never his fault, he was just their voice box. But this one was all on him.

It didn't matter that the driver's side door opened and arms grasped him. They pulled him away from her and he lost sight of her in the billows of smoke that had surrounded them.

"Don't move! Hands behind your back!"

He wasn't going to fight them. Not now.

A knee pressed into his back and he winced. "Matthew Pearce, you are under arrest . . ." the cop over him shouted. He continued to yell the Miranda rights to him but Matt only watched the car and the gaping hole from which they removed him.

"Is she in there?" someone called out.

"Is she still alive?"

"Get an ambulance out here, now!"

Several officers surrounded the vehicle and soon obscured his view of her through the smoke. It was bad. He had seen how she looked, and now they were getting their first view. And he saw it on their faces too. Pale and wide eyes, men and women on their hands and knees crawling into the car to help the lifeless woman.

Tears blurred his vision and he cringed again when the officer forced his fractured arm behind his back and locked the cuffs on his wrist.

"Do you understand these rights as I have read them to you?" the cop shouted.

His head dropped against the wet grass and cried, his eyes pinched shut. All he could see – and would ever see – was her bloody hair hanging down to the roof of the car.

The red phone rang, breaking the dread silence in the emergency room. Paul didn't turn away from the television. He couldn't. What if he looked away and that's when she crawled out of the car into the welcoming arms of all the cops that surrounded her? Everyone hated the red phone, because that meant an incoming call from paramedics. But tonight was different. The ring of that phone sent goosebumps across everyone's flesh. This time, they knew what was coming.

The crackled sound of dispatch sending out its nearest on-duty EMT's screeched throughout the nurse's station. *En route to Kennedy Expressway. MVA, two occupants in the vehicle, one is stable on the scene, the other . . . .*

He couldn't hear it. Paul didn't want to hear it.

Second occupant, female, unresponsive on the scene. Will need immediate extraction and crews en route.

Paul closed his eyes. He couldn't watch it either. Seeing the Jaws of Life rip open the mangled remains of the car and pull Evan out of there was too much. Unresponsive. There was no way she could have survived that.

Margaret's perfume wafted over him and her arm weighed heavy over his shoulders. "Oh, honey," she said and pulled him in close. She was old enough to be his grandmother, and he had always joked around with her about that. Margaret was one of his favorite nurses, and her embrace now was everything he needed. But he didn't break. He kept his eyes closed and allowed her to squeeze him as tight as she needed to. "The Lord will be with her. We're all gonna pray for her."

It's no use. Prayers won't bring her back.

She held him for long enough that he remembered his own grandmother at that moment. This is exactly what she would have told him too.

The sounds of the ER drifted into a muffled mess even after Margaret let him go. He still didn't let his eyes open, but she stayed by his side and muttered quiet prayers under her breath. He couldn't tell her right now, but he was glad she didn't leave.

The dispatch scanner crackled. The EMTs had arrived and called in the report from the scene. This was it. Everything he didn't want to hear.

Female occupant has active vitals, tachycardic at 156, BP 83/35. Extraction imminent. Will proceed with lines and intubation en route to St. John's, over . . . .

Paul's eyes flew open. Evan was alive. His gaze flew up to the TV again. The helicopter light shone down on the crew prying open the passenger side door. The EMTs blocked his view, but he was sure he saw them grasp her arm.

Copy that. St. John's Trauma crew: be advised, incoming with MVA, unresponsive passenger being extracted now. Further details to come, over . . . .

The ambulance was coming here as soon as Evan was pulled from the car. Here. In his trauma unit.

The overhead PA system clicked on throughout the hospital. *Code Trauma.* The call for all trauma-based staff to make their way to the emergency room. Trauma surgeons, blood bank, anesthesia. The ER was about to get chaotic.

"Dr. Williams," a booming voice sounded out to him. He flashed his glance on the other side of the nurse's station. The other ER residents had already gathered around Dr. Timmons, their proctoring physician and supervisor. He stood a foot taller than everyone, his clean-shaven head reflecting the harsh light of the ER on his dark skin. "I need your attention here, son."

Paul clenched his fists. The other residents looked back at him and they each had wide-eyed fear pasted on their faces. Paul approached their circle and Dr. Timmons scanned each of them over the top of his reading glasses.

"I need everybody to listen carefully," he said, his voice firm but calm. "This will be difficult, I understand that. Dr. Jensen is one of our own, and that is why everyone needs to stay focused. I want this orderly and controlled."

A few of the residents nodded in agreement.

"You know your jobs, people. Time to get the trauma bay ready," Dr. Timmons said, and the residents dispersed.

Paul started to follow his fellow residents when Timmons called out to him. He didn't need this right now, especially not from his attending physician. Holding it together took enough effort without another person trying to console him.

"I think it would be best if you let another resident handle this one," Timmons spoke low and only to him.

"With all due respect, sir," Paul said, his jaw tight, "I'm not leaving."

Dr. Timmons remained silent for a moment and studied his face. He nodded and removed his glasses. "Very well. But I need you, more than anybody else here, to keep it together. Are you comfortable running the code?"

"Yes sir. I wouldn't want anyone else to do it."

Paul believed it, but he hoped that he could keep his composure when she came through those doors. *Whatever happens next, I'll be okay*. He had to be.

Chapter 9

Paul knew everything had changed forever. There was no going back.

He stood at the end of the trauma bay, the other residents waiting in silent anticipation. Each of them represented different years in training, and the interns stood in the back, eyes darting to the others and hoping that they wouldn't screw anything up. In his three years as an emergency medicine resident, he had seen just about everything. Gun shots, drug overdoses, car accidents, and plenty of narcotic seekers. And each of those things came with some inevitable deaths right there in the ER. But nothing could prepare him for what came out of that ambulance.

The doors at the end of the hall opened, but it was around the corner and out of view from the trauma bay. The other residents stood stiffer, but Paul leaned back against the wall, arms crossed over his chest. Clattering wheels of a gurney echoed down the corridor. Half a dozen voices talked over each other, rushed and persistent. Somebody called out the listing of vital signs, none of them promising. The sound of all the chaos flowing down the hallway curled in his shoulders and up his neck.

Three paramedics rolled the gurney into the trauma bay and the room changed into a hive of bees.

"Belted passenger, roll over MVA," the lead paramedic called out to everyone standing in the room as he pulled the gurney completely into the bay and locked the wheels in place. "Unresponsive on the scene."

Paul peeled himself away from the wall and stepped up to the gurney just like the rest of the residents. It only took a second, but it felt like forever before he could bring himself to look down at her. To his trauma patient on the gurney right in front of him. Dr. Timmons marched into the room, his glasses once again perched on his nose. Paul stood at the head of the bed and finally gazed down at Evan. His chest tightened and the ringing in his ears blocked out anything else going on around him.

This couldn't be her, limp strands of blonde hair soaked in blood and strewn about her head, some of it sticking to the sides of her face where a painting of her own blood had already dried. Both eyes had swollen and a concerning dark bruise covered the right side of her face. A rigid white collar bound her neck in a straight line with her spine. A clear tube protruded from her mouth and the paramedic continued to pump regular breaths with the attached hospital-green respirator bag. Her chest rose with each artificial breath. Blood soaked her clothes down to her scrub bottoms, and that was when his mouth went dry.

The fabric looked like it had been shredded by a bear. Beneath the scrub bottoms, her right leg rested in an odd and unnatural position below the leg straps that held her secure to the gurney.

"Give me the run down," Timmon's voice boomed over the cacophony in the room.

"Head injuries, likely direct contact with the windshield despite the airbags. Right arm appears fractured and crush injury to right lower extremity. Pulses present in all limbs."

The paramedic stepped back and one of the residents took over the job of ventilating her. Others cut away her clothes and the twinge of regret pinched in Paul's chest. They shouldn't see her like this, he thought. They all know her; she wouldn't want them to see her naked and helpless just lying here. But it had to be done. To save her life, they needed to examine every inch of her.

The scissors cut up the center of her scrub top and Paul flinched at the exposure of her breasts as the cloth fell away. The breath caught in his throat when he realized something was missing. It can't be gone . . . . The chain with the ring didn't hang from her neck anymore. She had kept it there all the time because she didn't want to lose it.

His gaze darted along the streaks of blood along her neck, but the silver chain wasn't there.

No, please, no.

The resident to his left shifted her gait and his eyes stopped at Evan's still hand. Although her skin had been coated in dry blood that flaked at every touch, the glint of the silver chain caught his attention. His throat tightened. Evan had placed it on her finger, chain and all. Heaven only knows when she did it. Maybe when she was first pulled from the ER. Maybe when she sat in the passenger seat and racing down the freeway. But she had done it, probably so it wouldn't be lost. She must have known something bad was going to happen.

"She's getting harder to ventilate, Paul," the resident pumping the bag said.

He glanced to her chest. It rose unevenly with every artificial breath. Over the sounds of the ER, a hiss of air bubbled out from the pools of blood on her chest. She was his patient now, and he had to get his job done. Just like he did every night he worked here. And every night after this. His gloved hand moved along her sternum and outward where he felt the crunch of shattered bones beneath her skin. Somewhere under that pool, just below the skin, a rib had fractured and punctured her lung and every breath administered escaped from the lung and slipped inside her chest.

"I can place a chest tube, Paul," Dr. Timmons said as he stepped beside him. "You just finish the neurologic exam."

He had to look at her bruised and bloodied face again. Right. The neuro exam. Okay. The cranial nerves . . . Paul took in a deep breath and placed his fingers to her swollen eyelids. The pen light in his hand clicked on and shone brightly into her eyes. White light flashed back and forth over both pupils while he kept her lids pried open. His chest tightened: the right pupil contracted with the light but the left pupil remained unusually large and still.

Shit. This was bad.

"Left pupil fixed and dilated," he called out to Dr. Timmons.

It had to be coming from the all that bruising along her face. The swelling had grown in the few minutes since she had arrived in the ER. His fingers moved along her temple, where a laceration pumped fresh blood into her hair. Paul pulled an otoscope from his back pocket, leaned over the bed and gazed through it into her right ear. The eardrum bulged black and purple.

"There's blood here," he said.

"Alright," Timmons said and stood from the site of the chest tube he had just placed. Paul stood with him, careful not to stare at the blood that flowed out of the tube. "CT is waiting for us. Let's get her over there ASAP. And call the neurosurgeon. We've probably got an intracranial hemorrhage that he needs to be dealt with as soon as she's out of radiology"

Paul rarely followed the transporters with patients to radiology, but this was definitely an exception. He stood behind the lead glass that separated the monitors from the CT scanner and its radiation. Even with just a pane of glass separating them, seeing her on the scanning table, unconscious and dying, he felt so far away from her. Everything behind the monitors stayed quiet and subdued compared to the noise of the ER.

The technician finished securing Evan to the table and stepped into the monitor station. With a push of a button, a beeping sounded from the CT scanner and lights blinked around the donut-shaped mechanism. The scanning table moved, sliding Evan through the scanner circle. In seconds, the radiologic images appeared on the monitors.

He didn't need to wait for the technician to review the images or for the radiologist to give him an official report. The images of her skull told him everything he had suspected. The tech speed-dialed the main desk and a radiologist came in within seconds. A doctor he had only seen a few times leaned over the desk and examined the images. She squinted at the screen and moved the mouse to scroll through several more pictures.

"Looks like a fracture of the right temporal bone with an epidural hematoma forming just below it," the radiologist spoke and pointed out the fracture lines. "It looks like there may be the start of herniation here." She pointed to the brainstem and the absence of a defined line at the junction.

That was the worst news yet.

Paul made the phone call back to Dr. Timmons: Evan had a dangerous brain bleed and there wasn't much time to spare before it killed her. She needed surgery now. It didn't take long for transporters to send her directly to the operating room by orders of the neurosurgeon on call. Paul followed them up there and as soon as they arrived, a collection of grave faces met them at the elevator. Word had already spread throughout the hospital. The general surgeons and residents that Evan frequently worked with stood along the corridors and watched her drift by on the gurney. There was nothing they could do. Nurses and scrub techs came out of rooms to see what had happened to Dr. Jensen.

The transporting team wheeled her through the double doors that plunged into the hall of operating rooms, a place where Paul needed to be in sterile coverings. He covered his hair with a surgical cap and hurried to catch up to her before they took her into an operating room. She disappeared into the room before he could get to her, and he wasn't allowed any further. He could only watch her from the small window that peered into the cold room.

An operating room nurse stepped beside him and gazed through the window, her hand covering her mouth. "I can't believe this is happening. I mean, it's . . . it's Evan."

It had been almost three years since he had done his rotation in the operating room. At least since he was an intern, and he had never wanted to go back. But now he didn't want to leave. A lump formed in his throat as he watched them maneuver her onto the operating table, situate her breathing tube, and then they brought the electric razor to her head. When the bloody clumps of blonde hair fell to the floor and revealed the bleeding gash in the side of her head, he turned his gaze to the ground. The rest of the surgical prep looked too much like the preparation of a body for a funeral.

The door opened and he glanced up to see a nurse standing there, her face covered in a mask. Her gloved fingers moved a clear zipped plastic bag toward him.

"I thought you might want to hold on to this," she said, her voice muffled behind the mask.

His hand shook but he didn't care as he reached to accept the bag. The door closed and he pulled open the zipper. The chain curled in silver coils around a polished ring at the bottom of the bag. It had to come off before surgery, he knew that. But looking at it here, in a bag like a dead woman's personal effects made it hard to breathe.

A bone saw came to life and hummed with harsh vigor on the other side of the door. A shiver rattled down his spine and left his ears ringing. He had never come close to fainting, but he knew he was there now. The neurosurgeon was about to open Evan's skull and, as much as he wanted to stay with her, there was no way he could watch that. He had to leave it in the surgeon's hands . . . and God's will.

Chapter 10

Evan had never felt such warmth, a solace that hugged her in the way that only her father could. And when she opened her eyes, it was not what she had expected. Heavy fog spilled around her feet and obscured most of her surroundings. Quiet and still. Stretched, lean shadows of trees peeked through the mist and guided her attention to a growing but soft golden light beyond the fog.

Whatever that light was, she wanted to be near it more than anything. The fog held quiet and peace, but it wasn't where she was supposed to be. She stepped forward and glanced down to her bare feet and the soft moss that covered the ground. The further she moved, the more the fog thinned. At first, she had assumed she was alone, but that wasn't true at all. In the depths of the fog, others moved through the trees just as she did. Their bodies remained as indistinct shapes in the mist and all of them moved along with her.

The warmth of the light beckoned her, tingling against her bare skin. A smile formed on her lips. She didn't remember how she got here, only that there had been pain but now it was gone. Everything felt wonderful now. She was finally ready to see beyond the fog.

A shadow caught her attention at the corner of her vision. Somewhere through the trees, it lingered and didn't move like the others. Evan's step faltered as she turned to face it. The shadow stayed in its place, frozen and watching the others pass through the mist. The other figures continued on without her, and Evan stopped to face the form that watched her.

The fog thinned between them and the bright light withdrew through the trees, leaving them in a gradually darkening haze. The mist drifted away from the shadow and revealed a woman. She stood motionless, her body covered in a loose, tattered and blood-stained white gown. Her long, brown, unkempt hair fell over her shoulders and concealed most of her face. The others that moved through the fog abandoned her and this woman, unaware that either of them existed.

"Hello?" Evan called out to her, but her own voice sounded hollow and distant. The woman didn't move and, for a moment, Evan thought she was only a statue or a painting. Everything about that figure was different, like she didn't belong here. Maybe she didn't want to be lost in the mists that surrounded everything. Somebody as violated as that woman might need help.

The warmth that had come with the golden light faded. A chill drifted over Evan's bare arms and she shivered. The fog still hung about them but it now carried an uneasy vibration, like the change in ions just before lightning strikes. It squeezed at her insides and urged her to move on.

She couldn't turn away from the still figure in the woods. Something about her made Evan's feet heavy and her legs like wood. Maybe that woman wasn't a person at all, but why would that thought even occur to her? There she was, arms and legs and hands and feet. Just like her.

The woman's hand twitched. Evan almost missed it with the mist swirling around the both of them, but it made her flinch. Then she stepped forward, but her frail and thin legs streaked with blood pushed through the fog in jerking and broken motions. She moved with hesitant and awkward steps over the uneven ground, the fog curling over her dirty feet. Even her arms twitched and her spine bent at odd angles, barely keeping her upright.

Frozen air spilled across Evan's body and it came from the broken entity that moved toward her now. Just looking at this thing pained her and seized at her chest. Whoever this woman was reeked of desperation and anger. The entity didn't belong in this place, not like Evan and the other figures that had moved in the fog. It pulled away from the fading light and wanted nothing to do with it. It wasn't lost at all. Evan turned toward the fading light. She had to get to it as fast as she could before it disappeared and left her in the fog with the thing in the woods.

She forced her legs to move, like slogging through mud. One step at a time. Anything to get away from the woman that approached her. The closer the entity got, the colder her surroundings.

Another step. The light was just through the trees. Only a little further.

Was the thing getting closer? Evan glanced over her shoulder and a breath caught in her throat. Fog thickened along the edge of the trees, but it wasn't so thick that it could hide the entity that ambled over the forest ground. Yet, the figure had vanished, perhaps swallowed back into the woods and away from the light. It didn't matter, as long as it no longer followed her.

Evan turned back toward the light, but stopped only inches from the entity that stood directly before her, so close that she could smell the blood that dripped down its arms and legs and soaked her gown. Acrid and tart. Its stringy hair shadowed every inch of its face, but Evan smelled its swampy breath as it rattled from its chest. Evan gasped and her throat tightened.

The thing raised its hand, a distinct hospital bracelet dangling from its thin wrist. Fingers twitched and twisted as it reached to touch her face. Evan stood frozen, unable to move. Whatever power it held bound her to this place. The entity's skin was not only pale, but almost blue. Cold and dead like a cadaver. Blood dripped from its mouth and oozed over its chin, as dark and thick as tar. Stiff fingers touched Evan's cheek. The icy shock of it seared into her brain. Anger and hate surrounded them. It raged at her, every ounce of its turmoil bleeding into her soul.

Evan screamed. It would never let her go. It wanted to keep her in this place, lost in the fog, forever.

"There she goes again," the nurse spoke, the alarms of the cardiac monitor blaring in the dimly lit room. The digital green lines pulsed across the screen in a rapid series. "She's getting tachycardic again."

The other nurse at her side squinted at the monitor, watching the heart rate climb: 136, 152, 178. She glanced down to the still body on the bed. Dr. Jensen hadn't opened her eyes or made any response in the days since the last surgery to fix the bleeding on her brain. Her heart made these unusual changes in activity periodically with no explanation.

"I don't know why she keeps doing that." The first nurse pulled the cap from a syringe and injected it into the IV line. The heart rate slowed again and the alarms stopped.

"Do we need to call the resident?" the younger nurse spoke.

She shook her head. "Not yet. The rest of her vitals are holding just fine. But if she keeps doing it, we'll give him a call."

She turned away, leaving the younger nurse behind to gaze down on their patient.

Dr. Jensen was just here a week ago, actually tending to the dying man in this very room: ICU 9. Now, this hardly looked like her at all. Swollen eyes, a crescent scar along her shaved left temple glittering with silver staples. The rhythmic hiss of the ventilator that kept her alive inflated her chest at regular intervals, just like most of the patients that resided here.

Why did this have to happen to her? What would make a mad man kidnap her and almost kill her? Maybe he *had* killed her: her heart stopped twice during surgery and they had to perform aggressive CPR to bring her back. She hoped he rotted in Hell for what he did to her.

And every time Dr. Jensen's fiancé came to visit, the nurse had to leave. It made her cry every time and it was hard enough taking care of such ill patients when her eyes were red and nose stuffy. She just hoped that Dr. Jensen couldn't feel anything. Not the broken bones now held together with pins and screws. Not the horrible chest tube that still drained blood from around her lungs but allowed her to still absorb oxygen. And definitely not the opening in her skull below the shaved scalp.

She turned away from Dr. Jensen and stepped from the room, just as Evan's finger twitched from where it rested on the blankets.

Chapter 11

"The EEG looks promising," the neurosurgeon said and stepped away from her. "Looks like we can back off on the sedation even more and see what happens."

Paul didn't want to be too hopeful, but that was the best news he had heard in over a week. A puff of the ventilator expanded Evan's ribcage and then retracted. At least there were signs of neural activity, but there was no way of knowing if that meant she would ever wake up.

The neurosurgeon nodded to him and backed out of the room. Alone again, with all the machines and tubes that kept her alive. He pulled the chair beside her bed and took her hand. The ring on her finger still held its silver sheen even in the dim light of the ICU. It was the one thing he could do for her after she had come out of surgery, and it didn't seem right to keep the engagement ring in a plastic bag.

As soon as the nurse stopped the sedation, that would be the true test of what the future held.

Just squeeze my hand. Move your fingers. Something, he thought.

The last remnants of bruising along her face just looked like faded splotches of green and yellow now. The white gauze dressing wrapped around her head concealed the track of staples that still ran along her shaved temple and hid the drain that snaked into a canister by the bed. Puffs of condensation gathered in the endotracheal tube with each of her exhalations.

Sometimes, the nurses gave her a sponge bath and left her legs above the blankets to cool. The right fragile leg wrapped in fiberglass and gauze with traction rods protruding from the casting in silver spindles. Everything about her looked so broken.

What if Paul had just had the guts to grab the guy that night? Wrestled the gun from his hand. Maybe she wouldn't be lying here like this.

Such thoughts made his throat tighten. He leaned back in his chair and listened to the rhythmic hum of the ventilator. The sound of each inhale and exhale crackled under his skin like bugs that he couldn't shake. And when he closed his eyes, it just got louder. Sure, the machine was keeping Evan alive, but it also meant she couldn't live without it. Every single breath was not her own.

His fists clenched and he leaned forward with the ever-growing tightening in his shoulders. Every day was the same now. The EEG looks promising. The blood work looks better. The MRI shows decreased swelling around the brain. But when would it translate into Evan opening her eyes and fighting back?

"Excuse me," a man spoke from the door.

Paul lifted his head with his heart racing in his ears at the unexpected sound. Two men in suits and long coats speckled in dots of moisture stood at the doorway. The first man took a hesitant step into the room.

"Is this a bad time?" he said, his dark eyebrows raised.

"A bad time for what?" Paul said with a sigh. He hadn't meant it to sound terse, but he was too tired to care anymore.

The man extended his hand, the edge of his coat pulling back from an expensive silver watch on his wrist. "Clint Parks," he said and Paul shook his hand. "I'm from the state prosecutor's office. This is my colleague, Doug Richardson."

"Paul Williams," he responded, but couldn't keep the little knit from forming between his eyes.

"Ah, yes. Dr. Williams," Clint said. "I recall seeing your name on the initial report."

"I'm sorry," Paul said and leaned back in his chair again. "Why are you here?"

The lawyer pointed to the two padded chairs along the side wall. "May we?"

Whatever. Paul nodded and the men removed their damp coats and sat to face him. Clint reached into the pocket of his suit jacket and withdrew a business card that he gave to Paul. Richardson pulled a small note pad from his pocket with a pen and began writing as they talked.

"I am the lead attorney on this case involving what happened that night to Dr. Jensen," Clint said, his head ticking toward Evan's quiet body. "Mr. Richardson and I will be the prosecutors against Matthew Pearce."

Paul kept the card between his index finger and thumb, studying the thick, textured paper and silver ink like it would tell him something that the lawyer hadn't.

"We just wanted to stop by and get an update on Dr. Jensen's status," Clint continued. "But it's fortunate that you are here as well, since you were a witness that night."

Paul glanced up to him. What he had experienced was more than just being a witness. He had stood by helplessly while the gunman took Evan out of the emergency room and into the night. And he could have done so much more to stop it. Everything could have been prevented had he not been so scared.

"I know that now is not an ideal time to discuss things," the lawyer said. "But I would like to speak with you at length maybe sometime next week, get a full statement on your recollection of the events of that night. Every little bit will help to make sure Pearce never sees the light of day."

The card clicked once under his thumbnail and Paul pocketed it. "Next week."

"Just give my office a call and we can set up an appointment." The man feigned a smile, something to imply that it was the end of the small talk. His gaze drifted toward Evan again. "How are things looking for her, if you don't mind me asking?"

The ventilator hissed with another inhale and exhale cycle. Paul knew why the lawyer asked this right now. He wasn't particularly interested in Evan's personal well-being, but in the maximum charges that he could apply to his prosecution. If she didn't make it, maybe he could charge Pearce with murder. Although he might not have Evan's personal interest in mind, at least the lawyer did what he could to give her justice. That was all Paul could ask for right now.

"It's just a waiting game," Paul said. Evan's swollen eyes remained closed and her chest rose and fell with each artificial breath. "She hasn't responded to anything yet, but her testing is looking a little better each day."

Richardson's pen scratched frantically on the notepad.

"Do they think she'll ever wake up?"

The question squeezed in Paul's chest. "They don't know yet. It was a pretty big bleed on her brain."

He had expected the lawyer to ask more questions, but the three of them just sat in silence. No more pen sliding over note paper. Only a quiet and reverent silence despite the cyclic hiss of the ventilator.

"I won't take up any more of your time," Clint said and stood. His partner rose with him, folding the notebook and slipping it back into his pocket. "Please give my office a call next week."

Paul nodded. He really did plan on doing it, but he only hoped that he wouldn't forget to call.

"And please let me know if there is any change in Dr. Jensen's status, if you would."

"Will do."

The two men slipped from the room as quietly as they had entered, leaving Paul alone with her again. His hand moved to cover hers where it rested on the bed. At the point he decided to call the lawyer, he hoped that it would be to give him good news.

When his cell phone buzzed in his back pocket, Paul looked up to Dr. Timmons, who gave him a nod and let him go. His attending physician understood well enough, and knew that Paul worked diligently during his shift. But he just couldn't stay here when the nurse paged him to come to the ICU. Things had changed up there.

The elevator took too long to drop down to him on the first floor, so Paul rushed up the stairs to the third floor. By the time he got there, he didn't care that he breathed hard. Especially not when he saw the small collection of nurses standing outside Evan's room.

They turned to face him as soon as he entered the main corridor.

"What is it?" he said, his shoulders already tight. He wasn't prepared for this.

"Just go on in," Evan's assigned nurse said and pulled open the sliding glass door to her room.

His heart pounded against his ribs so hard that he thought they might shatter. Whatever this was, he had to face it now. Paul stepped through the open door.

The neurosurgeon stood at Evan's bedside, his resident at the foot of her bed. He turned as soon as Paul entered.

And he smiled at him.

"Glad you came," he said to Paul. "I had them page you. I thought you would want to see this."

The pulsing of blood in his ears made his whole head ring. Had he heard the surgeon right?

The neurosurgeon turned back to Evan. But she still lay there, the ventilator tubing still snaked into her mouth like a parasite. The bandage was still wrapped around her head and her eyes were closed. Nothing had changed since Paul was there last night. The heart monitor continued its steady thrum. Her pulse was just as regular as ever.

"Evan," the surgeon said. "Can you give me a thumbs up?"

Her fingers moved, just slightly, but it was unmistakable. Paul held his breath, and Evan's thumb shifted to point toward the ceiling. His eyes burned but he blinked them fast and swallowed. She had actually responded to a command. This was a huge milestone.

The neurosurgeon placed his fingers against her palm. "Good. Now can you squeeze my fingers?"

A few seconds drifted by and she didn't move. But then her hand tilted until her fingers had wrapped around his. Although the squeeze wasn't tight, it had happened.

She could hear him. And not only that, she could process everything she heard and responded accordingly.

"Very good, Evan." The surgeon turned back to Paul. "This is excellent progress."

"When will she wake up," Paul said, but he couldn't turn his gaze away from her.

"That's hard to say. Could be hours or even days. The CT scan this morning looked better. I think she may finally be turning the corner." He placed a hand on Paul's shoulder. "I'll see her again this evening. Hopefully she'll be breathing on her own soon."

Paul moved toward her bed and took her hand. He didn't care if the surgeon and his team left them alone. He knew that she could hear him now.

"Evan," he said and smiled down at her still face. "It's Paul. I'm right here."

Her hand twitched and her fingers wrapped around his in a light squeeze. "You're doing great," he said, but his eyes blurred with tears. It didn't matter. *Let them see me cry. I don't care anymore.*

"Can you understand me?" he asked.

She squeezed again. Weak, but her fingers still moved at his question.

"Okay," he said and worked to calm down his breathing. "One for yes, two for no."

Squeeze.

"Are you in pain?"

Squeeze. Squeeze.

Good. He let out another slower breath.

"You know I love you."

Squeeze.

"I'll be here for you, okay. You're gonna be alright."

He couldn't wait to tell everyone downstairs. They had been asking every day if there was much change. Now he could finally tell them that something great had happened.

"I need to go back to work, but I'll be with you again in about five hours. Okay?"

Squeeze.

He leaned across the bed and kissed her forehead. Hopefully, she felt that too. It pained him to leave her, but things were so much better now. It was the first time she had communicated to him since that night before she was taken. She would be speaking in no time.

Chapter 12

The sunlight left Evan's eyes in a mess of stinging tears that ran down her cheeks. It was the only thing she saw when she first opened her eyes. A bright yellow-white glow that blurred out anything else.

"Good," the man standing beside her bed spoke, someone she didn't recognize by his face but his voice sounded so familiar. How did she know him?

Her eyelids drooped, too heavy to keep open anymore. Back into the darkness, where everything was quiet and still. But his voice still bored into her ears.

"Can you do it again?"

Why did he want to pull her away from the darkness?

"Come on, Evan. You can do it."

The second time was much more difficult. It shouldn't be this hard, but yet she could barely open them enough to see the sunlight again for a fraction of a second. That was it. Back to the darkness where everything stayed silent and peaceful and nothing hurt.

And then another voice called to her in the black, one that stirred her back toward the sunlight. She forced her eyelids to open again. Evan held them open long enough to see that the room had grown dark, lit only by a faint glow beyond the door at her feet.

"Evan," the voice said again, and it wasn't the man who had spoken to her before, when everything was coated in daylight. Somehow, she had been plunged through time, from morning to evening in a few seconds. Without the piercing light, her eyes didn't water and she allowed them to focus.

"That's it," he said. A warm hand grasped hers, and she realized that it was the first time she had actually felt touch in so long. There had been those brief moments when she heard their voices in the dark and she moved her hands when they told her to, but she had never felt anything until now.

She blinked and her vision cleared. The sound of his voice coaxed her through the dimness in the room until she found its source.

Soft brown eyes, short cut dark hair. When he smiled, she recognized the dimples. Paul. Yes, that was his name. She remembered speaking to him, but how long ago was that? And there was a star.

No. Not a star, but something sparkling and beautiful. A ring.

An engagement ring. She had it around her neck, or at least that's the last place she remembered it.

Paul. I remember.

But when she tried to speak, pain shot through her throat. Her larynx spasmed with each attempt until beeps and alarms sounded from behind her. *What happened? Why can't I talk?* The muscles in her spine and legs flexed, sending sharp pain throughout her body.

Paul stood and placed a hand on her shoulder. "No, don't try to speak."

But I need to tell you something.

"Shhh." He touched her face.

Please, hear me. I saw someone. There is someone else in here with me.

The alarms rose and an army of blurry figures rushed into the room, shadows silhouetted against the light in the doorway.

"Excuse me," a woman said and Paul disappeared, his hand falling away from her face. "It's okay Evan. You have a tube in your throat, so don't try to speak, okay. I'm just going to give you something to help."

The room grew silent, and then a warm fog drifted into her bones. The pain in her throat and legs slipped away but she could no longer keep her eyes open. She fell back into the darkness, where everything was still and quiet again. But Paul wasn't here. He still lingered on the other side, out there where things hurt, and she no longer desired to stay in the dark. Even if she had to face the pain, she would do it to find him.

It could have been hours, maybe even days. Time moved differently here, tethered to a bed by cords, oxygen tubing, and drains. Of all her senses, hearing remained the strongest. Maybe it was because she couldn't keep her eyes open long enough to see anything. The tube in her throat numbed any sensation of taste except the tartness of the medications pumping into the IV lines. Sometimes the smell of antiseptic hand wash stung her nose when it stirred her into consciousness.

But her ears heard everything as long as she was awake. Everything, including the scratching sounds coming from the doorway. Irregular and grating. Nails tearing against the wood. She didn't need to open her eyes to see goosebumps along her arms. Something about that sound crawled up her spine like an insect ratcheting along a broken staircase. A shiver moved across her skin, cramping the muscles in her leg under the cast that bound them. Cold, damp air settled around the bed, and with it, the smell of wet dirt and rotting detritus.

She had smelled that only once before, accompanied by the same chill. The thing that skulked in the misty woods carried that scent with it. And now it was here. How did it get out of the fog?

Evan forced her eyes open despite the haze of morphine that still dulled her thoughts. The bed sat in the darkened room of the ICU, lit only by the few indicator lights on the machines around her. A thin strip of white light shone through the gap in the door from where it stood open just a few inches. But those small slips of illumination were enough for her to see the shape that stood at the door inside her room. The swampy, twisted thing just waited there, its fingers scratching along the door frame.

Long dark limbs twitched and its weedy hair hung limply over its face. A seething wraith in the emptiness of her room. Everything about this entity screamed hatred and despair, even when it stood far from her.

Evan's ribs seized when she tried to sit up, to shout for anyone that could hear. The damned tube in her throat wouldn't allow it, though. This entity should have stayed in that forest where she had left it. But somehow it followed her into this world.

The thing watched her from the doorway, just a black silhouette with willowy limbs that twist and bent in strange angles. Evan knew it had eyes but they were lost in its dark face.

What do you want from me? Go back to where you came from. She tried to shout but it only made her cough and choke against the tube. Why did it just stand there? It waited there as though anticipating something from her.

And then it stepped forward. The motion of it sent Evan's cardiac monitor to an increasingly rapid pace. The swampy smell of it flowed over her. Another step, its legs creaking under its broken posture.

Shit. No, no, no.

Evan's fingers shifted and curled around the sheet under her hand. Nobody knew that this thing crept toward her. None of the nurses outside the room. None of the other sick patients in the ICU. And if it got any closer, it could destroy everything left of her.

Where was the nurse call remote? It was usually one of the only things she could feel except the tingling in her fingertips.

The thing jerked toward her again.

Her fingers found the hard, plastic edge of the remote, but she didn't dare look away from the shadow that approached. Its breath wheezed out in a cold and decayed sigh. Evan walked her fingers over the surface of the remote, the series of buttons encased in a silicon cover squishing under her frantic touch. She had to find the call button, to get someone else in here as soon as possible.

The weight of the morphine settled onto Evan's eyelids. *Please, not now.* The cardiac monitor paced faster. Her fingers inched to the wide button at the top of the remote. She depressed the button.

And then her eyelids drooped. The morphine was far more powerful than her weak eyes. The alarms sounded on the heart monitor. At the pace beeping in the room, her heart rate must have been at least 140. Why wasn't the nurse coming? Her fingers clicked onto the button again and again.

The swampy smell burned into her nose, a sickening whorl of mildew.

So cold now, like the bite of a deep freezer.

If she didn't do it now, she may never be alive to do it ever again. She forced her eyes open. And there it was. The creature now perched over her, black stringy hair falling down from its face in a curtain. Darkness still shrouded its features, but its hatred and pain dripped across Evan's skin. A cold and slimy poison of death and destruction.

The morphine burned out of Evan's system in a fraction of a second. Someone had to hear the alarms, the call button. Where was everyone? Evan's eyes opened wide and she tried to scream again, and that sent a whole new set of alarms from the ventilator.

But the creature didn't care. It leaned down toward her while still in its insectoid crouch. Evan's heart hammered like a V8 engine.

In the shadows of its face, the wraith's mouth opened. At first the sound was only a guttural groan, but it grew until it had become a scream so loud that it hurt Evan's ears. It drilled into her brain with hot threads of white lightning. She pinched her eyes closed and screamed against the endotracheal tube. Raw pain seared into her throat along with the copper taste of blood. It didn't matter if anyone heard her. She couldn't die like this without trying to stop it.

The chorus of alarms brought in at least two nurses. One of them flicked on the overhead lights and the other moved to the ventilator.

"Whoa, hold on Dr. Jensen," she said and silenced the alarm with a push of a button.

"She's tachycardic," the other nurse said over her shoulder.

"But it's still sinus rhythm." She placed a hand on Evan's shoulder. "Dr. Jensen, relax."

Evan bucked against the tube skewered in her throat and her eyes flew open. Bright fluorescent lights burned into her pupils and her vision blurred around the forms of the two nurses that stood next to her bed. Her heart still pounded at full throttle, an effect mirrored by the rapid beat of the cardiac monitor. But other than the three of them in the room, there was no other person. No dark figure crouched over her screaming like a banshee. Her vision throbbed in and out of focus, but she was now sure that only three women occupied the room.

"That's it," the nurse said, her fingers patting against Evan's shoulder as her eyes drifted back to the monitor. The rate began to slow to a less frantic pace.

Evan let her shoulders loosen. It had to be the damn drugs. Morphine. They didn't name it after the god of dreams for nothing. More like lucid nightmares.

Where was Paul? Why wasn't he there right now? In the few moments she remembered him being at her side, none of the horrible visions came into the room.

God, no more. Please make the dreams go away.

Chapter 13

The removal of the endotracheal tube was both agonizing and a sweet relief. Evan's ribs throttled with deep, hacking coughs, each one clearing her lungs.

"Good," Paul's voice spoke to her between each hack. "Deep breaths."

The ICU doctor stood over her with the remnant of the tube in his hand. He threaded the elastic band of an oxygen mask around her head and the flow of humidified air mixed with the scent of plastic rushed into her nose and mouth. It didn't help with the coughing much, but it brought some relief when she took in a breath.

"Your throat's going to be real sore," the doctor said.

The same story she had told so many patients. Of course it was going to hurt: a rigid plastic tube stuck in the throat for weeks tended to do that.

The doctor leaned over her with a stethoscope to her chest. "Speaking will be difficult too, at least until the inflammation subsides."

Warm air filled her lungs with another inhalation. At least for the time being, the spasms in her throat had died down and allowed her to relax back against the bed.

He stood and pulled the scope from his ears. "Everything sounds nice and clear." His fingers moved to the palms of her hands. "Can you squeeze my fingers?"

She did as he asked. Not the strongest of grips, but it would do for what he wanted.

"Excellent," he said and continued with more of his exam, a checklist of neurologic testing that she knew she passed, if only barely. The weakness had taken over more than she had realized. When he finished his exam, he pulled the glasses from his face and tucked them into the chest pocket of his white coat. "I think we can go ahead and start physical therapy tomorrow."

Paul slipped his fingers into her hand from where he sat next to the bed. Though she closed her eyes and allowed the oxygen to fill her lungs, she clenched her hand around his.

"When do you think she can get out of here?" he asked the doctor.

"Well, if all goes well with therapy in the next few days, she could probably move over to the transitional rehab unit at that point."

The rest of their conversation sounded hollow and distant. It was amazing how just trying to stay awake left her exhausted. No matter how hard she tried to stay awake, the thickness of fatigue slid over her. If they discussed her care further, she had no idea. And whatever they talked about, she trusted Paul to tell her later when she could keep her eyes open.

Why am I here? That's what she wanted to say, but her lips didn't move the way she wanted them to. The question came out as a garbled mess. She tried it again, at least just the word *why*.

The occupational therapist sitting next to her bed glanced up to her from the foam ball that she had fitted into Evan's palm.

"Why?" the woman repeated. A pitied smile crept at the edge of her lips. "Why do I want you to squeeze the ball?"

Evan shook her head, a slow and tedious motion. It took so much effort just to form a word. She filled her lungs. Maybe if she could move more air through her larynx she could say it better. Her mouth tightened around the word again.

"Why . . . here . . .," she said and her shoulders fell with the difficulty of it.

The therapist glanced down to Evan's hand that weakly grasped the foam ball. "You want to know why you are here? In the ICU?"

Finally. Someone got it. That was the first time since she had opened her eyes that she formed any semblance of a phrase.

"You were in an accident, a really bad one." The woman still didn't look up at her.

How could that be? Evan looked down the length of the bed, to the fiberglass cast that held her right leg in a rigid line. She had seen the cast before, many times actually, but she had no idea what it had meant at the time. What kind of an accident could have left her trapped in this shell of her former self?

"The car you were in rolled and crushed your leg," the therapist continued. "And you had a severe head injury."

The bright morning light coming through the window stung her eyes and Evan blinked. But maybe its wasn't the intensity of the light after all. A shot of pain pierced into the side of her head. Thankfully, that happened less every day. And now she understood where it came from: that must have been the location of her head injury. The right temporal region of the skull.

"How . . .," she forced out through weak lips.

"I really don't know the details of how it happened," the therapist said and smiled at her again. It was that pity-smile, something that didn't extend to her eyes. The therapist was lying. She knew more about what happened than she had let on, but trying to call her out on it took too much effort and Evan grew tired.

The therapist touched her fingers to Evan's hand. "Okay, now try to squeeze again."

Just go through the motions. Gripping the ball turned out to be more difficult than she had expected, just like speaking. And that's why the therapist was here. Not to make small talk. Not to explain her injuries or why her own mouth wouldn't say the things that Evan wanted. Her fingers curled around the foam ball and repeated this motion several times until the therapist was satisfied. No more trying to form words, not to someone who couldn't tell her the truth. There was only one person who would do that, and he was usually here every night. She would have to wait for him and hope that she wasn't too tired to try and speak by then.

The fatigue hadn't set in too much that evening, not when she had slept most of the day after occupational therapy. She could keep her eyes open long enough to see Paul, and the woman he had brought with him.

Brandy smiled when she entered the room behind Paul. The family practice resident and her friend was never a good liar, though. She didn't have to say anything for Evan to know how horrified she was when she looked at her. This must have been Brandy's first time up here since the accident. Her eyes glistened with tears that she tried so hard to hold back. Paul always kept his poker-face when he was in the room, but it must have taken Brandy by surprise. The traction casts. The surgical scar on her head. Brandy now looked at her as though she wasn't the same person she used to be.

"Hi, Evan," she said, her voice weak and trembling. Her hands clenched together and she stood a decent four or five feet from the bed.

Evan smiled, but the lines around Brandy's eyes faded. Just like her words, her face didn't work well. That smile must have looked horrible.

"Paul said you were doing so much better," Brandy said.

"I think so," Evan said, but it sounded like a mess. Nothing like the words she had intended.

Brandy staggered a little, and Paul motioned for her to sit. He pulled up his usual chair next to her bedside. Evan reached her fingers toward him, and he grasped her hand like he always did. He knew what she needed, sometimes before she did.

"She wanted to come and see how you were doing," he said and leaned in close to her. Maybe he didn't have a poker-face, like she thought. He was just so used to seeing her like this.

Evan cleared her throat, a noise that sounded more like a choke. She forced her lips to move. "How . . ." she started.

Just as she had known, Paul could understand the simple one-word questions that she asked. Her chest tightened as she listened to him relay the tale of how she ended up here. But none of it felt real, like listening to an audiobook about a dramatic car chase. Evan shot an occasional glance to Brandy, her face drawn and pale and her eyes turned downward to the floor. Somewhere in the back of Evan's mind, she expected to suddenly remember any of it but there was nothing. There was only a memory of performing surgery on a gunshot victim, going to the ICU to watch Mr. Ceglinski die, and then she woke up in the very same ICU with an endotracheal tube down her throat and her leg heavy in a fiberglass cast.

Paul finished the story, his warm brown eyes glistening in the bright morning light that shone through the window. She believed him. Every word of it. The last few days of therapy prepared her for this moment. She raised her hand, slow and shaky, but with concentrated effort. Her fingers touched the right side of her head, moving along a train-track of staples that coursed through a bristle of short hair that had begun to grow again. She swallowed against the tightening in her throat. She knew that her hair had been cut, but to finally feel it made it real. The crooked course of staples overlying a scabbed incision probably hid a dent in the temporal bone. She had witnessed enough craniotomies to know that the skull never quite looked the same again.

"It'll, be okay," Paul said.

"Hair grows back and will look just as beautiful as it did before," Brandy said, this time not hiding the tears that trickled from her eyes.

She wanted to smile at them but it would likely just look crooked and ridiculous on her lips that didn't properly work yet. And it would be forced anyway. It wasn't the loss of her hair that bothered her the most. It was the fact that underneath that incision and the craniotomy, her brain was bruised and traumatized enough to have erased her memory. That it had created memories and visions of its own. Horrifying hallucinations of a shadow that sometimes crept into the light.

But only sometimes.

She dropped her hand and let it rest against the bed again. It took too much effort to keep her arm up like that. Her eyes drifted toward Paul.

"Were you scared?" she mumbled through lips that twisted in ways that she didn't want. Somehow it came out less garbled than she had expected.

He nodded. "Yes. I thought I was going to lose you. Technically, I did. Your heart stopped at least once in the operating room."

I died. The hammering of her heart responded through the cardiac monitor in increasingly rapid beats, as though it responded angrily to the accusation that it could possibly have given up at some time. *I died and I came back like this.*

"And when the neurosurgeon told me what he had to do to your brain . . .," he said but Evan's thoughts wandered.

That place in the woods, with everything shrouded in fog. Had that been Heaven? That moment was the only thing that her mind brought with her from the time she had been taken from the emergency room to the moment she awoke in the ICU. A place where others walked toward a cloudy light.

And that moment also carried something dark. Maybe it was just a mental manifestation of the hemorrhage in her head. A physiologic event projected as a seething, angry form. The brain could do such marvelous things when we are conscious, but maybe it tries to make sense of things when unconscious too. Such entities tormented the mind until the person awoke and organized those images into something real and tangible. Neurons mis-firing in a moment of low oxygen, when the heart stops if even for a few seconds.

Maybe those neurons remained scarred long after the heart beats again, leaving ghostly shadows at the periphery of her vision. There one second, and gone the next.

Whatever Paul said, she missed it. He just smiled at her now and held her hand like he always did when he stayed at her bedside. She would force a smile back to him if she had the strength, although it would come out crooked.

Evan glanced over his shoulder, beyond Brandy and to the closed door of her room. The same place where the shadow had stood only a few nights ago. The smell of it still lingering in her nose. Mud and mildew. Like the way the smell of a campfire settles on your clothes and hair. It was always there no matter what you did to get rid of it. Nothing stood next to that door in the mid-day sun. And perhaps nothing ever had.

Just oxygen-starved neurons trying to come back to life. That's all it had been.

Chapter 14

The eventual move to a post-surgical floor started with a little good-bye party in the ICU, with the many nurses and other residents that had cared for her in the weeks she had been there. Now Paul carried all those balloons and flowers behind her as the nurse wheeled her bed to the elevator and upward into the heart of the hospital.

This new room was at the end of the hall, thankfully far from the nurses' station. That was the noisiest place in any hospital, which meant Paul had looked out for her when the attending made the transfer. He had set her up in the nice, quiet room with windows that overlooked Lake Michigan.

No more huge ventilators and cardiac monitors beeping incessantly all night long. Fewer awakenings to check vital signs.

And hopefully, no more shadows by the door.

Once the nurse had gotten Evan set up in her room, Paul placed the flowers on the window sill and turned to her with outstretched arms. "Penthouse suite," he said with a big grin. "Almost."

"It's great," she said with mumbling lips that still didn't work well.

"Well, it was the best I could do on short notice."

He opened the vertical blinds to let the afternoon light into the room. "It's really not a bad view. You can see Navy Pier from here."

"Anything is better than the ICU."

"That's true." He turned back to her. "And you're only here for a little while as long as therapy goes well. Then it's up to the rehab floor. That's the best view of all. Top of the tower, babe."

He stuffed his hands into the pockets of his shabby jeans and stepped up to the side of her bed. "I gotta work a 12-hour tonight, but I'm thinking I'll bring up some fresh bacon and pancakes from George's down the street tomorrow morning. And some real coffee, not the tar that they heat up in the cafeteria."

"Sounds great." Her stomach already grumbled for something other than the hospital food, and even that had only been gelatin and pudding since she had become strong enough to eat again. Before that, her only nutrition had come from a tube fed through her nose and into her stomach that dripped a milky fluid filled with vitamins and calories. Thankfully that tube had come out shortly after the endotracheal tube. The thought of it made her throat tighten.

He leaned down and kissed her forehead. "I'll try to stop in and check on you tonight during my break, but I won't wake you up."

"It's okay if you did."

"I know, but I not going to. You need your sleep. How else are you planning on getting out of that bed to walk in a few weeks?"

"The Force," she said and smiled when it sounded like *forsch*. Paul understood it anyway.

He winked at her and then slipped from the room. The smile faded from her lips. She knew what he was doing. His optimism seemed unending, but she didn't think that he actually believed she would walk well or even be able to speak like she used to. Sure, her finger motion and dexterity had already improved. But those were just fingers. She rested her head back on the pillow and stared out the window until her eyelids grew heavy. Nothing else to do around here but eat, sleep and watch TV. At least time moved faster when she was asleep.

The first visitor of the afternoon was a man about her age and a physical therapist. She hadn't participated in any physical therapy yet, just the occupational therapy. But her doctor must have deemed it time to get those larger muscles functioning better. The session was about an hour and worked only her arms and shoulders. Such simple movements proved to be much harder than she had expected, though. Innumerable days, bed ridden in the ICU, could do that to a body.

And just an hour later, the occupational therapist paid her a visit. Not so much a visit, but rather another session. She was the same woman that had worked with her in the ICU, the one that didn't want to tell her what had landed her in the hospital.

"Hello again," the therapist said with a beaming smile. "You're moving up in the world."

"Looks like," Evan said and reflected her enthusiasm with a grin.

"I know that you're probably tired from the PT," she said, giving the common acronym for physical therapy, "but every little bit helps."

Evan knew it had already made a difference, especially in her hands and fingers. But these sessions left her fatigued, and it wasn't long after the therapist left that she let her eyes close again. She hated sleeping so much, but maybe Paul was right. And she had worked with enough head injury patients to know that sleep healed the brain better than anything.

Her mind still threaded through so many thoughts of the day and they wouldn't stop just because she closed her eyes. There was still a lot of work to do in order to get her mouth moving correctly, and that possibility seemed too far away right now. Forget the remote chance of walking any time soon. All of it only made her stomach hurt to think of it. What if she never got out of this bed? What if her speech always sounded distorted? This might be as good as it gets.

The shudders first started in her chest. A surge of panic that brought tears to her eyes. She clenched her eyelids tighter and shut off the waterworks, but that only made it worse.

Stop thinking like that. It doesn't help anything.
Neither does lying here all the time.

The door creaked open, slow against the metallic hinges. The sound was loud enough to wake her and her eyes opened to a dark room. Her heart jumped against her ribs and her pupils dilated. The foreign smell of the place made the breath catch in her throat. How had she gotten here? Silence permeated every inch of the darkness, even into the sliver of light that shone through the open door from the hall.

It's okay. That's right. I'm not in the ICU anymore.

Evan turned her head and peered through the dark room to the clock on the wall. The light from the hallway shone on the face barely enough for her to make out the time. 11:47. Not quite midnight. She had slept longer than she expected. At some point in her own self-pity, she had actually fallen asleep.

Then her gaze moved back to the door. That had to be the sound that had awakened her. She had distinctly heard it. Maybe it had been a nurse checking on her and she awoke just as the nurse had left. She pushed up onto her elbows with her eyes still pinned to the door. The thrumming of her heart left her hands shaking, but the door didn't move and nobody filled the space outside in the corridor.

But there was someone there. She knew it. Whoever stood out there breathed in shallow and quick bursts, loud enough that she heard it above the sound of the air in the heating ducts above her bed.

"Hello?" she whispered. She sucked in a quick breath. The word came out so clear and distinct.

The ticking of the clock snapped through every second, louder and louder as Evan held her breath and waited to hear a response.

"Is someone out there?" Her fingers searched for the remote that operated the bed and pressed the button that brought her head upright. Holding herself up on her elbows had drained her too much to keep it going, but she needed to see who stood out there just beyond her vision.

Tick. Tick. Tick. The clock had grown so loud, she wasn't sure that there was even breathing out in the hallway anymore. Or that there ever was.

She rested her head back against the pillow once again, but kept her gaze to the narrow slit of golden light that shone through the open door. Tick. Tick. Her ribs expanded in another breath.

And then she heard an exhale that wasn't her own.

Evan pulled herself up along the side rail of the bed, her eyes darting around the room. Her fingers searched along the rail, among the myriad of buttons. One of them had to be a light. A main room light, a small reading light above the bed. Something. Anything to chase away the shadows. The dark oozed over every aspect of the room and hid too many things.

The shaft of light blackened and Evan's gaze shot up to the slit in the open door. Her heart raced in her ears with the pounding of the clock. Someone stood just outside the door, a single eye peering through the opening. It stared at her, a dark shadow in the corridor. But its eye bored into her as it breathed again.

Evan's fingers frantically pushed every button on the bed remote now. A nurse call button was the largest button at the top of the remote. Someone had to have heard it signaling at the nurse's station.

But the thing just stood there, mostly concealed by the door and cast in shadows.

A buzz of static chirped through the PA speaker in the remote. "Can I help you?" the nurse spoke from her safe place at the central nurses' station.

"Help me, please," Evan stammered, her words mangled and desperate. "There's someone outside my room." *Damn it. That didn't sound anything like it was supposed to.*

The shadow still looked at her, but the air in the room chilled until it bit at the skin of her fingers and left her breath in puffs of fog.

She wasn't sure if she had blinked, but the shadow vanished and left the room in dread silence. One moment it was there, and then the next: gone. The sound of the clock no longer pierced into her brain every second. She held her breath and listened into the dark, her eyes searching the sliver of light that now fell across the floor once again. Her fingers still clutched the remote with white knuckles.

But there was nobody there. Maybe no one had ever stood there staring into her room. Misfiring neurons and broken synapses. All a result of her skull being cracked in a deadly car accident.

Her grip on the remote loosened and she allowed a cautious breath to escape her lips. A puff of white fog billowed with her breath.

The door slammed open, banging hard enough against the wall that a loud crack echoed through the room. She screamed and pressed back against the bed. The doorway remained empty despite the creak of the hinges as the door rebounded back from the wall.

A nurse rushed into the room with a start, her hands to her face and eyes wide. "What the hell was that?" she said as she stood at the door.

Evan couldn't speak anymore. The words just sounded like grunts and her lips wouldn't move correctly. She pointed a shaky finger toward the door and the nurse followed her gaze. She pulled the door back and flipped on the overhead light. Harsh fluorescent light filled the room, casting a white glare on the back of the door and the crack right through the middle of it.

"Was there someone else in here?" the nurse said, her fingers running along the damage in the door.

Tears flooded Evan's eyes. She wasn't sure anymore. But something had happened to that door, big enough to nearly snap it in half. Maybe there actually had been someone standing outside her door just a minute ago. Someone messing with her, trying to scare her.

She closed her eyes and clutched at the side rail. Misfires and broken synapses; but what if it wasn't?

What if someone followed her from the ICU, intent on doing her harm?

Chapter 15

"Whoa," Paul said and stopped in the doorway, a stack of Styrofoam take-out containers in his arms. "What happened here?"

The maintenance worker gave him a sideways glance and continued working at the screws on the hinges of the fractured door. "A gust blew through last night."

Paul looked from the man to Evan, who lay against the bed with the back propped up. She didn't smile when he came in, not like she usually did even if it was lop-sided and weak. Her glassy eyes stared toward the empty door frame and to the remains of the door, now disconnected from the hinges and leaning against the wall.

"Everything okay?" he said and sidled next to the bed. The aroma of bacon and eggs drifted off the boxes that he placed on the bedside tray.

She didn't look at him, but just kept her gaze fixed on the door. His throat went dry. Seeing her now like this was just like having her back on sedation with the tube in her throat. No response. No emotion. Nothing.

Paul turned back to see the door that Evan had fixated upon, and that's when he saw the huge split right through the middle of the wood. It hadn't cracked all the way through the board, but whatever caused that to happen had been strong.

"The door broke," she finally muttered.

He grasped her hand and watched her eyes. They still stared hard and unwavering at that broken door. "I see that. That must have been some kind of wind."

A tear streaked down her cheek. "It wasn't—," she started but winced.

"Hey," he said and leaned close to her. He lowered his voice below the sound of the drill on the hinges. "It's okay. Just tell me. Take your time."

"I don't know what it was," she said and brushed her hand against the wet trail on her face. "I don't know what I'm seeing anymore. Everything's been so confusing since I woke up."

"I get it. None of it has to make sense. Do you want me to see if I can get you a different room?"

She shook her head. "No. The nurse said the floor is full." Her head ticked toward the maintenance man. "He's fixing the door. It'll be okay."

"So," he said and squeezed her hand, "you don't think it was the wind that did that. What do you think happened?"

She shook her head and forced a smile that didn't reflect in her eyes. Her lips mashed together, trying to hold in the words. Whatever had her this scared made her afraid to speak, too.

"I think I'm going crazy." A choked sob squeezed through her throat. Tears flowed freely down her cheeks now.

He was afraid that this would happen to her. Not that she was going crazy, but that the overwhelming emotion of everything would finally catch up and collapse on her shoulders. And with a head injury, emotions could be such difficult things to handle. There was no way of knowing if there had been damages to part of her brain to cause swings of depression or anxiety.

He slipped a tissue from the box at the end of the bedside tray and handed it to her. She tried to smile again as she accepted it, but it was also forced.

"You're not crazy," he said. "You just need to get well. And you're definitely not imagining a giant door almost snapping in half. That had to scare the shit out of you last night."

A quick laugh escaped her throat. There it was: a true smile this time.

"It did." Evan dabbed at her eyes. She leaned toward him and her voice dropped, like she didn't want the guy across the room to hear her. "Ever since I woke up, I keep seeing things."

"What kind of things?"

She groaned, a sound that tried to stop her from saying any more. A grimace formed on her face and her eyes pinched closed. "Things that aren't there. A shadow or a person – I don't know."

"Do you see it every day?"

"No," she said and opened her eyes again. "Most of the time, everything is fine. Only sometimes, like last night. And it gets really cold, and I can smell it sometimes, too. Like a swamp or a damp basement. And it happens only at night so far."

Naturally, some degree of hallucination had to be expected with the kind of trauma she had experienced. Maybe they were a form of seizure zapping through the brain. Visual, even olfactory hallucinations were not unusual. Still, it made his chest get tight to think that this might be the devastating side effects of her accident.

"And when it happened last night, I just freaked out and the nurse came," she said, her words melding together in rapid succession.

Paul couldn't help but grin for a moment. The faster she talked, the clearer her speech became. She definitely didn't hear it in herself.

"They gave me some Ativan, and everything got quiet after that," she said and looked up at him again. Her eyebrows knit together and she paused. "What? Why are you smiling at this?"

The grin must have been wider than he expected. "Evan, did you hear that? You spoke clearly. I understood every word."

She sucked in a quick gasp of air and looked down at her hands, to the tissue that her fingers now finely held.

"I did," she said. Her eyebrows rose symmetrically and her jaw dropped. "I'm doing it again." A wide smile spread over her lips, and the fog of anxiety slipped from her face.

"See," he said. "You're getting better. It just takes time. Even these hallucinations are just a part of the healing."

"I hope so. I can't take much more it. They're absolutely terrifying."

Paul nodded. "You'll get there. I'll just talk to your doctor, see if we can get you something to help you sleep at night. If you're asleep, the hallucinations can't get to you." He glanced back to the broken door. "Except those wind gusts could still pick up. No guarantees about stopping them. A cold front moved in last night, and any doors or windows open in the building can cause a pretty good wind shear."

The maintenance man turned a side eye to him and gave a tiny nod in agreement.

"So only good dreams from now on," Paul said and turned back to her. "And time for breakfast, as promised. Georgie's had fresh bagels too. I got us a bit of everything. You're getting too skinny, I need to fatten you up."

He flashed her a smile, the one with the dimples that he knew she loved. The lines around her eyes softened and she relaxed back against the bed again.

"Thanks," she said.

The first take out box was still hot against his hand. It must be the bacon lying on the foil liner. Still sizzling in grease.

A small table setting was all he could organize because the bedside tray couldn't fit everything that he brought. "See, breakfast in bed. The best bagels in town. Can life get any better?"

Her fingers reached for a slice of bacon and her teeth crunched into it while she smiled. "I don't think it can."

The orange juice cartons would probably prove to be a little too much dexterity for her hands, so Paul popped them open and placed one before her. "And why don't I stay here with you tonight. I'll just get a fold-out bed from equipment supply. We can just hang and I'll be here when you go to sleep and when you wake up."

"You don't have to do that."

"I don't *have* to do anything. I want to."

She smiled. "Thanks."

"I'll just make sure the boogey man stays away and doesn't break any more doors."

The little glance she shot toward the door left a hint of emptiness in the space between them. That thing, a symbol of whatever she thought she saw, represented everything that had scared her last night. Even if it wasn't real, there was nothing Paul could do to take that away from her. The least he could do was to stay beside her and reassure her if she hallucinated again. His company, and a little nightly lorazepam, could get her through this rough patch.

When she asked about his shift in the ER last night, the tension melted off her shoulders. He droned about things that she would normally lose interest in, but she seemed fixated on them this morning. Probably anything to get her mind off the events of the last few weeks. And it occurred to him that he hadn't been able to converse with her like this since before the accident. Every once in a while, her speech halted like she tried to find the right word for something, but it had become so much clearer in just the last twenty-four hours.

Yes, things were healing. There was still so much for her to learn again, and she hadn't even been able to start walking yet.

The hours ticked on and the door was finally fixed, allowing the noise of the busy hallway to lull into a muffle. Paul sat beside her bed and they both watched the small flat screen TV mounted on the wall. Something they both enjoyed: home-made robots battling to the death in an arena surrounded by cheering crowds and raucous announcers. Occasionally he glanced to her, to the smile that had grown less crooked, as she watched the TV. Her eyes sparkled again. And her worries had dissolved, even when the sky darkened beyond the blinds.

A nurse knocked on the door and pushed it open just slightly. "Doctor Jensen," she said and stepped into the threshold.

"Come in," Evan said.

The young woman approached, her long brown hair tied back in a pony tail. Her hands held two small plastic cups. "I have your evening meds."

Paul glanced up to the clock. 9pm. The day had escaped them both, and now the work had to start. Keeping the monsters at bay. Keeping her safe.

The sparkle disappeared from Evan's eyes.

He turned back to her and whispered. "Remember. I'm right here, all night."

The nurse placed the cups on the bedside table and picked up the empty water mug. "I'll refill this and be right back." She turned and disappeared from the room.

Evan faced him. "You promise you'll stay here. All night."

He nodded. "I'm not going anywhere."

The nurse returned with a full mug of water. "Can I get you anything else for the night?"

Evan shook her head.

"Is there Ativan in there tonight?" Paul said, shooting a glance at the cups.

"Of course," she said. "After last night, she needs to get a full night of sleep. No more nightmares."

Evan grasped the cup and tossed the myriad of pills into her mouth. A swig of water from the thick straw shoved them down her throat.

"Now don't hesitate to call the nurses' station if you need anything else tonight, okay." The nurse smiled at her.

Paul watched her, at the lines that had creased around her eyes. That's how she looked when she worried about something but didn't say it. She kept it to herself, bottled until it broke her into a thousand pieces. Whatever she thought she saw still haunted the edges of her vision. He could tell by the way she shot a glance back to the door long after the nurse had left.

"Hey," he said and distracted her attention from the door. "I got you. It's gonna take about thirty minutes for that Ativan to kick in, and there's some robot fighting that needs to be done."

She smiled, breaking the mist of concern into nothing again. Her eyes turned back to the TV, but he still watched her from the corner of his eye. As soon as she closed her eyes, he would shut down the lights and the television. Nothing to distract her or trigger any more hallucinations tonight. If he had to stay up all night to make sure she slept, then he would do it. Just like in the scary movie with the guy who haunted the kids dreams and killed them in their sleep: he would watch out for her and make sure nothing happened. Except, in that movie, didn't Johnny Depp die doing just that?

He shook the thought from his head. This wasn't some scary movie. This was a serious case of a brain injury that needed to heal. And he would make sure that happened, no matter what it took.

Chapter 16

Evan sat across a table from a man she recognized but couldn't place. A hazy bright light flowed through the big windows of a restaurant – no, a café or a diner. Something like out of the 1950's with the old soda fountain and everything. Just like the one back home in Colorado where she and grandma used to go when dad was having one of his bad days. Bright and cheery and smelled like fresh baked pie.

But the guy across from her wasn't grandma. He wasn't even a relative as far as she could tell. His long thin face tapered to a pointed chin below a head of short dark hair. Soft brown eyes looked out the window, melancholy and waiting.

"Did you die too?" he asked but continued to watch the bright street outside.

The question was strange, but somehow, she had expected it. "Yes. That's what they tell me."

His narrow rib cage expanded and retracted in a deep sigh. "So, you crossed over."

"I guess so." Evan nodded and looked down at her hands on the worn red surface of the table. Her fingers splayed out between the placement of the fork and the knife. A diamond ring glinted on her left hand. "Paul told me that I died, but they brought me back. I'm fine now."

She raised her right hand to her head. Long blonde hair flowed between her fingers and cascaded down her shoulders. There once had been a crooked incision somewhere in her scalp. Or maybe she had imagined it.

"I was there too," he said, still watching the empty street. "I saw them. All dark and angry."

Her hand swooshed back down to the table, fast enough that it pulled at her hair and some of it came out in a bundle of corn silk. Not just some of it, a lot. She gasped and looked back up to him, her throat tight now.

"It's not real, Matt," she said and nearly swallowed the last word. Yes, she knew him. She remembered his face and his name and the worry etched across his eyes. "None of it is real. We were sick, but we'll get better soon."

"It never goes away. It's who we are now. See," he said and finally turned to her. His eyes flashed down the length of the table and signaled that she needed to look down as well.

She didn't want to see the wad of hair all tangled and loose on the table, but when she glanced down, the table wasn't there anymore. The light had vanished and left them surrounded in darkness with only the occasional flash of orange. The streetlights that raced past the window. A seat belt held her to the chair and her legs stretched out along the dark carpet of the passenger side of a car.

"It's all we'll ever be," Matt said, now from her left side.

Her fingers found the seat belt strap across her chest and gripped it, tight with white knuckles. Matt sat behind the wheel of the car, streetlights moving faster and faster with each second.

The race of her heart strummed against her ribs. "We're going to crash. Please slow down."

"She still wants something, you know. She won't go away until she gets it."

The outside world blurred into dark highlighted by color. No road, no signs. Just a dark oil painting that hadn't quite dried yet and the colors just ran together.

"Stop the car." Evan pulled at the seat belt.

Matt turned back to her, his face drawn and pale. "They never go away unless you do something about it."

The oil paint colors exploded and blinded her in a fog of black.

Evan startled awake and caught a shriek in her throat. Her eyes flew open and took in the early morning sunlight that streamed through her room window. The oil paint faded into sparks of memory that extinguished with her first deep breath.

Her tongue rasped like sandpaper against the roof of her mouth. For a moment she had forgotten where she was. The buttons along the side railing reminded her quickly and she elevated the head of the bed enough to see Paul stretched out along the length of the narrow fold-out bed next to her. The pulse in her ears faded as she controlled her breathing.

Just dreams, weird ones. About the crash and Matt.

Wait a second. Matt. Who was Matt and why did she need to remember him?

He was there that night, the night of the car accident. Was he the one driving? Did he do this to her?

Evan pinched her eyes closed and searched in the dark for any last vestiges of his face. Little bits here and there, including the sound of his voice. The way he looked at her. Everything about him was so sad and desperate. She remembered not being as much afraid of him as she was worried *about* him.

"Hey," Paul's voice stirred her from the vague thoughts.

She opened her eyes. Paul sat up and moved his legs over the edge of the sleeper.

"How'd you sleep?" he said, his voice still rough. "You seemed pretty quiet most of the night."

"I —," she started and her mind searched through the visions that quickly faded from her waking thoughts. "I think I remember something about the accident."

He rubbed his eye and looked at her with a single raised eyebrow. "Did you have a dream?"

She shook her head. "I don't know. I remembered sitting in the passenger seat. I yelled at him to slow down."

"Okay." The word fell from his lips slow and careful. He stood and moved closer to her bed.

"But he was scared." The flash of a memory flooded back to her. She had screamed at Matt until her throat hurt but he hadn't wanted to go back to the hospital. There had been something terrible back there and he needed to get away from it.

Paul nodded. "Yeah, scared to get caught."

"No, something else." But she couldn't remember what had frightened him so much. But it had to be bad enough that he risked running away from the cops. Yes. There were cars with flashing lights chasing them that night. And sirens.

"Do you remember anything he said to you?"

Only the sound of his voice rang in her head, not really full words or sentences. Well, maybe a few words here and there, but she couldn't tell if that was just from her dream or an actual memory. She clenched her eyes again. Anything to focus the jumble of images that ran through her scarred brain.

One sentence. *Matthew . . . but everyone calls me Matt.*

Her eyes flew open again. "Who is Matt?"

Paul's expression hardened and a stiff crease formed over his upper lip. "You *are* remembering." But he didn't seem happy about that.

He pulled up a chair next to the bed and sat down, his arms crossed over the edge of the railing and his chin rested on his forearm. "Matthew Pearce."

The name stirred a dust devil of a memory that started in her chest. Yes, that was his name. Matthew. But she called him Matt.

"Who is he?" she asked, but she wasn't sure she wanted to know the full truth. From Paul's steely gaze, it wasn't too good.

"He did this to you," he said, his voice dropping an octave.

That much she remembered, but everything else about it still hung like an intangible vapor in the air. What little she recalled of him didn't strike an angry nerve in her spine, though. Not like it did to Paul. She only felt a swell of remorse for him. Matt didn't mean to do any of this. It wasn't his fault.

"Pearce kidnapped you at gunpoint, right out of the ER that night," he said. His gaze didn't waver from her, but a dark storm shadowed his eyes. "Right in front of me."

Kidnapped. Is that what happened to her? That can't be right. She would have felt it, sensed it, when she remembered Matt's face and his voice. No. That wasn't what happened.

"He pulled you out of the hospital with the gun to your head and stole a police car. He drove away with you inside."

The muscles in her chest tightened. No, Matt didn't do that. He wouldn't. He worried about her and wanted to keep her safe. He never would have hurt her.

"That can't be right," she said and shook her head.

Paul tightened his lips and took in a steady breath. "That's exactly what happened."

She pulled herself upright, her hand clenched against the railing. The words started to stumble over her lips again, twisting into garbled fragments. "Matt would never hurt me."

He turned away from her and reached into the back pocket of his jeans. The smart phone filled his hand and he awoke the main screen. "I didn't want to show you this soon, but maybe it's time." His thumb scrolled across the white screen, the reflection of moving pages flashing against his skin. Once he found the right page, he turned the phone to her.

The phone was warm in her hand, a product of Paul's own body heat. The screen showed an article from one of the Chicago news affiliates. The headline scrawled across the top in bold letters.

Local Doctor Kidnapped By Armed Patient

This was all wrong. They had the story wrong. Her thumb scrolled down the page and stopped on a black and white security photo. From the angle, it looked like it had been taken at the trauma bay doors of the ER. She knew that area of the hospital all too well. Standing in front of the doors were two people. A man behind a woman, his left arm around her neck and the other hand with a pistol pressed against her head.

She would have remembered this. There's no way that it went down like that. Someone must have altered the picture.

But there it was. Sure, the resolution of the picture wasn't great, but she recognized her long hair that had fallen free, the white coat. Even the glint of a ring dangling on a chain around her neck. The man behind her stood obscured by her own hair, though. Maybe it wasn't Matt who had held the gun to her head.

Black typeset flowed down the white page.

On Thursday night, trauma surgeon and resident Dr. Evan Jensen was kidnapped at gunpoint from the emergency room of St. John's hospital. Officials say that the alleged assailant, Matthew Logan Pearce of Glenview, was a patient in the emergency department at the time and was being evaluated before proceeding to the Cook County Jail for processing. Eyewitnesses say that Pearce was able to obtain a weapon from one of his accompanying officers and he used this to take Dr. Jensen hostage. The assailant then proceeded to leave the St. John's campus via a stolen police cruiser, which evolved into a high-speed chase along the Kennedy expressway. The chase ended in a rollover when the vehicle being controlled by Pearce struck the police blockade. Pearce was detained at the scene. Dr. Jensen, who was still a passenger in the car, sustained life-threatening injuries and was flown to St. John's Hospital. A spokesman for the hospital states that Dr. Jensen's status is critical at this time and an update will be provided with a press conference at 5pm tonight. Pearce has been charged with multiple counts of kidnapping, use of a deadly weapon, attempted murder, and other charges which are still pending. These may be upgraded if his victim succumbs to her injuries.

Evan's throat tightened as an image appeared at the bottom of the article. Three color mug shots of a man's face from the front and both sides. Several lacerations across his forehead had butterfly tape across them and a purple-black bruise darkened is left eye. But she recognized him anyway. His long, gaunt face. A shock of dark hair on his head.

It was Matt. The same man who asked her in a dream, "*did you die too?*"

The words on the screen blurred and her hand shook. Paul grasped the phone and turned it off. "I'm sorry. I wanted to wait on that, but now seemed as good a time as any."

"That's what happened to me," she muttered, the words halting at each breath.

"It's what happened," he said and placed a hand on her shoulder. "But it's not who you are. You survived it. You got away from him and he'll never lay a hand on you again."

Paul couldn't understand, and there was no way she could make him. She wasn't afraid of Matt. Sure, maybe at first. But he had no intention of hurting her. He tried to help her. She knew it to the very bottom of her soul. Matt knew something and he had wanted to warn her.

It never goes away. It's who we are now. Matt said that before she woke up to this new nightmare.

Chapter 17

When Paul reassured her that everything would be okay, Evan nodded. There was so much she still needed to understand – to wrap her mind around – that she just needed to keep it to herself. He would only worry if he knew the things that still hung in her thoughts. So, for now, this would have to do.

A tap sounded at the door. "Knock knock," a woman's voice sounded from the hall. The door opened and the therapist stood at the threshold.

Thank heavens, someone to break this never-ending stream of disturbing thoughts. And someone to help distract Paul from the questions.

"Good morning," the woman said with a smile and a clipboard tucked under her arm.

Paul turned back to Evan. "I'll be back tonight, okay." He leaned down and quickly kissed her forehead. The tension around his eyes had eased and his dimples returned with his grin.

"Well, she won't be in here after noon today," the therapist said.

"What?" Evan said and sat up straighter. "I can leave?"

The woman smiled. "Not so fast. Looks like your doctor has approved a transfer to the rehab unit."

Evan's shoulders fell. Still in the hospital, but at least it would be a different view. "Oh, okay."

"Hey, it's not so bad," Paul said. "Those rooms up there are more like a little apartment. And fewer interruptions at night."

"And hours of therapy," the woman said with a tilt of her neck. "All meant to get you literally back on your feet."

Evan leaned back against the bed. "Well I guess I'm checking into rehab."

Paul glanced at her and his smile had deepened his dimples even more. "Yeah, you are, Winehouse."

She laughed and he leaned down to kiss her again. Then he bounded off, leaving the last vestiges of his lips on her forehead. He dodged past the therapist, gave Evan one last glance with a wink, and he disappeared.

The therapist shut the door behind him. "The other thing it means is that you're getting the cast off today too."

If she couldn't go home, getting the hot and heavy cast off her leg was the next best thing. "Alright, I'm ready."

"Sorry, not by me," the therapist said and pulled a chair up to the bed side. "The orthopedics resident will be stopping by later this morning."

The morning exercises with the occupational therapist went as usual, but her thoughts drifted beyond the routine that she did every morning. Snippets of memory, like sun-bleached video tape, reeled through her thoughts. The rawness in her throat from yelling at Matt to stop the car. The sound of his voice repeating in her head.

So, you crossed over.

This is who we are now. It's all we'll ever be.

They weren't even real memories, as far as she could tell. Just thoughts from a dream brought on by Ativan and a brain injury.

The time with the therapist had vanished and she wasn't sure that she did all that well, but the woman didn't say anything but, "see you tomorrow."

The sound of the saw grated at her nerves and left a roar in her ears. But it was enough to drive away the persistent visions of the dreams. The ortho resident leaned over the bed, the cast saw in hand and protective goggles on his face. But Evan couldn't look at it. She knew all too well that the saw wouldn't hurt her if it penetrated the cast. That sound, though. It had been used in way too many horror movies to settle right in her gut.

Then the loud steely whir silenced.

"There we are," the resident said. Kyle. If she could remember correctly, that was his name. He had said *hi* to her a few times in the resident lecture auditorium.

For a moment, she didn't want to look. What if her leg was so mangled under the fiberglass wrappings that she didn't recognize herself anymore? Crack. Pressure instantly released from around her calf and her eyes opened before she realized what she had done.

The cast had been split down the middle and the resident spread the edges of it until the rest of the fiberglass behind her leg crunched open. The ambient air of the room settled cold against the skin of her calf under the fabric wrapping just below the fiberglass. He ran his bandage scissors down the length of the gauze, and her leg was free for the first time since she woke up.

"Okay," he said and placed his hands around her ankle and knee. "I'm going to lift it out. Just let me do all the work."

His callused fingers rubbed against her skin, the flesh tingling and alive like a new baby, and it left the nerve endings especially sensitive. His grasp almost tickled and she bit her lip

134

just before he lifted her leg out of the remnant of the cast. With the cast brushed out of the way, the resident rested her leg back down on the surface of the bed. Finally, she took the chance to inspect her leg.

And it was nothing like she had expected.

First of all, since she started seeing Paul, she had always made sure that she stayed "well-landscaped". Just because. And if things were landscaped before, then the hedges had definitely overgrown. Her leg looked like sasquatch had been nesting just under the cast for the last several weeks. No wonder it itched so often. The hair growth there was astounding. And then there was the long track of silver staples along the front of her shin, all evenly spaced over a thin bluish-red incision line. Round purple scars dotted at regular intervals along the length of her tibia, evidence that at some point she had traction rods protruding from her flesh. Thank heavens she had never been awake to see that, or the aftermath of when they had been removed and replaced by the cast.

"Staples will come out today too," he said and gave her a sideways glance. He must have seen her eyeing the steel track.

"What's under there?" she asked.

His eyebrows raised. "Well, a plate along the tibia, and some pins holding the fibula together. Nothing that needs to come out unless they bother you."

And what would his definition of bother be, she wondered.

He worked at removing the staples, each one embedded into the skin for several weeks. She turned her gaze out the window to distract from the pinch of each one leaving her flesh. There had to be a hundred of them, but she had lost count when she gazed out to Navy Pier in the distance.

The young doctor didn't say much as he worked. Just silent and get the job done.

"Were you there that night, Kyle?" she asked.

The resident lifted his head. "I'm sorry?"

"The night this happened to me," she said and ticked her head to the half-removed line of staples. "Were you in the operating room?"

He swallowed and she could swear that the hand holding the staple remover faltered. "Yeah, I was there."

"How much of everything did you see?"

Kyle looked away from her and set to the staples again. "I was there for most of it."

"Even with the neurosurgeon?"

He nodded.

"So, did you see me die?"

The hand holding the staple remover now trembled and he stopped again. His head hung for a second. "Why are you asking me this?" he said.

"Because nobody understands what it's like to hear about your life like it's a TV show or something. I can't get anyone to tell me the truth unless I beg. So now I'm begging. Did you see me die?"

He sighed and placed the instrument on the next staple. "Yes. Twice."

That stopped her breath for a moment. It wasn't what she had expected to hear.

"Twice?"

"Yeah. You coded twice. The first time you went into ventricular fibrillation. Your skull was open and everything. They shocked you a few times until there was a normal rhythm. And the second time, you just flatlined."

The room began to spin, a sickening whorl of too much sunlight and the smell of antiseptic. Ringing sounded in her ears and she rested her back against the bed.

"The anesthesiologist was doing CPR, chest compressions and everything even though your ribs were already cracked."

Her hand drifted to her sternum, to the tender spots that still lingered there when she breathed deep or sneezed. Somewhere under her skin, scar tissue held together multiple rib fractures that must have happened from the resuscitation.

"How long?"

"What?"

"How long was I flatlined?"

"I don't know," he said and shook his head. "Five. Ten minutes, maybe. It felt like an hour. And then the rhythm just popped back on the monitor, slow but it was there. They finished evacuating the hematoma on your brain and closed you up before it happened again. The ortho team didn't fix your leg until four or five days later. You were too unstable."

Matt's voice echoed in her thoughts again. *So, you crossed over too.*

Paul had never told her what happened in the operating room that night. She already knew that she had likely coded, but this was the first time hearing the actual account of it.

"Thank you for being honest, Kyle." She pressed her fingers against her closed eyelids.

The next few staples pinched at a quickened rate. The feel of his rough fingers against her skin sent ripples of irritation along her leg.

"I'm sorry that this happened to you," he finally spoke after several minutes of uncomfortable silence. "But I'm glad you're getting better."

She opened her eyes to face him. The resident stood and gathered the remnants of his work. He gave her a weak smile and turned away.

"I'll see you around, okay," she said as he crossed the threshold.

Kyle stopped and nodded, the kind of quick and sure motion that an army recruiter would give. Distant. Emotionless. "You can count on it."

Then he left her alone with her bare, hairy leg resting uncomfortably on top of the bed. She pulled the rest of the blankets from her other leg because it was too difficult to try and move it above the linens. In the bright morning light that shone through the windows, she gazed at them both. The left leg had been free and unbound, although not used. But the right leg had withered, covered with sasquatch hair and flakes of dry skin that hadn't had the chance to escape in weeks. There was no way it would be able to walk. For all the effort she put into moving her toes, there should be a lot more than just a twitch in either foot.

This is how you are now. This is how you will always be.

There was only the Before and the Now, and only one of those would ever be experienced for the first time.

Chapter 18

Evan's fingers gripped the arm rests of the wheelchair. An actual chair. Not a bed that someone just pushed around with her laying on top of it and everyone staring at the *poor girl in the bed*. At least being upright felt more dignified. The nurse pushed the chair into the transport elevator and up they went. Straight toward the seventh floor. The top of the hospital.

The pull of gravity drew against her equilibrium and made her head spin. Moving vertically in an elevator always made her kind of dizzy, but it was a whole new experience sitting in a wheelchair. Her fingers gripped the rests harder.

"You okay?" the nurse said. The elevator let out an electronic beep as it moved past the next floor.

"I will be as soon as we get off this thing," Evan said and gave her a weak smile.

"Soon enough. At least you're moving up in the world." The nurse grinned and winked at her.

"Finally." Nausea welled at the back of her throat. Another beep. Only two more floors to go. She squeezed her eyelids tight and swallowed. Beep.

The last beep sounded three times and the elevator slowed to a halt. The doors slid open to a brightly lit corridor lined in tinted windows. The nurse pushed the wheelchair into the hall.

Everything smelled new here, and that wasn't by chance. This unit had opened up only about seven months ago and it was the first of its kind. A full-blown inpatient rehabilitation unit that incorporated all modes of therapy. Patients were transferred here from all over the city, but only if they could get a bed. Evan had never come to this unit before today, but she had never expected she would see it like this. From a wheelchair.

Doors lined the corridor on both sides, but these didn't look like hospital rooms. Instead, the walls and floor looked like a luxury apartment building. Large potted plants nestled against the walls about every 3 doors. Sky lights shone down, which added to the bright and open feel of the unit.

"I think you're gonna like it here," the nurse behind her said and continued toward the central station and hub of the unit. Each floor of the hospital had been designed in the same X-shaped floor plan, with a north, south, east, and west wing. This place was no different.

They neared the central desk, set in the crossway of the unit. A woman stood behind the desk as soon as she saw them approach. With a smile, she rounded the side of the desk. She kept her hands clasped behind her back and leaned down a little as the nurse brought the wheelchair to a stop.

"You must be Dr. Jensen," she said. "I'm Sally Higgins and I am the floor supervisor here. So good to finally meet you."

Evan nodded and met her smile as well, but Sally still held her hands behind her back. "Good to finally be here."

"I bet," she said. "Well, I really think you will do well here." She glanced up to the nurse. "Let's just get you checked in and then we'll start your orientation."

Sally's hands made an appearance to accept Evan's patient folder from the nurse. The two of them chatted about transfer orders and the proper signatures on the correct papers. All just mundane red-tape sort of things that got lost in the background noise of the unit.

Evan arched her neck and felt a small pop as her fatigued bones and muscles pulled back into alignment. It still surprised her how tired she got from just a little more activity than her current normal. Simply sitting upright in the chair for ten or fifteen minutes was enough to make her want to take a nap. As great as this place was, she would kill to lie down for a while and recharge with nobody putting on airs for her. She craned her neck to the left and felt another pop. That one felt good.

Her eyes peeked open and the rest of the noise fell silent. The north wing of the unit extended down from this central hub, but it wasn't like the corridor that greeted the elevator. That wing looked like it had been abandoned years ago and never incorporated into the main rehab unit. Part way down the hall a set of double white doors with two slim vertical windows blocked the path further into the wing. A heavy chain wrapped across the two push bars, locking the entrance beyond it. Those doors had sat there, neglected for years, the white paint chipped and yellowed at the edges from the years that had tainted them.

Whatever stood behind those doors remained secured and forgotten with that steel chain. Although the two little windows only showed darkness beyond them, Evan couldn't turn her gaze away from the doors, like they stared back at her. The sunlight that flowed through the corridor windows didn't seem to penetrate the space in front of the barrier, and neither did the heat. The cool air that drafted from under the doors chilled against the flesh of her newly-bared leg despite it being wrapped in an ACE bandage.

"Don't let that place bother you," Sally said from behind the desk now.

This drew Evan's gaze away from the doors. Sally had the folder in front of her and she continued to sign the designated pages. She didn't look up at Evan but she must have seen her watching the doors.

"That wing has been locked for so long, we forget it's even there," Sally continued. Her thin fingers pressed the ballpoint pen down on the paper with a quick tap to emphasize the completion of her work on the patient transfer.

"What's beyond there?" Evan asked.

Sally shrugged and glanced back up to her from the paperwork. "Storage, I think. It's been locked up since before I started at St. Johns, and that was three years ago this coming March."

"It was the old maternity unit," the nurse behind her wheelchair said. "It closed about eight or nine years ago when the department got moved down to the second floor."

Evan turned back to the door when another trickle of cold air drifted across her toes, like something breathing frost from down the corridor. The doors remained closed and still with their dark, black eye windows looking at her.

"Why did they never open it again?" she asked.

"I heard that there was safety issues or something." She leaned down, her face only inches from Evan's, and her voice dropped to a near-whisper. "I think it was something else. It closed down after a patient died, I guess it was pretty gruesome. I've heard stories."

"What kind of stories?" Evan whispered and turned to face her. The nurse's eyes were wide and she gave a quick glance to Sally, who disregarded their conversation in favor of completing her signatures. The nurse leaned in just a little closer. "The patient was pregnant, of course. Both her and her baby died. I guess there was blood everywhere and things were just never the same. Several staff members quit in the few weeks after that, said they were seeing and hearing things."

"What kind of things?" Evan whispered.

"Things that weren't there," the nurse said with a slow nod and then stood, the signal that she didn't have the opportunity to say more because her time here was done.

Sally withdrew something from her drawer and then stood from behind the desk with the closed folder tucked under her arm. She held out the object in her left hand, a device with a black strap like a smart watch. "This is for you to wear at all times. This is how you call any of the floor staff day or night."

Evan accepted the watch and glanced back up to her.

"Alright, I think we've got everything squared away. Let's show you to your room, and we don't have to go far." She started down the corridor to the east wing.

The nurse grasped the wheelchair and started to turn it, but Evan gave one final glance to the doors. A shiver moved across her skin, the same sensation that had crawled along her spine when she had seen someone peering at her through the door of her room. Or when she saw it standing in her room in the ICU and she couldn't move or scream to get help. The chair continued to turn and Evan could no longer see the black window eyes, but she knew they still watched her. The same eyes from the ICU and the thing at the door.

Sally led her just around the corner to the first room on the left. A black pad at the level of the door handle held a steady red light within its structure until Sally pressed her thumb to the black plate and the door clicked open. It swung inward on its own and they entered into the room.

"Well, here it is," Sally said and stepped aside while Evan's wheelchair moved into the room.

Paul was right. This place was definitely not like a hospital room. It reminded her more of a nice hotel, with a normal twin bed and a dresser topped with a flat screen TV. A white-tiled bathroom was off to one end of the room and a wide window with accordion blinds looked out to the city beyond the hospital. A night stand with a lamp and cordless phone station stood next to the bed. A small sofa under the window, the kind with a pull-out bed that would be the most uncomfortable thing ever slept upon. Everything she needed to hopefully get her sanity back.

"The entry is with thumbprint or a card," Sally said. "I'll bring in the thumbprint coder to get you started with your own entry. We can give you extra cards if you want to provide any to visitors." She opened the folder and withdrew a manila envelope that she placed on the dresser. "In here is the full welcome packet and your personalized schedule."

"I have a schedule?" Evan said, her eyebrows raised.

"Absolutely. Your life up here will be planned out for the most part, in hopes of getting you the most accurate therapy for your particular needs." Her bony hand patted the envelope once and then she pointed across the room. "The dining room is at the end of the east wing. All meal times are provided in the packet, but you can also get room service as well." She turned and pointed again. "The south wing will be where all your therapy is located, and the packet has your times and room locations. If you need to get a hold of me, my number is on speed dial programmed into the phone. There are more contacts listed in the packet as well, including your lead therapist should you need to get a hold of someone." She clasped her hands before her and stood with a smile. "Can I get you anything else right now?"

All this information flooded her already tired brain. She forced another smile. "I can't think of anything right now, but I'll call if I do."

"Excellent. Well, Dr. Jensen, it's a pleasure to have you here with us and please don't hesitate to reach out. Now, I will have one of our staff members help you get transferred into bed so you can get some rest before orientation."

"Thanks," Evan said and looked back toward the window. Well, this would sort of be like regular life again, although her life was all planned out for the foreseeable future. If it meant being able to walk and speak clearly even when she was tired, then she would do whatever they asked of her.

It only took a few minutes to get her situated into bed with help from her nurse and the staff member from the rehab unit. And then she was alone behind the closed door of her own room. No beeping monitors echoing from the nurses' station. Nobody in the next room shouting at the nurse about his pain and he needs more narcotics. Just quiet, in a soft bed that didn't have rails.

She let her eyes close and took in a steady breath. This place was a fresh start, the next door she had to walk through to get her life back.

This is who you are now. And you will walk out of this place on your own two feet.

Chapter 19

The knock at the door woke her from the quietest sleep Evan had had in days.

"Dr. Jensen," a man's voice came from the other side of the door. "It's time for orientation. May I come in?"

She cleared her throat. "Sure."

The door clicked and opened to a large man in a polo shirt and a name tag, the kind of guy who had probably played rugby in college. He stayed at the threshold and gave her a timid wave. "I'm Jake, with the therapy staff. I've come to take you to orientation."

Evan glanced to the digital clock on the night stand. Three in the afternoon. Right on the dot. She moved to her elbows and this was enough to get Jake moving into the apartment. Without any direction needed, he moved the wheelchair from its place against the wall to the side of her bed. She stopped to watch him lock the wheels and shift toward the lower half of the bed.

He looked up at her from where he stood. "I'm also your MTA."

"My what?"

"MTA. Mandatory Transfer Assist," he said with a smile. "That's what it says on your chart. You're to have assistance with all movement to and from your chair, at least for now."

As much as she hated the idea of someone always needing to be there to put her to bed or take her to the bathroom, there was a good reason for it. She could act like she was independent, but her upper body strength was just not there. She barely had enough to feed herself for a meal now, and that had only been happening for about a week.

With a nod of her head, Jake grinned and held out both arms for her while he gave instructions. Of course, it was awkward at first, with both his arms around her upper body in an uncomfortably close embrace while he hefted her upright. As big as he was, he still treated her legs with gentle ease. The wrapping on the right leg maybe gave him some clue that there was something to be cautious of, but it didn't matter. Evan believed he would have done it anyway.

Jake planted his feet and leaned in close again, his arms moving around her. "Now, just let me do the lifting. Don't try to help out yet. That comes later."

His arms went taught and she nearly buried her face in his broad chest when he lifted her upright. Her backside left the surface of the bed and then settled onto the seat of her wheelchair. The effort of it made her heart rate rush for a few seconds.

Jake moved behind her and pushed the chair toward the door, but not without picking up her manila envelope. Together, they moved to the therapy wing.

The wheels rolled closer to the central confluence of the wings, and the first whisper of cold air drifted from the shuttered doors of the north wing. *I'm not going to look.* Evan craned her neck the opposite direction as the central hub neared, an exaggerated movement but it was what she had to do to avoid looking at the locked doors. Sally was still nestled behind her desk and the computer screen. Evan caught sight of her broad smile toward her just before she turned away and the chair veered toward the south wing. But in the corner of her eye, the double locked doors beyond the desk still looked out into emptiness. Evan closed her eyes for that moment. She didn't want to think about them, not even once. There's nothing behind them but dust and outdated medical machines. Forgotten and left behind. That's it.

She opened her eyes again and gazed down the long corridor. The wheelchair passed door after door, but she knew where they were headed. Bright colored gym equipment and racks of various forms of weights surrounding a center of rubber mats lingered at the end of the corridor.

A woman stepped out from one of the side doors and beamed at them from the end of the hall. She easily stood taller than Jake with the build of a sprinter. A blue polo shirt also carried her name tag, just like her Transfer Assistant. Her thick, curly black hair was tied back in a rigid bun, but it left her face bright and her dark brown eyes clear.

"Hi, Dr. Jensen," she said as the wheelchair approached the edge of the gym. Jake stopped the chair and the woman stepped around her to sit along a weight bench. She must have wanted to be at eye level with Evan. "I'm Samena Lomu, your lead therapist."

Evan extended her hand, although it still trembled with the effort when her arms moved far enough away from her torso. The muscles in her shoulders fought to keep her arm up, a reminder that she needed to be here in the therapy unit.

Samena waved her off with a smile. "We don't do that here. A lot of our patients can't move their arms for whatever reason, so we just take that off the table so nobody has to worry about formalities"

Smart. That must have been why Sally kept her hands otherwise occupied when they first met.

"Alright, I can get on board with that," Evan said. "And call me Evan, please."

"Okay, Evan." Jake handed the envelope to Samena and she opened it. "So I am your therapy coordinator as well as your physical therapist. We're going to be a solid team from here on out."

She withdrew the stack of papers from the envelope and flipped through them until she found the schedule. A blocked table of times and locations splayed out over the paper and Samena turned it around to Evan.

"This is your daily schedule. Seven days a week. That's what it takes to make you independent, and that is our ultimate goal here. You start at 8am with speech therapy in Room 1," she said and pointed back down the end of the hall. Jake stepped aside for Evan to see. As much as she hated to admit it, her words still failed her occasionally. The sentences halted and her lips stammered for the right phrase, especially when she was anxious or tired.

The therapist continued down the entire block of her schedule, but there was no way Evan was going to remember any of this. Her brain already swam with information overload.

And Samena must have sensed it.

"It's okay, Evan," she said and let the pages rest on her lap. "We are all here to help get you where you need to go. For now, you just go along for the ride."

In just the short ten minutes she had been with her, Evan now felt the fatigue setting in again. "Thanks. I can't process things like I used to."

"I understand, and we are here to get your life back for you." She turned over the envelope and held it up for Evan to see the bright orange sticker with black print on the front: MTA.

Mandatory Transfer Assist. "You see this? This is the first thing we are going to get rid of. This is the first step in recovering your independence."

The conviction in Samena's voice left the burn of appreciation start in Evan's chest. Yes, it was exactly what she needed.

"I like you already," Evan said.

"Well, you say that now," she said with a wink and a grin. She stood and stuffed the papers back in the envelope. "And that means we need to get started right away. You will start the day with speech and occupational therapy. The afternoon is for physical. We'll start off with just a little today, and be aware, you may be sore tonight."

Jake left her with the therapist at that moment, and everything started. At first, Evan didn't know what to expect. The rigid schedules and times felt a little daunting, something she wasn't sure that she could maintain. At least, not in her current state.

Thankfully, Samena was patient. Demanding, but patient. And that's what she needed, because every time she pulled back, the fatigue threatened to take over and urge her to quit.

And the most unexpected and delightful moment came at the end. Samena moved a chair and instrument table next to the wheelchair and opened a jar of ointment that filled the space between them with the scent of peppermint.

"The best part," Samena said. "The massage at the end for doing such a good job. And to loosen up some of those tendons that have gotten so tight."

Her strong hands moved the ointment across Evan's right forearm, stretching the cords and muscles under the skin.

"You do this for everybody?" Evan asked.

"I do," she smiled. "It really helps to increase circulation and breaks up some of that scar tissue. As we progress, it will do a world of good for your ribs and the thoracic spine. I understand you had a chest tube in at one point. That area could definitely use some TLC. And when you can breathe better, you'll have so much more energy."

Evan wished she could do that now. She had worked so hard to ignore the pain between her ribs when she took a deep breath that she had just become dependent on the shallow ones.

"Samena. I've never heard that name before."

The therapist worked at the tendons in the palm of Evan's hand. "It's Tongan. Means *secret*."

"Tonga? Is that where you're from?"

She nodded. "It is. I still have family there."

"I've heard it's beautiful."

"Oh, but Chicago is so wonderful when its twelve below out and Lake Michigan freezes over," she said with another wide grin and Evan laughed.

Talking with her was so easy, like she had known her forever. Thank heaven she was her therapist.

"And you can call me Sam," she said and started on the other arm. Her fingers moved around the black band on Evan's wrist. "Don't forget about this thing. You just tap the screen and speak into it if you need anything. It can read your location anywhere on the floor, so if you need assistance, it's like your own Life Alert."

"So, if I've fallen and I can't get up, I talk into the Star Trek watch and you'll come running?"

"Exactly." Sam laughed. "Or Big Jake will come and find you. One of us will be there."

She finished the massage, leaving them in the cooling aroma of mint. "Alright, I'll call Jake and you can head back to your room. Dinner is at six, so he will be around to take you to the dining room. And you just buzz him on the watch when you're done and he'll get you home. Just like the best date ever. And I'll see you tomorrow."

"Sounds good," Evan said just as Jake appeared down the hall. She almost felt a sense of regret that their session was done. Being able to talk to her made things better, less uncomfortable. She hadn't even thought of her fatigue until it was time for Jake to take her away.

The distance back to the room went quickly, and it wasn't until the wheelchair moved through her doorway that she realized she hadn't tried to look at the double doors again. Not even once. She had actually forgot about them until now. And no cold chill to numb her toes.

"Do you feel like sitting here or would you like to transfer to the sofa or the bed until dinner?" Jake said. He sounded so helpful and kind, and he probably was. But she had to remind herself that it was also his job. After all, she has a Mandatory Transfer Assistant.

"Uh, I think I'll just hang here, watch some TV or something until then."

"Okay," he said. "I'll be back in about an hour."

"I'll be waiting with baited breath," she said with a half-smile. He waved at her and then stepped through the door, leaving her alone in the room.

Chapter 20

As soon as someone called into her room and said that she had a visitor, the aching muscles in her arms eased. It had to be Paul.

"Yes, let him in," she said into the phone receiver and eyed the door, ready for it to open with a wave of an entry card on the security pad. The lock clicked and the door automatically swung open.

But her throat tightened and she tried to sit a little taller in her wheelchair when she saw the man standing at the threshold, grey on black hair, a handsome face and endearing smile.

"Dr. Sorenson," she said, the words garbled and numb on her lips. Damn, why did her voice fail in times of need? Was it ever going to get better?

"Dr. Jensen," he said and stepped into the room. As the chief medical officer of the entire hospital, he always looked like he had just come from an important board meeting. The last time she had seen him, he had grilled her about *Pneumococcal* pneumonia in front of all the residents in the lecture hall. And now he was here. And she couldn't believe that she remembered that embarrassing moment in lecture. Of everything she had forgotten, why couldn't that be one of them?

He entered the room and extended his hand to her. Right. He probably didn't know the therapy unit's guidelines about the hand shaking. But Evan extended her right hand, although it quaked with the effort. Sorenson cupped his other hand over hers as well while he kept eye contact.

"I apologize for stopping by unannounced," he said and released her hand. He pulled one of the chairs into the room and sat across from her. "And I should have come sooner."

Thank heavens he hadn't, especially when she couldn't speak and the nurses had to continually wipe the drool from her lips right after the endotracheal tube had been removed. That would have been far worse than being called out about pneumonia.

"That's okay," she said and gave him a forced smile.

"I just wanted to see how things are going for you. I hear that you are making a remarkable recovery."

Did he really care that much? She wasn't even sure that he had known her full name the entire time she had been a resident here.

"So far so good," she said. The trembling in her voice made the words blur.

"I also want to assure you that there will still be a place for you in the surgical program. As soon as you are on your feet, we would love to have you back in the operating room." He nodded, his gaze firm.

Damn. She hadn't even thought of that this whole time, and she knew she should have. Maybe something else had happened to her brain to make her apathetic to the whole residency thing right now. That was the absolute last thing on her mind. She had only been thinking about trying to speak again and hopefully walk without falling.

"Thank you," she said.

"This is the best place for you. And if you need anything, and I mean anything, please call me." He reached into the inner pocket of his suit coat and withdrew a business card. The white and black design of it flashed in the lamplight when he placed it on the end of the bed. "This is my personal cell number as well as a direct line into my office. Please rest assured that you have no concern for any expenses incurred here. Whatever you require, I'll make sure it's done."

A lump formed in her throat. He had just offered to cover everything. That must be why she had so easily gotten a room in the therapy unit, a place that was highly sought after for premier rehabilitation. Maybe that was why everyone here was so nice to her. Her shoulders fell at the thought.

The phone beeped again and the speaker sounded. "Dr. Jensen, you have another visitor."

"Okay," she called out and the phone clicked.

Dr. Sorenson stood and smoothed the front of his jacket. "Well, I won't keep you any longer."

"I really appreciate everything," she said.

The door automatically clicked open and Paul stood at the door with a backpack slung over one shoulder. His eyes widened slightly and he stalled as soon as he saw Sorensen in the room.

"Ah, Dr. Williams," Sorenson said and reached out a hand. Paul accepted it, but Evan recognized the slack in Paul's jaw.

"Dr. Sorenson, good to see you," Paul said with a vigorous hand shake.

"You take care of our young doctor here," Sorenson said with a nod to Evan.

"I will, sir." Paul grinned just enough for the dimples to appear.

Sorenson stepped around Paul and gave a final wave to Evan. "I will check up on you again soon. Have a good evening." Then he disappeared into the hall and the door shut behind him.

The grin fell from Paul's face and he turned to her with wide eyes. "What the hell?"

"I know, right," she said and laughed at his dismay. "He just showed up a few minutes ago."

"Just to say hi?"

"I guess," she said. The lines pinched between her eyebrows. "And I'm pretty sure he just told me that either he or the hospital is covering every expense up here for me."

A quick laugh came from his throat. "I'm not surprised."

"Really?"

"Yeah. I mean, you were kidnapped, assaulted and almost murdered all starting on hospital property. It's workplace violence all stemming from a lack of security in the ER. I bet they've been sweating about a lawsuit ever since it happened."

She shook her head. "I would never."

"But they don't know that, so don't let them know that. Make them worry. Maybe it could change things for the better. Looks like they'll bend over backwards to keep you happy."

Her spine sank and the pain started in her head again. "I don't want them to be afraid of me."

Paul smiled and leaned forward, grasping the arms of her chair. "They need to be afraid. Very afraid. My girl is a fierce warrior that takes no prisoners."

The smell of his body wash drifted over her and she had expected him to kiss her, but he backed away with the smile still painted on his face.

"I brought you some stuff from your apartment." He lifted the backpack and rested it on the end of the bed. "Picked up your laptop and tablet." The computer slid from the top of the pack and he placed everything across the bedspread.

Finally, a link to the outside world. She hadn't realized how much she needed them until now. How long had it been since she connected with anyone else besides the people in this hospital?

He withdrew a wad of clothes: a blue and white Star Wars print. "Your pajamas. Thought you would want something other than hospital gowns." He peered into the top of the bag. "A bunch of shirts, pants. And some intimate things." He turned to her with a wink.

A rush of heat moved over her cheeks. Oh hell. Hopefully he hadn't spent too much time in her underwear drawer.

"That's what I got for now. I can always go back for more if you think of something else you need me to pick up."

All of this stuff was more than enough for now. It was more than she had had the whole time she had been in the hospital.

She shook her head. "This is so great. Thank you."

"Of course." He settled into the chair that Sorenson had moved into the room. "So, how is everything here so far?"

She told him about the therapy and Samena. It was probably the most she had talked in a long time, but with Paul it was so much easier. The words didn't stumble as often.

"This unit is awesome," he said and looked around the room. "I've only been up here during orientation when I started residency. And the room is bigger than my apartment. Maybe I'll just move in here with you." He grinned.

For that second, she wished that he could. Spending hour after hour alone with her thoughts was starting to get on her nerves. A memory of the chained doors in the north wing danced through her thoughts. Just another one of those things that always lingered in her distant consciousness, like the nightmares and the flashes of everything that happened that night in the ER.

"Do you want me to stay tonight?" Paul said, his voice dropping.

The edge of worry in his voice drew her attention. He must have detected the anxiety that had started in her brain.

"I don't know if it's allowed, but yeah," she said.

"I'll make it happen." He leaned forward and placed a hand on her knee. "I brought the laptop. Maybe we can Netflix and chill."

She laughed. "Well, Netflix anyway."

Having Paul with her at dinner helped to ease the tension in her shoulders. It took her mind away from the thoughts that she was here only because Sorenson made it happen. She believed that the residency would welcome her back, but looking at the way she could hardly grip a fork made the singular fear start to boil. This was just a fork. A simple, straight utensil. It wasn't a scalpel and the pile of salty green beans on her plate wasn't a human being bleeding out from a gunshot wound. Her fingers had to work better than this or she wouldn't trust herself to operate on anyone. She angled her hand to stab at the beans, but most of them fell off the end.

"Let me help you with that," Paul said from the chair next to her.

Evan shook her head. "I got it." It came out more forceful and twisted than she had expected.

She tried again and most of the vegetables stayed there this time. The fork angled to her mouth and trembled with the quaking in her hand. But it worked and she fed herself. And it only took about four minutes to just get that mouthful.

A sigh breathed out from her chest while she chewed.

"It's okay," Paul said, low enough so that the other patients in the dining room couldn't hear him. "You'll get it soon."

"I know. I'm just being impatient," she said.

"Hey, only a week ago you couldn't even hold a tissue. Baby steps."

She smiled at him and placed the fork back on the table. The muscles in her hand threatened to cramp if she continued to hold it. "I want big girl steps."

"You will. It's just gonna take time."

"I hope so," she said and glanced down to the plate with more beans, a mound of mashed potatoes and a grilled chicken breast that still needed her utensils. "I won't be able to operate again if it doesn't."

He said nothing and she pressed her lips together in an attempt to hold back the tears that threatened to come. They always tingled at the edge of her eyes when the emptiness started in her chest. That deep, hollow pit that sucked in every thought that raced through her mind and turned them into despair.

"You will. I know you will."

She turned to him again and blinked her eyes until they felt dry. "Well, for now I'm hungry. I need your help. The chicken isn't going to cut itself."

He laughed. "Sure thing."

Every bite of dinner with him was worth it, even if he did have to help feed her like a toddler. The way he looked at her didn't make her feel like a freak, not like when so many others stared at the scar on her head or the way her hands didn't work quite right. All they saw was something to be pitied, but not with Paul.

They went back to her room together and the knock sounded at the door at 8pm. Right on time for her Mandatory Transfer Assistance. It wasn't Jake this time, just some other big guy that wouldn't allow Paul to help. It probably had to do with liability – everything in a hospital comes down to that in the end. But he moved her from the chair to the bed and then the guy left, no questions asked about Paul being there so late after visiting hours. They must have figured that Sorenson would probably intervene if they kicked him out. After all, she had his personal cell number now. If anyone gave Paul trouble about staying late, she would definitely use that card.

Evan leaned back against the stack of pillows and eyed Paul as he moved around to check out the sofa bed. She bit her lip and a flutter of moths started in her gut. This shouldn't be so nerve-wracking.

"That won't be very comfortable," she said.

He glanced back to her. "What? This? Well, what Hide-A-Bed is?"

"Come on, Paul. Don't make me beg," she said.

A smile crept across his face. "Oh, you mean, share the bed."

She rolled her eyes. "I can't believe I have to ask."

"Ask no more," he said and sidled up to the bed. He nestled down next her and rested along his side, his head propped up on his hand. "Is this better?"

"A lot better." She turned on her side as well but lay back against the pillows. His deep brown eyes studied her face and the grin didn't fade. He was so close now, closer than he had been since all this happened. Sure, he had held her hands and kissed her forehead and stayed in the room with her to ward off the nightmares. But that was it. Like he was afraid to break her.

That boyish smile still made the moths in her stomach swarm. There was something she wanted to ask, and it had been simmering for a while. Now would be as good a time as any. She had to know.

"Can I ask you something?"

"Shoot."

She cleared her throat. This had to be as clear as possible. No more slurred words. "Do you still love me?"

The smile disappeared and those lines appeared around his eyes. He moved up to lean on his outstretched arm and looked down at her. "Of course I do. Why would you ask that?"

"It's just, I haven't looked at myself in a mirror since all this, but I know I'm not pretty. And I can barely speak without drooling, and who knows if I'll be able to walk. I wouldn't blame you if you wanted to just part as friends and move on—"

"Stop," he said, his voice tight and his eyes narrowed. "Just stop this. No, you haven't looked in a mirror. And you should. There's nothing wrong with how you look. And I happen to love drool." He drew his finger up to the corner of her mouth as though to clean her face.

She laughed and that made him smile.

He leaned down, his torso pressed against hers. His fingers trailed along the side of her head, tracing the line of the incision along her temple. "This thing that happened to you, it changed things. It would be a lie to say it wasn't true. But so what? This is part of you. It's part of us." His hand then moved to the silver ring that glinted on her hand. "For better or for worse."

"But—"

"Hey," he said and touched the point of her chin. "Nobody's gonna love you more than I do. I'd like to see them try."

Paul closed his eyes and leaned toward her. The touch of his lips on hers sent shivers of goosebumps across the back of her neck. And it was the first time he had kissed her – really kissed her— since she awoke. Unafraid and true. She wouldn't break. Not ever.

When he leaned back, his face had relaxed and the tingle of the kiss still danced over her lips. "Now, I don't ever want you to think that again."

"You're not the boss of me," she said as clear as she could manage and then flashed him a quick grin.

"That's true." He settled back down beside her and draped his arm across her waist.

She didn't remember when she fell asleep, but when her eyes blinked open, the room had plunged into darkness. Paul must have turned out the light at some point, but he lay behind her with an arm around her and his torso pressed against her back. His body heat kept her warm despite the chill in the room. The even cadence of his breath lulled her eyes to close again.

But the sound of a woman crying in the corner of the room made the breath catch in her throat.

Chapter 21

The sobbing continued, somewhere in the shadows beyond the slit of light that shone through the window. Evan held her breath to hear the sound. At first, she thought it had come from outside in the corridor, but when she could listen better, she knew it came from inside the room. The tremors started in her arms and came out as an uneven exhale. The heat from Paul's body pressed against her had kept her warm, but now she realized that the air in the room had gone frigid. And the sound coming from the corner bounced on the cold atmosphere.

Evan lifted her head, anything to see better into the shadows. The weeping sounded louder, more frantic, like the sound came through clenched teeth. A sound that ebbed with desperation, rage, and hopelessness.

"Who's there?" Evan whispered, but regretted it as soon as she said it. If someone had broken into her room, they could be angry and confused. The last thing she needed was some other patient attacking her because he was startled by her voice.

The cries didn't change but stayed consistent in their gasping waves.

Paul shifted in his sleep behind her and his arm unconsciously wrapped around her midsection a little firmer. Evan held her breath again and listened into the dark, waiting for whoever it was to stop and run out when Paul moved. But it didn't change. The same weeping, ugly crying continued in the shadows.

"You need to leave right now," she whispered at the crier in the corner. The weeping stayed the same, hollow and alone.

Evan moved her hand to Paul's and patted it, increasing the speed the longer she had to do it. "Wake up." She didn't want to speak in more than a whisper but the urgency pinched in her voice.

The weeping stopped, abrupt and now uneasily silent. Although she couldn't see into the shadows, Evan knew that whoever it was still crouched in the corner. She paused for a moment and Paul still didn't move.

She grasped his hand tighter, digging her nails into the dorsum of his hand. "Paul."

A dark form arose in the corner, blacker than the shadows around it. The crying had stopped, leaving only dread quiet now. The thing stood there and watched, no sound coming from it at all, not even a breath.

The familiar and heavy scent of wet mud and swamp water drifted across the room. Evan froze, but her heart pounded against her ribs.

Not again. Oh God, please wake me up please wake me up please wake me up.

The temperature plummeted enough to leave her breath in fog. The thing only stood there, though. If she hadn't seen it rise, she easily could have mistaken it for just a shadow cast from the edge of furniture in the room.

"Wake up," she whispered to herself. "Wake up." Why couldn't she just wake from this nightmare?

A tormented wail rose from the corner of the room, increasing like a tornado siren and just as loud. The sound gripped in Evan's chest like a cold hand. Someone had to hear it. Paul must have heard it, but he didn't move. The sound rose to a scream.

Evan cringed and pulled her hand to cover her ear and pressed her other ear into the pillow.

The darkness folded in on itself. In a swirl of cold black, the form rushed at her, its scream so loud that she only heard a roar now. She clenched her eyes closed but felt its damp breath in her face. The swampy odor choked her and stifled her own cries.

Paul jolted behind her, his arm grasping around her and his head jerked upright. He jumped out of the bed and scrambled to the light on the night stand. Without his body heat against her, the skin of her back now crawled with frigid goosebumps.

The night stand light flicked on as soon as Paul found the switch. Evan gasped when his hands touched hers.

"Evan, wake up," he spoke to her. He was so close now she could smell the hair gel he had used earlier in the day. The hair gel, and nothing more. No cold, musty stench that clung to wet clothes and dirty skin.

Her eyes flew open to see him leaning over her, his eyes wide and his hands on her shoulders shaking.

"Did you hear that?" she said and darted a glance back to the corner, now illuminated by the lamp, but it was silent and empty.

"Hear what?"

"There was—" she started and scanned the corner. "There was someone over there."

Paul followed her gaze. "I don't see anything."

"How did you not hear that?"

He shook his head. "I didn't hear—"

"She was screaming. How is it possible you didn't hear that?"

Paul relaxed his hold on her shoulders and settled back down on the bed. "You had another nightmare."

"No. This wasn't a nightmare. She was real."

"I know it scared you."

She glanced back to the corner. It wasn't her imagination and it wasn't a dream. Someone had been crouching there crying. She had smelled it and she didn't dream of it screaming at her. The cold of it still danced against the skin of her forearms.

"Please, you have to believe me."

He leaned close to her and took her hand. "I believe you saw something."

"But you don't believe it was real."

A beep sounded at the door and a nurse stood in the doorway as soon as it opened. "I heard a scream," she said, her arms rigid and ready to help. "Is everything okay?"

Paul nodded. "She had a nightmare. She'll be okay."

The nurse gave him a quick look with a single raised eyebrow. That same look that asked what he was doing here, but she said nothing of it. She glanced back to Evan. "Do you need anything?"

Evan controlled her breathing and let her arms fall back down to her chest. It was no use trying to convince either of them of what she had seen. She had sustained a brain injury and everyone knew it.

"No, I'm fine."

The nurse nodded. "Okay. If you change your mind, just use your watch and call me." She turned and stepped away from the door, but not before eyeing Paul one last time.

He lay back down next to her. Her heart still raced in her chest and there was no way she planned on closing her eyes again tonight.

"Hey," he said, still holding her hand. "I believe you."

"No, you don't." She couldn't look at him right now. It

would only break her heart and she didn't have any reserve left to deal with that.

Whoever was in the room had let herself in and disappeared by the time Paul had turned on the light. The sound she had made was only for Evan's ears.

Maybe she *was* going crazy. Nobody could have done something like that without Paul hearing it. It was impossible. Tears streamed down the sides of her face and soaked into her pillow.

"I think I need help," she finally said and pulled his hand closer.

Chapter 22

"Are you sure you want to do this?" Paul said, looking at Evan in the mirror from where he stood behind her wheelchair in the bathroom.

Evan's assigned nurse for the day stood between them, electric razor in hand. She glanced between the two of them, just waiting for the go-ahead.

"I need to take control of something in my life," Evan said. The face in the mirror didn't feel like her own. This was the first time she had actually seen herself in weeks. Dark circles under the eyes. Her blonde hair that had grown out unevenly around the arcing incision along her scalp. She looked like a kid had gotten a hold of scissors and took to the doll in her lap, cutting off the locks in huge irregular swipes. And this was the end result. The incision along her temple barely peaked out from the hair that stood straight out from it.

"Just shave it all, right down to the scalp." She said and looked back to the nurse through the mirror.

"Alright," the nurse said with a half-grin. The razor clicked on and buzzed in her hand.

The first touch of the device to her head sent shivers down her spine. The sound of it vibrated deep into her skull and probably rattled against the metal plate that sat in there. It mowed down the little spikes of pale blonde hair and they rained down like snowflakes, some falling on her nose and tickling the side of her face. Evan closed her eyes to prevent any of the hair from falling through her eyelashes, but mostly because she didn't want to see it until everything was done.

When the thought first came to her to shave her head, it gave her pause. She had always had long hair. But that all changed the night of the accident. The moment she saw herself in the mirror, she was disgusted by so many things. The one thing she could change was the ridiculous fuzz that grew from her head and itched along the incision.

The swath of the razor came from the back and moved toward her forehead again. Although the hair falling was small, an enormous weight shed from her head. *Finally, I can say that I made a choice in all this.*

After the last pass, the nurse clicked off the razor and brushed her small hands over Evan's head, dusting off the last of the shavings. "How's that?"

She opened her eyes and let them adjust to the light again. The face that looked back at her smiled. "Perfect."

"You feel better now?" Paul said and uncrossed his arms. He stepped behind her and placed his hands on her shoulders. "I like it." His hand smoothed over her scalp and he leaned down to plant a kiss right on her crown.

"Are you ready for a shower? Now would be a good time to get the rest of the hair rinsed away," the nurse said.

"I think so," Evan said and arced her neck back to glance at Paul.

"That's my cue, I guess," he said. He crouched down to see her at eye-level. "You gonna be okay after last night?"

She nodded. "I think I was just tired and didn't sleep well."

"Okay. I'll be back again after my shift tonight." He turned away and slipped out of the bathroom.

Alone now, with the impending state of humiliation. Definitely something she didn't want Paul to see. Someone to help her naked self onto the bench in the shower. Someone to shave her legs for her because they were driving her crazy and she couldn't do it herself. Just get it over with. At least there was somebody in here with her, a person she could actually see and hear.

As soon as that was done and breakfast had ended, it was time for therapy. Her Mandatory Transfer Assistant (aka Jake) showed up again and wheeled her from the room.

"When am I not going to need you anymore?" she said as he pushed her into the corridor.

"When you can move yourself and wheel your own chair," he said.

"So never, right?" she said and turned her face up to smile at him.

"Not with that attitude," he said with a laugh and kept going.

They entered the central hub, the place where Sally watched everyone come and go between each of the therapy wings, and conveniently ignored the locked double doors in the forgotten wing. Jake pushed the chair into the hub, and Evan glanced to the quiet doors, more out of habit now than anything else. And like habit, her brain had expectation of seeing the steel lock, the two black windows and the chipped white paint on the doors.

But there was something else now.

The breath left Evan's lungs and her ribs locked for only the short moment before Jake turned the chair toward the therapy wing. How can it be, in the middle of the morning, with everyone walking around and phones ringing and televisions playing behind the closed doors of the patients?

The dark figure stood there, but not a shadow like she had seen so many times now in the hospital. It was just like it had been in the foggy woods of her thoughts, that moment between life and death when everything had gone still and quiet. The thing stood there, as plain as Sally who sat behind the desk. Only, nobody else seemed to notice the figure with long, stringy black hair and a dirty hospital gown, blood dripping down her legs and pooling on the floor as it stood right in front of the double doors. It – or probably, she – stood there motionless, her arms still at her side and trickles of crimson running downward and dripping from her fingertips.

Evan's mouth went dry and the wheelchair turned, leaving the figure behind them to watch as they rolled away. And she knew the figure still stood there, unseen by everyone else. Jake didn't seem to even notice or falter when they rolled into the hub and then back out again. But the woman still stood back there. Evan knew it because she could feel its gaze on her back.

She swallowed and never needed a glass of water so badly in her life. Then Jake took her into the first room: speech therapy. Oh, god. How was she supposed to make coordinated sentences now?

By the end of the day, therapy of all kinds had left her fatigued, but it didn't take away the memory of what she had seen by the doors. When Jake had come to take her back, it was time to see if the figure still stood there. Despite the weakness in her hands, Evan situated herself to sit tall in the chair to begin the harrowing journey back to her room. The hall had grown more dim with the early evening hour and fading light of the setting sun. Too dark to see from the end of one wing all the way to the doors on the north wing.

They moved together, while Jake made small talk. Just things that Evan only said *yes* or *no* to. She barely paid attention because the only thing that mattered were the locked doors of the north wing and who stood in front of them. They neared the central hub but the desk now stood empty. No Sally with her tall blonde and perky persona.

And, most importantly, the north wing remained vacant. Just two doors and no depressing dark figure standing there. A regular and uninteresting locked unit.

Evan realized that she didn't feel relief, but almost disappointment. If the woman still stood there, then maybe she wasn't crazy and seeing things again.

Jake turned the chair and rolled through the door of her room. As usual, he said, "You want to stay in the chair until dinner or would you like to transfer?"

"I'll stay here for now, but could you hand me my laptop?"

"Sure thing," he said and grasped the closed device from the night stand. "I'll be back for you in about an hour."

"Okay," she said with the best smile she could fake.

He nodded and closed the door behind him.

The niggle of doubt had first spread into her thoughts the moment she saw the figure this morning. *What if I'm not crazy?* She needed to find something – anything – to give her an answer either way.

She opened the laptop and started the browser. At least she could still use her private physician's Wi-Fi up here instead of the hospital's guest access. She didn't have the patience tonight to wait for pages to load. The search engine opened.

Her fingers froze as they hovered over the keyboard. What in the world should she search? She was sure that typing in *creepy woman down the hall* probably wouldn't yield much useful information. Come on, think. Just like the speech therapist said today, picture the words right in front of your eyes and then use them. Maybe, find out why the doors are locked.

St. John's Hospital Chicago maternity ward.

That should yield something.

She pressed enter and the list of pages appeared. The first several results gave articles on new baby announcements, all of them dated in the last week. No. Not specific enough.

St. John's Hospital Chicago maternity ward Closed

A new list of articles came up, and it looked more promising. The first article was titled "St. John's Hospital Opens New Maternity Ward." She clicked on it and perused the body of the article. Some stuff on the ribbon cutting of the obstetrics ward, accompanied with pictures of nurses, a couple of doctors including Dr. Sorenson holding the oversized scissors opened up against the wide ribbon. Smiles adorned everyone's faces.

There wasn't a lot of useful information in the articles. Mostly a list of donors, including Dr. Sorenson and most of the other obstetricians that worked at St. John's. Nobody else looked familiar, and probably because it was dated almost 7 years prior. Nothing about why they had locked up the previous ward and moved, except a sentence here and there on more rooms available and a bigger nursery.

She clicked back to the list of articles and scrolled down several more pages, but the information became less relevant. Her mouse hovered over the page close icon and then she stopped. A title at the bottom of the page drew her attention and she opened the article.

Evan opened the page wide and a picture of a candlelight vigil around an illuminated water fountain preceded the body of the story. The photographer who took the picture held the faces of a woman and her teenage daughter in the center of the scene, the light of golden candles in their hands falling against faces streaked in tears.

> *The town of Glenview holds a candlelight vigil to remember one of their own tonight. Only yesterday, sixteen-year-old Angela Sinclair was a vibrant high school student who had been making plans to welcome a baby daughter into the world. She had just attended a baby shower with her closest friends and family, who anticipated the birth of her child in a few short weeks. The young woman had complained of labor pains to her mother, Judith Sinclair, on Wednesday night. She went to the hospital for evaluation, but things took a turn for the worse. Angela, or Angie as her best friends knew her, had developed a fatal illness while in the hospital. Resuscitative efforts were started but deemed unsuccessful. She suffered cardiac arrest and neither she or her baby were able to be revived.*
>
> *Angela will be remembered with a memorial service at St. Catherine's and interment at Rose Hill cemetery.*

Evan checked the date again. That would have been almost a year prior to the date that the new maternity ward had opened. Maybe this was the reason the north wing had been closed. She scrolled further down the article and another photograph filled the bottom of the page. A young woman, long dark and wavy hair that framed a pretty, smiling face. Her green eyes looked at the photographer, probably her mother or someone else she knew because her smile was genuine. Two zirconium ear studs glistened through the locks of her hair and a gold locket hung around her neck. Innocent. Still a child herself. And she was dead with her fetus.

At least the rumor she had heard about the locked unit was partially true. A tragic death had occurred there, but who's to say that it was why the unit was closed now.

One mystery solved.

So many more to go.

Chapter 23

"Ready to go to dinner?" Jake said from her doorway.

Evan startled and glanced up from the computer screen. Had she lost an hour already?

"Yeah," she said and closed the laptop. The research would have to wait.

Jake wheeled her down to the dining room. Fewer patients ate here tonight than yesterday, or maybe it just felt a little emptier because Paul wasn't there. She ordered her food and nibbled at it, but her thoughts continued to drift toward the locked doors and what had happened behind them so many years ago.

Angela's green eyes peered into her, happy and unaware of what was to happen to her. Pregnant at such a young age but accepting her fate. A baby shower had probably brought in many gifts, pink things. She thought the article had said the baby was a girl.

Her fork moved around the peas on her plate until they were a tight circle of green. Could a memory of something be so profound to affect the location? The rumor said that the maternity floor closed after something bad happened, and the staff noticed unusual things after that.

"Not hungry?" Jake said from behind, startling her again.

"I guess not much," she said.

"Do you want them to box that up, take it back. Maybe you'll have an appetite later."

"Sure," she said and sat back in her chair. He took care of getting her food ready and then carried it back in a plastic sack as he pushed her back to her room.

He situated her back into the bed and placed the food on the nightstand and the laptop at the end of the bed in case she needed it.

"Anything else I can get you for now?" he asked.

She shook her head and he turned toward the door, but she stopped him. "Hey, just a question, maybe you can answer. Do you know much about the north wing? Why it's closed? Why they never expanded the therapy unit down there?"

He shrugged. "I don't really know much about it. I heard someone say it was because it wasn't up to code, but I never really asked about it. Sorry. Anything else?"

"No, thanks. See you tomorrow," she said and waved at him as he stepped away.

She pulled the laptop back to her thighs and rested against the stack of pillows. The fatigue of therapy still lingered in her muscles and made her eyes heavy, but she wasn't about to give up on her quest for answers. At least it was something else other than thinking about how her hands didn't work well or that she wasn't even close to being able to walk again.

The screen blinked on and she typed in her four-digit passcode. The photo of Angela Sinclair immediately came back up when it connected.

"What about the real you?" Evan whispered to the computer. She moved the cursor to the search tab and typed in *Angela Sinclair, Glenview Illinois.*

More lists came up, several of the articles about what had happened to her. A few obituary listings from the newspaper as well as the mortuary websites. Even an obituary for the baby that had died with her. Everything you would expect to see about a young woman who had tragically died. No specifics. Just variations of the same photo, plus a few others from a yearbook and maybe from some cell phone stills. But the girl was just an image on the internet. A fragment of the past.

She leaned back and glanced up to the black TV screen. Her eyes had begun to blur and the words slurred in her thoughts. They didn't even have to make it out of her mouth to be garbled. Therapy had totally drained her and she couldn't stay awake much longer. Paul hadn't made it yet, and he wasn't technically off work until after seven. That wasn't too far away, but she knew she wouldn't make it until then.

With the laptop closed, she moved it to the night stand and situated herself lower in the bed. The light of the lamp cast down on her but left shadows streaking across the room, especially in the corner where she had seen and heard the figure last night.

An idea formed in her brain. She pushed it away, but it came bubbling back every time. *This is ridiculous.* What if Angela was still here, somewhere on the floor or in the hospital? *That is the stupidest thing I've ever thought.*

But what if? She bit her lip for even thinking it. *You're talking ghosts, and ghosts don't exist. And if the ghost of Angela Sinclair exists and is stalking this unit, then we have a problem.*

Regardless, the lamp light didn't need to be off tonight. It's good to have a little something there in case she woke up again. Something to chase away shadows.

She closed her eyes, but her thoughts still raced with the image of something standing outside those doors of the north wing.

And Matt's voice spoke to her again just like he did on the night of the accident. She remembered his face, panic lacing every line around his eyes and across his forehead. *That door allows us to step into the realm between us and that other place. And that's where they live.* Evan recalled what he had said when she asked what he meant by *they.*

The dead.

Matt believed it. Hell, he committed several felonies in one night because he believed in it so much. He had claimed he saw something in the emergency room that night. One of *them.* Matt had described what he saw, but Evan didn't remember anything about it. Just that it scared him to death.

And she remembered when Matt started seeing them. He had told her everything. The details were fuzzy, but the important parts came back to her, like the story of him traveling to the Bahamas and he had been seriously injured.

They said I had died for two minutes in the ambulance.

Something about the brain changes after it has crossed over.

His voice came around again, like a music track on endless repeat. Matt had died, if only for a brief time, and he was brought back with this ability to see things nobody else could see.

Sound familiar, Evan?, a voice that sounded like him spoke in her head.

Her eyes flew open and she squinted against the lamp light.

Damn it. None of that is real. Remember. Broken synapses and overly-sensitive nerve endings. *Things that make you paranoid and make you hallucinate.*

But what if? It didn't matter. That was the kind of thinking that sent someone down a psychological rabbit hole, and sometimes they can't find their way back out.

She let out a tired sigh. If it meant clearing her head so she could sleep, then she had to do it. Just get it out, release it to the wild, and never think about it again. The more she thought about it, though, the more her hands trembled.

Just do it.

She cleared her throat and spoke the words, although barely a whisper. "Angela Sinclair, are you still here?"

The breath stopped in her throat and she listened. Several seconds ticked by, thankfully without a wall clock to remind her. The room sat in silence and the only thing she heard was the pulsation of blood in her ears. She let out the breath, her eyes dancing across the shadows cast from the lamp light against the furniture and back to the corner.

"Angela?" she said again. Maybe it didn't hear her the first time.

The crinkle of the sheets echoed loudly and she had to remind herself that it was just the motion in her torso that made the noise. Nothing else was out there. Not even a drip from the faucet in the bathroom.

She rolled her eyes. Naturally. There was nobody hiding in the corner. Nobody hiding in the bathroom or behind the curtains. The room was otherwise empty and quiet. She swallowed back the tension that had built in her neck and she reached out for the light switch, but she stopped short. Probably best to keep it on, at least for tonight.

The pillow curled around her head and she rolled away from the light with her eyes closed. She just had to focus on her breathing and no more attention toward the news articles on the internet or the things her brain wants to see in strange places. Her mind pushed those things aside until they left her alone and sleep drifted over her.

Chapter 24

"Excellent," Samena said, her hands just below Evan's but not touching.

Evan gripped the weight in both hands, her arms outstretched and moving parallel to the ground. Almost there, but not quite yet.

"Keep going, keep going," Samena coached her.

The weights weren't huge, but they were the heaviest she had lifted so far and she had never been able to lift them this much until today. Not to exact parallel, but it was close enough before she had to give up and let them ease down.

"That was great." The therapist said as she took the weights from her hands.

"I'm a regular body builder now," Evan said and Samena laughed.

Samena grabbed a pair of fingerless gloves from the bench and handed them to Evan. "Well, these are for you."

Her eyebrow lifted as she accepted them. "Gloves. Thanks."

"I believe that you can ambulate your own chair now. So you'll need those to avoid calluses."

The lump in her throat came out of nowhere. "Really? No more Mandatory Transfer Assist?"

"It looks like we can take that off the chart now."

"Don't get me wrong," Evan said as she pulled the gloves on. "I love Jake and everything, but a girl needs to do some things on her own."

"And it helps when you start sleeping better," Samena said and brought out her jar of peppermint therapy cream. She leaned over the chair and pulled Evan's weakened right foot up to her own thigh. "Looks like your bad dreams have improved."

Samena's hands worked at the healed incision sites on Evan's leg. The lower leg exercises she had done left her calves quite sore.

Evan nodded. "Yeah. Sleeping like a baby now. No more hallucinations."

"I guess a few weeks up here makes a difference. You're speaking clearer all the time now. Just need to get these legs stronger."

She rested back against the chair and watched Samena massage the tight tendons. Her toes and ankles moved at her command but the rest of the legs still needed work. Sensations had fully returned, but just like her speech previously, the muscles didn't respond right all the time. At least the strength in her arms had improved well enough to be able to transfer herself. No more embarrassing bathroom sessions with a nurse required to stay by her while she did her business. She could now shower and use the toilet at her own discretion. Mandatory Transfer Assistance could burn in Hell.

And most importantly, no further visions of the woman. Not in her room, screaming in the corner. Not standing in front of the north wing doors. Those parts of her brain must have healed since the night she saw it in her room and then later standing in front of the north wing. No more visions of monsters. Thank heavens, because she had started to think she might need to get a psychiatrist involved.

"And is Paul ready to take you on now that you're more mobile?" the therapist said.

"I think so," Evan said. She held her smile in place, but deep in the back of her thoughts, she wondered about that. Paul had been visiting a little less now that he wasn't as worried about her. And he didn't spend the night any more. Just hung out with her watching TV or Netflix when he got off shift until visiting hours were over. When he snuggled beside her in the bed, those worries tended to dissolve away, but they came right back when two or three days went by without seeing him. Sure, he made the effort to call on the nights he couldn't make it. But still, she just wished she could get out of here and they could move in together finally and put all this behind them.

"Don't you worry about him," Samena said, the smile gone and the lines hard across her forehead. "That guy loves you."

She must have sensed the tension that had built in Evan's shoulders. "I know he does."

"Oh, I forgot to tell you," Samena said and reached a hand into her pocket where she found a sticky note. "Dr. Sorenson called to check up on you. I told him you'd call him back when we were finished."

Evan rolled her eyes. The man called at least once a week and she couldn't help but think that Paul was right about the CEO of St. John's making sure he didn't have a million-dollar lawsuit coming out of her. "Thanks." She took the paper, wadded it up and tossed it in the small garbage can at the end of the bench.

"Look at you, making trick shots." The therapist smiled again. "You couldn't have done that a week ago. I take it you don't want to talk to Sorenson?"

"Not really, but I will. Gotta keep these bills paid, you know."

The fluorescent lights above them flickered in a series of half a dozen flashes. Samena glanced up as soon as they steadied. "Must be a power surge."

Evan followed her gaze and then looked out the windows. Large snowflakes fell in swarms just beyond the fading daylight now shrouded in thick clouds. "Looks like a storm."

"Yuck. That's the kind that brings down powerlines," Samena said as she looked out the window as well.

"At least I don't have to drive in it." Evan turned back to her and smiled.

She smirked. "Thanks a lot. It's going to be slow getting back to Glenview."

Evan lost her smile but Samena didn't seem to notice. She continued massaging the tendons, but the swarm of nerves started in Evan's stomach. She hadn't thought about that town since the night she had searched the internet three weeks ago. "You're from Glenview?"

"Yeah."

"You lived there long?"

"Most of my life." Samena smiled up at her. "My parents still live there."

Evan steadied her breath and clenched her hands. "Oh, I just came across something about that place not long ago."

"Ask me, I've probably heard all about it. Doesn't seem like it, but it functions like a small town."

"Do you remember anything about Angela Sinclair?"

Samena looked up to the lights and squinted, like she searched her brain for the name. She nodded. "Yeah, I remember her. We went to the same high school, although I was a senior and she was a sophomore. We really didn't hang out, but I remember her though. Well, I remember what happened to her."

Evan sat upright, her hands clutched to the arms of the chair. "I found an article about it, said it happened up here."

"That makes sense," Samena said and glanced down the hall toward the north wing. "That's when the old maternity unit was open."

"Did you ever know what happened to her?" Evan said, trying to keep her words slow and not too eager.

"Not much. Everyone knew she had gotten pregnant, and it wasn't a great thing for her. She started getting bullied a little bit, especially the more she showed."

"Did she know who the father was?"

Samena shook her head. "That was probably the biggest thing that got her bullied. Nobody knew and she wouldn't tell. Her mom took her out of school not long before she died. Everyone said she was being homeschooled at that point. And then that whole thing happened and so many people acted like she had been their best friend. So many two-faced people in that school when I was there. So glad I got out of there, but I always felt bad for what happened to her."

Evan nodded her head. She felt sorry for the girl too, and she didn't even know her. "Anybody ever hear how she died?"

"I heard so many things, it was hard to tell rumor from truth. Drug overdose, suicide attempt. The one I believe is that she had labor complications, something really serious, but I don't know enough about that world to know what is serious enough to kill her and a baby. Could have been anything, I guess."

The image of Angela's photo danced across her thoughts again, something that had not bothered her in a long time.

"Her mom still lives in Glenview," Samena added, finishing the massage and placing her foot back down on the chair foot rest. "My parents see her at the grocery store sometimes."

Evan nodded, pretending that the comment didn't intrigue her.

"Okay, that's it for today. I'm not going to call Jake. I think the finale for therapy today will be you making it back to your room on your own."

She smiled. "Will do, boss." Her gloved hands grasped the wheels, clicked off the wheel lock and turned herself to aim down the hall. She stopped and glanced back to Samena. "Hey, drive careful out there."

"You too," she laughed.

Evan turned back and pushed the wheels in unison, keeping in even strides despite the burning in her muscles. Slow and steady. Each stroke didn't get her terribly far, but it was something and she did it on her own. And she was grateful for the gloves because it didn't take long for her palms to get sore.

The wheels stroked together with each push. Evan glanced between both wheels, at her hand placement. Was she doing it right? No doubt Samena watched her from down the hall. She couldn't let her down. Keep going. *Show her that you can make it back to your room.* The lights above her in the hallway flickered again, a different bank than the ones in the therapy room.

Evan glanced up to see if she was still in a straight line heading down the corridor or if she had veered off course. The grip on her wheels faltered when she saw it. Her palm slipped and the chair made a 45-degree turn, but she hardly noticed.

The figure stood at the doors again just like she had a few weeks ago. Still and silent. Standing in a pool of blood. Her stringy hair falling over her face and shoulders. Somewhere behind that curtain of hair, an eye watched her. A green eye.

"Everything okay?" Samena said and walked past her.

Evan's heart jumped into her throat and she looked up to

the therapist for only a second. "Oh, yeah." She glanced back down the hall, to the dark figure that stood before the doors. Evan swallowed, her gaze unwavering. "Just catching my breath."

"Take as many breaks as you need," Samena said and continued down the hall, a back pack hanging on one shoulder. "I'll see you tomorrow."

The therapist continued down the hall, facing toward the north wing. Nothing about the north wing seemed to concern her. Not the flickering lights. Not the locked doors or the bleeding woman standing there. It didn't bother Samena because she couldn't see it.

Evan gripped the wheels again but didn't look down this time. She pushed the chair further toward the hub and ever closer to the hall leading down the north wing. The figure stood there, as still as a photograph except for the trickles of blood and expanding pool at her feet. As she neared the hub, a chill drifted from the north hallway across the carpet and to Evan's feet. The air had grown as cold as frost and the lights flickered above her now.

She stopped in the central hub and stared at the woman. The thing only stared back and left the scent of mud drifting toward her.

I won't let you scare me anymore, Evan thought. *Whatever you are, you have no power over me.*

And then it moved, the things bloodied legs stepping around until it faced the doors. Dark hair flowed down her back, along the opening in the hospital gown. The thing – this dark woman – stood there for a moment, her backside visible through the open gown.

Blood poured down from between her legs, bright red and running like water. The copper smell of it wafted toward Evan.

The figure stepped forward and plunged through the doors as if they were nothing but an illusion. The smell of blood and swamp disappeared with her as did the pool that had soaked into the hallway carpet.

Her heart beat roared in her ears. She loosened the iron grip that she had on the wheels and looked down at her own legs. For a moment, she forgot where she was but the gloves on her hands and the leggings that covered her legs reminded her that she was in the hub. She glanced around her, to the quiet center of the therapy unit. But she was alone and the lights had stopped flickering.

No further chill emanated from the doors, but Evan turned her gaze back to them. This wasn't a hallucination, she knew that now. There was something behind those doors that harbored a secret, a truth. There was no point fighting it or trying to forget about it. That thing was never going to leave her alone. Pills wouldn't help, either. It wasn't psychosis.

This was a damned ghost and demanded her attention, for whatever reason, and she needed to give it the attention it wanted.

Chapter 25

Evan turned the wheelchair away from the north wing doors, but those dark window eyes watched her as she wheeled back to her room. When she was safely in her own apartment, she turned the chair around and stared at the dark gray paint of the door. The figure – or the spirit, or whatever it was – could get through that barrier if it wanted. It had managed it before. The thing had even thrown the door open when she was on the third floor.

And she realized that it could follow her anywhere. Maybe even outside the confines of the hospital. What if it followed her home once she was discharged?

The worst part of all of it was the fact that nobody believed her. She hadn't even believed herself until now. They all thought it was just a manifestation of a head injury. At one time, that might have been true. But this thing was real. She had seen it and felt it and smelled it enough at this point to trust her instincts. If no one else believed her, they wouldn't help her either. She had to do it herself.

She turned away from the door and to the laptop on the night stand. The screen lit up as soon as the top flipped open and she typed into the search engine: hospital hauntings.

The list of searches filled the page, hundreds of them. A grid page full of alleged photographs of ghosts plastered across the image search, most of which were clearly faked. Each article she clicked on described personal accounts, some stories from so-called ghost hunters, and retellings of old stories that sounded like myths.

This really didn't help. Sure, the stories were great for teenage girl slumber parties, but not when she was stuck on the seventh floor with an angry entity that kept showing itself to her. None of them told her how to deal with it, to make it go away. The articles only detailed what people saw. That's it.

She sighed and tried the search engine again: contacting a spirit.

Another entirely new list of articles appeared, just as numerous as the first. Seances. Ouija boards. Tarot cards. And more of the ghost hunters that thought they were communicating with a spirit but, at least to Evan, were only talking to sounds made by a settling house. There was the occasional listing for services from people who claimed they could get rid of ghosts, but that just wouldn't fly on the inpatient therapy floor at St. John's.

Page after page of this stuff filled the search. She scrolled down and stopped at a single article. It sounded different than some of the other repetitive stuff. Worth a try.

The article pulled up: My Home and My Ghosts.

Although the author wrote it on a blog over five years ago, the things he said sounded familiar. The man had described buying a home and renovating it with plans to eventually sell at a much higher price, but that all changed when he experienced strange things as soon as he tore down the first wall. Noises. Odd smells. And then he saw a ghost.

I tried everything. Every priest, pastor, spiritualist in town came to my home in hopes of getting rid of it. But the footsteps continued to run back and forth upstairs all

A quick set of knocks sounded on the door followed by a click of the key pad in the hallway. Her stomach dropped and she gasped at the unexpected noise, her hands covering her mouth to stifle the noise. Paul stood in the open doorway and paused.

"Hey," he said. "Did I scare you?"

She steadied her breath. "Yeah."

"Sorry." He smiled and stepped into the room, raising a white paper sack. "I brought dinner. Something not from the hospital food services menu."

The smell of burgers and fries followed him. He moved to the chair beside Evan and opened the bag as he glanced up to the computer on her lap. "What's so interesting on there tonight?"

She folded the screen down and shook her head. "Nothing important."

A foil-wrapped burger filled his hand and he gave it to her. The heat of it told her that it was fresh enough to make her mouth water.

"Hey," he said with a mouthful of fries. "Look at you." He pointed to the fingerless gloves on her hands. "You must be moving yourself now."

She held up her right hand, her fingers splayed open. "Yeah."

His brow furrowed. "You don't seem too excited."

"Oh, I am." She sat up straighter and tried to clear the vision of blood pooling under a dark woman's feet. "It's been a long time coming. I guess I'm just a little tired tonight."

Paul chewed but his gaze still bored onto her. "Everything okay?"

The wrapped hamburger warmed her hands too much and she placed it on her lap. Her stomach turned, the initial sense of hunger now waning with each passing thought of the locked doors and the thing that lingered there. No, everything was not okay and she couldn't tell him about it.

She painted a smile on her lips and tilted her head back. "Definitely. I really am just worn out."

"Hmm," he mumbled and swallowed. "You're not upset that I haven't been up here in a few days, right?"

That made her more nauseous. "Paul, no. Seriously." She placed her gloved hand on his knee. "I swear. I'm not mad at you."

He smiled again and his shoulders relaxed. "Okay, because I totally plan on staying tonight."

She hadn't expected to see him tonight. There was so much more she wanted to research on line and she couldn't do it with him here. With the way he looked at her now, he would be devastated if she told him to go home. Although her chest tightened at the thought of it, she had to let him stay.

"Good," she said and peeled open the hamburger.

Paul's arm draped around her waist and he breathed slowly. He had been asleep for hours now, but Evan lay beside him and stared at the ceiling in the dark. For a short while, they had talked and laughed and she forgot about the thing that hid in the shadows. But now those thoughts trickled in again when there was nothing else to think about in the middle of the night and insomnia set in.

Her laptop lay on the chair across the room. Too far for her to just grab it without waking up Paul. But her mind wouldn't shut down, thinking about Angela Sinclair. It had to be her, roaming the halls of St. John's. For some reason, she couldn't move on from the tragedy that she suffered here.

Paul shifted and rolled over, his arm lifting off her torso. She lifted her head and watched him through the dark, but he settled into deep sleep again, leaving her to deal with sleeplessness on her own.

A beep sounded beyond the noise of him sleeping. The door to her room creaked open on the automated hydraulics in response to an entry on the key pad. Evan pulled herself up to her elbow and looked to the gaping door. The longer that the threshold remained empty, the faster her heart raced. Nobody stepped into the room, not even a shadow.

As dark as it was outside, it had to be late. She glanced to the digital clock on the nightstand: 3:41. Who in the world would just come into her room at that hour of night? But she knew exactly who.

She sat upright, her eyes pinned to the threshold into the corridor. The floor remained quiet. No staff members walked the hall. No patients wandered aimlessly, opening random doors. Whoever opened it was still out there, though. Waiting.

Chapter 26

Evan's hand reached through the dark until she found the arm of the wheelchair. She pulled it closer and lifted herself into the chair. With one final glance to Paul, she listened for his even breathing. He still slept, unaware that anything had happened. She moved the chair to the door and peered into the hallway. Occasional wall lights illuminated the corridor, but they were dimmed for this time of night. There was no one standing there.

The wheels rolled across the threshold and into the hallway. She surveyed the length of the corridor, still quiet and lonely. But the shadows that filled the hub of the unit breathed with energy that trickled into the hall. Everything inside her said to turn around and go back to the room, safe and sound with Paul. The man who wrote the blog did that, and it didn't help. It only got worse. And what did he say? He finally spoke to the spirit that tormented him, and it spoke back to him.

She turned the chair toward the dark of the hub, the gateway to the north hall. With each stroke of the wheels, the deeper into the shadows she went until she turned to face the north wing. The east wing lay behind her, as far as another country at this point. She gazed into the dark as her eyes adjusted to the thin slivers of city lights that came through the windows and cast across the empty corridor.

The light fell over the open door to the north wing, the silver chain crumpled in a heap on the floor.

Her fingers gripped the wheels and her neck stiffened. Cold, musty air oozed from the gaping door like the entrance to a cave. There had to be an explanation. Someone must have opened it. Everybody kept saying that it might be used for storage, so maybe a staff member had unlocked it and just forgot to put the chain back. But the thickening air that surrounded her told her that wasn't true.

It was open for a reason. It was open for her.

She pulled in a deep breath and forced the wheels forward. The chair rolled further into the hall and approached the open doorway. The quaking in her arms made it hard to keep the momentum and she stopped at the threshold.

Wind rattled at the windows in the closed wing, echoing likes rats running along the floor. She listened for anything else. Movement. Footsteps. Whispers. Anything. Only the sound of the wind filled the space.

She pushed the wheels into the corridor, swallowed by the cold damp air and the blackness that filled it. Her breath came out in shaking bursts, but it was too difficult to control. At any moment, something could step out of the many rooms that lined both sides of the empty corridor. She moved past the first open doors, where city light poured through the bare windows and into the hall. The light cast enough into the rooms to show her the empty space, devoid of any stored equipment. The faintest sound of the wheels rolling along the floor echoed down the hall in reverberating squeaks. Her hands pushed the chair further down the hall. Without the gloves, the wheels chilled her fingers.

Although the wing appeared empty, she felt eyes that watched her from every shadow and corner. The energy of it danced over her bare arms and raised the hair across her skin. The wheels squeaked forward again, approaching the next pair of empty patient rooms. Hollow chattering came from the next room as snow pelted the windows.

A light clicked on in the room toward the furthest end of the hallway, casting a solitary golden beam into the corridor ahead of her. Evan's hands stopped the forward momentum of the chair and gripped the tires with stone fingers. The breath stopped in her throat with the roaring of a heartbeat in her ears. Someone was in here with her. There was no other way that could have happened. Whoever had opened that door was over there now, maybe just a mechanic or another nurse, like she had suspected before she crossed the threshold.

But no sound came from the room, either now or when she first entered the wing.

Her tongue had lost all its moisture. "Hello?" she called out, her voice echoing down the hall and back to her. "Is someone down there?"

Still no movement or sound. Just the triangle shaft of light that poured into the abandoned corridor.

I shouldn't be here. I shouldn't be here.

The voice that pleaded to her to turn around started to scream in her head. Nothing good could come of this. At worst, somebody might discover that she had entered the north wing and maybe even accuse her of unlocking the door. And that could get her removed from the therapy unit entirely.

But someone unlocked those doors. Someone had turned on the light. Someone waited down there for her.

The cold grip she had on the wheels loosened. *You came here to find an answer, you can't turn back now.*

The wheels moved forward with her shaking arms. Her breath chattered with the trembling of every muscle in her body. The chair inched closer and still no sound came from the room.

No shadows cast by a form moving around beyond the door. Just the solitary beam of light.

Cold winter wind pounded against the glass in each room that she passed. It chilled every inch of the north wing, where the furnace no longer worked. Evan glanced up to the ceiling, lined with empty fluorescent light banks and exposed wiring from old security signs and other fixtures. All of it had been removed, probably a long time ago. So why did a single room still have a functioning light?

The cold air coalesced in wisps of fog that drifted from her lips with every breath. Her wheelchair rolled to the edge of the beam of light, but not so far that she could see into the room. And, most importantly, not so far that anyone inside could see her. What if there was a person standing there? A maintenance worker? Anyone? They were bound to wonder why she was wandering around in here at three o'clock in the morning. But even worse, what if nobody was there?

She flexed her fingers again, trying to fight the cold that had settled in her joints. *You've come this far. Time to prove your worth.* She gripped the wheels and pushed forward. The light cast across her feet, her knees, the front half of the chair. Golden light poured over her lap and she turned the chair to face the threshold when she stopped.

A single hospital bed stood in the center of the room, its head against the back wall. The glow came from the light bar over the head of the bed, fully intact with bulbs and a frosted casing. Clean linens made up the bed, folded down from the top and finished with a crisp white pillow as though someone had just made it up minutes before. Vertical blinds covered the windows, hardwood floor clean and shining, all in preparation for accepting a patient at any minute. Just like every room in this hospital, only this one had been closed for almost a decade.

She glanced down to the floor again and followed the light out into the hall. A layer of dust coated everything in this place, thick enough that she traced the lines of her wheels going clear back to the entry doors. It covered the door knobs, the plastic signs next to each door indicating the room numbers. The plastic sign with the number 706 beside this very room had a layer at least a half-inch thick. But not the floor of room 706, nor the bed or the seemingly brand-new light fixture and blinds.

This room was as fresh as the day the maternity unit closed.

Evan pushed the chair into the room. The moment that the gold light flooded over her, the temperature rose. A comfortable seventy degrees. This place broke the rules of time and space, existing only before tragic events shut the unit down forever. Her breath no longer puffed in bursts of fog. The joints in her hands warmed. She wheeled in further and a glint of gold on top of the bed caught her attention.

You probably should leave now, that little voice in her head started to nag again.

Her hands gripped the wheels and she rolled forward again. Can't stop now.

The warm light fell on a round pendant – no, a locket – with a long gold chain that spread out straight over the white blanket. The necklace looked as new and fresh as everything else in this room. Burnished to a high golden gloss, the locket lay untarnished with its round shape and carved finish.

If someone left this here just for her, to lure her into a trap or something, it was the most elaborate thing she had ever seen. She glanced behind her, into the darkened hallway where a dozen eyes most likely watched her and waited for her to act. No sound ever echoed down the hall louder than the snow against the window panes. That, and the squeak of her wheelchair.

And nobody else but her had left tracks in the dust that had settled over this place in the last nine years. Not. One. Person.

She turned back to eye the locket. This was impossible, and yet there it was. This entire room, in fact, was simply not possible. Not without evidence of someone else in here.

It didn't matter how much she tried to resolve it in her own brain, she knew what this was. She knew who did it, at least she suspected as much.

Evan cleared the spasm in her throat and glanced around the walls, half-expecting to see or hear someone there.

"Angela Sinclair," she called out to the empty room. After all, the guy who wrote the blog said he started talking to the thing in his house and it talked back.

She wasn't sure what she had wanted. If someone had responded, she probably wouldn't be able to handle it and bolt out of there with her tail between her legs. But nothing happened. The only thing she heard was the sound of her own breathing. She chewed her bottom lip. This locket and this room weren't here by chance. It had to be just for her.

Her hands moved the wheels to the edge of the bed while she eyed the locket. If she was to learn anything more about this place, that piece of jewelry was the start. It had to be. She leaned forward and grasped the locket, but nothing special happened. No big reveal. It was just a simple piece of jewelry, and probably wasn't even real gold.

She pressed the tab that unlatched the casing. It sprung open like a clam shell and she held it up to the light. A small color photograph filled the frame inside the case, a picture of a smiling woman with long dark hair with a child of about four or five on her lap. The girl's dark hair had been braided into a long cord that rested over her shoulder. It didn't appear to be an old photo, either. Something maybe done cheaply at the mall, and the little girl wore a printed T-shirt for the movie *Independence Day*, the original one. That photograph had to have been taken sometime in the mid-nineties. But neither of the faces in the picture looked familiar.

Her fingers closed around the locket and it latched. She stuffed the piece into the side pocket of the wheelchair and turned back to the open door and the dark hallway beyond it. This is what she was meant to find, she knew it. And going back out there could be horrible. Or it all could end right now. The spirit that kept following her might just disappear because Evan did what she needed to do.

She steeled her arms, gripped the wheels, and pushed herself into the hallway. The moment she crossed the threshold, the gold light extinguished. The breath stopped short in her chest and her ribs froze. She turned back to the room only to find that it was empty. No hospital bed. No vertical blinds, but the same bare window pounded by the coming snow storm. Just as empty as every one of the rooms.

No. She didn't imagine this. Her fingers fumbled in the pocket of the wheelchair and curled around the clam shell shape of the locket, the metal still warm. It was real. Everything in that room had been real. And it was all gone, like a dream.

The cold air grew dense and tainted with a hint of mildew that must have crept into the corners of every empty room. Her breath escaped in wisps again. At the end of the corridor, the door still gaped open with the chain piled on the ground in front of it: the finish line. Her spine shivered, maybe from the cold but maybe from something else. She had to get out there. Now.

Her arms pumped the wheels forward, each stroke pushing her faster toward the exit as though she might not make it before someone closed it and locked her in there forever. And then she would moulder and mummify before anyone missed her. The muscles in her arms and shoulders burned, screaming for her to let up, but she couldn't. Every second wasted could be the end. Blood pounded in her ears with each beat of her heart.

The front wheels crossed the barrier and she pushed through with a single and final burst of strength. She gasped for breath and turned back to the doors. She thought they would slam shut the moment she moved through, but they didn't budge. The corridor behind her still remained dark without the golden light from room 706.

Good. *It needs to stay that way. I did what you wanted.*

She turned the chair and rolled quietly back to her room, where Paul still lay in deep sleep, unaware that she had been gone. Unaware that she had crossed into another time, possibly into a place that still lingered at the end of the north wing. She settled into bed, but not before collecting the small locket and tucking it away in the drawer of the night stand.

Chapter 27

It could have been a dream, but Paul's kiss woke her from the deepest sleep that she had had in weeks. No more nightmares and no visions of shadows moving in the corner of the room. When Evan opened her eyes, morning light filtered through the edges of the curtains that made her squint. Paul lay across from her in their tiny twin-size bed. His arm draped around her ribs and pulled her closer to him.

"Morning," he said with a smile.

She glanced beyond him and to the gold and pink sunlight spread against the wall. The heavy energy of last night had vanished and allowed her to fall asleep as soon as she had crawled back into bed. The memory of everything she did was just that now: a memory. Her task done and the spirit – or whatever it was – crawling back into the fog, never to return.

"What's wrong?" he asked, following her eyes that scanned the room.

"Nothing," she said and rested her head back onto the pillow to face him. "And that's just it. Nothing. Everything is right."

"Good." He pressed his forehead against hers. "I don't have a shift today so I thought I would hang out with you, get through some therapy and stuff."

"It's gonna be so boring."

"I doubt that. Samena said she has some good things planned today," he said.

"You've been talking to my physical therapist?" she said with a light finger pressed against his shoulder.

"Not really. She just said I might want to be here today."

The flutters started in her stomach. What did Samena mean by that? Sure, she had made progress in the last week, strengthening her arms enough to make it easier to transfer herself. But that was to be expected at this point.

An alert beeped on Evan's watch, the signal that the dining room was open for breakfast. And then speech therapy followed by the occupational therapist. Another long day.

"Well, if you really want to come, then who am I to stop you?" she said. Evan moved herself to the wheelchair and to the shower, insisting she do it herself despite Paul's pleas to help. And just as he had said, he stayed with her throughout the day, listening to everything that each therapist instructed. They included him in some of the exercises as well. All things to help her more when she went home.

Physical therapy always came after lunch, and Evan hadn't expected what Samena had planned.

The therapist clasped her hands in front of her as soon as Evan and Paul settled into the therapy gym. "Excellent. You made it Dr. Williams."

"Paul," he said and shook her hand.

"So, I hope you're both ready. We're going to start working on walking today."

The floor seemed to fall out from under Evan. She hadn't fathomed being ready for anything like this so soon. Her legs were still weak and didn't like to follow her commands yet.

Evan opened her mouth to express her doubts but Samena stopped her.

"No pun intended, but it's baby steps," she said. "We have to start somewhere."

That's true, but Evan didn't want to try and then find out that it wasn't going to work. She had wanted this so bad, but the niggle of worry had always stayed in the back of her thoughts that she would always be in the wheelchair.

The exercises started like usual, though. Warm up with the "sand box", the warm circulating sand that loosened up her stiff tendons and muscles, making her joints move better. Instead of the recumbent bicycle, though, Samena moved her to the hip-height parallel bars. She instructed Paul to stand inside the bars and then moved the wheelchair to the device.

"Okay," Samena started. "I'm going to help lift you to the bars and you will work on steadying yourself with your arms."

Evan glanced back to her. "I can't do this."

Samena smiled and pulled a wide white strap around Evan's torso. "Yes, you can. And I have this to help you." She cinched it snugly and buckled the strap around Evan's waist.

The shaking started in her hands first. *Sam is crazy, I'm nowhere near ready to do this.* The tremors intensified when the strap tightened around her.

"You ready?" Samena said as she crouched in front of her.

"No," Evan said.

"Yes you are. You need to start somewhere and it's time." She placed a warm hand on Evan's knee. Blood pulsated through her veins just under the skin, activated by the warm up she had done so far.

Oh, God. Please don't let me fall.

Evan nodded. Samena wasn't going to take no for an answer, so she had better just get it over with.

The therapist stepped behind her and wrapped her strong arms under Evan's shoulders, just like Jake used to do when he was her Mandatory Transfer Assist. She could tell what Samena's intentions were and Evan braced her arms. Paul watched them both, his eyes wide and his forearms tight.

"Remember," Samena said right behind her ear. "I've got you. I won't let you fall, and neither will he."

The color drained from Paul's face. Apparently, he wasn't ready for this either.

Evan swallowed hard and her fists clenched.

"Ready?" Samena asked.

She couldn't say anything; her throat was too dry. So she just nodded. The therapist tightened her grip and lifted her from the chair. The world got awfully high at that moment as she moved upright toward the bars. Her fingers reached until she found both wooden bars. Paul took a step forward and Evan was sure that he had no idea he had done it. Her hands gripped the bars and the muscles flexed in her arms.

Samena kept her grip around Evan until her arms no longer shook.

"Good," she said to her. "Do you feel your feet under you? Make sure they are flat on the ground and as wide as the bars."

Thank heavens Sam was strong enough to do this. Evan glanced down to her feet, but she could feel them. Seeing them against the mat just made her feel a little steadier until her feet moved into position.

"Okay, I think I've got it," Evan said, her heart pounding now.

"I'm going to let up a little, but you need to tell me if it's too much." Samena waited for a moment and then her grip loosened, although her arms still contacted Evan's ribs.

The weight was more than she had expected at first. Her arms trembled but straightened, elbows locking. Pressure formed against the bottom of her feet for the first time in months. She knew it was hardly anything because Sam was doing most of the work, but the sensation made the bones and tendons in her feet tighten and her toes to curl. All muscle memory. They knew what they were supposed to do.

"Make sure you breathe," Samena said.

Evan let out a little gasp from the breath she didn't know that she held. The therapist let up a little more. Her thighs quivered, springing to life and trying to keep her knees steady.

"You're doing it," Paul said.

She glanced up to see the dimples in his cheeks and smiled at him, nodding her head.

"I just want you to stand there for as long as you think you can," Samena said from behind her. She slowly relaxed her grip and grasped to the white strap around Evan's waist.

The concentration required to do this was too much to respond verbally to anyone right now. She shifted her weight between her shoulders and her hips. The joints in her pelvis and knees ached at first, but dulled the longer she stood there.

Samena's grip on the strap remained steady. "You're doing great."

The weeks spent on the unit had built up to this moment. The pain of strengthening her arms and hands was all worth it to see the world at this height. To look Paul directly in the eye so he didn't have to crouch to speak to her.

Her quadriceps quivered and her right knee buckled a little. The strap around her waist tightened with the therapist's grip.

"Okay, I think that will do for now." She reached around Evan's torso again and lifted the weight off her legs.

And just like that, it was lost. She was back in the wheelchair and looking up to Paul again. But Samena was right. A few more seconds and her legs weren't going to hold her up anymore.

"Don't worry. We'll be doing a lot more of that," Samena said and unbuckled the strap. "Remember, baby steps. Back to the bike and isometric exercises."

Those were boring compared to the exhilaration of standing. All necessary evils and they were important to keep her muscles strong so they would eventually hold her up without needing support on the bars.

"That was awesome," Paul said and stepped from between the bars.

"There will be more of that every day."

Evan's muscles quivered from the bottoms of her feet to her head. Most of it was out of exhilaration, but some came from the fatigue of doing that for only a couple of minutes. As much as she wanted to stand again, she knew it wouldn't be possible today. But there was always tomorrow.

She spent the remainder of therapy with the peppermint lotion massage of her legs and then Paul took the opportunity to push the wheelchair back down the hall.

"I'm so glad I didn't miss that," he said from behind her.

"Me too." The smile on her face wouldn't go away, nor did she want it to. She reached back and touched his hand where he gripped the back of the wheelchair. Finally. A breakthrough that meant significant progress. Before too long, she would be able to go home and hope that she never had to stay on this floor ever again.

Paul leaned down and gave her a quick kiss on her cheek, something that took her by surprise and tickled down her neck. He laughed and pushed her faster, the overhead light banks moving past them with ease. Evan gripped his hand tighter.

The wheelchair moved toward the hub of the unit and the muscles in her shoulders tightened for only a moment, drawing the smile from her face. The twilight shadows cast in shades of blue and indigo across the hallway and against the double doors of the locked unit. Locked. The heavy chain bound through the door handles as though nobody had opened them in years. And they stood silent and abandoned. No dark form waiting there. The north wing was empty, as it should be.

Her eyes fixed on the doors but nothing moved there. She allowed her shoulders to fall again and her spine to relax. Paul turned the chair and left the north wing behind them. Everything was now the way it should be.

Chapter 28

Evan moved her right foot forward. It didn't rise much off the ground, but she had air between the bottom of her shoe and the mat.

"Good," Samena said, her hand holding the waist strap firm in case Evan's knee gave out from under her again.

She shifted her weight to that foot as soon as it rested on the ground. The parallel bars trembled a little under her grip but she didn't put nearly as much pressure on her hands as she had the last few days in therapy. Most of the work was directed down her legs.

Now the left foot.

"Make sure you lift it completely from the floor," Samena said.

Evan had never had to think this much about foot placement before, but now her mind rolled through the series like a list. Heel. Ball. Toe. Heel. Ball. Toe. All of that coordinated with the muscles contracting at the right time in her thigh and the knee bracing when she needed it too. It was amazing that humans could ever walk at all.

Then her weight shifted to the left leg but it wobbled. Samena moved in close with the strap tight.

Evan stiffened her arms. "I got it."

The pressure on her shoulders eased the shaking in her knee, but that was the sign and Samena knew it.

"I know you do, but that's probably enough for today."

She hated to admit it, but Evan knew when her legs had faced their limit. But at least she had been able to walk the length of the parallel bars. That was a first since she had taken the initial stand only four days ago.

Samena moved the wheelchair closer and helped ease her into it, but her legs did most of the work. The fatigue left her muscles trembling and her heart racing, though. And Paul wasn't here to see it this time, or to wheel her back to her room. Her own shaking arms would have to do it tonight.

"That was great," Samena said while she started the massage along Evan's ankles and feet. "I think you'll be able to move to a full walker by this time next week."

"You really think so?" Getting out of the wheelchair for good would be the next best thing to going home.

"At this rate, yes. And if you can graduate to that, I think it's time to make preparations for discharge."

"I could kiss you right now," Evan said. The tears threatened to well in her eyes.

"Well, it wouldn't mean that you're totally on your own. You still have months of therapy to go, but you could do it as an outpatient a few times a week."

Evan released a steady breath. She didn't want to be too hopeful, but she had to ask. "And what about being able to go back to work?"

Samena shrugged. "Occupational therapy has said your hands are working very well. I think you could get back to seeing patients, but surgery may still be little much. Not until you're able to fully stand again."

"But it's possible."

The therapist nodded. "I do. But you have to be patient with the process. There's still a lot of work to do to be able to get you there."

Evan didn't expect changes to happen overnight, but the worry of her own future had always sat at the back of her thoughts. She was on her own, with no help from family, and she had worked too hard to lose everything because of this accident. Years of school and residency couldn't be worthless. There had to be something.

"Alright," Samena said, wiping her hands on a towel once she finished the massage on both legs. "Same time—"

"Same Bat Channel," Evan finished with a grin.

"See you tomorrow."

Evan pulled on her socks and shoes while Samena put away the equipment for the day. Her muscles still quivered, but the peppermint oil left her legs energized and the blood pumping through them in vital bursts. She pulled the wheelchair around to face down the south wing corridor.

And the air rushed from her lungs in a sudden and silent gasp.

The spirit stood in the dim areas between the bank of lights that shone down in the center of the corridor. It stood there, long stringy black hair falling over its face and shoulders. Blood pooled at its dirty and bare feet. The warm air from the floor vents pushed the smell of mildew down the hallway and wafted across Evan's chair.

It was supposed to be gone. She had done what the thing wanted her to do, so why had it returned and blocked her way back to her room?

"Everything okay?" Samena said as she stepped beside Evan. She followed Evan's gaze down the hallway.

Evan tried to breathe but her ribs had spasmed. The spirit stood there, watched her from under its cold, limp hair. Her fingers clenched around the wheels and wouldn't move.

She closed her eyes, the trembling chattering down her spine and into her legs.

"Evan?" the therapist said, her hand resting on Evan's shoulder.

"Yeah," she finally said. "I just –," she said and turned away from the spirit, "I just don't have any strength left in my arms tonight." That was the best lie she could come up with on the spot.

"That's understandable," Samena said and stepped behind the chair. She grasped the chair and pushed her forward. "You did a lot of work today. I'll take you back if you don't mind."

Evan kept her gaze averted but the figure still stood there in the middle of the hallway and now her chair moved directly toward it. She clenched her eyes tight and held her breath against the thick smell of mildew that neared her. It was only a matter of seconds and the chair would be right on her. A sudden burst of frozen air moved through her, straight into her core and it forced the air from her lungs like jumping into a cold lake. Her eyes flew open.

The corridor lights moved past them in even strides with every step Samena took. The hallway remained empty all the way to the hub. It was only her, the chair and her therapist.

Evan controlled her breathing and balled her fists on her lap. The thing hadn't gone away. It still stood back there, watching her as they rolled back to her room. It would know where she slept tonight and it would come back, just like it always had.

Everything she had done to get rid of it was for nothing.

As soon as Samena brought her to the apartment, she forced the brightest smile she could and thanked her for everything. But when the door had closed, she wheeled back and watched it. That thing was bound to come through there searching for her. It just needed to walk the halls – or whatever it did – but eventually it would creep back into her room.

The pounding of her heart drowned out any other sound from the hall. And the room was too dark. She spun around the edge of the bed and flicked on the side table lamp. The lights on the dresser. Even the bathroom light. Anything to chase away the shadows in the room.

She faced the door again.

The air around her chilled, prickling against the hair that rose on her forearms, tainted with the odor of mildew. Everything had gone dead quiet. Nobody walked in the hallway outside her room. Usually the sound of patients returning from therapy interrupted the quietness of the evening, but not tonight. She clasped tight on the wheels, her knuckles peaking white at the edges of her fingerless gloves.

A scratch, like a finger moving down the face of a chalkboard, sounded on the other side of her door. It moved steady and slow, echoing into the room. Evan pulled away from the door, her wheels backing toward the open threshold into the bathroom, but her eyes fixed on the door. That thing could get in if it wanted to; it had done it before. So why did it continue to taunt her like this?

The sound vanished, leaving the room in silence again. Cold bursts of fog escaped her lips with every breath.

"What do you want from me?" she whispered. She wished that it was a foolish thing to do, to speak to something that she couldn't see, but she knew it heard her.

The lamp on the bedside table rushed from the surface and crashed into the far wall. Evan clasped her hands over her mouth to stifle the scream, but someone must have heard the sound of the breaking lamp from outside her room. Then the other two lamps in the room flew from the dresser and collided against the foot of the bed in a cacophony of broken ceramic, glass and brass fittings. Shards of the ceramic bodies cascaded against her arms as she crossed them up to shield her face.

The cold pierced the skin of her fingers but she moved them swiftly to the wheels and backed into the bathroom. Her eyes darted to the main room, now plunged into darkness without the lamps to drive away the shadows. The bathroom now felt like a deep freezer, frigid against her shaved head.

"Why are you doing this?" she said, her teeth chattering. She waited for the shadows to move and undulate, but only the silence peered back at her.

The bar of three lights above the sink flickered in short bursts. If those went, she would be left in absolute darkness. *Please, no. Don't let the lights go out.*

Short pings and clicks popped from inside the bulbs with each strobe of light. She gazed to the center bulb, willing it to keep working just a few minutes longer.

Between the flashes of light, a shape filled the reflection in the mirror over the sink. Someone stood in the threshold of the door, but only in the reflection. From where Evan sat, with her hands clenched to the wheels of her chair, the doorway remained empty. But in the mirror, she could see the profile of the dark figure. It stood motionless in the doorway, its dark hair falling over its face.

The figure transfixed her, keeping her frozen with its dead stance through the mirror under the steady light of the bulbs above the sink. This thing seethed of rage and it wanted only to take it out on someone that could see it, hear it, smell it. And Evan was the only one here.

The only one, but others were nearby. They had made sure she could summon them whenever she needed help. She drew her glance away from the thing in the mirror quick enough to eye the black square watch face on her wrist. Her finger tapped the surface and a soft aqua display lit against the black background. The light flashed twice, but she wasn't sure what she had to do next. She had never used this thing before, and she could only hope that someone was on the other end.

"Help me," she cried at the flashing light on her wrist. They had promised her that it should work if she ever needed them. Well, now was the time.

The thing turned toward the mirror, its reflection staring down at where Evan sat. Maybe it could hear her; maybe it didn't care. A pale, boney hand rose to the glass and its shaking fingers touched the mirror. The glass suddenly exploded in a shower of fractured silver shrapnel.

Evan screamed and covered her head with her hands. The shards clattered across every surface of the bathroom, clinking against the sink and white tiles around her. The scream made her throat raw with the seizing of the muscles between her ribs and the shaking in her spine.

The main door opened and two nurses burst into her room, but she could barely hear their calls for help down the corridor. She held her arms around her head and her chin pressed against her chest. Hands touched her shoulders and someone called out to her.

"Are you okay?"

"What happened?"

The voices sounded hollow, like in a dream or too far away to even expect a response. She didn't dare look up for fear the three bulbs above the sink would go out for good, because nobody in that room could help her now.

Chapter 29

"Are you sure you want to stay in here tonight?" the nurse said from where she crouched in front of the wheelchair.

Evan didn't look at her, but kept her gaze on the custodian in the bathroom who swept the last of the mirror fragments into a dustpan. The other two nurses had already picked up the shattered pieces of lamps that had been strewn about the room.

"I'll be fine," she muttered. The tinkling of glass kept her attention as it moved across the tiles with the broom. That sound was the only thing that prevented her from breaking down into tears. Just focus on that. Of course, she wasn't going to be fine, but there was nothing this nurse could do to make it any better.

"I can work on finding you a different room."

"I said it's fine," she said and turned her gaze away from the bathroom. "No need to go to so much trouble."

It wouldn't matter where she went. That thing would follow her anywhere. It had already done it where ever she went in this hospital.

"Okay," the nurse said and stood. "But if you need anything, please just call." She turned toward the custodian. "Have you ever seen anything like this?"

"Well, I've heard of big gusts of wind knocking things around on the penthouse floors of some tall buildings. Just never seen anything like it here. It was either that or an earthquake."

The nurse shot Evan a questioning glance. There was no point in telling them what really happened. Who would believe her, anyway?

"He's almost done and then we'll get you to dinner, no problem," the nurse said with a nod.

"I'd rather stay here, get room service tonight," she said. She wasn't about to go out there and have that spirit stand next to her throughout supper. It was one thing seeing it in the privacy of her room, but an entirely different thing in public where nobody but her could see it.

"Okay. I'll at least have someone get you a couple lamps, though. You need some light in here."

Fine. Whatever she needed to do to make herself feel useful. *And how about an exorcism, while you're at it.*

The nurse finally left, and the custodian shortly afterward, with his garbage bag full of clinking broken glass. Alone, to face that thing whenever it decided to come again. And when it did, there was nothing left to do. It could get through locked doors and solid walls.

She glanced to the laptop on the surface of her bed. There had to be something she could do to protect herself, and someone out there knew how to do it. She was sure of it.

She wheeled herself to the bed, grabbed the computer and opened the screen to the search engine: *stopping a haunting*. More of the same stuff she had already seen. Exorcisms. Communicating with spirits. She read the titles and even some of the articles until her eyes hurt. A spirit haunted her, of that she was sure. But an exorcism seemed to be for people or homes possessed by demons and devils. This didn't seem like a demon, not that she would know a demon from a ghost from a banshee.

No. This was a dead person, and it was probably Angela Sinclair. It had to be her, right? So, it probably couldn't be exorcised.

More articles about Ouija boards, crystals, sage. So much of it seemed like nonsense, and truthfully, made up to sell whatever magic thing that would get rid of ghosts for good. She sat back in her chair and rubbed the headache that had started between her eyes. So much of this was false hope packaged to look pretty. A séance here. A haunting investigated there. And enough information contradicted between articles that they rendered all other advice useless. Hadn't anybody ever really gone through this before?

Her eyelids opened and she gazed through the window with the realization that struck her. Of course, someone had, and nobody had believed him either. She straightened the computer on her lap and cleared the search engine again. The cursor blinked as her fingers froze. Did she really want to go down this abyss? She wasn't sure how she felt about seeing his face again.

She took in a deep breath and typed: Matthew Logan Pearce.

A new list of search topics pulled up on the screen. The original news articles dated from the night of the accident filled most of the feed. She scrolled past them. The last thing she needed tonight was to relive the video footage of the accident. The mouse pointer stopped on an article dated only a few weeks ago.

Pearce Charged With Kidnapping Chicago Doctor,
Trial Set For June

The article pulled up and his mugshot appeared at the top. Her eyes squinted to read the print, the story detailing the events of that night, some of it still absent in her memories. The article continued with how Pearce appeared in court on the 15th where the charges were read and plead *Not Guilty* with a lawyer by his side: Janet Lynch. Defense lawyer and the woman who was supposed to make sure he got a fair trial.

*Pearce was remanded to Cook County Jail
where he will await trial set for June 9th.*

Matt, more than anyone, understood exactly what was happening to her. He had even warned her, and she didn't believe him at the time. He knew that something in this hospital had been following her, and it scared him enough to take action. So, maybe, he would know what to do about it now.

If she could just talk to him, maybe he could help her.

Cook County Jail.

Could she call him? Or did she have to go visit him in person? What did it take to speak to an inmate? She had never thought she would have to figure this out, but now she searched it out on the internet: *how to speak to an inmate, cook county jail.*

Luckily, this search yielded much more specific and useful results than her previous searches. Speaking to an actual person was apparently easier than trying to communicate with the dead. But the further she researched, the more her jaw tightened. If she was even going to be able to talk to him on the phone, he would have to agree to accept the call. There was no guarantee that he would want to speak to her. After all, he was in there because of her.

But he would most likely talk to his lawyer.

No. No way. That had to be illegal.

Evan had the lawyer's name right there: Janet Lynch. She only needed a few minutes of his time. If he hung up on her, then at least she tried.

She fished her cell phone from the night stand drawer and lit up the keypad with a single push of a button. The numbers glowed against her skin as her thumb hovered over the screen. If she used her own phone, anyone could trace it back to her cell. That's how it seemed to work on every TV show, anyway. She glanced to the cordless phone on the night stand, the one linked directly to the hospital network. Any call from this number came up as a generalized hospital number or *Unknown* on a caller ID.

She grabbed the cordless and punched in the main number for the jail before she could talk herself out of it. With each ring on the line, her heart pounded harder. What if they knew right away that it was her?

An automated operator answered and she waited until an option came up that sounded right. It might not be what she needed, but if a human being answered, it was a start. Another series of rings sounded while the line waited to connect.

A person finally answered, sounding like she was tired of answering the phone by the end of the day. She introduced herself, but the name sounded like a mumbled mess and Evan didn't catch much of what she said until, "how may I help you?"

"Yes," Evan said, straightening in her chair. Maybe it would help her sound as official as possible. "This is Janet Lynch and I need to speak to my client, Matthew Pearce."

"Pearce," the woman on the other line repeated like she scanned a list of inmates and looked for his name. "Oh, yeah. Pearce. He'll be available to call you back between seven and nine this evening. When he calls, be prepared to accept the charges. Phone calls are limited to twenty minutes. What number would you like him to try you at?"

Evan rattled off the number listed on the label on the back of the phone. With a bored "good-bye", the jail operator hung up before Evan could say anything else. She held the phone on her lap, her hand still shaking. Sometime tonight, that thing was going to ring and it would be him. Every once in a while, she still heard his voice in her head and not just when she dreamed. Sometimes he pleaded with her, just like he did that night.

It doesn't matter if you believe in them or not, if you see them or not. They're still there and they see you.

Everything that he had said now manifested. Somewhere outside the walls of her small therapy apartment, that spirit waited and grew angrier every day. It wanted something and Matt had warned her. It might have even listened to her just now, perhaps laughing at her desperation to call an imprisoned man for help.

Chapter 30

Evan's palm had grown sweaty holding the phone for the last couple of hours and sitting alone in the room with only her laptop to keep her company. The single lamp on the night stand and the one on the dresser weren't nearly as bright as the previous ones that had died a grizzly death at the hands of an unseen force. The shadows that crawled from the edge of the chairs and the foot of the bed left too many dark places for something to hide, so she kept as close to the light as she could.

When the phone rang, it jangled her already loose nerves and sent the shivers down into her toes. Her fingers tightened around the phone and it rang again. It was now or never.

She pressed the green button and placed the phone to her ear.

Another automated voice answered before she could say anything. "You are receiving a phone call from a Cook County detention facility. If you accept the charges, please press '1' now."

With a trembling finger, she pressed one. The system directed her to place her credit card information, which she punched into the keypad. The system beeped twice and the voice came on again.

"You will be connected momentarily."

The sound of her own breathing magnified in the mouthpiece of the phone. A rhythmic series of beeps continued as the system worked on connecting the lines. Then a distinct click.

"Hey, Janet," his voice came from the other end. "I wasn't expecting to hear back from you until tomorrow."

Evan's mouth went dry and her breathing shuddered. She wanted to say something, so why wouldn't it just come out? The words formed on her lips, but hesitated just like they used to when she first awoke. *Calm down. Think out each word before you say them, just like in speech therapy.*

"Janet? You there?" he said.

She swallowed and licked her dry lips. "Matt. I'm sorry I called you but I need help."

"Wait a sec. Who is this?"

"Um," she stammered and sighed. "This is Evan. Evan Jensen."

Now it was only his breathing coming through the phone for several seconds.

"Please don't hang up me," she said. "I really need to talk to you."

"I – uh —," he started. "I don't know what to say."

"I'm sorry I lied to get you on the phone, but I didn't know what else to do."

She heard him clear his throat. "I definitely didn't expect to hear from you. Um, are you doing okay? You sound good."

"I'm okay," she said and forced a smile, even though he couldn't see it. He still talked to her, and that was something for the positive check list. "I mean, I'm getting better. Still in the hospital just taking it a day at a time."

"Christ," he said. It almost sounded like his throat had tightened and he cried. Echoes surrounded him in the background, possibly of other inmates on phone calls as well. He took in another breath. "I can't tell you enough how sorry I am that this happened to you."

She shook her head. "I know that you didn't mean for any of this, but that's not why I'm calling. Honestly. I'm improving every day."

"Okay. What else can I do for you?"

The voice trembled from her lips. Why was this so hard to say? "I remembered a lot of what we talked about that night." He said nothing and she still heard him breathing. Good, at least he still listened. "All that stuff about seeing something in the hospital, and you said that it was angry."

"I remember," he said, his voice stiff.

"I—" she said, but it just wouldn't come out.

He spoke again, but this time it was lower like a whisper. "You can see her now, can't you?"

The long-held breath fell from her lips and she relaxed back into the chair. "I can see her, and she won't leave me alone."

"What have you seen so far?"

She leaned into the phone and mirrored his tone, in case anyone else listened through the door. Everything that she could remember from the first memories in the ICU to the events of tonight came rushing out to him. He listened without comment, at least she hoped he listened because she didn't give him a moment to respond until she finished.

"Do you know who she might be?"

"I think so," she said.

"So have you figured out what she wants yet?"

"That's just it. I thought she wanted to show me the room in the north wing. I did everything she wanted me to do. I found a locket and brought it back with me. And she still won't go away."

"You still have the locket?"

Her eyes darted to the closed night stand drawer. "Yeah."

"And you're sure it's hers?"

She hadn't really thought about it, but had just assumed. "I guess, I'm not sure."

Matt paused on the other line. "You know how she died?"

"I don't know the details, just that she died in childbirth up in the north wing. I know when it happened."

He sighed and it almost roared in the phone. "Evan, she's really angry about something and is trying to get your attention. She one of the most violent entities I've ever seen, that's why I tried to get you out of there. All of this tells me that there's something about her story you need to find out. Something happened to her that nobody else knows and she wants you to discover it."

Her shoulders fell. "How am I supposed to do that? I'm still stuck in this hospital and she's getting worse all the time."

"I'm not sure how to help you there. You just need to find people that were there, talk to them. Piece it together until she's happy with what you have, and then she'll just go away."

That was all he said in that breath, and Evan had hoped that there would be more. "And what if she doesn't?"

"She will follow you until you end up like me."

Evan chewed on her lip. That's not the advice she wanted to hear.

"I wish I could be there to help you, to at least take the brunt of it," he said, his voice now slow. "It's my fault you have to deal with this."

Muscles tightened in her throat. "Matt, for what it's worth, I'm really sorry that you've had to face this alone all these years. You're stronger than I could ever be."

"You're gonna have to get that strong in order to beat this. I wouldn't wish it on anyone, especially you."

She nodded, another useless gesture that he couldn't see. But it was for herself and nobody else.

"You doing okay over there?" she asked.

He gave a quick snort. "Sure. Peachy. Just taking it a day at a time." He repeated what she had just told him, and then she knew they had lied to each other. Whatever made it easier to swallow, right?

An automated voice interrupted the conversation. "You have five minutes remaining."

"Ah," he said. "Looks like our time's up."

Her fingers clenched around the phone. In a few short minutes, the sound of his voice would be gone. The only person with whom she had ever discussed this topic. He was the one that understood, more than anyone. And he believed her, which is more than she could say about herself when she first met him.

The line had gone silent and she panicked. "Matt?"

"Yeah," he responded.

"I thought you had already gone," she said, the tears already starting in her eyes.

"Hey, it's alright. You know, you can call me anytime. And you don't have to lie about who you are. I'll put you on the call list."

She smiled as a tear rolled down her cheek. "Thanks. I'm sure I'll need to. I'll talk to you later."

"Ditto," he said, but then his voice broke through before she could end the call. "One more thing."

"Yeah," she said.

"I would start with the girl's family," he said. "They always know more than they say."

"Okay."

Then the line went dead. She turned off the phone and stared at the earpiece as though his voice might come through it again.

Start with Angela Sinclair's family.

Samena said that she had gone to school with the girl back then, and that her family still lived in Glenview. No. She said her mother still lived in Glenview.

Just like Matt said, she needed to start with the family and she could track her down through public records. Maybe even Samena had a phone number or an address. A perfect place to dredge up the horrible death of the woman's daughter.

Great. This didn't promise to be easy.

Chapter 31

The knock on her door made Evan's heart jump into her throat and she nearly dropped the laptop. A click from the outside keypad released the latch and Paul stepped through the door, a smile on his face and another bag of fast food in his hand. But the smile faltered when he saw her face.

"What's happened?" he said. "Something's off."

That didn't take long. He glanced around the room and absently placed the sack on the dresser. "The lamps are different."

Evan nodded and glanced up from the computer screen. "You could say that."

He stepped through the room and into the bathroom, flicking on the lights. "The mirror. What happened to the mirror?"

"Well, they say it might have been a big gust of wind, just shook the whole building, but it only really affected my room," she said in the most sarcastic way possible and placed the laptop on the end of the bed.

He turned away from the bathroom and stepped toward her. His eyebrows rose and he squinted at her. "Everything okay? Because I'm sensing that you're not telling me something."

Evan looked away from him and to the glowing computer screen with the page displayed. The picture of Angela Sinclair looked back at her, side by side with a photo of her mother at the candlelight vigil. There was so much to tell him, but every time she tried, he just chalked it up to her medications or her head injury. She understood that tendency, but why couldn't he just listen the way Matt did?

She leaned over her laptop to close the screen down but Paul stepped in to stop her. "Hey. You can tell me anything, you know that, right?"

Angela's green eyes watched her from the bright screen, the innocent 16-year-old smile on her face that creased at the corners of her eyelids. Nothing like the horror she had become after death, pacing the halls and looking for answers to some hidden question.

Paul sat on the edge of the bed, his hand still over hers that grasped the screen of the laptop.

"What happened today?" he asked.

She pinched her lips together and slipped her hand away from his. The wheelchair creaked as she leaned back into it. A weight of anxiety danced across her chest. It pressed so deeply that she couldn't look at him and just eyed her hands clasped over her lap. She picked at the edges of her fingernails.

"Paul," she said and turned her eyes back up to him. The smile left his face when he met her gaze. "I need you to try your very best to listen to me and believe me."

"Yeah." He nodded and swallowed, his lip quivering just a little. She didn't talk to him this pointedly very often, but she had to do something. "Whatever you need."

She leaned toward him and placed her hand on his knee. "No. It's what you need to do. Everything I am going to tell you is absolutely true, so you need to work very hard to believe me. Whatever I tell you."

"Of course."

"And no questions asked. Just listen to me."

"Evan, geez," he said with a weak smile. "You're starting to freak me out."

"Good," she said and didn't return the forced smile. "That's a good place to start."

She moved back to the laptop and turned it around to face him. The white glow illuminated his face in the dimly lit room. His brow furrowed while he studied the picture.

"Do you know who that is?"

He shrugged and shook his head. "I don't think so."

"Her name was Angela Sinclair."

"Okay." The way he said the word drew out the last syllable with an exhale. His dark eyes turned to her, one eyebrow cocked.

The muscles in her shoulders tightened and threatened to give her a headache, but she had opened this Pandora's box and now she needed to let him see what was inside of it. No matter how much it hurt to have him look at her the way he did now.

"You remember the stories of the patient that died up here, in the north wing when it was Labor and Delivery. The one that everybody says ended up closing the unit and it was the whole reason it got moved to second floor."

"Yeah. Every intern hears that story on their first night of call. It's supposed to scare everyone. An initiation into the fraternity, so to speak."

"That's her." She pointed to the screen with her head turned to the side for emphasis. The way he just spoke told her that he was already trying to be skeptical.

He turned to examine the screen again. "Wait, what? That's a real story?" His finger found the mouse pad and he scrolled down the length of the article. "How'd you find this?"

"She was only sixteen at the time and died giving birth up here, and so did the baby."

The words scrolled past him, the contrast of light and dark playing across his face from the computer screen.

"I'll be damned," he said with a half-grin that formed over his face. "The story is real after all. I seriously thought it was fake all this time."

He continued to read and didn't look at her, as though he was more interested in the story than what she had said to him. His lips moved silently as he read, eyes scanning quickly over the screen. "Damn, this is depressing stuff. Why are you even looking into this?"

The article rolled down, his finger still scrolling through the page and the photographs.

"Paul," she said and pulled the laptop from his grasp.

He finally looked up at her, his hands up in an innocent gesture. "What did I do?"

"You said you would listen to me."

The grin faded and he turned his gaze down. His shoulders fell. "You're right." He clasped both of his hands in front of him and then fixed his eyes on her. "Go ahead."

"Something terrible happened to this girl right down that hall," she said and pointed through the wall of her room toward the north wing.

"Yeah, but that was like ten years ago or something. There's nothing you can do about it now. Why are you worrying about this? Are you having trouble sleeping again?"

"I said no questions asked." Her eyes narrowed toward him.

"My bad. Continue."

"You already know why I'm worrying about this, but you didn't believe me," she said and leaned toward him. "She actually died eight years ago, but I saw her in my room tonight."

Every bit of humor that had lingered in his face vanished. The dim light reflected in his dark eyes and she could have sworn his pupils dilated just a little.

"She came in here and broke every lamp in the room," she said as clear as she could possibly speak. "And then she shattered the mirror."

His Adam's apple bobbed when he swallowed, his eyes wider. "You saw her here? In your room?" When he realized what he had just done, he shook his head and put his hands up in surrender again. "Sorry. No questions."

"Yes. She was in here just a few hours ago. And before that, she was in the hallway just outside of physical therapy. Before that I saw her standing in front of the locked doors to the north wing. And do you know when I saw her before that?"

He shook his head, unblinking.

"She broke the door in my room on the post-surgical floor. She came to me in the ICU, and nobody could hear me screaming. I saw her before I woke up. She's been following me ever since, and now I know who she is." She turned the computer screen to face him once again, Angela's face still glowing and innocent.

He raised his hand just above his shoulder like a school boy begging for permission. Evan nodded to him and his mouth opened, but his words came out carefully.

"How do you know it's her? I mean, can you see her?"

She leaned back again. "I told you I was seeing things. And feeling the cold. And the weird smells."

"But that was hallucinations—" Another glare and he held up his hands again. "Sorry. Just listening."

"They're not hallucinations. I thought they were at first too. But it's real." She ticked her head toward the empty space in the bathroom where the mirror was usually mounted. "I certainly didn't hallucinate that."

He glanced back and stood, stepping back into the bathroom. His fingers moved over the bare tile that once held the mirror, but now it only bore the scars of absent mounting screws and dry wall. The tile had cracked in the center, as though something had punched right through the mirror and almost through the wall behind it.

"You're saying that she came in here and did this." He glanced back to her, but the skeptical gleam in his eye had faded. The skin stretched over his cheeks now paled. "Did you see her then too?"

Evan nodded, slow and deliberate. "Do you believe me now?"

His fingers traced the fractured spider lines radiating from the wall along the tile. "Someone came in here while you were here as well. They came in here to scare you, and I think it worked on both of us."

"It wasn't just someone. It's her." She pointed to the screen.

He turned back to her and settled on the edge of the bed, but this time he avoided eye contact with the screen. "Okay. Let's say that she is still here. Why would she do this to you? Has anyone else seen her?"

Of course, this was bound to come up. "Nobody else can see her, just me." Well, her and one other person, and he was locked away at Cook County Jail. "I've been researching and sometimes people who have maybe seen the other side come back a little different. Like their eyes are opened wider than other people's."

"The other side? You mean death?"

"Yes. I mean death." There was the skeptic again, with his raised crooked eyebrow. "I found all kinds of stories about it, and

I think that because people like me have been there and came back, it leaves a sort of trace or a beacon or something. I don't really know. But whatever it is, they can see it too."

"They?"

Her jaw clenched. "Yes. They. Spirits. Ghosts. Whatever you want to call them. They know we can see them."

Paul clicked his tongue on the roof of his mouth and looked away from her.

"You've stopped listening to me," she said and pulled her laptop away from him again.

"No I haven't." He tried to grab it but she slammed it shut and placed it far out of his reach on the night stand. "Please, Evan. I swear. I'm listening, but I still don't know why she would do this to you."

His gaze bored into hers and he leaned forward, his hands resting on the bed. With her jaw still clenched, she didn't want to tell him anymore, but his sincere brown eyes still fixed onto her.

"Because she wants me to find out what really happened to her."

The lines creased along his forehead again. "But we already know what happened to her. She died giving birth. It happens all the time around the world."

"No, we don't know what actually happened." Evan clenched her fingers together and leaned on her elbows, narrowing the distance between them. An idea coalesced in her thoughts, something that might give Paul a tangible piece of evidence to cling to. "You know what, do me a favor."

"Okay," he nodded.

She glanced to the night stand. "Open that drawer for me."

Creases formed around the edges of his mouth and his dimples disappeared. He stood but kept his gaze on her for a second longer, as though he didn't trust what she had wanted him to do. He stepped to the night stand and leaned down.

The drawer slid open and he scanned its contents. "Alright. Now what?"

"You see a locket?"

"Yeah," he said and withdrew the piece of jewelry. The chain dangled from his fingers and he stared at it as though he had just gotten it from a prize egg he won at an arcade.

"It's hers."

His glance shot up to her and the piece almost dropped from his grasp. "What?"

"That belongs to Angela Sinclair."

The furrow lines formed on his brow again, another sign of his doubt. "How do you know that?"

"She led me to it. I found it in room 706 on the north wing, the old maternity unit. The room where she died."

He grimaced and tossed the locket onto the bed like it was too hot to hold anymore. "What the hell, Evan. How did you get into the north wing?" His voice dropped as though he suspected someone else could hear him, and if they did both he and Evan would get kicked out of the hospital immediately.

The fact that he could no longer hold the locket told her that some inkling of belief now settled in Paul's brain, even if he didn't want to acknowledge it.

She clasped her fingers together and set her stare at him. "I told you. She led me there. Angela provided a way for me to find that. I thought that it would be the end of it, that it was all she wanted me to do. But I was wrong."

He looked at the locket, waiting for it to slither back toward him. "It was still in there, after all this time."

Evan nodded. "And there's a picture of her and her mother in there. Finding it wasn't enough. She needs me to know more about her."

His gaze returned to her, the lamp light casting weird lines across his face. All evidence of skepticism had now vanished, replaced by the look she had seen so many times in her own mirror. "What more is there to know?"

"She was a healthy sixteen-year-old girl who was pregnant and nobody knows who the father was. And then she suddenly dies in childbirth. Why did she die? Did she have a heart attack? A seizure? What happened to her? That's what she wants from me. She wants someone to know what happened."

His nostrils flared a bit when he let out a slow breath and his dimples deepened. The slow nod of his head made her clench her fingers tighter.

"Okay," he said. "You're right."

She sat up straighter, a little smile at the edge of her lips. "I'm sorry, what? I didn't catch that."

He smiled. "You heard me. You're right about her. Everybody just accepts what happened to this girl as a given, but none of us know the real story. If that's what it takes for her to leave you alone, let's tell her story."

She shot him a sideways glance. "Serious?"

"Hey, you told me to listen. I listened. And I want to help you put her to rest, because she's clearly not happy with something." He turned back to the cracks in the bathroom tiles. "I can't have her taking it out on you next time."

Evan gave him a weak smile. She couldn't tell if he was serious. Did he actually believe her, or was he trying really hard to believe like she asked him to do? It didn't matter. She finally told him everything that had weighed on her and he listened. Not as well as Matt, but now he knew. No more secrets. Well, except the phone call to Matt, but he didn't need to know about that.

"Okay," she said.

"So, where do we start?"

Evan opened up the laptop again and scrolled back to the picture of the candlelight vigil. "I think I need to speak to her mother."

He nodded, that slow and methodical motion again. The thinking nod. "Alright. That could be more difficult than you realize, bringing up a subject like this to her."

"I know. But it's all I've got right now, and if it means that she will go away, I need to try. And she deserves to have her daughter's locket returned."

"So where do we find her?"

"Glenview," she said. "And I have a day pass that I can use to get out of here for a while. You and me, we need to see her together."

He closed his eyes and hung his head. It was a lot to ask of him. "Alright. I have a day off tomorrow. We'll hop in my car and go for a drive."

Chapter 32

Direct daylight was nothing to be taken for granted. Evan closed her eyes to the warmth of it on her face despite the snow that had blanketed the city overnight. The white stuff sparkled and left the city clean, a stark contrast to the often dull gray. Paul drove the wet streets northward through the city while she let the sun fall on her skin from the passenger window.

The last time she had been in a car, it ended in the most horrible way. And she had been a passenger at that time too. The hum of the Subaru behind the dash bought back flashes of a dark night broken by intermittent street lights that zoomed by them, and the sound of sirens in the background. With a deep and steady breath to fill her lungs, Evan pushed aside the memories that made her heart race and focused only on the warmth that covered her face.

"You doing okay?" Paul said.

She didn't open her eyes but she could still see the orange glow through her eyelids. "Yeah. I think so."

"Are you nervous?"

With the controlled breathing, it kept her anxiety at a minimum. At least about being in the car again. She supposed that she should be anxious about talking to the mother of the dead girl. But the idea of getting to meet someone tangible who actually knew Angela brought her a measure of comfort. At least she was trying something to put her to rest.

"Not yet," she said and turned toward him. "But I guess we'll find out."

The car meandered up the interstate and exited into Glenview, where the streets hadn't been plowed as well.

"The address I found is an apartment building," she said and watched the GPS directions on her cell phone. "It's not the original place where Angela grew up."

"Is that going to matter?" he asked, taking a right turn when the GPS voice directed him.

"I hope not."

After several turns and stop lights, Paul eased the car against a curb and eyed the building across the street. "That's it."

Evan looked past him and to the front entrance. It wasn't a grand building, but it had been kept well enough, with at least five floors with patios that looked out to the park filled with once-leafy trees.

"Apartment 314," he said, reading off the paper with the full address of Judith Sinclair. He turned to her and watched her eager eyes. "You ready to do this?"

"No turning back now."

"What do you plan on saying to her?"

She shook her head. "I'm not really sure, but hopefully I know when I get in there."

"What if she doesn't let us in?"

"At least we tried," she said with a shrug.

"I'm glad you're optimistic about this," he said and opened his door. He set up her wheelchair that had been tucked into the trunk and helped her into it.

Trudging through the snow-packed sidewalk toward the building proved to be more difficult than she had expected. Thankfully, Paul was here to do most of the work, because she was sure that she couldn't have rolled herself over the snow. They moved into the lobby and to the inner glass doors. As soon as Paul tried them, she knew that it was their first barrier. Locked until someone from inside buzzed them in.

Evan glanced to the left wall, where the PA system waited next to a list of apartment numbers and codes.

"Well," she said. "I guess this will be where we know if she wants to see us or not."

She dialed in the code and the speaker buzzed out a rhythmic series of beeps with silence in between each set. Her fingers trembled with each successive beep only met by silence afterward.

"Maybe she's not in," Paul said.

Just then, a click sounded and a pause. "Hello?" came a woman's voice.

Evan almost gasped. "Hello, Mrs. Sinclair?"

"Yes."

"My name is Evan Jensen," she started, trying to keep her voice steady. "I was hoping my friend and I could talk to you for a few minutes. I —," she said but hesitated. "It's about your daughter. I knew her, and I just wanted to connect with you."

She met Paul's gaze, and his eyebrows rose with anticipation. The woman on the other end of the speaker paused, and Evan was sure she was just going to hang up on them. Why should she let in two complete strangers who wanted to talk about her daughter that died years ago?

"Okay," the woman said. "Wait for the buzz."

The speaker clicked off and both of them looked to the double glass doors. The buzz sounded and Paul opened them, allowing Evan to roll inside. They found the elevator that took them to the third floor and down the hallway toward apartment 314.

She rolled to a stop and Paul stuffed his hands in his pockets. "I don't know why you're not nervous. I'm anxious as hell right now."

"Give it a few seconds," she said with a half-grin. "I'm sure I'll be right there with you."

Paul lifted his hand to knock on the door, but the latch clicked before he got there. The door creaked open just wide enough for the occupant inside the apartment to peer outside and hold the chain tight. Judith Sinclair stood there, her soft brown eyes scanning them from a safe distance. Thin strands of dark sable hair framed her face.

"Hi, Mrs. Sinclair?" Evan said.

"Do you have ID?" the woman said.

The question took her by surprise. Evan hadn't thought to bring anything with her. She didn't need anything like that in so many weeks.

"Uh, sure," Paul said and reached into his back pocket. He produced his hospital badge, with the St. John's logo and his picture. He passed it through the narrow opening and she took it.

After only a few seconds, she looked up from the ID and toward Paul. "You're a doctor?"

"We both are, actually," he said. "I'm emergency medicine. Evan here is general surgery. We're residents at St. John's."

She passed the ID back to him and closed the door. For a moment, Evan thought that she had just shut them out, but the click of the chain shifted against the door and she opened it again. Judith stepped aside and held the door open for them. She was prettier than Evan had first thought, her long tresses tied back into a pony tail. The color and style made her look younger than she probably was, and she had the same nose and eyes that she had seen in the on-line photo of Angela. And the only real difference from the locket photo was her hair. More modern, without the big bangs and perm.

"Come on in," she said, motioning them into the main room.

Evan wheeled across the threshold and Paul followed behind her. There wasn't a lot of space for her to turn the chair around and face the dark gray couch, but she found enough room on the other side of the glass coffee table.

"Sorry about the security check," the woman said as she moved to the couch and settled down in the center. "Please, make yourself comfortable."

Paul nodded and sat in the arm chair beside the sofa.

"I just can't be too careful," she said. "I had a lot of reporters right after Angela died. Most of it has stopped in the last few years, but every once in a while someone comes and wants another bit for their story."

"We're nothing like that, Mrs. Sinclair," Evan said.

"Oh, call me Judy, please," she said. "And I know you're not reporters. I think I recognize you." She painted a smile on her face, the one with eyes that showed her pity as she looked at the scar on her head and the chair beneath her. "I imagine that you've had your share of reporters as well. I saw you on the news, at least I saw what happened to you."

Evan glanced down at her own knees. This was something she hadn't anticipated. She should have expected that someone would recognize her, especially after all the coverage of the arraignment and charges against Matt on the news lately.

"Can I get you coffee? Tea?" Judy asked to both of them.

"Oh, I'm fine," Evan said and Paul just smiled.

"So," Judy said, the word drawn and slow. "What can I do for you?"

Evan cleared her throat. Now came the hard part. "I'm really sorry to come here about this—"

"You didn't know her, did you," Judy said, her head cocked to the side. Her face was still soft but her eyes had narrowed into curiosity.

Evan looked up at her and her heart jumped into her throat. Oh no. She was going to kick them out right now. But when she met the woman's gaze, she still held the knowing smile on her full and beautiful lips.

She swallowed and averted her gaze from Angela's mother. "No ma'am. But I want to know her."

Paul leaned forward in his seat and rested his elbows on his knees. "Mrs. Sinclair – sorry, Judy – Evan has been recovering from something terrible, as you are well aware."

"Yes, I am," she said and gave him the same smile.

Evan pushed down the rise of nerves that had welled in her throat. "I recently heard about your daughter." She licked her dry lips. "Her story has moved me in ways that I can't tell you. I'm currently living on the seventh floor of St. John's hospital where I'm doing rehab, and that's where I learned about her. I don't want her memory to die."

Judy's eyes sparkled and she wiped the back of her hand against her cheek. Her voice came out pinched. "I appreciate that. Every day that comes and goes brings it further away, but it still feels like yesterday."

Paul and Evan glanced to each other and he discreetly nodded to her to keep going. Evan let out a controlled breath. "I only know a little bit about her, but I was hoping you could tell me who she really was."

"Who she really was?" she repeated and smiled with another tear that flowed down her cheek. "She was the smartest and happiest teenager I had ever known." She laughed and glanced down to the cell phone she had produced from her pocket. She started the home screen and pulled up an album of photos. "And she was so smart. 4.0 GPA."

Evan accepted the phone and gazed down at the pictures of Angela, some by herself and others with friends. All of them with her smiling or laughing. One after another showed a girl that loved the people in her life.

"Her dad died when she was little. Pancreatic cancer," Judy said. "And she was my only child, so it was just her and I. We did everything together."

Evan handed the cell phone back to her. "She was beautiful."

Judy looked down at the picture on her phone, the smile still on her face. "She wanted to be a veterinarian. She loved animals, wanted to take in every stray she came across. But then everything changed when she got pregnant." The phone stayed cradled in her hand with the glow of the screen highlighting the edges of her chin and nose. "She was so afraid to tell me. It wasn't until she was about fifteen weeks along that she said anything at all, and it was only because I had noticed her pants weren't fitting anymore."

"How did she handle it?" Evan asked.

Judy looked up, her eyes brighter and the tears drying. "Once she told me, I think the stress of it all started to ease up a bit. We talked at first about what her plans were for the whole thing. Of course, we discussed adoption but that scared her. But she knew that having a baby at her age would change her whole future."

"Did the father or his family get involved at all?" Paul asked.

She shook her head. "You know, she never told me who it was and I never asked. I figured she would let me know some day, and I can't say that he even knew she was pregnant, whoever he was. After . . . everything . . . nobody came out and admitted it." The cell phone shook in her hand. She placed it on the coffee table and rose to her feet, straightening the hem of her shirt. "I'm going to get us some tea, okay. Excuse me."

Angela's mother slipped into the kitchen with her hands clenched. This had to be hard for her, dredging up the painful memories that ended in her daughter's death. Evan wasn't sure how any of this would help her situation, or the entity that walked the halls of the seventh floor. At least she tried, isn't that what she told herself? That had to be worth something. Without Judy in the room, the apartment felt empty and soulless.

"Hey," Paul said and Evan glanced to him. He ticked his head toward the wall behind her. He had dropped his voice to a whisper, so it must have been important.

She found the thing to which he had drawn her attention: a single 5 x 7 picture in a cheap frame. It rested atop a table just under the wall clock. Evan craned around the edge of the chair to get a better look, but it didn't take long for her to recognize it. The photo was a larger, clearer version but she had definitely seen it before. A simple color photo of Judy, although she was much younger, and a child at her side. Both with long dark hair and the young girl wearing a t-shirt with the movie logo for Independence Day.

The same photo in the locket.

"Oh, she loved that picture," Judy said from behind Evan.

The sound of her voice startled her and she turned to see the woman step into the living room with a tray displaying a porcelain tea set.

"We just noticed it," Paul said and shot a quick wink to Evan.

"She was about four or five at the time, I don't remember. And she found her dad's t-shirt. Insisted on wearing it that day, so I couldn't say no." She poured steaming liquid from the pot into small Japanese-style tea cups. The effort left her hands trembling but she lifted one of the cups toward Evan.

The ceramic had already gotten hot enough that Evan held it at the edges. A minty citrus aroma steamed from the caramel-colored liquid surface.

After she passed a cup to Paul, she held her own and sipped at it. She looked down to the steam, contemplating the soft curls of white before they dissipated forever.

"It happened so fast that day." Her voice broke, but she continued despite the shaking in her hands. "She was almost 35 weeks along. The pregnancy had been text book up to that point. She was having a little cramping and some contractions, so I took her into the hospital for an evaluation. Nothing out of the ordinary. I mean, I went into false labor at least three times when I was pregnant with her, so I was sure that's what it was. But we wanted to be safe than sorry."

Evan glanced to Paul again, but he leaned in further with the cup in his hands. He hadn't drunk from it at all, and neither had she.

"When we got there, the nurse put her in a room and told her to change and they were going to put her on a monitor. I had just gotten home from work before we left and I was hungry, so I told her I would be back and that I was just planning on picking something up for dinner for both of us." Her hands shook so bad now that the tea threatened to spill on her fingers.

"Mrs. Sinclair," Evan said and reached across the table, but Judy held up a hand to stop her.

"I'm okay." She placed the cup back on the tray and smoothed the hem of her shirt again, but it hadn't wrinkled since the last time she had done it. A deep sigh escaped her throat. "When I came back, there were alarms going off and people running down the hall. Never in a million years did I think that they were running toward my little girl." Tears glistened down her cheeks again. "When I got closer to her room, there was so much going on. Someone grabbed me and pulled me away before I could see her. They told me I couldn't go in there."

Her eyes drifted to the far corner of the room. The memories played across her face, a tin-type of everything she went through that day. "I remember now. It was room 706. Can't believe I forgot it for a second."

It seemed like Evan's heart stopped for a moment. She knew that very room. She had seen it as though it had been the day it all went down.

"What happened then?" Paul asked.

Judy swallowed the lump in her throat. "They sent me to a waiting room and it seemed like I was there for hours. Nobody would tell me what was going on. It wasn't until later that I found out she was dead before I had even gotten back to her room. All those people in there for nothing, because she was already dead on the floor in a pool of her own blood and nobody had known about it for several minutes. I guess all those people in that room were doing everything they could to find the baby's heartbeat, but she was gone too."

"Mrs. Sinclair," Evan spoke, but her voice wouldn't come out as more than a whisper. "I'm so sorry."

"Judy, please," she said and wiped a tear from her cheek.

"Did you ever get any answers about what might have happened?" Evan asked.

The woman stood and paced around the coffee table to a desk across the room. "There was an autopsy done at my request." She opened a drawer and withdrew a white envelope. The flap had never been unsealed, but the edges of the paper were plenty worn. "They sent me the report but I never had the stomach to read it." She handed the envelope to Evan.

"So you never knew the cause?" she asked.

Judy settled back down on the sofa. "Dr. Sorenson filled me in on the final results and spared me the details."

Paul sat up straight and glanced at Evan. The bottom of her stomach dropped. "Wait, Dr. Sorenson?"

"Oh, yes. He was her OB/GYN at the time, which was so great for us. We lived just a few houses away from each other. Angela used to babysit his two girls. He took such good care of her and stayed with me for all the funeral preparations and everything. I don't know what I would have done without him. But, yes, he had the full report. It's hard to remember everything he said and to tell you the truth, I don't really want to remember. But it's all in there." She nodded to the envelope in Evan's hand. "You can keep it. You'll probably understand it better than I could anyway and I never plan on opening it. You're lucky I still have it. There were so many times I almost burned it. Just promise me that if you read it, you never tell me what's in there."

"Okay," Evan said with a weak smile and held the envelope close to her torso. Such a valuable thing couldn't be allowed to slip from her fingers.

"You know," Judy said, placing her hands over her knees. "If you want to talk to Dr. Sorenson about what happened, I'm sure he would remember a lot more details. I know it's all protected health information, but I can call him and give permission to release it to you. He's a busy guy these days. I hear he is now the CEO of St. John's or something."

Evan nodded. "Yes. We know him and he's a great doctor." He was probably a saint at this point, considering what he had done for her as well as Angela's mother.

"I didn't get to see him much after the funeral, and then I moved here. I couldn't bear to stay in the house any longer without Angela. He and I lost contact after that. It'll be good to get in touch with him again."

"I think he would love to hear from you too," Evan said. She tucked the envelope between her leg and the side wall of the chair. "We have taken up so much of your time, and we both appreciate you for sharing this with us today."

Judy smiled and reached out her hand, which Evan accepted. The woman's fingers still trembled. "Thank you for stopping by, and I hope this helps to remember my daughter and grandchild in some way."

"I know it will. I'll make sure of it."

Chapter 33

Neither of them said much on the way back to the hospital. The envelope almost felt like fire in Evan's hand. There could be so many answers in here, everything that Angela wanted out in the open. But they needed to wait until they returned to the sanctuary of her own room before they opened it.

With Paul pushing her wheelchair from the parking garage and through the hospital, she moved with perfect quiet among the people that milled within the halls. Lab techs pushing a cart of needles and vials. Hospital executives in their suits and ties talking amongst each other, lattes in hand. Nobody noticed her or Paul as they skimmed down the corridors toward the main elevators. She held the most important information close to her midsection. These people had no idea what she carried, that this could be the answer to a young woman's death within these halls.

They rode the elevators with small collections of people that got on and off at different floors until they were alone to exit on the seventh floor. The silver doors slid open and Paul pushed her into the corridor until they arrived at the central hub. In the middle of the afternoon, patients and nurses moved between rooms, going back and forth from the south therapy wing.

But Evan grasped the wheel to stop the forward motion of the chair and Paul halted in his step. He followed her gaze toward the north wing, to the double doors held closed with the steel chain. And that was all they were. Two doors that locked the abandoned hallway.

Evan held her breath and listened beyond the murmur of general noise on the unit. Maybe if she tried hard enough, she would be able to hear someone on the other side of those doors. Although the two black windows appeared empty, perhaps Angela stood on the other side, watching her return with word from her mother. There was nothing but emptiness on either side of the barrier.

"Do you see anything?" Paul whispered.

She shook her head. Unfortunately, no. She wasn't sure what she had expected to see, but there was nobody standing there. "It's quiet."

Evan released the wheel and Paul pushed her back to her room. Behind the closed door, he opened the blinds to allow in the fading afternoon light. She held the envelope into the light and read the addresses printed over the front of it.

"Well?" Paul said and settled into the chair next to her. "I'm dying to know what's in there."

"Me too," she said. "But what if it's horrible?"

"What choice do you have? If her ghost is taunting you to do something, maybe it's just as simple as reading her story on those pages."

"I hope you're right."

Evan turned the envelope and dug her thumb under the edge of the seal until it tore in ragged edges across the entirety of the lip. The pages inside had been stapled together and folded in a thick bundle. It wasn't the first time she had ever seen an autopsy report, and they usually came with a large collection of information. Final blood and tissue results. A full and detailed examination report that was usually about five pages long. And sometimes there were photographs included. She silently prayed that nobody had sent pictures to this poor girl's mother.

She unfurled the bundle and flipped through the first couple of pages that were just official notes and letterhead from the coroner. The third page detailed the beginning of the autopsy.

"Okay," Evan said, scanning the document. "Looks like it was a complete examination." The first page detailed the date of the exam, which happened the day she died. The medical examiner hadn't wasted any time. The second page held the list they had been waiting for. "Cause of death . . . wow, I did not expect this."

"What?" Paul said and leaned forward to peer at the page.

"It says cause of death from acute hemorrhage secondary to disseminated intravascular coagulation, also secondary to amniotic fluid embolus."

Paul scrunched his nose. "Isn't that rare?"

"Extremely." She had only ever read about it during medical school, one of those things you learn in the first couple of years and in clinical rotations. Every medical student remembers it, though, because it's gruesome and almost unbelievable. It always showed up on a test but hardly ever in real life, thank heavens. Nobody seemed to know what caused it: a sudden, freak accident where amniotic fluid from the pregnancy can get sucked into the mother's circulation and drive right into her lungs. It causes a severe inflammatory reaction that happens as fast as lightning. The mother will go into rapid cardiopulmonary arrest and all of her blood coagulation factors will be consumed in the body's attempt to fix the problem. Then she won't be able to clot anymore, and every little microscopic breech in a blood vessel will open. The patient can bleed from any needle poke, from her eyes and mouth, and definitely from a third trimester pregnancy.

She leaned back in her chair, the image of the dark figure

standing next to the doors now playing in her mind. The spirit stood there in a pool of blood that ran down her legs like water. Just like it would have that day. How could such a rare event have happened to her? So suddenly and without warning?

The page crinkled in her hand and drew her attention back to the print. She read some of the details aloud, especially the lung and heart dissection. The medical examiner had found a significantly large bolus of amniotic fluid, complete with fetal cellular material, lodged in the main confluence of both pulmonary arteries. Dramatic inflammation had taken hold of her lungs, the initial spark of this girl's death.

"Her vessels were practically empty," Evan said and felt a surge of nausea. "She must have bled out in minutes."

"How did nobody on the unit know what was happening to her?" Paul said. "Aren't those ladies hooked up on monitors as soon as they get admitted?"

"It says here that there was lividity present in her limbs consistent with laying on the ground for some time," she said as she scanned the rough diagram the examiner had made. "She had already had IV lines put in." She turned the page so Paul could see where the medical examiner had detailed a line in the girl's left forearm. "So someone had already seen her and started an initial exam when she got there."

Evan turned the page and the nausea in her stomach churned. This page was the additional exam on the fetus. "I don't think I can read this part." She handed the pages to Paul.

He accepted them and leaned his elbows on his knees while he read. "Well, it was a baby girl, just like Judy said. Absolutely nothing wrong with it. Says cause of death was extravasation."

Extreme hemorrhage, just like the baby's mother. They both had died of a sudden and severe blood loss, all because a large volume of amniotic fluid somehow got into her circulation.

"It's been a long time since I had to know anything about amniotic fluid embolus," Evan said. "Looks like I'm going to be doing some studying tonight."

"Bright side," Paul said and folded the pages back together, "you now know how that girl died. Maybe that's all she wanted, was for someone to finally read this."

"But Dr. Sorenson would have read it," Evan said. "He was her primary obstetrician."

"True. But for some reason, she wants you to know about it."

Paul had a point. The ghost of this girl was following her and not Dr. Sorenson, as far as she knew. If Mrs. Sinclair gave him permission to look into her files, that would certainly help. And he probably knew more about the situation that day than was even on the coroner's report. Maybe she could use some of her influence with him to get as much information as possible.

Her shoulders fell and she accepted the folded pages from him.

"What is it?" he asked.

She shrugged. "I don't know. I just thought I would feel relieved when we read this, but I think I just have more questions."

"Yeah, I agree."

"Do you think Sorenson will talk to us?" she asked him.

His eyebrow rose and he smiled. "I bet he will. He'll do anything for you right now. You have the power. And I have another idea." He stood and clasped his hands together. "I'm going to make a visit to the current labor and delivery floor, see if any of the nurses working there now had worked when they were on the seventh floor. Maybe someone was there that day and remembers what happened."

"I love it," she said with a smile.

He leaned down and kissed her. "Alright. I'll leave you to it and report back, boss."

"You have to go now?"

"Unfortunately, yes. My shift starts in a couple of hours, but I promise I'll see you tomorrow."

After everything that had happened today, she had gotten used to having him nearby. The thought of being alone for the next twenty-four hours made her shiver. Going to Glenview was supposed to make all of this better, but it didn't settle well in her bones. And she suspected that Angela had not come to find peace by the simple discovery of the autopsy report.

"I wish you could stay" she said.

"Hey," he said and clasped her left hand, the ring on her finger pressed against his palm. "You can handle this. If she comes back, just tell her what you learned. Tell her to move on and find peace in the next life."

"And what if she isn't happy with that?"

A deep sigh left his throat. "Then she'll have to deal with me."

"I'm serious."

"I am too." He fished his cell out of his back pocket and flashed it in the light. "I'll have my phone on me. Text me if something happens."

She nodded and he stood. After blowing her a kiss, he slipped out of the room and the door latched closed with a resounding click.

Alone in the room with the coming twilight that left the furniture with drawn out bands of orange light across the bed. The autopsy report crinkled in her hands as they clenched tighter around the envelope. Tonight would come whether she was ready for it or not, and so might the things that wandered in the shadows.

Chapter 34

"You seem distracted today," Samena said from behind Evan.

She held to the parallel bars, upright and weight on her legs. Evan took another step forward. It wasn't far but it was so much further than a week ago. But even with the concentration she needed for walking, Samena was right. Her mind had been drifting through the pages of the autopsy report she and Paul read yesterday.

"Sorry," she said. "Had a lot on my mind lately."

"Nothing wrong with that. After what you've been through, it's good to be able to have that stuff on your mind at all."

The left foot moved one step ahead and she shifted her weight to that hip. Her hands adjusted along the bars as well.

"Getting a day out of here yesterday had to help a little, too. Some fresh air, even though it's cold and miserable outside." Samena kept a hold on the strap behind her, but Evan noticed that she didn't hold it as tight as she used to.

Her thoughts floated to Mrs. Sinclair – Judy – and the way she looked at the old pictures on her phone. Going outside should have lightened things for her, but Evan felt the same weight of everything on her shoulders. It should have helped, but she didn't feel any different.

The right foot stepped forward, but her toes didn't clear the mat and she stumbled. Her arms locked onto the bars and caught the weight before she fell.

"Whoa," Samena said, tightening the strap around her waist.

"Sorry," Evan said and straightened her foot. "I didn't lift my foot like I was supposed to."

"That's okay. It's the whole reason we are here doing this every day."

Evan settled her weight down through the right leg but her knee wobbled with the trembling of her quadriceps.

Samena stepped closer behind her. "I think that's enough for today."

"I can do this," Evan said and held tighter to the bars. She wasn't about to allow Samena pull her away from the rest of the walk.

"I know you can, but you also need to listen to your body. You can't push it when it's not ready to be pushed."

Evan knew that. It was the same stuff she had spouted to patients after surgery. Those patients who didn't listen were the ones that came back with popped stitches or hernias through their internal incisions. She understood very well the consequences of pushing too hard.

"Okay, fine," she said with a sigh.

Samena pulled the wheelchair closer and helped her settle into the seat before wheeling her back to the post-therapy massage.

"I don't want you to get discouraged," Samena said and placed the dollop of cold peppermint massage cream along her right shin. "It will always be three steps forward and one step back. But that is progress. And I still think you'll be out of here by the end of next week."

That was about nine or ten days. Only a week and a half or so to get the dark entity to leave her alone, and that was hard to do if she hadn't seen it in a few days. But she wouldn't bet any money on the fact it was gone forever just because she opened an autopsy report. The thing didn't show up every day. Just like a tornado, you know it's coming eventually but not really sure when or where it's going to hit.

"So what did you and Paul do yesterday? Something fun, I hope," Samena said while she did the slow stretch of the peroneus muscles on the outside of her shin.

I should tell her, she thought. Evan wasn't sure why, but the urge to say something about it continued to nag at her. It had for the last several weeks, but she always pushed it down and hid it away.

Tell her the truth.

What if Sam looked at her like she was crazy? The same way Evan had looked at Matt when he told her the truth.

"We went for a drive north," she said. That was not the whole truth, only a fragment of it. The pressure of her thoughts didn't lighten by only saying that much.

"It was a good day to do it. At least the sun was up and it had stopped snowing."

Tell her.

Evan's throat tightened around the next words, but she forced them out. "We went to Glenview."

"Oh," Samena said, her eyebrows rising, but her attention to the massage indicated that she still wasn't particularly interested.

Evan licked her dry lips. "You're right, you know. Something has distracted me lately."

Samena looked up to her but continued to stretch the tendons along Evan's foot.

"This place gives you a lot of time to think," Evan said and tried to smile but it felt so fake. "And I've been thinking a lot about Angela Sinclair."

Sam wrinkled her nose. "Angela? You mean the girl that you asked me about the other day?"

"Yeah. I've been looking into what happened to her, and it was really tragic." She swallowed. There was no way she could just say that she wanted to put the girl's spirit to rest. "I – I mean, Paul and I – were thinking about maybe starting a memorial for her or something."

"That would be great," Sam said with a smile.

"We went to Glenview and talked with her mother yesterday."

The therapist's eyes rose again and this time she stopped massaging. "Really? Oh my gosh, what was that like?" She leaned forward like she was ready to hear the latest gossip from her best friend.

"We didn't know what to expect, but she was great," Evan started and began the story of their trip to Glenview, including the photos and the story of what the poor woman had gone through.

Samena sat back, her hands still oily with peppermint cream. "Wow. You guys are so brave to do that. I would have buckled and bawled with her. What she had to go through, I felt so sorry for her." Then she leaned closer again and dropped her voice. "I'll tell you something I haven't told anyone else."

The butterflies started to stir in Evan's gut.

Sam glanced around them, to the empty corridor and physical therapy space. Nobody else stood there, and no one would hear what she was about to say.

"There was one time, maybe like four or five months ago, I was finishing up my shift and putting everything away. It was pretty empty up here and everyone else had gone home for the night. I had turned out all the lights and was walking back toward the elevators when I could have sworn I heard someone say my name right behind me. Like someone whispered it in my ear. I thought someone had stayed behind and was playing a joke on me. So I turned, ready to catch them, but there was nobody there."

The butterflies in Evan's gut now swarmed and sent shivers down her arms.

"And, you know, at the time I seriously thought it sounded like Angela. So when you asked me about her a couple weeks ago, I thought about that night."

The fluorescent lights flickered in a series of three blinks and then glowed steady again. Both of them stopped and glanced up to the light banks.

Samena laughed. "Geez. That made my heart stop."

Evan still looked up to the lights, but she didn't feel like smiling. She had experienced enough of the electrical disturbances to not just laugh them off anymore. She held her breath and listened to the silence around them, but there was nothing else. No cold. No footsteps. Just both of them with the aroma of peppermint oil in the air.

"Yeah," Evan said and gave her a half-grin. "Just bad wiring I guess."

Sam let out a deep breath and continued with her massage. "Anyway, when I heard that I just bolted down the hall. But I never heard it again, so who knows."

Evan looked at her, to the top of her head as she leaned over and worked the muscles in her leg. "I believe you, because I think I've seen her."

She glanced up and stopped rubbing again. "Really?"

The room around them fell into a deep quiet and not even the breeze outside the windows broke it.

Evan picked at her nails and chewed on her lip for a moment. "Yeah. Lots of times, in fact."

"You're serious?" Samena's face had gone white and her eyes widened.

"You know that day when my bathroom mirror broke?"

Her brow furrowed and she leaned in again to whisper. "You mean that was her? Did you see her do it?"

Evan nodded. Samena shivered and Evan could see the goosebumps on her forearms.

"My grandmother used to talk about seeing ghosts in her house," Samena said and finished the massage before wiping down her hands with a towel. "She called them *riorio*, said they were children that had died of influenza on the island and buried near her home in Tonga. She always said to take extra precautions when one was around because they could possess you. I never saw one but I totally believed her." She tossed the towel to the side and eyed her again. "Why do you think she destroyed your room?"

"She wants something, and I may have found it, but I'm not sure."

"Just be careful," Samena said. "*Riorio* are not to be messed with. My grandmother was terrified of them. I'll pray for you."

"Am I interrupting something fun?" a voice broke the silence from behind them. Samena jumped and Evan turned.

Dr. Sorenson stood just at the edge of the therapy room, a briefcase in hand. He smiled at them both and raised his hand with a slight wave.

"No sir," Samena said and stood. "We were just finishing up."

"So good timing then," he said. "I certainly don't want to detract from therapy."

"Not at all," Evan said and turned her chair to face him.

"See you tomorrow," Samena said with a knowing look to her and then turned away.

Evan nodded and wheeled toward Sorenson.

"May I walk back with you?" he said as she wheeled into the corridor.

"Of course."

"I received a phone call this morning and I'm bringing you some documents that I think you might be interested in." He patted the side of his brief case.

He must have talked to Mrs. Sinclair. That woman hadn't wasted any time in getting a hold of him.

The bank of lights flickered again, each blink accompanied by the slightest ping in the bulbs. Her hands tightened on the wheels. Not now, she pleaded to whoever might be able to hear her thoughts. Please, not now. Her eyes darted down the hallway, to the shadows between the lights and in the corners of the rooms. Nothing stood there, though. Nothing waited for her. The lights steadied again and left the hall in a glow of white.

Dr. Sorenson glanced up to the lights as he continued to walk. "Must be having some issues with electrical up here."

"Yeah," she said with a steady breath. "It's been doing that."

"I'll send someone up to look at it in the morning," he said.

They made it back to her room and she invited him inside, but not before glancing into the shadows to make sure nothing crouched there.

"I spoke to Judith Sinclair today. She said you and Paul stopped by." He sat in the armchair across from her and placed the briefcase on his lap. "Gave me permission to discuss her daughter with you."

"Yes," Evan said and watched him sift through papers inside the case.

He produced a large envelope and closed the case. "Just curious, but what made you ask about her? Angela, I mean."

She hadn't expected to lie to Dr. Sorenson, essentially the man that was her boss and could end her career at St. John's if he wanted to. But there was no way she was going to tell him what she had said to Samena.

"Well, being up here gives you a lot of time to think, and I have been learning a lot about her and what happened to her. Paul and I were thinking of starting a memorial for her."

He nodded and smiled. "That's a great idea." He handed the envelope to her. "Judy said something about that, and said you were asking about things that happened the day her daughter died."

"Yeah, she said that you had been Angela's doctor."

"I was. Not to go into too much confidential details, but I took care of her from beginning to . . . well, to the end."

Evan opened the envelope and glanced over the papers, which looked to be routine prenatal care forms. The patient's weight, blood pressure, the fetal heart rate and the age of the pregnancy at each visit.

"As you can see, everything was routine up until that day," he said.

"Did you see her that day, before it happened?"

He nodded. "Yes. I was already up there doing a procedure and the nurse told me she had arrived. I stopped in to check on her before I left. Everything was normal, just a simple labor check and she was supposed to go home after a few hours of monitoring. Very common. It happens every day up there. But then, you know the rest."

She glanced through the pages of the standard prenatal visits that he and Angela had back then. Her weight, the baby's heartbeat, her blood pressure. All of it was quite normal. There was nothing to suggest that something terrible was about to happen to her.

"They said it was an amniotic fluid embolus," she said and glanced up to him.

"Yes, that was the conclusive diagnosis. It caused the cascade of events that led to DIC and eventual hemorrhage," he said.

DIC. Disseminated intravascular coagulation. The consumption of all clotting factors in a person's blood until the patient can no longer clot and they bleed to death from every orifice and needle stick. A horrible way to die.

"My understanding is that amniotic fluid embolus is rare," she said.

He nodded. "Extremely. I had only ever seen two other instances in my whole career before her. Haven't seen one since and hope to never see it again. It's the most horrifying thing I've ever witnessed."

"And they're sure it was an amniotic fluid embolus?"

"Absolutely," he said. "Mrs. Sinclair said she gave you the autopsy report. It's all in there."

"Do you know how they test for something like that?" she asked.

"It's quite simple, actually. There was a bolus of fluid that was obvious in the pulmonary artery bifurcation. The pathologist just samples it and looks under a microscope. Amniotic fluid has very specific characteristics. It even carries fetal skin cells, and you can see that when you look under the scope. They found a substantial amount in Angela's arteries."

That's the part the bothered Evan the most. "Why would they find that much in her arteries? In my studying about this, correct me if I'm wrong, wouldn't that much be impossible if she wasn't in labor? I thought that much could only get into the vasculature if there was something like a c-section going on at the same time or something?"

"That's the thing about this disease. It's poorly understood and nobody really knows why it happens. We just know that it's devastating when it does and hardly anyone survives it."

She had read that part in her textbooks too. An embolus like that was fatal more than ninety percent of the time. Poor Angela didn't have a chance with an embolus that big.

"Is there anything else I can answer for you?" he asked and closed the latches on the case.

She shook her head. "I don't think so. You have been so incredibly helpful. I really appreciate this."

"Of course. And if you have any further questions, please call me. You have my number." He stood and turned back to her.

The lights flickered in the two lamps that left her room in dim light. They blinked only twice and then steadied, but it was enough to leave Evan's heart racing.

"There it goes again," he muttered and glanced between the lamps.

She steadied her voice before she spoke. "I'll keep in touch. And thank you for everything."

"I hope they are doing a good job up here for you," he said as he pulled open the door. "I think Dr. White and his team are anxious to have you back with them in the operating room."

"I'm anxious to be back."

"You just concentrate on getting well again, and don't worry too much about all this other stuff. There will be time enough to start a memorial when you're out." He nodded and stepped from the room.

The door clicked shut and the lights blinked again, this time in a series of three quick bursts. Evan glanced to the shadows again, checking her peripheral vision each time she turned her eyes.

"Is that you, Angela?" she whispered. If someone stood out in the hall, she didn't want them thinking she was going crazy in there.

The lights burned steady in their fittings now. The room had gone silent, except for the sound of her own breathing and the pulsation of each heartbeat in her ears. Her fingers curled around the tops of the wheels until the skin of her knuckles stretched tight.

"Do you need to say something?" she said and flashed her eyes toward the dark of the bathroom.

Everything stayed quiet and still. No more flashing lights.

It was going to be a long night if nobody answered her.

Chapter 35

Paul had a couple hours to kill before his shift tonight, but Evan would be in physical therapy right now. There was no point in going up there just to watch therapy and not be able to talk to her about everything they had done in the last few days. And he really needed to talk.

He did what she asked him to do. He promised he would try as hard as he could to believe her, and after everything that happened in Glenview, it didn't take much trying. That picture in the locket that matched the one in Judith's apartment was no mere coincidence. Evan didn't make that up. She had found it somewhere, and Evan was genuinely scared of something. He had to give her the benefit of the doubt.

And he had also promised to dig a little deeper for her.

Paul pressed the call buzzer just outside the double glass doors that barred entry into the second floor north wing.

"May I help you?" a woman's voice said on the other end.

"Uh, yeah. I'm Dr. Williams, from down in the ER. Can I talk to a floor supervisor or manager?"

"Sure," the woman said. The doors clicked and he pressed them open.

He hadn't ever been on this unit before. There was no need. The maternity ward was its own world, separate from the day to day in the rest of the hospital, including the emergency room.

Security stayed tight here all the time, especially in light of the abductions that had happened in other hospitals in the past. Nobody came in or out of the unit unless the main desk knew about it.

The hallways here were different than everywhere else in this building. The designs suggested professional decorators had a hand in the final outcome of the place. The corridor led to the central nursing station, a place of hardwood countertops, brushed nickel accents and soft lighting that you would typically find in a high-end spa. The unit secretary smiled at him.

"Dr. Williams," she said and stood. "Follow me. The unit manager is in her office right now. Her name is Felicity."

"Thanks," he said and followed her behind the desk to a closed door.

After two quick knocks, the door opened from the other side and a woman in a set of dark pink scrubs stood there. She didn't look much older than himself, but she held out her hand to him.

"Felicity Park," she said with a smile and shook his hand. "And you must be Dr. Williams. What can I help you with?"

She stepped aside to allow him into the office. As he settled into the chair across from her desk, he couldn't help but notice the professional photos of newborn babies decorating the walls.

"This may seem like a strange question, but I am doing a little historical research. I was just wondering if any of your staff up here used to work in the old unit up on seventh?"

Her eyebrows rose. "Oh, yeah. A few of them, actually."

"Great. I just wanted to interview one or two of them. A friend and I are working on a project about the old unit and I just wanted to get some perspective from someone that used to work there."

She smiled and pulled a pen from her pocket. The ink flowed quickly over a yellow sticky note before she handed it to him. "They would love to tell you stories about that place. These three in particular worked there for several years. And the second one – Asha – she's here right now. It's not too busy if you wanted to talk to her for a few minutes."

"That would be awesome," he said and flashed her his dimple smile, the one that usually got him what he wanted.

Her cheeks flushed just a little and smiled back at him. She showed him out to the nursing desk, with its panels of fetal monitors that projected the on-going heart rates of fetuses still in the womb of every patient that currently resided on the unit. Felicity walked to a woman that sat before a computer and clicked away at the electronic chart.

"Asha," she said and the nurse looked up. Her long black hair, peppered with an occasional strand of gray, was tied back in a ponytail. "This is Dr. Williams from the ER. He was just hoping to talk to someone who had worked on the old unit and I thought you would be the perfect person to fill him in on what he needs to know."

Her eyes brightened with a smile. "Of course."

Felicity left the two of them alone in front of the computers. Asha turned back to the keyboard. "Just let me finish this note really quick."

"Sure," he said.

She clicked through what looked like a saved version of one of the fetal heart rate tracings. With a snap of the enter key, she closed the chart and turned to him with a smile. "So, what can I help you with today?"

"Well, a friend and I are working on a memorial project," he started. It sounded as good as the time Evan had said it to

Mrs. Sinclair, so why not go with it? "I was hoping you might have some information on an incident that happened up there just before the unit shut down."

The smile faded a little, but the wrinkles still held around the edges of her eyes. "You're talking about the patient that died up there."

He nodded. "Yeah."

"Angela Sinclair."

That had taken him by surprise. "You remember her name?"

"Of course, I do. She was my patient that day. She died under my watch."

Knots turned in his stomach. That wasn't something he had expected. "I'm sorry."

"It's okay. It was many years ago."

"I've spoken with her mother and she filled me in on some details. Can you tell me anything that you remember from that day?"

She sat back against her chair and rested her hands across her abdomen. Her gaze wandered behind him, to the empty corners that only held a coat rack.

"I remember that she was young, fifteen or sixteen if I remember correctly. She'd come in for a labor check. These young girls do that a lot. They feel a few contractions and get all excited, until we monitor them and send them home disappointed a few hours later. She came in with her mother, but her mother left for a little while. The girl was sort of quiet, scared I guess. All wide-eyed and adrenaline pumping. I got her in a gown, put her on the monitor and watched it for a while."

"So, it all looked pretty normal at that point?" Paul asked.

She nodded. "She had several contractions." Asha tilted her head with a grin. "But there was nothing out of the ordinary about that. Contractions are a part of the third trimester. Doesn't mean they're in labor, and neither was she. But I started an IV and gave her a liter of fluid. Sometimes these girls get a little dehydrated and that's what causes the contractions. If you just get their tank full, the contractions stop and they end up going home. Her cervix wasn't doing anything, closed like a lock box as I say. The contractions fizzled out with the IV fluid and baby looked great on the monitor."

"How long was she up here before –"

"Before it all went to hell? About an hour, hour and a half maybe. She looked ready to be discharged because everything was back to normal for her. Her doctor, Dr. Sorenson, was on the unit doing a procedure – an ultrasound or amniocentesis or something, I don't remember. I flagged him down and told him she was in a room if he wanted to see her before I sent her home. He obliged and went in and saw her."

"The doctor doesn't usually see the patient's before they go home like that?" he asked.

"No need, unless they're already up here and we just let them know if they want to say hi or give them some instructions or something." She sat up straight again. "He went in and gave her instructions on if she feels more contractions to come back. She needed to go the bathroom before she left, so he disconnected her from the monitor and helped her to the bathroom. These third trimester girls have to pee all the time, especially after we give them IV fluid. He said he didn't want to hover around her while she used the bathroom so he left her there and told her to buzz the nurses' station when she was done."

"And then?" he said.

"And then he left. I was doing my charting and lost track of time, but it had been maybe ten or fifteen minutes by the time I had looked at the clock and realized I hadn't heard from her.

I got up and went into her room," she said and looked down at her hands. "And that's when I found her. She was crumpled on the floor just outside the bathroom in a pool of her own blood. I could still hear it running out of her like water from a faucet. I'll never forget that sound. And her IV site was oozing blood. She had blood coming out of her nose and eyes. It was everywhere."

Paul didn't say anything, but only listened to the silence between them.

"I called a Code Blue as fast as I could and then I ran to her. There wasn't a pulse and she was cold. Everything after that was such a blur, but the code team got her into bed and everyone tried to revive her. I remember hearing her ribs break while they did CPR. We searched for the baby's heart beat while they were doing it, but it was quiet in there. The baby was already gone too. There was nothing anybody could do."

Asha sighed and looked up at him.

"That must have been hard to deal with," he said.

"I've had patients die before and it's always hard. But that girl, she was so young and there was nothing wrong with her. To this day, it's unheard of, what happened to her."

"And I heard that Angela's death might have been the reason the unit closed and moved down here?" he said.

She shrugged. "Who knows. There were a lot of inspections that happened after that. I think everyone was nervous about a law suit, but it never happened. Angela's mother understood that it was just a freak thing that can happen out of the blue. It was nobody's fault. I just wish I had looked at the clock sooner. Maybe I could have done something."

"From what I know about amniotic fluid embolus, the ending might just have been the same whether or not you had gotten to her sooner," he said.

Asha smiled at him. "True. I need to hear that every once in a while. That case still bothers me to this day."

"I can understand why." Paul stood and extended his hand to her. "Thank you so much for your time. I probably need to get out of your hair and let you work."

She shook his hand and stood with him. "Of course. And please let me know more about the memorial when you get ready to do it. I would love to be a part of it. That girl needs to be remembered."

He nodded and stepped back down to the security doors. The more he learned about this case, the more he agreed that the memorial needed to happen. It was a convenient lie at first, but now he believed in it.

Chapter 36

The cold prickled against Evan's forearm, making the hair rise. That was the first thing that made her stir. Her throat had gone dry and she swallowed, but it only made her tongue feel swollen. The light from the small lamp on the dresser met her eyes.

At some point she had fallen asleep in her chair. The last thing she remembered was talking to herself in the dim light of her room, hoping that someone would talk back. She must have dozed off waiting for the response that hadn't come.

The light flickered, just like it had earlier that night when Dr. Sorenson had come to visit her. She had hoped that nothing happened with him there, and then nothing happened after he left, much to her dismay.

Evan straightened her neck that had tightened from leaning to the side while she slept. The bones in her spine popped into place as she forced herself upright and watched the light blink on and off like Morse code. The temperature in the room plummeted enough that now she could see her breath.

The short hair on her head bristled, and it wasn't just the cold. Between the flashes of the lamp, the room plunged into darkness and she could have sworn that someone stood just inside the threshold of the bathroom.

She steadied the shaking in her hands. "Angela, are you in here?"

The lamp continued its erratic blinking and an involuntary shiver moved up her spine. Her eyes squinted into the shadows of the bathroom. Maybe it was just a trick of the light, but something stood there, watching in silence.

"What do you want from me?" she whispered and hoped that nobody could hear her outside the room.

The light bulb exploded in a sudden ping and made her jump. Her hands grasped the top of her wheels, ready to move at any second. Darkness flooded the room but her eyes hadn't quite adjusted yet. The cold left her jaw tight and her teeth ready to chatter.

Shadows morphed and twisted at the edge of the bathroom door, the only place in the room not illuminated by any city lights outside the main windows. It drifted, smooth like fog across the forest floor, and stood just at the edge of the dark. Blacker than the shadows, it stood silently at the end of the bed, only the shape of a head and shoulders and darkness below them.

The sound of her breath moving in swift gasps through her lips deafened Evan's ears. She couldn't move, the cold left her muscles and joints almost frozen.

"Angela?" she whispered again, the words in a trembling phrase.

The shadow waited in still quiet, drawing every fraction of warmth from the air. That's how it built up enough energy to act, or at least that was what the blogs she had read on the internet led her to believe. One even said that the colder it got, the more the entity would act out. If that was true, this was going to be an act of violence.

Evan's lips quivered, and if she could look in the mirror, she was sure they were blue. "I don't know how else to help you."

It moved again, drifting soundlessly around the edge of the bed and into the shaft of pale gold light that poured through the window. The shadow had become the same twisted and bent woman with long stringy hair, but this time the light shone under the dark curtain of hair that framed her face. The skin of her face was pale and smooth, like cold porcelain with a hue of blue or purple. But it was the face of youth. The face of Angela Sinclair, only with milky eyes that looked out from her veil of death. Those white cataract corneas gazed at Evan as it moved toward her chair.

The energy that the spirit pulled from the room also left Evan stiff and unable to move her arms. The thing had her trapped as it drifted over the floor. No sway in her movement because her legs didn't move. The entity just flowed across the room in steady progress with a fixed gaze toward Evan.

Her ribs tightened and she gasped. The entity raised its boney white hand, the fingers outstretched toward Evan. The hospital gown, still soaked in blood, hung over the spirit's thin and ghastly form.

The closer it got, the more Evan could smell the mildew coming from its body. But there was something else underneath it. Cloying and acidic. Angela's spirit neared her and Evan finally realized that she could smell the blood that dripped down its arms and legs. Its outstretched fingers neared her and she pressed back against the chair. She wanted to close her eyes or hold her breath against the smell, but the entity had her under its control now.

The fingers reached for her and made contact against the center of Evan's sternum. Cold like stiff clay, its index finger bent against her flesh and Evan gasped. The cataract eyes turned down to look at her chest where its hand had opened and now pressed against her sternum. Evan tried to cry out, to move. Anything to get away from the entity that had her in its grasp, but she still couldn't move.

Those milky eyes flashed up to her as though it knew that she tried to scream. Angela's blue, cracked lips parted and trembled as she fixed her gaze into Evan's brain. Maybe it was the sound of her heart pulsing in her ears, but she swore that a breath fell from the spirit's mouth. The frozen clay hand pressed against her chest until it burned, a sharp and stabbing pain that relentlessly forced through her bones and made her breath catch. At the peak of the pain, the entity let out a single sigh.

"Not mine," it said in that one breath with trembling lips.

The pain seared into Evan's chest now and forced tears at the corners of her eyes. Her ribs suddenly expanded and she gasped. Her eyes and teeth clenched against the pain and she closed her eyes for only a second.

And then everything let go. The pain vanished and her eyes shot open to see an empty room. There was no cold hand pressed against her chest and definitely nobody looking at her with cataract-clouded eyes. Her shaking hands released the wheels but it had left her knuckles sore. The chill had receded along with the shadows and now the temperature began to climb again.

Evan had asked for a response. Well, she definitely got what she asked for, but what did it mean, *not mine*? Everything had vanished, but she still felt the aftershocks of the pain in her chest. Her fingers moved to the spot on her sternum that continued to throb and she pulled down her shirt. In the faint light, a bright red hand print had burned into the flesh between her breasts.

Right in the center of her chest. In the area just above the convergence of her own pulmonary vasculature. The very spot that the amniotic fluid embolus had lodged in Angela's own body.

Not mine. Was it possible? Maybe Angela had told her what to do after all.

The hours crept by throughout the night, all without a moment that Evan could close her eyes. She lay in bed the entire time, staring at the ceiling and waiting to be able to make the call when she knew it would be answered. There was only one person she could ask to help her with this, as crazy as it was going to sound.

The clock hit eight, and the morning sun had started its round above the cold city. Evan grabbed her cell phone and dialed the number. It might be still be a little too early, but she would try until someone answered.

After the fourth attempt, a woman's voice finally picked up on the other end.

"Pathology," the woman said.

"Dr. Barnhart?" Evan asked.

"Yes."

"Thank heavens. I was hoping it would be you. This is Evan Jensen."

There was a two second pause. "Oh my goodness, Evan. I can't believe this. It's so good to hear your voice. I never would have expected to hear from you today, not in a million years."

Evan smiled when she heard the excitement in Dr. Barnhart's voice. "Good to talk to you too."

"How are you doing? I mean, after everything you've been through . . . are you back to work?"

"No, not yet. Still in therapy, I haven't been cleared so far. I'm hoping soon."

"That's good to hear. You've had so much to go through, I didn't know when it would be a good time to come see you."

"You don't have to worry about that, I'm doing great now. Just started walking so I'm hoping to be out of here soon." She cleared her throat. Enough of the small talk; now it was time for the awkward part. "Um, I just need to ask you something. Maybe a favor of sorts."

"Sure. What can I do for you?"

"I don't know if you remember back about nine years ago or so, there was a sixteen-year-old girl that died of an amniotic fluid embolus up on labor and delivery when it was on the seventh floor."

"Oh, sure I do," she said. "Everyone remembers that case. I wasn't the medical examiner, but I know that Dr. Anderson did that one. He's retired now but I still have his case notes."

"Well, when I did my rotation with you as an intern, I remember that the department would save some tissue samples. Like for educational purposes or even open cases. Would you happen to know if anything was saved from that case?"

"Hmm. Let me check. If so, it would be in our archive," Barnhart said. The click of a keyboard resounded through the phone. Evan heard her breathing and the occasional mumble while she read her computer screen.

"You might just be in luck," Barnhart said and clicking stopped. "Looks like Anderson kept samples on file, and I'm not surprised. It's not every day that you see an amniotic fluid embolus, and these sorts of cases are good for teaching residents." She paused while she continued reading. "Yes. It looks like the family signed off for the department to keep several samples on hand. There's lung, liver, heart, kidney, uterus. Even some bone marrow. And there's a good sample of the amniotic fluid that Anderson extracted from the pulmonary vessels."

Jackpot. That's exactly what Evan had hoped for. "That's the best news I've had in a while."

"What's this about, if you don't mind me asking?"

Evan bit her lip. Dr. Barnhart was one of the best physician-attendings that she had had during her intern year, which was fraught with difficult doctors. And she had kept in frequent contact with her, especially when she let Evan join her during some autopsies. Barnhart had taught her so much, and she deserved to know at least a fraction of the truth.

"This might be a little strange, but I need you to trust me on this one. I've come across something that worries me about this case." She took in a deep breath, waiting for Barnhart to argue with her, but it never came. "I was wondering if it was at all possible to test the amniotic fluid, like for DNA or chromosomes or something if you could. See if you can match it to Angela Sinclair or her baby."

Barnhart paused, and then dropped her voice. "Yeah, I'm sure I could test it, but what's going on?"

"I'd rather not say quite yet. I just have a hunch," she said.

"Alright," the pathologist said, but her voice was still low. "I'll do it because it's you. But when I get results, I expect you to fill me in on what's going on."

"Will do," Evan said and the line went quiet.

Chapter 37

Paul glanced down to his phone's screen and read Evan's text:

Something's not right. Called Barnhart, pathology running chromosomes/DNA on amniotic fluid. We'll see . . . Going to therapy now. Let's talk later.

It made him stop in front of the elevator doors that would take him upstairs to see her. After his conversation with Asha on labor and delivery yesterday, he was sure that he had every bit of information in the story. The last of the puzzle pieces had fit into place. But, apparently, one of them didn't fit quite right.

If Evan was heading to therapy now, it would be no use trying to talk to her. They couldn't discuss these things in front of the therapist and he didn't want to get in the way. He didn't have a shift tonight, so maybe it would be best to come back at dinner. He turned around and headed for the garage.

"We're going to step it up a notch today," Samena said as soon as Evan rolled into the therapy unit. A semi-evil smile spread across her lips.

"I hope that's a good thing," Evan said and stopped the chair beside the parallel bars.

"No bars today." Samena stepped around her to the closet and brought out a walker, just like the one Evan's grandma used to have. "We are going to try walking with this."

"Then I'll be so stylish," Evan said with a laugh. "Everyone is gonna want one."

Sam laughed and opened it up before the chair. Just like with the bars, she strapped the white belt around Evan's torso for added support.

"Just like with the bars, just hold yourself up. When you feel steady, take a step and then move it just a little. We don't need to go far today." She tightened the strap behind her.

Evan looked at the walker, to the rubber hand grips down to the rubber skid stoppers on the legs. It might have looked ridiculous at first but it meant mobility and independence. She reached to the hand grips and slid herself toward the end of the chair until her knees were above her ankles.

A simple motion that so many people took for granted: rising from a chair. Her fingers gripped the walker and her leg and hip muscles flexed. The effort made her muscles quiver and her shoulders almost spasm, but she forced herself upward until she had support on top of the walker with her arms. Samena's grip on the waist strap tightened.

"Are you steady?" she asked.

Evan nodded. It was too much effort to speak right now and it might break her concentration. She glanced down to her feet and shifted them to the side in a wider stance, just like she had done before on the parallel bars.

"Okay," Samena said from behind her. "Whenever you're ready, take a step and then support your weight to move the walker."

She bit her lower lip and flexed her fingers around the grips. Just like walking on the parallels. Her right foot moved forward and she shifted her weight to the right hip. Muscles contracted, unsteady at first but held their own. She loosened her elbows, feeling more of the weight on that hip and up her spine. *A few inches, that's all.* The walker slid forward, barely above the ground. Her elbows locked again, putting more of her weight back onto the walker.

"Good job," Samena said, moving with her.

Without prompting, Evan's left foot stepped forward and her weight shifted again, just like the last time. It wasn't far, but the walker moved each time, and she got further away from the wheelchair. Turning around proved to be a little more of a challenge, but she managed it with a little extra support from Samena. She returned to the chair and settled back into the seat. The muscles in her legs twitched now that they had been asked to do much more work than they had in months.

The thrill of walking left her heart racing and her fingers shaking. "I want to do it again."

"Patience." Samena said and slid the walker aside. "Remember, baby steps. We'll do some cycling and then another round of the walker a little later. Then more and more of it each day until you no longer need the chair."

Evan smiled. She couldn't contain it any longer. "But I will eventually get rid of the chair for good."

"Yes," Samena said with a nod. "Absolutely."

The therapist helped her to the recumbent bike and left her to the workout. It warmed up her legs fast enough that she got in stride with the cycle quicker than usual until sweat began to drip from her brow.

Her cell phone vibrated in her pocket and she glanced down. Dr. Barnhart. That was fast. Fast enough that it made her palms sweaty and she took in deep breath before she answered.

"Hey," the pathologist said on the other line. "I've got some results for you."

"I wasn't expecting it so quick," Evan said and glanced up to Samena, who was busy putting away medicine balls.

"Well, we got a new electrophoresis machine and it's awesome. You gave me a chance to use it today, and it's good that you did."

She slowed the pace on the cycle. "What did you dig up?"

"I should be asking you the same question," Barnhart said, her voice dropping again just like it did last time. "I don't know what prompted to you ask, but your hunch was right."

Evan sat up and stopped cycling. She pulled her feet from the straps and sat upright on the seat. "What did you find?"

"First of all, DNA won't be back for a while. But I have some chromosomes here that I didn't believe, so I ran them a couple more times." Barnhart paused, and Evan wasn't sure if it was for effect of if she expected her to say something. A noise happened in the background and then silenced. Barnhart must have been waiting to be alone for this conversation. "I got back a set of XY chromosomes."

Evan's grip on the phone tightened. "But Sinclair's baby was a girl."

"Yeah," Barnhart said. "This is not amniotic fluid from Angela Sinclair's baby. Someone injected her with this."

It might have been from the effort of the workout, but Evan had a hard time catching her breath.

Not mine. That's what the spirit had whispered to her, and she was right.

"I'm not going to ask right now how you knew to look for this," Barnhart said in a near whisper now. "But I have to open this case now. There's enough with this sample to suspect foul play, so I need to inform the state board and the police. I think someone killed this poor girl and her baby. The DNA from the fluid won't match the patient or her baby, I'm one hundred percent positive of that."

No wonder the entity was angry. She had been murdered and nobody knew about it until right now. This was the answer she had been waiting to find.

Evan swallowed hard. Her throat had gone dry in the last few seconds and she just wanted water. "Thanks."

"Hey, Evan," Barnhart said before she could end the call, "don't tell anyone else about this for right now. Let me take care of things on this end. Once this gets out, it's going to be huge."

The pathologist hung up and Evan looked at her phone. Barnhart was right: this was going to not only be huge, this was going to be enormous. But she couldn't promise to keep it just to herself. There was only one other person she trusted with this information, and Paul needed to know about it now. Her fingers danced over the text keyboard and sent the message straight to his phone.

At least he had managed to get a few hours of sleep. But when his phone alerted him about a text message, Paul bolted out of bed and scrambled to the night stand.

Despite the heavy sleep still in his eyes, the message made his muscles stiffen. The key to everything Evan had gone through was in the amniotic fluid sample, and she had just proven it. She had told him to believe her, and now he was grateful that he had. Something out there had tried to contact her, to tell her its story and now she began to unravel it. And all because she listened.

He pulled a fresh t-shirt over his head and slipped into a pair of worn jeans. There wasn't time to shave. Evan had uncovered one missing piece of this puzzle, and he knew where he could find the next one. But he had to get to the hospital before shift change. He forced his feet into the unlaced shoes by the door and raced out of his apartment.

The drive back to St. John's took far too long, or that's how it felt in all the slow late afternoon traffic. It was the worst time to travel back downtown but he had no choice. He needed to do this for Evan. At least the garage was emptying out and he found a space on the second floor, something he could never do in the mornings.

He hurried into the building and up the stairwell to the second floor. There was no guarantee that she was here today, but he had to try. The glass doors on the labor and delivery unit stood closed with the entry system waiting along the door. He pressed the buzzer and listened to the series of beeps until the unit secretary answered.

"How can I help you?"

"I need to speak to Asha," he said.

"One moment." The entry system went quiet and his knee jiggled, mostly in an unconscious effort to will the doors to open.

A click sounded and the red light on the entry pad changed to green. He pushed the doors open and hurried down the corridor to the nurses' station. A group of women, all decked in pink scrubs, stood around the medication bay and computers. It was almost shift change and the fresh staff waited for sign out to the earlier crew. And one of those early nurses was Asha, but she didn't stand among the group.

"Can I help you?" one of the young nurses looked up at him from the computer where she charted.

"I need to see Asha? Is she here?"

"Yeah," she said and looked at her screen where the individual patient rooms were listed. "She's in room seven, but she should be out here soon. Do you want to wait or should I give her a message?"

"I'll wait." Hell, yes, he would wait. This was probably the most important task he had ever undertaken in his life. He wasn't about to just let it go now.

Paul stepped aside, out of the mayhem of women that milled around the station. From his time as a medical student, he understood labor and delivery nurses well enough to know they weren't going to tolerate someone getting in the way of their work. Everything they had to do involved two lives: a mother and a baby. There was no room for error. And that's why he had to see her. Asha remembered that day, and something she had said still troubled him. Now he knew why.

As soon as she stepped around the corner, her eyes creased in a smile. "Dr. Williams," she said as she removed a stethoscope from around her neck and draped it over a coat hook along the wall. "Back for more? Couldn't get enough of us last time?"

He wanted to smile and forced the best one he could, but this was too important. "Can I talk to you real quick? It'll just take a second."

"Sure," she said and motioned for him to sit at the computer station with her.

He grimaced and clasped his hands together. "I was hoping to talk in private."

"Oh, okay." The smile faded from her lips and she walked around him, encouraging him to follow her. She led him down the labor hall and into an empty patient room. The dim security light glowed above the neatly made bed, adorned with white linens and a patterned bedspread. As soon as they were in the dark of the room, she turned back to him. "What is it? You look troubled by something."

"I just . . . yeah, I just need to ask you one more question about that same thing we talked about before."

"Angela Sinclair."

"Yes." He glanced back out the door. Evan had warned him not to tell anyone about what she had discovered, but there was a way to learn more without revealing their secret. He faced her again. "You said something that I just keep coming back to. Now, you remember Dr. Sorenson being there to see the patient that night, but the doctors aren't usually there."

She nodded and her eyebrows rose. "Yeah, but he was on the floor already. And since he was here, he just went and saw her when he was done with his other patient. That's not unusual. All the docs will do that if they're hanging around anyway."

"What was he doing here? I remember you saying there was a procedure or something."

"I think it was an amniocentesis."

Paul had never seen one, but it was one of those procedures that he had to learn about as a medical student. It involved drawing off amniotic fluid from a womb with a needle and syringe under ultrasound guidance, usually for diagnostic testing of some kind.

"I'm sure it was," she continued. "I remember the ultrasound tech was here."

"Was it just the two of them?"

"No. There's usually three or four people there for the procedure, not counting the patient and her family. There will be a tech from radiology to do the ultrasound during the procedure, and usually a nurse or two to help prep the patient and to assist the doctor. I remember it was a woman with twins and she was having some kind of complication – I'm not sure exactly what kind – but Dr. Sorenson did an amniocentesis to assess for maturity. He was looking to see if the babies were mature enough to be delivered."

Paul clenched his hands. There were at least two others in the room that night besides Dr. Sorenson. And all of them had access to that patient's amniotic fluid. This was the key, the last piece of the puzzle.

"Do you remember the nurse that might have been in that procedure? Or even the ultrasound tech?"

She winced. "Ultrasound techs come and go. There's no way I would remember who came that night."

His shoulders fell, but then Asha smiled at him again.

"But I know the nurse. Pam Harper. She's a good friend of mine and works in ICU now. She actually quit labor and delivery shortly after that night. I think the whole thing freaked her out a bit."

"Pam?" he clarified, trying to keep his voice steady and not sound too excited.

"Yeah. You know her? She works tonight, probably starting shift real soon."

He grabbed her shoulders and she laughed. "I could kiss you right now."

"Please don't."

"Yeah." He nodded and rushed from the room, leaving her alone in the dark.

Paul hurried past the nurses' station despite the fleeting glances of the day and night shift. They buzzed him out of the unit. With the days he spent in and out during visitor's hours in the ICU, he knew very well how to get there from here.

Chapter 38

Paul's badge allowed him access through the security doors of the ICU, a privilege that he didn't have on the labor and delivery unit. As an Emergency Medicine resident, he was often required to accompany a patient from the ER to the Intensive Care Unit. But now, it allowed him access to find Pam Harper. And luckily, she was someone he had contact with on a frequent basis.

He rounded the first nurse station, but it was the third one where the shift change sign-out would happen. When he came on the station, the nurses there were in the middle of discussions, like a dozen different one-on-one huddles while they went over the events of the day regarding every patient.

Paul slowed and leaned against the wall, his eyes pinned to the woman who took notes beside her day-shift counterpart. Pam's short hair had been recently colored, shining a radiant copper (almost burgundy) to hide the grays that had started to sprout. Her dark-rim glasses perched on her nose, and behind them the thick mascara and dark eye-shadow of someone who was fifty trying to look twenty.

When the sign-out was done, the day-shift nurse stood and Pam tucked her notes into the pocket of her dark blue scrubs. Paul stepped into the station and she stopped with a smile when she saw him. Her rouged cheeks bulged with a smile.

"Dr. Williams," she said and scanned his attire. "You don't look like you're ready to work tonight."

"I'm not working, actually," he said and flashed her his dimple smile. Whatever it took to get her to open up to him. Under her heavy makeup, he always noticed the way she blushed when he came up there and said hello to her. She was a recently divorced woman and every single doctor on staff knew about it.

He stepped up beside her and stuffed his hands into his pockets. "I was hoping I could talk to you, ask you something."

"Sure," she said and pumped her eyebrows a couple times. She moved to the chair at the computer bank and he sat across from her. "What can I do for you, sweetie?"

Stay cool. Just let her flirt. "I talked to Asha today and she sent me to you for help."

"Oh, Asha," she said and smiled. The blush faded from her cheeks. "How's my girl doing? We're supposed to get drinks this weekend, make sure she remembers that."

He nodded, but he had no idea what she was talking about and wasn't going to be a messenger boy back to labor and delivery.

"Okay. Um, she sent me here because a friend and I are working on something and a question came up. Asha was hoping that you could fill in the blanks."

"I'll do my best. What is it?"

"It's about something that happened the night Angela Sinclair died."

The smile fell from her face and she leaned back in her chair. "Oh, that night. Yeah. I remember a lot from that night. Honey, it's why I'm not over there anymore. I'd rather be here, where half the patients are expected to die some time while they're here. These people have mostly lived their lives. They're sick. That poor girl wasn't sick. What happened to her was tragic, but I wasn't her nurse that night. I didn't even see the girl until they called a code. I ran into the room but there was a whole mess of people in there and she was already dead. I can't tell you much more than that."

Paul rested his elbows on his knees and leaned forward. Nobody else was in the station right now, but he still kept his voice low. "Well, it's more about what you remember from before all that happened. Asha said you were assisting on an amniocentesis."

She shrugged, the corners of her mouth depressing. "Yeah. A simple amnio, nothing special. Everything went normal. We finished the procedure, the patient did just fine."

"Do you remember who was in the room with you that night?"

Pam took in a deep breath and her eyes drifted to some point above his head while she thought. "Well, Dr. Sorenson was there. It was his patient and he was doing the procedure. And there was an ultrasonographer. The patient of course, and her husband. I think that was it."

"Do you recall who the ultrasound tech was?"

"Some girl, I don't remember seeing her before, but there are so many radiology techs. It's hard to keep track of them all."

She wasn't allowed to reveal the name of the patient or her husband, so there was no point in asking. And he knew it to be true: it was difficult to know every tech that worked in radiology.

"Was there anything else about that night that seemed odd or anything?" he asked.

The cheeky grin appeared on her face again. "Why are you asking about this?"

Of course, she would ask that. The one thing he couldn't tell her. He sighed and let his head hang. There had to be something to keep her talking, and then he swallowed the tight constriction in his throat. He glanced up to her.

"I can't say right now, but I'll buy you a drink sometime if you think of anything else," he said.

"I will definitely take you up on that offer."

He stood, but this was not how he had hoped to leave the ICU. There wasn't any more that Pam could add to the story that Asha hadn't already told him.

"Just give me a call if you think of anything," he said. "I'll see you around."

He turned away from her and stuffed his hands into his pockets again.

"You know, Paul," she said from behind him. "There was one thing."

The breath caught in his chest and he turned back to her.

She approached him and put her hands on her hips, the nails a bright lacquer of red and black artwork. "I'm not sure if this will be helpful, but there was something that always bugged me about that night. Something I had pushed out of my mind after everything else that happened."

"Anything," he said. "I'll take it."

"We did that amniocentesis and it was pretty routine. Dr. Sorenson pulled off three syringes of fluid. I remember that exactly, because I handed him each syringe. But when I cleaned up after the procedure, I only found two. I never knew where the third one had gone."

That was the missing puzzle piece, right there.

"Where do you think it went?" he asked in a whisper.

"I'm not sure. Dr. Sorenson left the room first, then the ultrasound tech. The patient and her husband stayed behind, but I don't think they would have swiped it. I had just assumed that I lost it in all the clean-up."

"But you never actually believed that, did you," Paul said.

"Not for one second, honey." She winked at him. "I hope that helps."

He smiled at her. Unlike Asha, Pam would welcome a kiss. He leaned in and pecked her on the cheek, which made the flush brighten under her make up. "You bet it does."

"Any time, doctor," she said with a smile as he turned away from her.

Evan would forgive him a single kiss on a lonely woman's cheek. Especially if it meant giving her some important information, something she desperately needed to know.

Chapter 39

The sound of the television chattered in the background, but Evan gave it little attention with Paul right next to her on the bed. He had already relayed the events of the last couple of days, especially the revelation from Pam Harper. All of it now swirled in her thoughts and drove out any possibility of concentrating on the TV. She rested her head on his out stretched arm and curled into his chest. With the rest of the lights off, the television flashed in colors of black and white with the classic movie channel playing.

"One of these days, we need to set a wedding date," Paul whispered. The lights glistened like tiny strobes in his eyes.

"One of these days we will." She smiled at him.

His hand moved through the short strands of blonde hair that had begun to cover the scar along her scalp. "Do you plan on keeping it short? Because I like it this way."

"It's low maintenance, so maybe."

When his hand slid down her neck, he leaned in closer, his forehead touching hers. "Do you still want to marry me?"

She pulled back just a little, enough to see his eyes in the flashing lights of the TV. Those dimples showed along his cheeks, but he didn't smile. The weight of the ring on her finger reminded her of the moment he had popped the question and the way it made her chest seize. But that had all gone away. Maybe that anxiety had been replaced by everything else since that time, and now she was sure of one thing.

"Yes, I do. And when I get out of here, I don't want to wait. I don't want a puffy dress or an expensive venue. I just want to get on with our lives, even if I have to do it in a wheelchair."

She placed her hands on both sides of his face and kissed him. At this moment, she knew this was the thing she wanted most.

"So, should we try to get you out of here tomorrow?" he said.

She drew back onto her elbows. "You mean it?"

"Yeah, why not?"

"I guess we could try. I want to do physical therapy first, and I should tell Samena."

"Okay," he said and grasped her hand, pulling it toward his chest. "I'll talk to the rehab doc and get him to discharge you a little earlier than they had expected."

"And then what?"

A yawn peeled from his mouth and he blinked his eyes to try and keep them open. "Then, I move you into my place for now. Until we have everything straightened out. Sound good to you?"

"Sounds perfect." She stifled the yawn in her throat that he must have triggered.

His eyelids closed and he took in a deep breath. "Good night."

Her fingers squeezed his hand and she closed her eyes as well. The television continued playing its movie marathon, and she found the occasional flash of light from it comforting under her eyelids. Voices of another time, the golden age of Hollywood, spoke in low tones. The sounds drifted into her ears like a lullaby, the cadence sounding like a Shakespeare verbiage that she might have heard in literature class back in high school. A man's voice, theatrical and dramatic, muttered the words of Hamlet, before her world plunged into deep sleep.

"Tis now the very witching time of night, When churchyards yawn and hell itself breathes out Contagion to this world."

A metallic, wet odor filled her nose. Evan's eyes drifted open to the dark room, her throat tightening against the smell of blood somewhere in the shadows. The sting in her vision cleared and she rolled away from Paul.

The wraith stood at her bedside, staring down at her in a steady gaze somewhere behind the curtain of long dark hair. Before Evan could cry out, the entity moved in a sudden twitch. Its pale arm and fingers reached out like a twisted aspen branch and touched her face. The instant cold burned against her skin. The cry froze in her throat and she couldn't move. It leaned in toward her, the moldy scent of wet earth enveloping her and turning her stomach.

Cloudy eyes held her in its gaze from between strands of hair. Its crooked fingers moved toward her eyes until the cold frosted over her corneas. Evan tried to back away, to scream. Anything to get Paul's attention. But the spirit held her fast in its unnatural power. The darkness in the room blurred and swam in a fog until she could no longer make out the figure before her. But it was still there. She knew it by the smell, even though it had blinded her.

Evan clenched her eyes, the only thing she was able to control. Her ribs couldn't take in a breath. There was only the cold, blinding touch of the spirit at the bedside.

The thing leaned close enough to her that she felt the tickle of hair on her cheek. In a single breath, the spirit spoke only one word. "*See.*"

A powerful breath filled her lungs in that moment and the cold vanished. Her eyes flew open, no longer blind. But something had changed. Darkness still covered everything, lit only by the city lights from the windows. The room was empty except the bed on which she lay, and now she lay there alone. Paul had vanished and so had the rest of the furniture.

Evan sat up and glanced around the room, but the spirit was no longer at her bedside.

"See."

The whisper filled the room again, its breath rushing just past her ear.

A latch resounded and the door creaked open. The spirit stood there, her dark hair now pulled back from her pale dead face and her eyes a milky white. Something had changed, though. Her hospital gown now hung over her frame without the blood stains that had previously soaked it. An ID band hung from her wrist, the same wrist that now reached its hand out to her.

Angela didn't need to say anything. Evan knew exactly what she wanted, what she needed now. This was her world, a plane in between life and death where fog drifted over a forest floor and she waited for someone to hear her. This place was where Angela had been stuck for eight years. Now, Evan could listen to everything the spirit needed to reveal.

The girl's hand stayed outstretched, waiting for her to respond. Evan swung her legs over the edge of the bed and let her bare feet touch the floor. The tiles were solid white, not the hard wood of her previous room. Not cold, not warm. Just there. In the place where things were not the same.

Her muscles tensed and joints moved with ease until she stood on the firm floor. There was no wobbling or weakness here. Angela made sure of it. Evan stepped toward her, to the open door. A single round mirror perched along the wall and she caught a reflection of her own face, lit by the city outside the hospital. The short light hair and thin neck were unmistakably hers, as were the clouded corneas that now matched Angela's.

She turned back to the girl with the outstretched hand. Everything about her and this place looked so clear despite her milky vision. She extended her hand and grasped Angela's. The skin of her hand stayed cold and stiff, just like she remembered from when the spirit had touched her the first time. But it didn't hurt. The girl turned and drifted into the corridor, and Evan followed with their hands clasped.

Everything around them had lost its sense of time and place, plunged into silence and emptiness. The hallway was dim, like no light would ever reach into the corners. Nobody walked the unit anymore. It was as abandoned as the north wing had been. Nothing moved here but the two of them – the dead holding onto the living.

Angela's ghost moved silently toward the hub and Evan followed without hesitation. Wherever the spirit wanted to go, she would stay with her in this realm. And then she turned to the north wing and drifted before the double white doors. Evan stepped up beside her when she stopped and stared through the windows, into the black abyss that was the old labor and delivery unit.

Her milky cataract eyes moved to gaze at Evan, and she looked back through her cloudy corneas. Their fingers curled together, locked in their bound fate.

"See," Angela said again in a breathy voice that hardly broke past her lips.

The doors opened inward without the chain that had once locked them. It was the only sound Evan had heard since her eyes had opened to this otherworld. A loud click resonated throughout the empty seventh floor. A gust of stale air breathed outward and danced over her skin, bristling the hair on her forearms.

When Evan followed the spirit into the north wing, everything morphed from the dull gray-blue light of this realm to a warm and colorful world again, just like the one she had left. No longer abandoned, the north wing teemed with life. Nurses in their characteristic pink scrubs stood along the corridor with their mobile charting computers outside of the patient rooms. Lights along the ceiling and dotted against the walls glowed a warm pink-gold to ward off the dark of night outside the windows.

With all the staff that bustled along the unit, nobody seemed to notice the two of them at all. Evan glanced to the spirit, her hand still holding onto its cold, clay fingers. Angela still carried the blue hue of the otherworld, dead and out of place with her white eyes that stared forward. And Evan's skin held the same pallor. She was sure that her eyes looked identical as well. Two spirits among the living now.

Angela moved with purpose beyond the nurses that crossed their path without noticing them. Evan glanced back just to see if there was any recognition at all, but the spirit's grip continued to pull her forward. This was not what she was meant to see, not yet. The thought crossed her mind to ask Angela where they were going, but the words just wouldn't form on her lips. Like the days after she first woke up in the ICU. Everything ran through her mind, all that she wanted to say and do. But they couldn't be spoken.

Evan glanced back down the hall and it all came back to her in an eerie memory. She had been here before, in the wheelchair of course. All the way down the hall and almost to the old nurse's station.

All the way to room 706.

She didn't doubt it, not once. The spirit slowed as they approached the very same room. A warm light came from inside the room, accompanied with voices. At least three of them, and all women.

Angela's white eyes turned back to Evan. She knew what the spirit wanted and she didn't need to say it this time. This was what she needed to see.

The entity released her hand and Evan stepped into the room, taking in everything with her cataract eyes, because they could now visualize what had once happened here. That's why Angela gave her this sight, so she could finally *see*.

A hospital bed stood in the center of the room, the same bed that was there the night Evan had come to this empty unit. But it was no longer in solitude. Someone was lying there, the head propped up so she could sit upright. Her long dark hair fell in thick beautiful waves down her shoulders and framed her young face.

The face of a sixteen-year-old, scared pregnant girl.

The face of Angela Sinclair when she was alive.

Chapter 40

Angela's spirit gazed quietly over the scene of herself lying in that bed, but she watched without emotion. None of the raging anger that Evan had seen coming from the shadowy corners of her room at night. She just stood there with her blue-gray skin and white eyes and watched the past unfold.

A woman came around the corner and Evan stepped aside, afraid she would run into her. And, at the same time, Evan knew she wouldn't because she wasn't really here at all. The woman approached the bedside and the living Angela looked up at her with hopeful eyes.

"You doing okay, baby?" the woman said, and Evan recognized her voice the moment she spoke. Judy Sinclair, Angela's mother.

Angela nodded. "Still cramping but I'm okay." The girl's pregnant belly bulged under the white linen blanket.

A shelf of monitors topped with a computer beeped with every beat of the baby's heart. Cords extended from the monitor and toward Angela's belly, diving under the blanket and surely strapped to her abdomen. A single IV pole stood next to the bed, running sterile saline into a line directly into Angela's vein. A nurse stood at the computer and typed in a series of notes, oblivious that Evan watched from behind her back.

"Hey, I'm going to run and grab some dinner real quick," Judy said. "But I'll be back soon. You be okay without me?"

Angela smiled and placed a hand over her swollen abdomen. "I'm fine. I'm not going anywhere."

"She'll be here for at least another hour or so," the nurse said and turned her head. This must be Asha, the nurse that Paul had met. "You've got plenty of time."

"Okay," Judy said and flashed her cell phone at her. "But call me if you need something before I get back."

Angela rolled her eyes. "Mom, just go."

Judy leaned down, planted a kiss on her daughter's forehead and stepped out of the room. Evan watched her leave, but she wanted to plead with her to stay. Maybe if she stayed, nothing would have happened. But it did happen. This wasn't like watching live TV. It was more like a recording: it would always be there, playing on an endless loop of tragedy.

"Alright," the nurse said and logged out of the computer. "I'll leave you to it for a while. We're just going to watch this baby and make sure you're not in labor. In the meantime, you can catch up on some television or I can bring you some magazines."

"TV's just fine." The girl said and grabbed for the remote on the side table.

"If you need anything, just use your call button." Asha signaled to the red button at the bottom of the remote.

"Okay."

The nurse turned and stepped back through the door. Another person who left this unfortunate girl alone.

Evan glanced back to the spirit again, but she stood still. Unwavering and staring forward as though she waited. As much as she wanted to ask what she needed to do, she knew it would be a futile effort.

The living Angela turned on the TV mounted on the wall across the bed and rested back against the pillow. Like the others on the unit, she was completely unaware of the entities that watched this all unfold. She just focused on the sitcom that played, with its canned laughs and fake sets. The rhythmic beating of the baby's heart continued, strong and healthy through the monitor.

It wouldn't be long now. Angela's final moments would be played for Evan to watch, and unable to ever intervene.

The sound of the monitor and the occasional laugh from the girl kept this moment as serene as possible. Evan didn't want it to end, but she knew it would when she felt the chill come from the spirit standing next to her.

The door opened and clicked shut quickly. Evan turned and saw Dr. Sorenson enter the room. His long white coat was still unbuttoned over his dark blue scrubs. As soon as the door was closed, he turned to face his patient. But he didn't smile. His pupils had dilated and his breathing had picked up just a little faster than normal.

"What's going on?" he asked.

The living Angela sat upright and turned off the television the moment she saw him. "I didn't know you would be here."

"Well, I am," he said, his tone brusque. Not sympathetic, like Evan would have expected a terrified pregnant teenager's doctor to be. "So why are you here?"

"I thought I was having contractions," she said, her hands moving to her abdomen again.

"Are you sure this isn't regarding the thing we talked about today?"

She shook her head, her eyes getting glassy and her forehead wrinkling. "No, I swear."

He stepped up to the monitor and examined the fetal heart rate tracing, including the contraction strip. "Well, I don't see many contractions here." He glanced over to her. "Is your mom here?"

"No. I mean . . . she was, but she left for a few minutes to get something to eat."

"Did you tell her?" His voice dropped and almost sounded like a growl.

Angela shook her head again, this time more frantic. "No, I didn't."

Sorenson put his hands on his hips and sighed. "Are you lying to me?"

"I promise." Her voice quivered and Evan thought she was about to cry. "But I need to tell her something. She keeps asking me."

His jaw clenched and his fingers dug into his hips. "I told you. You have to keep quiet."

Evan took a step back. She had never heard him speak like this to anyone. Like he was scared and angry and horrible all at once. Pressure tightened in her chest and she felt like she couldn't catch her breath. No. She didn't want to hear anymore. Another step back, but this time the spirit turned back to her. Its milky gaze caught her and wouldn't let her move again. It needed her to *see*.

Tears streamed down living-Angela's cheeks now. "I won't. I swear. I won't tell her."

Sorenson grabbed her arm and the girl cried out. "What did I say? This has to be our secret. You can't tell your mother, your teachers, my wife, nobody. Remember what I told you: if you say anything, your mother could get hurt. That baby could get hurt."

The hollow pressure in Evan's chest expanded and she wanted to vomit. *Please, I don't want to hear anymore.*

"Do you understand me?" he said with another forceful jerk of her arm.

She only nodded with tears soaking her face.

He released her arm and put his hands back on his hips again. "Now get up. Go in the bathroom and wash your face before someone sees you."

The girl could hardly see through her tears to remove the blankets and swing her legs over the edge of the bed. Sorenson moved aside and unplugged the monitors from the machine. The trail of cords dropped around her legs while she took a step, but the IV tubing pulled tight.

"You've got to take that with you," he said, his tone mocking.

She sobbed and looked back to the IV pole. Her small fingers wrapped around the pole and rolled it with her. She took waddling steps under her large abdomen draped with the hospital gown.

Evan looked back to the spirit at her side. She still gazed silently at the scene, but she wore the same gown, although it was cast in a blue-gray hue. And the biggest difference was the absence of her pregnant abdomen. She had come to this other-world without the child she had lost along the way.

The IV pole rattled with each step living-Angela took. Sorenson glared at her back as she moved. Then his hand slipped into the pocket of his white coat.

Evan knew what he had kept in there, but she hadn't realized it until now. The hollow pit in her chest grew. She wanted to double over and force herself to breathe, but it was too late.

A syringe appeared in his hand, the barrel full of straw-colored clear fluid. At least ten milliliters of it. His narrowed glare followed Angela, her steady gate still moving toward the open bathroom door.

The hollow pit exploded and Evan found her breath. She filled her lungs and shouted at the girl, but there was no sound in this world. All of it was a futile attempt to change something that could never change.

The girl's hand touched the threshold of the door. At that moment, Sorenson grabbed her and turned her around until her back slammed into the wall. She gasped and the IV pole tipped over. Before she could scream, his forearm pressed down against her neck and she cried, but the sound only came out as a low squeal. Her face went red and her eyes darted to the door, looking for anyone to help her.

And for a brief moment, Evan thought those eyes found her own and pleaded for salvation.

Sorenson brought the syringe to his mouth, pulled off the needle cap with his teeth and found the IV port. He plunged the needle into the port and pushed the fluid in as fast as it would go. The girl wriggled her hand free and grabbed at his arm. Anything to get air. But he held her against the wall.

A smile formed on his mouth and he pulled away from her, releasing the pressure on her neck. She almost stumbled but caught herself against the wall and coughed as she tried to fill her lungs.

"You won't ever tell a soul," he said and capped the syringe again, placing it back into his pocket.

She looked up at him, her hand against the sore spot on her neck. Her face was still red and wet with tears. "What are you doing? I said I wouldn't say a thing."

"What am I doing? Let's say it's a little experiment." His head tilted as he looked at her. "Something we read in text books in medical school. A little amniotic fluid in the wrong place. Let's just see what happens."

She coughed again and leaned over, her other hand supported on her knee. "What are you talking about?"

He didn't say anything else, but just backed away from her, his eyes narrowed and lips curled into a smirk.

Angela coughed again, this time a wheezing, choking sound. The hand at her throat moved to her chest, and she coughed over and over. Her frantic eyes glanced up to find him. The sclera had bloomed into hemorrhages. Another cough sent a spray of blood across the floor. The wheezing in her chest grew louder and her skin developed a pale shade of gray.

Her knees wobbled and she glanced down between the volleys of choking sounds in her throat. The IV site in her arm oozed with blood that dripped in faster rivulets down to her fingers.

Splash. Splash.

The sound came from under her gown. A burst of bright red fluid erupted under the white fabric and poured like water down her legs.

The metallic odor of the blood hit Evan and she tried to scream again, but she knew it was useless.

The girl fell to the ground, her limbs sliding in the growing pool of blood on the floor. Dr. Sorenson looked down at her, at the hemorrhages in her eyes that now trickled from the corners of her lids. Her shaking, bloodied arm reached out to him and a gurgling choke came from her throat. He stepped back, a grimace on his face, in case she touched his clean, white coat with her bloody fingers. Her lungs fought for air that would never come.

"That baby will never see this world," he whispered to her. "I did you a favor. Now your mother will never have to hear how

I knocked you up. If you had listened to me from the beginning and ended this pregnancy, this never would have happened. You did this to yourself."

Her fingers still reached for him with whatever life they had left, but he stepped further away from her. He glanced to the clock on the wall and then back down to her. "Just a few more minutes, I suppose. Then I'll be off to meet the wife for dinner." He smiled at her, a wide self-satisfied grin.

Angela's eyes gaped but no more sound came from her throat. Her arm went limp and collapsed in the expanding pool that surrounded her crumpled body. A finger twitched and her neck spasmed a few times, but that was all she had left in the neurons that supplied her brain. Maybe her open eyes could still see even though her pupils dilated. Those eyes looked blankly out into the room but didn't follow Sorenson as he stepped through the door and closed it behind him.

The spirit didn't move beside Evan. It's face still remained emotionless like cold porcelain. She followed its white gaze and it was then that she realized the body of Angela stared back at her with those wide open, hemorrhaged and dead eyes.

Evan wanted to cry more than anything else at that moment. She had seen enough, everything that she was meant to *see*. She leaned over and supported her hands on her weakening knees, but the tears wouldn't come. And maybe they never would with her cataract eyes that could see into this world.

The spirit turned its milky gaze toward her again. Its cold fingers reached out to her, but it didn't want to lead her anywhere this time. The first two fingers extended toward her face, just like it did when it came to her in the apartment and woke her up to bring her here. Those fingers twitched before they touched the side of her face.

When they made contact, the cold zapped into her flesh and Evan gasped.

"*See*," the spirit whispered again.

Evan's eyes flew open and she sat up with a powerful gasp that resonated through the room. She grasped at her chest, at the residual pain left from the gaping hollow of pain and rage that the spirit had bestowed on her.

Paul jumped out of bed and stumbled across the floor. "Shit," he shouted. "What the . . . Evan! What the hell?"

Her eyes searched the dark of the room, now plunged into inky darkness and not the blue gray of the otherworld. The ambient sounds of life returned: the clock ticking, the rustling of the bed linens. And her skin was no longer the color of death.

That must mean her eyes were normal again too.

She breathed hard, her heart beating like it had just fought through a marathon. The images of what she had just seen raced through her thoughts, burning at the edges and screaming at her to *see*. She balled her fists and pressed them against her temples, especially at the edge of the plate just under her skin. The flesh rubbed against the metal, causing just enough pain to make the images fade.

"Evan," Paul said again and placed his hand against her back.

She flinched, his skin hot against hers. Everything hurt now, but at least it kept the truth at the edge for now.

It wasn't going to stay there, though.

Angela Sinclair would make sure of it.

Chapter 41

"Are you sure it wasn't a dream?" Paul said, his arms around Evan and her head wedged in the angle between his neck and shoulder.

"What I saw was the truth," she said. Her hands still trembled despite holding him against her.

His fingers brushed against the short hair growing at the back of her head. "I believe you. But it means I need to get you out of here today."

Evan pulled back, her eyes still wet. "How are we going to do that? We have nothing prepared. I'll need a wheelchair and a walker and –"

"Just let me worry about all that," he said. Paul released her and stood, pacing the room. "I'll talk to the floor supervisor and get them started on discharge stuff. The therapists can pull something together for now, and I can always come back to get anything else we might need later. We can do it."

Evan's shoulder's fell. A simple discharge from the therapy unit wasn't going to be enough. Eventually, Paul would have to come back here to work. And so would she, if everything went well. And Dr. Sorenson was their ultimate superior.

"How am I supposed to come back here knowing what he did?" she muttered.

"I'm going to work on that too. A transfer or something. There are training hospitals all over the country. We'll find something together. Maybe it won't matter. You said Dr. Barnhart was going to get the police involved. They are bound to discover this too."

When she looked up at him, he had turned away with his hands up behind his head and his arms tense. He made it sound simple, but it just wasn't that easy.

"So what do we do until then?" she asked.

"Just like Dr. Barnhart said. Don't tell anyone else what you know." He said and turned back to her. "If I can get things rolling this morning, you can be out of here by sundown."

Her fingers clenched into fists, but the sickening feeling still welled in her chest. Right in the same spot that the spirit had placed her fingers. The skin never looked the same there and ached now more than ever.

"Hey," Paul said and crouched down by the bedside. He placed his hands on her shoulders. "Just get through therapy today and I will come get you when everything is ready. Okay?"

She nodded but the ache intensified.

He leaned in and placed a quick kiss on her lips, but she wished he had lingered there a bit longer.

"Keep your cell on you," he said and flashed her his own phone in his hand. "I'll text you as I know more."

She picked up her phone from the night stand. This wasn't going anywhere, especially not today.

He opened the door and stopped. His dimpled smile turned back to her. "I love you."

"Love you too." She hadn't said it enough these last few weeks. There was no way she could say enough today.

Paul stepped through the door and the latch closed with a resounding click. Evan's fingers gripped tighter around the phone and glanced back at the oncoming sunrise over Lake Michigan.

Hopefully, the last one she would have to see from this room ever again.

Evan forced her knees to keep straight, contracting the quadriceps in the right leg until the wobble stopped. Her hands gripped onto the walker but supported most of her weight on her leg with the end of the step.

"Good," Samena said, "but just don't force it. You seem like you're trying to rush it today."

Evan probably was and didn't realize it. After everything that happened this morning, she knew that she needed to walk now more than ever. There wasn't time left to wait for it to get better.

You can't tell anybody. She bit her lip at the thought and moved her left leg forward in another step. "Just getting anxious to walk, that's all," she said. Not really so much of a lie, but it wasn't the whole truth.

"I don't blame you. Just make sure that you're not pushing it too hard. That's when you get injured."

But she was determined to push it anyway. Her legs needed to get stronger, and she had to make it across the room with the walker, even if it took her the rest of the session to do it. Speech and occupational therapy this morning went well enough that she was comfortable to do without them. Now, if she could just walk . . . .

"That's far enough," Samena said from behind her. "Time to turn around and head back."

But she wasn't even half-way across the room. She had to make her legs go farther. "I can keep going."

"I know you can, but you need to turn around and head back before your legs get too tired to do it."

She stepped forward again and pushed the walker further.

"Evan." Samena's voice hardened, a sound like she had never heard from her before.

"I can keep going." She pushed her other foot ahead and her knee wobbled. The quadriceps didn't want to respond this time and trembled under her weight. The walker shook with her grasp and Samena hurried behind her with the wheelchair.

As soon as she felt the edge of the chair bump into the back of her thighs, Evan released her weight from the walker and fell into the seat. The walker toppled to its side, but her insides fell like a drop from a roller coaster. Her legs didn't care what she wanted. They could only go so far. Evan hung her head, the tears filling the edges of her eyes.

"What was that about?" Samena said and stepped around the chair. She sat on the edge of the weight bench and placed a hand on Evan's back.

Evan pressed the heels of her hands into her eyes. "I – I just wanted to make it."

The therapist's hand moved in warming circles over her spine. "I understand. You're tired of this chair. But you have to be forgiving to your body. Be patient."

The muscles in her legs still quivered with a deep ache. "I'm tired of being patient."

Samena leaned in closer. "Is something else wrong?"

She can't know anything. It's just safer for everyone that way. Evan shook her head. "I just want to go home."

"Yeah. I see that Sally has submitted Discharge Planning paperwork for you." Samena leaned back on the bench and her hand slipped from Evan's back. "Looks like Paul may be trying to pull some strings for you."

After her legs gave out, she knew that it was a little premature, but she had to go even if Sam would be disappointed. "I'm sorry. I'm getting stir crazy. I promise I'll keep up with the therapy, though. I swear."

"I know you will." She tilted the walker back to upright and situated it in front of Evan again. "But I must say that I'll miss you. You've been a great patient."

Her therapy with Samena was one of the few things she looked forward to in her time on the therapy unit. Unless she found herself back here again, she might never see her after tonight.

"I'll miss you too," she said.

"Enough of this sappy girl talk." The therapist smiled and stood. She tapped the rubber grip of the walker. "Let's do it again, but stop when I say stop. Got it?"

Evan smiled and nodded. "Got it."

A vibration moved through the seat of the chair as Evan placed a hand on the walker. She reached into the side pocket of the chair and found her cell phone. The screen glowed with a new message.

Got the discharge started. Will have a wheelchair by 6pm tonight. Then we're outta here!

The tension in her shoulders eased and she slipped the phone back in the pocket.

"Everything good?" Samena asked from across the room with her clipboard in hand.

Evan smiled at her. "Oh yeah."

Chapter 42

The sunset had long faded, casting an inky blue haze across the city that spilled into Evan's room. The lamp lights on the night stand and dresser lit up the space where she collected everything that she had left to pack.

The room light barely reached into the dark of the bathroom, but she couldn't bring herself to go in there again. Not with the new mirror above the sink looking down on her. It wasn't the same one that had broken, but it still held a reflection that could look through from some other place. She hadn't seen Angela's face, with her empty white eyes, since she woke up that morning. And if she didn't see it ever again, it would be too soon. She had gathered everything out of the bathroom, or so she assumed. Whatever was left in there would have to stay.

Evan rolled away from the gaping door of the bathroom and faced the remainder of the apartment. Anything personal that belonged to her now lay in one of the two plastic bags resting on the bed. A monument to the end of her time on the therapy unit, and maybe even the hospital entirely. The thought left an empty void in the center of her abdomen. Her last three years had been spent at St. John's, including hundreds of sleepless nights in the operating room. And it was all about to dissolve.

She pushed the chair to the night stand and opened the drawer, just in case she had left anything there.

The glint of gold caught the light on top of the stand. She never would have seen it, all tucked in the back of the drawer behind the generic bible that had sat unopened in there for the last several weeks. Her throat tightened.

Her fingers grasped the chain and the locket dangled from her hand. It was a good thing she thought to look in here. Ever since she found it, she wanted to give it back to Judy Sinclair but just couldn't find the will to do it yet. The latch popped open under her thumb, revealing the small picture of a young Angela and her mother.

When she was finally out of here and back at Paul's place, she would make the effort to send it back to Mrs. Sinclair.

A loud buzz startled her and the locket slipped from her fingers. It dropped in her lap and the vibration of the cell phone shook the frame of her wheelchair again. She swallowed against a dry throat and reached into the pocket of the chair for her silenced phone that continued to buzz away with each ring. She grasped the locket – can't lose that – and turned the phone screen toward herself.

Her hand shook the moment she looked at it.

Sorenson's number. And it vibrated hot in the palm of her hand.

With a trembling thumb, she tapped the "Decline" button at the bottom of the screen and it went black again, taking the rhythmic buzzing with it. She closed her eyes and pressed her forehead down on the phone.

Just don't answer it. Once you get out of here, you never have to answer it again.

The incessant buzzing started again, making her jump and her heart start at a sprinting pace. The phone screen faced toward her, and she released the breath that had caught in her chest. She pressed the green button and put it on speaker.

"Hey Paul," she said. The effort to catch her breath was harder than she had expected.

"Hey. You okay?" he asked. "You sound funny."

She licked her dry lips and glanced back out to the darkening night through her windows. "I'm fine, just a little jumpy tonight. I'm ready to get out of here."

"Me too. I'm just parking the car and I'll be up in a few minutes, unless the elevator is broken again and then maybe a little longer."

"Hurry." The word sent shivers into her abdomen and she shot a glance to the dark bathroom mirror. "It's getting late and this place is starting to give me the creeps."

"Starting to?" he said. In the background, the car's engine shut down and a click of the driver's side door echoed into the phone. "I've been creeped out for days now."

The phone buzzed in her hand. Another incoming call. She turned the screen toward her and looked at the number.

Sorenson again.

She closed her eyes and declined the call once more. "Please hurry," she said into the speaker.

"I'm coming, I swear it."

"Okay. See ya soon."

The line went silent and she gazed at the black screen in her hand. Two minutes to walk from the garage to the central scheduling desk of the main floor. Wait for the elevator, which could take anywhere from thirty seconds to five minutes. And maybe a minute up to the seventh floor. It shouldn't take too long for him to get here, but it seemed like it had already been hours as she slipped the phone back into the pocket of her chair.

Just five or so minutes. And then gone for good.

She looked over the top of the lamp and out the windows. The city lights twinkled in the mid-winter chill that had settled with the coming fog. It floated over the lake and drifted toward the city, like something out of a Stephen King novel. There might be monsters in that fog. Or, even worse, angry spirits that called out for vengeance.

The locket pressed into her palm, the hinge still open and the picture looked out at her. Young Angela's smiling face rested in eternal youth and happiness in that moment of time. She would never have known that she would be dead in a few short years. And her killer still walked free for more years than that.

Not for long.

She closed the locket and strung it about her neck, tucking the locket under her shirt the way she used to with the engagement ring that now adorned her finger. It was a place to keep things safe. The ring had never left her side, and neither would the necklace until she sent it back to Judy.

The door latch unlocked behind her with a resounding click. Its mechanical hinges swung open with a low whir.

"That was fast," Evan said and glanced up to the reflection of Paul in the window.

But it wasn't Paul.

Her heart hammered in her chest at that moment and she turned back as much as the chair would allow, but all she saw was a man moving behind her. Peppered gray hair under a surgical cap. Dark blue scrubs. He stepped around her so quick that she didn't have time to see his face before a hand pressed a cloth painfully to her face, covering her nose and mouth.

Evan tried to scream and her hands grabbed at his thick forearm. Another arm clamped around her torso and pinned her arms down. The sound of her scream muffled against the cloth. A quick breath drew in a pungent smell like alcohol and it filled her nose and mouth. It pinched in her throat, making her pull in another breath just to clear the first one. But each attempt forced the chemical deep into her lungs.

Drowning on dry land. A clean breath never came, but the alcohol smell permeated into her skin and bloodstream. With each pulse, it closed the world around her and threw her into a darkening world where she couldn't hear herself scream.

But the cloudy white eyes looked at her through the dark. They watched her, and the girl screamed at Evan to wake up.

Chapter 43

"Wake up."

Something touched Evan's face hard enough to sting. The voice came at her again, but this time it wasn't Angela's. Her brain reeled with a swell of nausea. The alcohol smell still lingered in her nose, but almost beyond her ability to smell it. It left a sour lemon taste on her tongue, though.

Another sharp sting on her cheek made her eyes open, but nothing stayed in focus. It was all a little too dark to make out any other shapes but the person who stood in front of her. And even he was blurry.

He bent over and looked at her. A single beam of bright light flashed in her eyes, sending a white-hot shard of pain into her skull. She squeezed her eyes closed against the light, but a distinct slap against her face exploded into her cheek. She tried to move her hands to shield her face from another strike, but they wouldn't budge. Her muscles contracted and her bones shifted, but something held them down.

"It's time to wake up," he said.

The light moved and then settled off to her left, leaving the rest of the room in darkness again. Evan opened her eyes and focused on the one standing before her. The white LED beam of a flashlight shone from the surface of a table to her left and cast onto the man's form.

Dr. Sorenson glared as he stood in front of her, the light sending shadows across his face. He wore the same colored scrubs he had the night he killed Angela. There must be something about that dark blue that helped him deal with the things he did. Her eyes still tried to focus in and out on his face with the diminishing alcohol odor at the back of her throat. With the way her mind distorted the image in front of her, the nausea pinched in her stomach.

"Nice deep breaths," he said and leaned down to look at her again. "Gotta clear the chloroform out of your lungs."

She turned away from him. He had the same look in his eyes that he did with Angela when he stood there and belittled her. She couldn't stand to see it now. The harsh beam from the flashlight cast onto the strips of surgical tape that bound her wrists to the arms of her chair. No wonder she couldn't move her hands. Evan tugged on the tape but it held fast.

"You're not going anywhere." He straightened and stepped to the table that held the flashlight. "Not tonight."

She turned away from the light again and tried to focus her vision into the room. Expansive and dark. With a deep echo. Wherever they were, it was huge and dark and mostly empty. Except for the rows of big square shadows.

Washers and dryers. They were in the laundry room of the hospital. And at this time of night, it would normally be locked up and quiet. Nobody would be coming to work here until morning.

"I told you to let it go," Sorenson said from her left where he stood at the table. "I wish you would have listened to me."

Evan took in a deep breath. The air rushed oxygen into her blood stream and the dizziness lifted from her head.

He moved his hands in front the flashlight beam. A plastic cap clicked from the base of a needle and he dropped it to the surface of the table. The needle plunged into the bottle before him. Small in his fingers, with a clear liquid inside that he pulled into the syringe he held.

Evan tugged on the tape that bound her left wrist, then her right. It slipped only a little, but not enough to make a difference.

"I don't know what you're talking about," she lied and squinted toward the light.

A quick laugh escaped his throat, coarse and hard. "Of course you do." He held up the syringe to face-level and pushed the air out until a tiny squirt erupted from the end of the needle. He rested the syringe back on the table and produced two blue vinyl gloves from the back pocket of his scrubs.

"But what I still can't wrap my head around," he said and pulled a glove onto his left hand, "is how you figured it out. It's been all these years, and then you come along with your damaged brain and somehow put it all together." The other glove slipped onto his right hand.

"What —" she said but he moved in front of her like an angry wolf.

"Don't lie to me," he said, his jaw tight. "I got a very interesting phone call from Judy Sinclair this morning. She said that she got a call from the pathologist telling her that Angela's case was being re-evaluated, that the police and even the FBI are getting involved. She wanted to know if I knew anything about it. And you know what? I didn't. But now I do."

The thick, stale odor of liquor emanated from his throat when he spoke to her. The blood shot in his eyes pointed at her like daggers. He leaned closer to her, and Evan pressed back against the chair. The tape on her wrists pulled tight and pinched at the hair on her arms.

"I just need to know," he whispered, each word smelling like vodka. "How did you figure it out?"

She cringed away from him, from the anxious sweat that dripped from his temple and dampened his hair. The tape that bound her to the left arm of the chair slipped under the metal bar.

Evan eyed him and tried not to take in a breath. "You wouldn't believe me if I told you."

Sorenson's eyes pierced her as though they willed her to tell him. He stayed like that for a second and then grinned. "Fine. You know what, I don't care."

He backed away from her and turned to the table once again. His blue-gloved hand grasped the syringe.

"Well, if you know about Angela, then you know I'm good at making things look like a terrible accident," he said and drew the syringe to the edge of the flashlight.

She pulled on the tape again, her wrist dragging even further under the strap.

"What is that?"

"This is Fentanyl," he said and looked at the clear liquid as though it were his crowning achievement. "One of the most abused narcotics in and out of the hospital. You've been abusing it since you woke up from your accident. Dr. Williams has been supplying you with it from the drug dispenser in the ER. And when they find you in the morning, you will have suffered a fatal overdose, I'm afraid. Just another loss of a brilliant mind quenched too soon by opioid addiction."

The tape still held despite another tug. Sorenson moved in front of the chair and his hand grasped her forearm. She tried to pull her arm away, but he squeezed her with a vice grip. The needle glinted in the light and he drew it toward the hollow of her elbow.

"Wait," she said. "You don't have to do this."

"Of course I do." He said and flashed an angry look up to her again. "You gave me no choice. Just like Angela. This is my career. And both of you . . . girls," he said as though the word was sour on his tongue, "want to ruin it."

Her throat had gone dry and her heart pounded in rapid beats. "If you kill me, your secret will still get out. The pathologist knows about the amniotic fluid from Angela's chest."

The smile that formed made her stomach drop. The needle pulled back for a moment. "Yeah. Those samples will have a way of disappearing, I guarantee it. I can get in and out of anywhere in this hospital if I want. Including the pathology lab. Just like I did your room tonight." He focused on her arm once again and the needle approached her skin.

"You won't get away with this." Evan's voice trembled. The adrenaline that pumped in her veins kept the tears from her eyes, but it crawled down her spine and ached in her legs.

The needle tip touched the surface of her skin.

"I've gotten away with it before. I can do it again."

"Not if I'm still around," a voice said from behind him.

Sorenson's eyes widened and he quickly stood. The needle slipped away from Evan's arm. She glanced up at the moment Paul stood at the edge of the light beam and swung a heavy bar against Sorenson's head. The thud echoed throughout the vast room.

The syringe dropped and so did Sorenson. Evan let out a gasp as she looked at Paul, who stood with the pipe still in his hand. But Sorenson hadn't gone all the way down, just to his knees as blood trickled from the side of his head.

Paul stepped back and wound the pipe back again like he was ready to hit a fast ball. Evan pulled at the tape again, the adrenaline fueling power in her muscles. The tape ripped at the edge and her wrist pulled free.

With her attention down to freeing her other hand, she didn't see Sorenson reach behind his back. His fingers scrambled for something tucked into the waistband of his scrubs. When the light fell on his hand, it was too late.

The pipe in Paul's hand readied to come down again, but Sorenson lifted back and swung his hand around with the thing he pulled from his waistband. Evan cried out and tugged helplessly at the bonds on her right wrist. They slipped but it wasn't soon enough.

A loud crack resounded in the room with a flash of small and sudden light. The sound rang in her ears and her whole body tightened around her core, the flinch leaving her shoulders sore. The room plunged into sudden silence, with her ears deafened from the shot.

A gun shot.

The bright flash still lingered in her eyes and she could barely see into the dark beyond the beam of the flashlight. But Paul no longer stood there. A dark shape writhed on the floor before her, and then it rose with his vodka breath and sweat.

He just shot Paul.

Before her chest could seize, she leaned across the arm of the chair toward the flashlight. Sorenson moved back up to his knee and grunted to push himself to his feet. Her fingers barely touched the stem of the light. It rolled a few millimeters away from her and she stretched harder. The tape on her right wrist creaked with the strain. She gritted her teeth against the pain of the stretch, her fingers reaching further toward the light.

He groaned as he leaned on his knee to stand.

Her fingers found purchase and rolled the flashlight toward her palm. She grasped the heavy stem, her knuckles white and her arm strong with the weeks of physical therapy and lifting herself in and out of the chair hundreds of times. Sorenson lifted off his knee and moved to stand when she dropped the heavy flashlight against the back of his head as hard as she could.

He dropped again and she tugged against the tape. The adhesive ripped over her skin and hair, leaving raw exposed dermis as she pulled at her wrist.

The wheelchair shifted with a powerful jerk. Sorenson grasped at the wheel and pulled her toward him. The pounding of her heart urged her faster and she pulled her wrist free. At that moment, he shoved the chair hard. Her fingers gripped the arm rests and the chair no longer had any balance. It tipped, and Evan held her arms over her face at it toppled to its side and dumped her on the ground.

The flashlight tumbled out of her lap but she caught it as the beam spiraled against the walls and the machines around the room. Evan's back hit the metal beam along the side of the chair as it fell and she rolled away from the wheel.

Sorenson's hand grabbed her shoe and pulled her back into the dark. Her fingernails scratched along the linoleum, trying to take purchase of anything before he pulled her closer. The flashlight clattered against the floor, but her hand caught it again. He tugged her further until she could feel the weight of his torso on her leg.

This was her last chance. Somewhere on that dark floor, Sorenson had a syringe of Fentanyl, and it would definitely kill her. And in that dark, beyond where she lay, Paul was there. Maybe bleeding to death. Maybe dead already.

Her fingers wrapped around the stem of the flashlight. She forced herself up until she sat on the edge of her hip and swung the flashlight in the dark again. It struck home with a sickening thud and the light shattered. Sorenson groaned again and fell back, his grip on her leg loosening.

She had to go now, to leave Paul wherever he lay in the dark, and get away from the man who was trying to kill her. If she could walk, it would be a completely different thing. But this was all she had, and she had to do it or she would die.

Evan turned onto her abdomen and propped up on her elbows. She crawled with the weight of her mostly useless legs behind her. Each arm reached forward to pull herself across the linoleum into the shadows before Sorenson collected his strength again and came after her. The cold floor slid under her torso with each stroke forward, taking her further into the dark of the laundry room.

Chapter 44

The muscles in Evan's shoulders burned, even with the weak attempt at propelling her forward with her legs as well as her arms. But she continued, each nudge taking her down between a row of dryers. The effort left her breathing heavy, like she had been sprinting. She couldn't quit now.

A screeching sound of metal on metal echoed from somewhere in the center of the room. Too much indistinct noise to make out what it was, and she didn't have to. Sorenson moved again, and he no longer had the flashlight to find her. There was only the faint light from the upper windows, which wasn't much since the laundry room was in the hospital basement.

Evan lifted her head to see a desk half-way down the dark aisle, situated between dryers. The legs of a chair jutted into the aisle. Maybe a place to hide. She pulled herself toward the desk, each stroke making her breathe harder.

"Jensen," Sorenson's voice rose like thunder in the room and rebounded off the walls. He groaned after he said it. Something crashed from where he stood. Probably the wheelchair rebounding off one of the washers after he threw it. An exasperated laugh came from his throat. "You can't walk. You can't even stand. What's the point? I'll find you, you won't get far."

This made her pull faster. His voice still sounded like it was coming from the center of the room but it wouldn't take him much to start walking the aisles until he came upon her. She approached the desk and pulled herself up to her knees and glanced back in the dark. Only shadows back there, but his footsteps echoed all over the place.

She held her breath and turned back to the desk. Her hands grasped to the edge of the desk to steady herself when she saw the land line phone at the edge. A red light glowed steadily on the keypad screen. With trembling hands, she reached for the receiver and pulled the pad toward her. Her fingertips found the buttons and memory told her what to push. 911.

The ring on the other end came so loud she was sure that Sorenson could hear it.

By the third ring, a woman answered. "911. What is your emergency?"

"I'm in the basement of St. John's hospital," she whispered. "I need help now."

"Can you speak up?" the woman said. "You said you're in a basement. Are you injured?"

She repeated her location, but glanced back down the aisle as she spoke. Any louder and he would definitely hear her.

"Is there someone there with you?"

"My friend's been shot, and someone is trying to kill me," she said.

"Jensen," his voice came louder and closer.

Her hand trembled and quietly set the receiver down on the surface of the desk. The operator's voice still came out of the speaker but grew faint as she lifted herself up against the edge of the desk.

He was coming, and there was no way she would get away from him crawling on her belly like a serpent. She pulled up onto her legs and steadied her knees while she supported herself against the desk. Just like in therapy. She stepped one foot forward and walked her hands across the desk. The next dryer stood right beside the desk. She reached out for it and moved her other foot forward. Her knee trembled and she held tight against the machine.

You've got to keep going.

Another step. She moved her hands along to the next dryer. The burning ache started in her quadriceps, the same feeling just before her legs gave out in therapy. *Please, not now.* Just a little further. She clenched her teeth and dug her nails into the edge of the dryer, holding herself up. Her hand reached for the next machine, but there was a gap between the dryers. Too far for her to reach and too far to step.

Sorenson's voice called out to her again, and he must have been in the next aisle.

Her hands released the edge of the machine and she collapsed to the ground. The sound of her knees hitting the floor rang in her ears and the pain shot up into both hips. There was no time to stop and assess the damage. She crawled into the space between the dryers and pulled her legs in to her chest, hugging herself in the black shadow cast between the machines. She pressed her lips together and listened into the dark despite her rapid breathing. With a hand pressed against her mouth, she stared with wide eyes into the dark aisle.

"You can't get away from me," he said. His voice resonated against the metal siding of the machine where she pressed her back. A footstep sounded and then another, an uneven shuffle. She had hurt him enough to slow him down to a limp. "Evan?"

She held her hand tighter against her mouth. The sound of his footfalls was only a few feet away now.

"You have to understand," he said. He turned his head in all directions as he spoke. "I couldn't let her tell anyone. She could have ruined my career. I could have lost my license, my job, my family. All because of her. What else was I supposed to do?"

His head flipped around and the last word carried off in an echo across the room. The sound came from the machine right behind her now.

"I wasn't going to let that happen," he said. His voice dropped now, no longer a shout. "And I won't let it happen now."

She held her breath and watched from her shadowy place. A hand shot out from the aisle and clamped down on her foot. She screamed as he pulled her from the shadows. Her fingers grasped for anything to gain purchase, anything to prevent him from pulling her from the shadows, but she slid along the metal siding of the dryer. He yanked her across the floor with a grunt.

Evan twisted but his weight fell on her. She cried out again. His hand struck fast and hit her hard enough to leave her dizzy and her ears ringing. Her arm pulled up to shield her face and he pinned it down. A ring of metal pressed to her forehead and she froze. The barrel of the gun still held heat from the last shot, and it burned against her skin

Sorenson straddled her, breathing hard and wiping the blood away from his eye. The continuous stream flowed back into it, though, leaving his sclera even redder than it was before. The hammer of the gun clicked into place and the barrel pressed harder against her head.

"This was supposed to look like an accident," he said. A drop of blood fell from his eye and landed on the floor just beside her ear.

"Please don't do this," she said, her eyes blurred in tears.

He took in a steady breath, his eyes burning down on her as he did it. The hand holding the gun trembled and the index finger barely contracted.

Evan's chest ached with the muscle spasm between her ribs. She closed her eyes, and that was the moment the chill moved over her skin, as cold as the deep of winter. It frosted against her cheeks and nose. Her eyes flew open and her breath escaped in a burst of fog.

Angela Sinclair had just arrived.

A footstep echoed down the aisle from where Sorenson pinned Evan. The cold spilled over the floor, and another step sounded. Sorenson glanced up and the barrel's pressure lifted only a little.

"Who's there?" he called out into the dark.

A cracking, like the sound of knuckles or broken bones, resonated from the shadows. He pulled the gun away from Evan's head and pointed it into the dark.

"Show yourself," he demanded. The gun now shook in his hand. Evan tilted her head back and followed his gaze into the shadows.

At first, the darkness twisted and contorted like oil in water, moving with uneven grace. It took form as the entity drew into the faint light from the windows. A head, then a neck and shoulders. Arms appeared at its sides and a torso draped in a bloody hospital gown. Long, stringy black hair fell over its face and it stepped forward in a twitchy, broken cadence.

Sorenson's breathing quickened and he moved both hands to the gun. "Who are you?" he demanded.

Evan's throat tightened. Sorenson could see her. He could *actually* see her.

The entity moved forward, its twisted and crackling limbs reaching out for him. It lifted its head and the hair fell away from its face. Her cold, porcelain-blue dead face with the milky cataract eyes that stared at him with all her anger and hatred for what he had done.

The color drained from his face. "No, it's not possible. You're dead."

The spirit moved toward him in the crooked way she always did. He shouted into the dark and pulled the trigger. A volley of shots in continuous sequence, but each one went right through the entity that approached him. Evan pulled her hands to her ears to shield the sound of the gun and his screaming.

And then Angela smiled, revealing grey, stippled tiles of teeth barely visible through a dark mouth.

A door at the other end of the room opened and a half-dozen flashlights appeared. From her place on the floor, Evan couldn't see what stood out there and her ears still heard everything in muffled sounds from the rapid-fire gunshots.

"Put the gun down!"

"On the ground! Now!"

Sorenson shouted at the horrible thing that had stood in front of him, but it had faded in the sudden burst of lights that poured through the main door into the laundry room.

"Put the gun down!" another shout came from the door.

Evan pressed her hands closer to her ears. Sorenson still hovered above her, and the gun now moved in the confusion of the moment from the disappearing entity to the door.

An eruption of gunfire exploded again. Evan clenched her eyes and screamed with her hands to her ears, but the sound bellowed in her brain. A warm mist drifted over her and the taste of copper filled her tongue with a spray of blood that rained down from the dark. His body shifted above hers and then he fell to the side and away from her.

The room went dark and quiet. She didn't want to move or open her eyes. The copper taste still lingered in her mouth and she was sure that her face was stained with a coat of blood. The loud pop still rang in her ears, one after another until it made her dizzy.

A hand clasped against her wrist, but it wasn't the brute force that Sorenson had.

"Ma'am, are you okay?" a man's voice sounded in the distance, so far away. But he must have been right next to her. It didn't matter, because she wasn't going to open her eyes. She didn't want to see what had happened around her.

He released her wrist. Evan turned to her side and pulled her knees up to her chest, but she never let her hands fall from her ears. So many footsteps pounded around her and flashes of light burned through her closed eyelids.

"Paramedics," someone called out from behind her. "We've got two in critical shape here, and the perp is deceased over there."

"Tube him!" a woman called out from far across the room, away from where Evan lay beside the still body of Sorenson. "Start compressions. Andy, get him up and out to trauma, now."

Evan's legs pulled up closer to her chest. *They're talking about Paul.*

Another hand touched her back, this one smaller and gentle. "Dr. Jensen," a woman said. "I need to examine you, okay?"

The woman's fingers moved to Evan's wrist, feeling her pulse. "Are you injured?" she asked.

A cold surface of a stethoscope slid under her shirt and against her ribs. When they moved near the scar from the previous chest tube, Evan flinched. The nerves tingled and burned there ever since it had been pulled.

The clatter of gurney wheels on the linoleum made her eyes open, but the sound moved away from her. They were going to Paul. She craned her head around, every noise in the room muffled in her ringing ears, and looked beyond the paramedic at her side. It was going to happen, although she willed it not to. Everything drowned away in a muffled chaos as she watched a group of paramedics carry Paul out on a gurney. A tube protruded from his mouth and a man at his head pumped oxygen into his lungs. Another sat astride the gurney, his hands pressed together on Paul's chest, pumping in a rapid rhythm.

Chapter 45

"What are you thinking?"

Paul's voice stirred Evan from her attention on the gold locket around her neck. She tucked it back under the neckline of her shirt and turned to him from where she sat in her wheel chair.

"I'm thinking that I have never been more ready to leave this place." She smiled and glanced back to the IV pole that hovered over him from the hospital bed where he lay.

He groaned with the effort of shifting to his side. A black sling wrapped his left arm and bound it to his side, and the Velcro straps of it creaked as he leaned enough to press the button along the side of the bed. The back of the bed rose with electronic whirs and came to a stop once he could face her without craning his neck. "Just one last evaluation and we're out of here for good."

"I wish they would hurry," she said. She rolled the wheels of her chair to his bedside.

Paul turned to reach for her but he stopped part way and winced.

"You okay?" she said.

He placed an even palm over his sternum. "Still hurts sometimes."

"Well, you had three cracked ribs from CPR, so . . ."

"The price we pay to stay alive," he said with a smile. He shot a quick glance to the door and turned back to her. "Any more signs of her? Of Angela?"

Evan shook her head. "Not since that night. Everything's been quiet, and the air has been so much lighter. I think she's gone."

The door opened and Samena walked in, a young man with a wheelchair right behind her. A wide grin appeared on her face when she looked at Paul.

"My two favorite people," Samena said.

The man with the chair entered the room and readied the chair beside the bed.

"Looks like everything is ready to go," Samena said and held up the envelope of final discharge papers. She glanced to Evan. "We've got all your therapy appointments scheduled as an outpatient now. You are officially discharged. And so are you, Dr. Williams."

That was the best news Evan had heard in a long time. Her legs still ached from the events of last week, things that still made her wake up in the middle of the night, sweating until her sheets were wet. Sometimes she could even feel the cold metal of the gun barrel against her forehead.

Things got a lot better when Paul began to recover. The bullet had torn through his upper chest and shoulder, but it was enough to cause cardiac arrest. CPR, an ICU admission and a blood transfusion helped, but she knew he still relived that night when he closed his eyes too. And she didn't want to leave the hospital without him. With both of them here, there was no need to rush out of the rehab unit. She could continue her therapy until he was good enough to leave with her, and today was that day.

They were both going home now, together. And she had meant what she told him. There was no point in waiting to get married with an expensive dress and an even more expensive venue. She was ready to do it this weekend. Hell, why not tonight.

The transport courier pushed Paul out of the room while Samena pushed Evan with them. Paul extended his hand to hers and they intertwined fingers as they moved through the sterile corridors of St. John's hospital. Staff members bustled through their day, oblivious to their presence. A cacophony of dance and sound that helped save lives.

The elevator opened to the lower level, with streaming morning light that poured through the grand stained-glass windows opening into the atrium. Just through the crowded foyer, the sliding doors to the outside world awaited them. The courier pushed the chair across the rainbow hues of light cast down through the windows.

A rush of cold air brushed over her face with the opening of the sliding doors as a couple walked into the hospital. The doors closed, but the sensation lingered over her skin.

And a tickle of electricity etched across the back of her neck.

The pull first came from her left, and Evan urged Samena to stop for a moment. The muscles in her shoulders softened when she saw a young girl, no older than six or seven, standing just outside the emergency room doors. Her small hand waved toward her and a bright smile formed on her lips. The white dress on her small frame looked like fresh frosting on a cupcake over her tiny white shoes. Evan smiled back and the girl turned around to walk back into the emergency room.

The tug forced from her insides and she could no longer ignore it. Evan turned back to Samena. "Can you give me a second?"

Sam and the courier nodded and Evan pulled at Paul's hand. "Just go with me on this. I'll be right back."

He didn't ask a single question. Not after everything they had just been through. "Sure."

The chair moved forward, leaving everyone in the lobby to watch her move into the emergency room entry.

Cool, alcohol-laced air drifted through the doors as the wheels bumped over the threshold. There was no sign of the little girl and her poofy white dress, but the pull still remained. She turned to the left corridor, one that she had traversed so many times as a resident. The back entrance into the main section of the ER.

A nurse moved down the hall and smiled with her clipboard in hand. "Dr. Jensen. So good to see you." She continued down the hall as she nodded in acknowledgement.

There was no time for pleasantries. The pull still drew her down the hall and Evan had to see why. The chair rolled around the corner, to the open nurses' station that bustled with people. Doctors, residents, nurses, and EMTs. Nobody paid her any attention or even noticed that she waited there.

The chair stopped the moment she saw the girl again. Her dress still hung in flawless white tufts of lace and the smile had never left her face. Dark brown eyes looked at her, a glint of sweet kindness there that should be in every young girl of that age.

A curtain behind the girl opened, revealing a patient bay and the chaos that happened back there. A resident Evan recognized held oxygen tubing and a pump to an endotracheal tube inserted into a very small patient. A child on the gurney. Nurses swarmed around the room, injecting syringes into the IV tubing as a man and woman clung to each other in one corner. The child's parents.

The little girl still faced Evan, the smile still present on her lips, completely oblivious to the tragic scene behind her.

The clutch of nurses around the gurney cleared long enough for Evan to see the little body on the gurney, a body with small feet in shiny white shoes and a puffy white dress stained in blood. The doctor still worked over her with his oxygen pump as the heart monitor beat in erratic and ominous rhythms.

Another nurse rushed down the hall and bumped against the wheels of her chair. Evan stopped her for a moment. "What's going on here?"

The nurse recognized her and leaned down, her voice lowered. "Hit and run at a kid's birthday party. She's not gonna make it." The nurse turned away and hurried back to the room where the child lay.

She already knows that. Evan knew it as she looked on the little girl standing outside the trauma room. Her small white shoes turned and the girl walked into the room. She stood next to her father and placed her head against this thigh, but he would never feel it or know she was there.

But Evan knew, because the little girl wanted her to know.

The courier pushed the chair to the car in the round-about at the front lobby of the hospital. Paul stood with careful ease, a slight grimace on his face when the pain in his chest pinched again. Evan slid into the passenger seat as the courier took the chair away and closed the door. The quiet inside the car let all the images of what she had just seen replay in her head in a never-ending loop.

That child had wanted her to see what happened, and that was it. No anger, just a witness. And she was the chosen one.

The pull happened again, but from so many different angles, all with a single tether inside her chest. It was the same place where the ghost-Angela had placed her fingers and left a mark that night. Now it pulled and tugged with sharp pins that burned into her sternum. She turned her gaze up to the windows of the hospital, hundreds of them looking down on where she sat in the car.

And most of them held pale faces that watched her, milky eyes staring down, knowing that she could see them.

It would never be over. They would always see her.

The End

Acknowledgments

A medical residency is one of the most difficult things I've ever experienced, but it consisted of so many great experiences and even greater people. Five years of training after graduating from medical school. Working eighty hours a week (that's the limit based on rules set down by those that run graduate medical education). The intense training doesn't allow much time for a social life outside of residency. Those people with whom you work day in and day out are your circle of friends. Together, you see some of the best and worst things in humanity.

My training program in OB/GYN occurred mostly in a hospital on the north side of Chicago. Unfortunately, just months ago (when I sat down to write this acknowledgment), the labor and delivery unit of that facility was closed by the corporation that has now taken over the hospital. Those nurses and other staff members that I had worked with are now scattered among other hospitals. For all of us, even those of us who no longer work there, it was the end of an era.

So many unique experiences occurred there during my time. They shaped who I am now as a practicing physician. And those experiences trickled into aspects of this novel. Of course, it's a work of fiction, but there are tidbits of truth and real interactions that had occurred during my residency. Medical training is a frightening time, and more so when the facility you work at also has an element of terror.

This story started during the final year of my residency. I was Chief Resident at the time, and the idea of Time of Death began to formulate. During the month of November that year, the fifth month of my Chief year, I worked nights. Seven at night to seven in the morning, five days a week, for a month. I took over the duties of labor and delivery as well as any gynecologic emergencies that came into the hospital during those thirty days. And believe me, a Chicago-area hospital is never a dull place to work. Pregnant women with gunshot wounds from a drive-by shooting or cocaine overdoses, women from foreign countries with no prenatal care coming in with extremely complex health issues (including female circumcisions, but that's a topic for an entirely different book) can fill the days and nights. Walking the halls and empty stairwells at night in a large hospital begins to mess with your head after a while. A hospital in the middle of the night can be a little creepy. There, I said it. And to make things worse, the resident call rooms were located in a closed unit of the hospital one floor below labor and delivery. Closed, because it had been the former psychiatry lock-down unit, and someone thought "hmm, let's make the residents sleep here at night". So, if you were able to have some time for sleep, you had to go to the old, empty psych ward with wall paper peeling off the walls, the windows rattling in the wind, and few of the light bulbs in the hall worked. Yeah. That psych ward.

And that's when the idea of this story first came to me. Hospitals can be terrifying places, especially at night. Especially when the nurses who have worked there for years begin to relay tales of spooky experiences they have had on the various units throughout the hospital. Yes, many of them stood solid in their beliefs that they had witnessed paranormal events throughout their years working at that hospital.

A collection of tales from battle-hardened nurses, a creepy old psych ward where I had to sleep at night, and a daily battle for life and death in my own patients brought about the story of Time of Death. The first four or five chapters came easily during my month of nights, drawing on my own experiences and intertwining them with the ghost stories told to me.

Then, residency became busier outside of the night shift. I graduated from residency, started practicing as a private OB/GYN and life was even more hectic. And this story sat on the shelf, unfinished for many years.

In 2019, my thoughts came back to that story and to my experiences during residency. Since leaving the Chicago area, I have still kept in contact with so many of those nurses and my fellow residents, but we have also drifted apart in many ways. Thank heaven for social media, otherwise I don't think any of us would be communicating to this day. One of those nurses, Asha Fasino, was one of the only people who had read the first few chapters of this book when I had started it during residency. She has periodically kept on me to finish it, and I'm grateful that she did so. I also apologize to her for those chapters so many years ago. I didn't write well back then. Not that I'm great now, but things have improved dramatically since that time. Thank you, Asha. You have been immortalized in this tale as a nurse that cares, and someone who helps the protagonists solve the mystery.

Thank you to all the nurses at St. Francis hospital. Being a nurse that has to put up with us residents for years, and a new batch of us every July, can't be easy. I don't want to leave anyone out (my memory sucks), but thanks to: Anne, Dorothy, Kelly,

Lisa, Nancy, Kasia, Rose, Maureen, Kathy, Liz, Maria, and anyone else I forgot.

My fellow residents deserve a shout out, especially to those of you that shared some of those spooky times with me: Charlie, Amal, Craig, Calvin, Michelle, Kim, Lisa, Theresa, and Migdalia. And to the attendings we all had, a big thank you: John, Marco, Sandy, Gina, Tom, Jan, Brenda. Especially to you, John. Thanks for believing in me and accepting me into the program. I wouldn't be where I am without your illegible signature on that residency acceptance form.

About the Author

When she isn't delivering babies, Carrie Merrill is a prolific writer who has put pen to paper since the age of 8, when she wrote her first story about a dragon that lived in a cave across the river from her house in Idaho. A day has not gone by since that time when she didn't have a story floating around in her head.

Her widely-read and praised Angel Blade Series received great praise. *The Key, The Outlaw and The Treasure*, is an exciting YA novel that takes place in the old West and is filled with adventure and anger.

She is currently a full-time OB/GYN in Wyoming with her six rescue cats when she isn't writing about the things that lurk in the dark.

CarrieMerrill.com

www.ingramcontent.com/pod-product-compliance
Lightning Source LLC
Chambersburg PA
CBHW061049190726
48286CB00006B/1673